HATTIE'S MILL

HATTIE'S MILL

Marcia Willett

HEADLINE

First published in 1996
by HEADLINE BOOK PUBLISHING

10 9 8 7 6 5 4 3 2

British Library Cataloguing in Publication Data

Willett, Marcia
Hattie's mill
1.English fiction – 20th century
I.Title
823.9'14 [F]

ISBN 0 7472 1754 8

Typeset by Palimpsest Book Production Limited,
Polmont, Stirlingshire
Printed and bound in Great Britain by
Mackays of Chatham PLC, Chatham, Kent

HEADLINE BOOK PUBLISHING
A division of Hodder Headline PLC
338 Euston Road
London NW1 3BH

To Susie

Prologue

1986

James Barrington bade farewell to his friends in the small Devonshire village of Strete, folded back the hood of his MGB and settled himself comfortably for the long journey back to Oxford. Driving along the coastal cliff road, he glanced as often as he could at the placid shimmering sea stretching out to the misty horizon and smiled with pleasure as the golden crescent-shaped beach at Blackpool Sands appeared below him through the trees. Three years ago he'd lived in this part of Devon when he'd been articled to a firm of lawyers in Dartmouth and, as he drove the familiar route with its breathtaking views, his mind fled back across those years.

He turned inland from Dartmouth heading towards Totnes but, at the junction by the Sportsman's Arms, decided to cut across country. How often he'd driven these lanes in his old battered Citroën Dyane, looking forward to those summer evenings when he could relax and sail his Mirror dinghy on the creek. Even as he thought of it, the signpost caught his eye: 'Abbot's Mill Creek 2 Miles. No Through Road.' On an impulse he swung the steering wheel and headed down the narrow track. Here, in this deep secret lane, the bluebells grew thickly and the May sunshine was warm on his head.

He rounded a bend, caught his breath and abruptly braked, switching off the engine. Cut deep in beneath the sloping rounded fields, the creek spread out below him; its waters smooth and dark, the trees crowding at its banks, their boughs just tipping the surface. Small boats rode at anchor and the sound of hammering, from the boatyard which was hidden from sight by a bend in the river, echoed up the valley. James sat quite still. The mill, at the head of the creek, was not visible but he could see it quite clearly in his mind's eye; the mellow stone walls, the water wheel, Hattie pottering out to feed the ducks, the two little cottages crouching

1

under their golden thatch close at hand. How happy he'd been there. Why had he left it so long before returning? Supposing they'd all gone: Hattie, Joss, the Admiral, Miggy . . .

His heart gave a little twinge of remembered joy and longing, and he thought of Daisy, waiting patiently on the hard in her old shorts and sandshoes, her copper curls bright in the sun, her twelve-year-old face lighting up when she saw him. Her voice came clearly down the years.

'Oh, James! You're late again! We'll miss the tide if you don't hurry.'

'Can't help it. Messrs Whinge, Whinge, Bellyache and Moan have kept me at it all day long.'

'Shoulder to the wheel?' Her small face was alight at their silly joke.

'Nose to the grindstone!'

And Miggy, waving to them from the lawn as they sailed past . . . Miggy.

James swallowed some strange obstruction that seemed to have lodged in his throat, started up the engine and followed the winding lane down to the head of the creek.

Chapter One

1979

'I wish you weren't so set on buying on the coast,' said Sarah Farley as she and her old friend Hattie Wetherall sat at breakfast. 'There are lots of lovely properties for sale round here and it's not that far from the sea. Tell her, Nick.'

Nick Farley, one of the partners in a busy legal practice in Plymouth, glanced up from *The Times* and smiled at his wife.

'My dear Sarah, I should have thought you knew Hattie far too well to imagine that I could tell her anything at all that might change her mind. I'd be far too frightened to try.'

Hattie, retiring from a senior position in the QARNNS after a lifetime of service, grimaced at him. 'Quite right, too. I want to live by the sea. Or, anyway, water of some kind. Not stuck in the middle of Dartmoor.'

'We've got rivers,' protested Sarah, faint but pursuing. 'There's the Dart and the Tamar and the Tavy . . .'

Nick shook his handsome distinguished head as he folded the newspaper and pushed back his chair.

'Give in gracefully, my love, and let her get on with it. She won't be far away. Closer than she's been for most of the last thirty years, anyway. I must dash. Enjoy your day.'

He kissed Sarah, waggled his fingers at Hattie and went out. Sarah sighed and Hattie watched her thoughtfully.

'Nick's on top form,' she observed presently, spreading marmalade on her toast.

'Mmm.' Sarah sounded preoccupied. 'He is.'

'All well?'

Sarah pulled herself together and looked at her. 'If you mean, "Is he having an affair at the moment?" the answer is, "No, I don't think so." None of the usual signs.'

'Oh dear.' Hattie shook her head. 'I'd hoped that as he got older it all might . . . well, drop off a bit. If you see what I mean.'

3

'No such luck.' Sarah stopped crumbling her toast and pushed the plate aside. 'Rather the contrary. He's always needed to have his vanity soothed. Middle age makes him more insecure, if anything. And he's not that old! Only forty-four. Don't forget he's nearly five years younger than I am.'

'It's not that much. You're five years younger than me but who's counting?'

'It's different somehow. Anyway, let's not worry about that. So what are you going to view today?'

'Several places.' Hattie shuffled the papers beside her plate. 'There's a cottage at Torcross and a house in Dartmouth but the one that takes my fancy is the mill.'

'Oh, yes. You showed me. Honestly, Hat! Don't you think it's a bit much all on your own? A derelict mill with two old cottages. What will you do with it all? Probably cost a fortune to do it up.'

'Probably.' Hattie rumpled her short grey hair, frowned abstractedly and shook her head. 'I've got a feeling about it, that's all. Want to come?'

'No, I've got a charity lunch, I told you.' Sarah began to clear the table. 'Well, have a good day but for goodness' sake don't do anything rash!'

Hattie smiled affectionately at the younger woman. In the past, during their nursing careers, they'd often been taken for sisters: both were short and rather dumpy, both kept their hair cropped short, both tended towards old casual clothes and a love of the outdoors. Then, at thirty-five, Sarah inherited a considerable amount of wealth from her parents, met the delightfully charming Nick and immediately resigned her commission. Many there were who said that he'd married her for her money and her connections but there was no doubt at all that Sarah adored Nick. They were happy enough, thought Hattie, but she gave Sarah's arm a quick squeeze as she collected her belongings together.

'I've been subject to rules and regs for thirty-five years,' she said lightly. 'The one thing I'm simply longing to do is something rash. Don't be an old spoilsport!'

'You're hopeless.' But Sarah was smiling. 'I'll be longing to hear all about it. You know the way?'

'By heart.' Hattie gave her a tiny wink. 'Nick showed me with maps and diagrams. I wonder he didn't set it to music. Relax. Enjoy your lunch and I'll see you later.'

She went out, pausing to collect her Newfoundland dog who

4

was drinking lavishly at the fishpond. She'd always vowed that, on her retirement, she would buy a house by the sea – or a river – and a dog. The dog had come first – Admiral Jellicoe – a large handsome puppy bought from a breeder friend. She'd trained him whilst she lived in the cottage in Hampshire – left to her by her mother and used by Hattie as a holiday retreat – waiting for it to sell, and now she had all her savings, her gratuity and her inheritance lodged in the bank, a twelve-month-old dog and very little else.

Hattie bundled him into the back of her Renault 4 and set off across Dartmoor. She was by no means inured to its majesty on this blowy March morning – she loved the great sweeping vistas and misty distances – she simply didn't want to live on it.

'We'll come and walk on it, won't we, Jellicoe?' she murmured, glancing at the dog in the mirror and seeing him put his head on one side, ears pricked, as he listened to her. 'What we want is water.'

She mused on this as she drove, glad that Sarah wasn't with her. Fond though Hattie was of her, she knew that her input would have been discouraging. Sarah would like Hattie to live as near to Buckland Monachorum as possible but – geography aside – Hattie had no desire to be drawn into the charity lunches and bazaars that filled Sarah's days and took her mind off Nick's infidelities.

'How does she bear it?' she muttered. 'How does her sense of self-worth remain intact?'

Though she'd spent many leaves and weekends with women friends who'd left the service to marry and raise children, she'd never been tempted to revise her opinion that it was so much simpler to remain single. Only once would she have been prepared to give up her freedom but the sacrifice had never been demanded of her. Nearly thirty years before, she'd had an affair with a senior consultant which had ended in his abandonment of her when she became pregnant. When Hattie realised that his stories of an unhappy marriage were lies, and his promises to divorce his disinterested wife and marry her were empty words, she took her life back into her own hands and had an abortion. She'd long since ceased to regret the consultant but she never recovered from the loss of the child. How often she'd regretted her decision, which at the time had seemed the only possible one open to her, was known only to herself.

· She pushed her memories aside and gave her mind to the confusing network of lanes that lies in the hinterland between Totnes and Dartmouth. Her relief when she saw the signpost was

great; she'd already apologised mentally to Nick for regarding his
minute instructions as unnecessary fussing. 'Abbot's Mill Creek
2 Miles. No Through Road.' Hattie turned into the narrow lane
and started the descent to the creek. As she rounded a bend she
gave a cry of pleasure and braked for a moment, gazing down at
the scene below; the water of the creek glinting and shivering in
the sun, the trees that appeared to be paddling in its shallows, the
high wooded promontories topped by sunlit fields. Hattie took a
deep, deep breath, let in the clutch and drove on.

Down she went between the high banks where catkins danced
in the March wind and celandines, enamel bright, glowed amongst
the dead leaves and new shoots. Down, until the lane levelled out
and she was running along beside an orchard, and glimpsed the
mill pond and the empty leat moments before she came upon the
mill itself. She drove past the gate and slowed beside the creek. It
opened up away from her, widening into a deep channel, whilst
the lane, starting to climb again, wound away behind the woods
that crowded to the creek's edge.

Hattie parked the car and climbed out. The tide was ebbing
and a small dinghy was beached on the foreshore a few yards
away. Further down the creek a boat rocked at its moorings and,
as she watched, a man appeared through the companionway and
stood gazing around him. She raised a hand to him and, after a
moment, he returned the salute but, before she could hail him, she
heard the sound of an engine and presently a car appeared and
pulled in beside her own. It was the agent. They shook hands and
together they returned to the gate that led into the mill's grounds.
For Hattie it was love at first sight and, in a daze, she attempted
to take in all the information that the garrulous agent was intent
on bestowing upon her.

The mill, he told her, as he unlocked doors and led her round,
had been in the early stages of renovation when the young couple
who owned it had run out of money. The agent shook his head.
Very sad and such a nice young pair . . . But the plumbing and
electrics were done and a nice new roof. Did she see the roof?
(Hattie nodded obediently. She saw the roof.) The cottages now,
were different again. One was done up a treat since they'd been
living in it whilst they worked on the mill . . . Very comfortable
and tastefully done. Wouldn't she agree? (Hattie nodded again.
Oh yes, she would. Certainly.) The other half wasn't too bad at
all. Merely a lick of paint and a few odds and ends, new window
frames, perhaps, but no real problems there, nothing to mention.

(Hattie shook her head. Nothing to mention.) As for the mill itself, well, the opportunities were limitless. He'd been showing a couple round only two days before and they'd come up with a brilliant suggestion . . .

Hattie's brain clicked into gear and her heart jumped anxiously.

'I suppose there's been quite a bit of interest?' she suggested casually.

The agent laughed a little, in a gently reproving manner. Naturally there was a *great deal* – he emphasised the words – of interest. The almost ludicrously low price reflected the work still necessary. But one only had to imagine the possibilities . . . letting the cottages out for income . . . bed and breakfast always in demand in this area . . . incomparable setting . . .

Hattie did a violent mental sum and threw years of discipline and caution aside. 'I want it,' she said.

The agent, who had strolled on to the tiny quay and was now extolling the virtues of owning one's own moorings, was silenced for a moment. 'You wish to make an offer?' he asked cautiously.

'Certainly. A cash offer.' Hattie did another sum, retrieved a small measure of cunning and named a sum which was three thousand pounds below the asking price. 'And I want the answer today,' she added firmly.

Resisting the urge to tell her that she could have it at once, the owners being in such desperate straits that they would have accepted an even lower offer, the agent looked grave. He would do his best but there would be telephoning to be done and – given the *very great* interest – they would have to consider the offer carefully.

'By this evening,' Hattie insisted. She would die if she had to wait any longer. 'Take it or leave it. It's not open to negotiation.'

The agent nodded. He quite understood. And, seeing that a mortgage wasn't involved and things could move quickly . . .

Resisting, in her turn, the urge to manhandle him bodily into his car and rush him back to his office, she waited with clenched jaw whilst he promised to cancel her other viewing appointments for her, made his farewells and drove off.

She listened to the sound of his engine dying away and then strolled back on to the hard where once the boats would have come alongside the wall to be loaded. Beside the hard was a slip where another dinghy, newly varnished, rested upside down on two planks of wood. She leaned on the wall and looked towards the ketch where the young man was sitting on the cabin roof, a mug in his hands. Hattie could almost smell the coffee and her mouth watered. She waved again and hailed him.

'Ahoy!' Her voice carried easily across the water. 'Have you got a minute?'

The young man put down the mug and came to lean on the rail. 'Good morning. Been looking at the mill?'

'I have. D'you know it well?'

'I overwintered in one of the cottages and I used to lend a hand occasionally with the renovation.'

'I'm going to buy it.' If she said it aloud, it must make it true.

'Goodness! That was quick work!' He hesitated. 'Like some coffee?'

'Oh, I would! Only I've got Admiral Jellicoe in the car.'

There was a silence and the young man straightened up. 'Sorry?'

Hattie grinned to herself. Thinks I'm a nutter she thought, fairly accurately. 'My dog,' she said. 'I thought I'd give him a little run up through the woods. But I'd love some coffee and perhaps you could tell me all the things that our friend with verbal diarrhoea didn't think worth mentioning.'

She saw the flash of teeth in the young man's face and smiled in relief.

'Take your time,' he said. 'Give a shout when you're ready and I'll row across and fetch you.'

Admiral Jellicoe leaped thankfully from the back of the car and ran nosing about. Hattie wandered back into the mill yard, looking at the mellow stone, the new slate roof and the huge unmoving wheel. The whitewashed cottages looked cosy under their heavy thatch and, beyond the fence, the orchard was carpeted with daffodils. She gave a nod of pleasure and determination and followed the Admiral out along the lane beneath the overhanging trees.

'You must be mad,' announced Sarah, later that evening as she juggled deftly with the supper plates. 'I should have come with you. For heaven's sake get a surveyor's report before you sign anything. Tell her, Nick.'

'I never argue with a woman who's made up her mind to something,' said Nick, pouring three large brandies. 'Waste of breath. D'you want me to ask Paul Hicks to do the conveyancing for you, Hattie?'

'That's very nice of you, Nick, but I've got my own chap, thanks. Saw to everything when my mother died. I'll stick with him.'

'Fair enough.' Nick passed Sarah her brandy. 'Cheer up, my love. Sounds as if she's made friends already.'

'But what if this Joss goes off on his boat?' cried Sarah. 'You'll be stuck all on your own. Oh, I do wish you'd reconsider!'

'But I shan't be alone,' said Hattie. 'As soon as the mill's habitable I shall move in and let the cottages. There will be people just across the yard.'

'Very risky!' said Sarah darkly. 'You never know who you might get.'

Nick and Hattie burst out laughing.

'You're hopeless,' said Hattie affectionately. 'Anyway, I shall have the Admiral. He'll protect me. And that reminds me,' she added before Sarah could cast aspersions on the Admiral's abilities as a guard dog, 'he's been outside rather a long time. I think I'll go and check on him.'

She left the room, glad to get away from Sarah's anxieties which she'd been voicing ever since the agent had phoned to tell Hattie that her offer had been accepted. Outside in the cold March night, she called to the Admiral, who appeared from the darkness and thrust his nose into her hand before disappearing again almost immediately. She thought about the mill and the cottages, the creek with its hard, the track up into the woods, and felt it was all too good to be true.

In six weeks, she thought, I could be in. Living at Abbot's Mill.

She sighed with happiness and excitement and, calling again to the Admiral, turned back towards the house.

Chapter Two

On still, early summer mornings the creek was a magic place; the soft white low-lying mist suffused with golden light, the incoming tide – bearing on its breast two graceful swans – sweeping in across the mudflats where the heron stood in lonely contemplation. A wren fossicked in the bushes at the water's edge and, higher up the valley, the hollow drumming of a woodpecker echoed round the thickly wooded hills. As salt water met with fresh the ketch anchored in the deep channel stirred, lifting as the tide slapped gently round her hull.

Observing the eternally changing scene from his lawn, which ran down to the creek, Toby Dakers relaxed into the overwhelming atmosphere of tranquillity. He knew how lucky he'd been to find this retreat; a pair of cottages on a tidal creek, off the beaten track. He'd been told that they'd formerly belonged to the fishermen who worked the river for eels and salmon and he and Ruth had knocked the cottages into one roomy house, renovated it and slowly transformed it into a charming, comfortable home. That was in the early days, before Ruth had become bored with the novelty of country living and had urged him to return to his job in the City. Fifteen years in a merchant bank – with the last seven trading in futures – was more than enough in Toby's view and he'd refused. He had a very good portfolio of investments, they owned the cottage outright and he'd bought himself in as a partner in the boatyard which was further down the creek. Why go back to the pressure, the noise, the rat race?

The rising sun was drawing up the mist, touching the tree-tops with fire, and the soft pale mud had all but vanished beneath the encroaching tide. Toby stared out over the creek, his mind running over the scenes that had been played and replayed.

'You love this place more than you love me!' she'd shouted. 'Or Georgia!'

'Be fair,' he'd pleaded. 'You know that's not true. I can't just stroll back in and take up where I left off. You know it's not that easy. I've been out of it for three years. It's not that kind of job.'

'You could do something else. You've got masses of contacts.' But her voice was less sure. She knew he spoke the truth and that it would be impossible for him.

'I don't want to do anything else.' He'd held out a hand to her. 'Come on, Ruth. Be reasonable.'

'It's you that's not reasonable.' She'd stared at him, unmollified by his expression of love and beseeching. 'You won't admit we got it wrong. That this sort of life is fun for a bit but it soon wears thin. We could keep the place for weekends and holidays.'

'I don't want to use it for weekends and holidays.' His hand dropped back to his side. 'I want to live in it. I don't think we made a mistake. I love it here.'

'That's what I said! You love it more than you love me . . .'

On and on it had gone whilst Toby tried everything he knew to make up to her for all the things she missed. He knew that she pined for the social life and, more importantly, the status his position and wealth had given her. To begin with, the idea of taking off to live in a creekside cottage with Toby and the ten-year-old Georgia had been exciting. It was different, and their friends had been impressed and envious. These friends had travelled down for weekends and fallen in love with the creek and the cottage. They'd been loud in their admiration but, as the months passed, Ruth felt it harder to settle down when they'd gone. Much though they professed to love it, she noticed that none of them was prepared to follow suit and move down and their talk of mutual friends, new plays and parties unsettled her. For Ruth the experiment had been a failure; for Toby it was a tremendous success.

He simply couldn't imagine how she could begin to want to go back to London and tried to alleviate her boredom by taking her out more and making no objection to the house being used as a weekend retreat for a continuous flow of people. It wasn't enough.

Had he been justified, he asked himself for the millionth time, in standing firm; in refusing to go back? After all, when he'd asked Ruth to marry him she couldn't have known he'd want her to leave London and settle in such a place.

'A godforsaken hole . . . cultural desert . . . interminable rain . . .'

Her disdainful words echoed in his ears. How quickly she'd forgotten her own early raptures and that she'd loved it as much as he did.

The heron's unhurried flight downstream recalled Toby's attention and he smiled a little to see the swans – back-paddling in the hope of breakfast – beside the ketch. He loved the seasons on the river, the continual cycle of life, the familiar yet exciting pattern of it all. Ruth had accused him of becoming a vegetable and the arguments became more frequent and more acrimonious until she'd announced that her former boss had been promoted, was offering her a job as his PA and that she intended to take it.

She'd been defiant and determined; Toby, wondering whether she might not be as happy as she imagined back amongst the bright lights, had made only a small effort to fight it. That was two years ago and, ever since, she'd lived at her flat in London with Georgia. To begin with, they'd come home for weekends and holidays but gradually he'd seen less of them. Georgia was old enough to travel down alone by train and she came at half terms and for part of her holidays but Ruth came rarely and discouraged his suggestions that he should make the journey to London. He'd already decided that she'd met someone else or – more likely – had resurrected the friendship she'd had with Alan, her boss. She'd remained in touch with him, and Toby had always suspected that theirs had been more than just a working relationship.

Toby watched the Lysander swing round on her mooring ropes. He'd built her himself; a little two-berth estuary cruiser. A worthy successor to the Goblin dinghy he'd built in his mews garage in London all those years ago. Ruth had been unimpressed by his skill: unable to comprehend his immense satisfaction in creating something with his own hands. She'd watched with an expression very close to disgust when he returned from the boatyard in dirty overalls and with paint staining his hands.

'If I'd wanted to marry a labourer, I'd have done so,' she said icily when he tried to share his sense of fulfilment. 'How you can be satisfied with this after what you've achieved in the past, I simply can't imagine.'

It was at this time that she'd begun to escape back to London; a day's shopping here, a weekend there, a few days with friends. Georgia was a weekly boarder at St Margaret's School in Exeter and Ruth had plenty of time to herself. She and Toby were drifting further and further apart and neither of them seemed inclined to make a real effort to halt the process. When she'd sprung the news of the job upon him, Toby wondered whether she'd been seeing Alan during those visits and, when she blocked his own visits to London, he felt quite certain that something was going on.

13

Then, out of the blue, he'd received a letter from her telling him that she wanted a divorce. She saw no point, she wrote, in carrying on in this indeterminate state. She'd heard that a divorce might be granted on the grounds of an irretrievable breakdown of the marriage and she trusted that he had no objection.

Toby packed a bag and went straight to London but Ruth was adamant. Either he moved back to London and took a sensible job or the divorce would go through. It took him a week to decide. Those few days were more than enough to make him realise that he didn't belong in the big city any more but he begged her to think carefully about divorce. It was such a huge step and there was Georgia to consider. Ruth told him that she'd given it all a great deal of thought. Naturally, Georgia would continue to visit him regularly and spend holidays with him and occasionally she, Ruth, would come too, just to show there was no hard feeling and to make it easier for Georgia to adjust. However, she pointed out, there would be hardly any difference as far as Georgia was concerned.

'There's a psychological difference,' he'd insisted. 'We're still married and your home is with me, even if you don't spend much time there. At any moment we might get back together properly.'

He saw the flash of contempt in her eyes and raised his eyebrows.

'You know how I feel,' she said, shrugging. 'You say you won't come back. As far as I'm concerned, that's that.'

'Did you only love me because of what I was?'

'You know it's not that simple,' she said, avoiding his attempted embrace. 'You've changed. You were exciting, sharp, powerful. Now you amble about in old clothes like some sort of dropout.'

'Can you imagine what life's like on the trading floor?' he asked, exasperated. 'Taking crucial decisions in thirteen seconds flat for eight hours a day? I've known people who burn themselves out by the time they're thirty. Is it wrong to want to relax and enjoy the rewards of all that pressure?'

'You don't have to live on a muddy creek in the back of beyond to relax,' she cried, and he turned away at the reiteration of the things she'd been saying for the last few years. 'We could have relaxed here, going to the opera and the theatre and dinners with our friends.'

'I didn't want that,' he said bleakly.

'Oh, no! And it has to be what you want, doesn't it?'

'You wanted it, too.'

'OK. To begin with it was fun and I'd have been perfectly happy to go down for weekends and holidays . . .'

'Oh, Ruth,' he said wearily, 'let's forget it. We've been over it a million times. We had fifteen good years here but I needed a change. I couldn't come back now.'

The sharp smack of *Westering*'s hatch being pushed back echoed across the water and Toby saw Joss's fair head emerging from the companionway. It was not the time for shouted greetings or exchanges, shattering the peace and dispelling the magic of the morning, and Toby slipped away leaving Joss with the swans as company.

A few hours later Toby walked the short distance to his car which he kept on the hard as close as he could to the cottage. He heard the rumble of a heavy vehicle coming down the lane and paused to watch the large removal van pull into the mill yard. He'd already met Hattie, brought along to the cottage by Joss, and had approved the short sturdy woman with her determination and excitement at the prospect of her new project. It would be good to have a neighbour again. Of course, Joss was always there, making his boat seaworthy, preparing for the great voyage he planned, but it would be fun to have another member in their tiny community.

He drove over the bridge and headed for Dartmouth. Georgia would be arriving for her half-term holiday in a few days' time and he needed to stock up. Being so far from civilisation, he tended to do a big shopping run once a month, loading the car up and then buying himself lunch at the Royal Castle as a kind of reward. This morning the town was fairly quiet and he parked on the Embankment. The river was busy again after the winter; most of the local boats were back in the water and the passenger ferry was chugging across to Kingswear. Toby paused to watch a line of cutters from the naval college heading down river and then turned his attention to his shopping list.

Miggy Hardcastle, standing at her bedroom window in the Royal Castle Hotel, stared out across the boat-float to the river. She was still wondering how she'd had the courage to tell her husband that she needed to go away, to be alone for a few days. Stephen was the type of man who looked upon such dramatic flights of fancy as foolish and unnecessary. Even more difficult had been leaving her ten-year-old daughter, Daisy, who'd been outraged when Stephen had refused to allow her to miss school and accompany Miggy. Poor Daisy! Miggy smiled a little sadly to herself. During the five years between the death of her husband Patrick – Daisy's father – and her marriage to Stephen she and Daisy had been continually together and it had been hard for the child to understand that their relationship must adapt and expand to take Stephen into their lives. Despite the efforts made, it hadn't taken long for Miggy – and Stephen – to realise that they were totally unsuited as a couple. She'd married him in a rush of loneliness, impressed by his ability to know his own mind and go for what he wanted. She was in need of adult companionship and Stephen, so different from the youthful, easy-going, optimistic Patrick, flattered her by his attentions.

Opposites may attract but – after the novelty has worn thin – they can also irritate. Stephen liked an efficiently run home and enjoyed a busy round of entertaining and socialising. Poor Miggy had come sadly unstuck in this demanding routine and had fallen well short of Stephen's demands. He was an extremely erudite barrister and she and Daisy were easy targets for his ironical – and hurtful – humour. His friends, who had been amazed at his infatuation for this Bohemian widow of a struggling artist, had quickly seen which way the winds of disillusionment were blowing and made no attempt to hide their prejudices or opinions of this unlikely match. Soon Miggy was lonelier than she'd ever been, even after Patrick's death, and had long since felt little more than a rather unwelcome guest in Stephen's gracious house in Chelsea.

She turned her back on the busy scene beyond the window and wandered over to the bed. She'd chosen Dartmouth because it was the first place that had come to mind when Stephen had asked sarcastically, 'And what romantic venue has been selected for this *retreat*?' She'd come to love the town whilst visiting her friends Jo and David Harper, who lived a few miles away at Dittisham. They'd been surprised when Miggy had insisted on staying at the Castle. Jo was a supply teacher, David ran his own small engineering company from premises in Townstal and both of them were out during the day. Miggy had used this as a reason for staying in the town but Jo saw behind the excuse and suspected that Miggy needed time on her own. She'd picked her up from the station at Totnes and, much to Miggy's relief, had accepted her explanation that it was sensible to be central. They'd had supper together and David had promised to take her out to lunch since Jo was on dinner duty and couldn't get away from school. Miggy glanced at her watch. He should be here at any moment and, picking up her key and her bag from the bed, she went downstairs.

An hour later Toby was in the back bar at the Castle with a pint in front of him, his shopping done. He sighed with relief and relaxed comfortably. Of course, the unloading of the car was yet to come; the trekking to and fro with the bags from the hard to the cottage. This had quickly become another bone of contention, especially on wet winter days. Ruth had cursed the inconvenience of it until Toby had come up with a solution. The shopping would be unloaded into a large plastic wheelbarrow, kept only for this task, and wheeled straight into the utility room to be unpacked at leisure. It had worked well enough until recently the big ball of the wheel had split and Toby was back to trekking to and fro. It really didn't bother him enough to do anything about the wheelbarrow but it was sad to think how quickly the things that had begun as fun deteriorated into causes for complaint.

The bar was filling up and Toby ordered his lunch, nodding at one or two locals as he finished his pint. His attention was caught by a striking-looking girl who came in rather hesitantly, waited her turn at the bar and then carried her glass of wine to a seat in the far corner. Toby studied her covertly. She was tall and slender, pale-skinned and delicate-boned, with short coppery curls; her loose navy-blue cotton jersey and short denim skirt emphasising her rather fragile appearance. She seemed sunk in thought; her head dropped forward, chin on chest, her long legs stretched out in front of her, crossed at the ankles.

Toby was very taken with her and wished that he could catch her eye. It was a long time since he'd had any female company, apart from the social round with the friends that they'd made during the last six years and which he'd kept up with since Ruth left. Until recently he'd regarded himself as a married man whose wife, though absent, may wish to return at any moment and, with Georgia visiting so regularly, he didn't want any sordid muddles. However, since Ruth came home so rarely and now with the shock of the divorce proceedings, Toby felt that he was at liberty to make his own life. He finished his pint and, out of the corner of his eye, saw the girl look up. He saw David Harper come in, glance around and go to greet her. He kissed her lightly as an old friend might. Toby took his elbow off the bar and was waiting for him when he came to order.

'Hello, David. How's life? Haven't seen you on the river lately.'

'Toby!' David clapped him on the shoulder. 'Never seem to get the time these days. We must get together. What are you drinking?' He glanced across his shoulder and lowered his voice a little. 'Just meeting a friend for lunch. She's down for a few days.'

'Lucky old you,' said Toby lightly. 'Pretty, isn't she? I was just getting up the courage to talk to her when you arrived.'

'Why not join us?' asked David at once.

Toby pretended to hesitate. 'Won't she mind if I butt in?'

'Be relieved I shouldn't wonder. She's more Jo's friend than mine but Jo's tied up at school. Come and meet her.'

Toby followed David to the corner table.

'This is Miggy Hardcastle,' said David, putting the drinks down. 'An old sailing friend of mine, Miggy – Toby Dakers.'

'Hello.' Toby held out his hand. 'Miggy? That's an unusual name.'

She grimaced a little as they sat down with her. 'It's short for Mignonette. I know!' She grinned at his expression. 'Flower names for girls is a tradition in our family and I was named after a wealthy spinster aunt in great expectation.'

'And did it materialise?'

'Afraid not.' Miggy shook her head. 'Left it all to the cats' home and I was lumbered with the name.'

'I think it suits you.' David smiled at her. 'After all, it could have been worse. Think of some of the alternatives!'

'Gloxinia?' hazarded Miggy. 'Wood Spurge? You're probably right. I've called my daughter Daisy,' she told Toby. 'She seems to like it at the moment but she'll probably curse me when she grows up.'

So she had a daughter. Toby had already noticed the rings on the third finger of her left hand.

'I've invited Toby to join us for lunch,' David was saying. 'Can't leave him to eat all alone, can we? If you ask him nicely he might take you out in his boat while you're here.'

'Oh.' Miggy looked a little taken aback. She liked the look of Toby in his old flannels and jersey but felt that David was being rather high-handed in putting his time and boat at her disposal.

'I'd be delighted to,' said Toby, blessing David for his suggestion and trying not to sound too keen. 'If you think you'd enjoy it?'

'Well, thank you.' She hesitated, wondering whether anyone else might be included in this unexpected expedition. 'It sounds rather fun although I have to say at once that I'm no sailor. So you have your own boat?'

'I do. Just a little cruiser but she's got an outboard engine and you'd be quite safe.'

'He's quite trustworthy,' David assured her. 'On all counts. Terrific afternoon to be out on the river.'

'I'd love it,' said Miggy, making up her mind and Toby smiled at her in relief.

'Let's order,' said David. 'I mustn't be too long.'

Toby stood up to fetch them a menu from the bar, his heart beating fast with anticipation and excitement. He'd already decided to set her mind at rest as much as was possible during lunch by referring to his divorce and to Georgia, and would try not to do or say anything that could be misconstrued during the afternoon. He gave her a few moments alone with David, so that she could ask any questions about him without embarrassment, and then took the menu back to where they waited for him.

Chapter Three

Hattie soon had one of the mill cottages looking habitable although the furniture from her mother's house overflowed into the adjoining one and several of the larger pieces into the mill itself. Joss and Toby dropped in to offer assistance, which she instantly accepted, and advice, which she considered more carefully, whilst dithering between whether she should renovate the mill first or the second cottage. She wanted to start letting as soon as possible so as to boost her income but, when Joss suggested that she'd get a much higher rent for the mill than she would for both the cottages put together, Hattie was adamant. She wanted to live in the mill. Both men had been privy to the previous owners' ideas and plans and were very willing to make suggestions as to how her ideals could be achieved. They gave her the name of a local builder she could trust and Joss offered his own services for the smaller jobs.

Once everything was costed out, Hattie decided that she could afford to get the mill together first and then turn her attention to the second cottage whilst letting the one she presently occupied. Relieved to have come to a decision, she began to get herself organised. By keeping things simple and retaining many of the mill's original features, it was possible that she'd be in by the autumn. Meanwhile, whilst the major alterations were taking place, she would do as much as she could to the cottages.

Joss, amused by her inability to wait calmly for anything, teased her about her impatience.

'You'll never fit in down here if you don't relax a bit,' he told her when she waylaid him on the hard with yet another timesaving idea for the renovation of the cottages. 'You know what they say about West Country people? They use the word "directly" as you've probably noticed. "I'll do it directly," or, "I'll be round directly." Foreigners think they mean "immediately". But when the locals say "directly" you should interpret it as meaning "*mañana*" but without the same sense of urgency. You'll have to adapt to the local pace.'

'I can't afford to hang about,' said Hattie. 'I can be getting on with the cottages whilst Mr Crabtree is working on the mill. What an old duck he is! The Admiral adores him.'

'But does he adore the Admiral?' countered Joss. 'He carries old Crabbie's tools into the orchard and I can hear him swearing from halfway down the creek.'

'I know,' said Hattie indulgently. 'But he doesn't mind a bit really. You should see him when he thinks no one's looking. Chats to him and brings him biscuits. The Admiral may look enormous but he's still a young dog. He likes a little game.'

'God help us all when he grows up,' remarked Joss, looking at Admiral Jellicoe as he sat on the hard, ears pricked, gazing in astonishment at a family of mallard that had just taken to the water. 'Look. When the autumn comes I shan't be able to work on the boat full time so I can lend you a hand with the cottages. Don't bust a gut.'

'You told me that you overwintered in one last year.' Hattie looked at him questioningly. 'Will you want to do that again this winter?'

Joss hesitated. 'I might, if that's OK. I'm not quite sure yet. If I do, I'll work for you in lieu of rent. We'll get them both shipshape ready for the spring. I've got a long way to go with *Westering* yet so I'll be grateful to have a bolt hole during the rough weather.'

'It's a deal,' said Hattie at once. She watched as he untied his dinghy and settled himself at the oars. Admiral Jellicoe watched too. He wondered if he might be needed to do a spot of rescue work if Joss suddenly took to the water.

'Stay!' said Joss severely, and the Admiral's ears flattened and his tongue lolled out but he still watched closely. 'If he starts trying to rescue me again I'll sock him with an oar,' Joss shouted to Hattie.

Hattie chuckled and put a restraining hand on the Admiral's head. Not long after Hattie's arrival Joss had decided to go for an early morning swim. Presently he found the Admiral paddling beside him, urging him in to the shore. Joss resisted with imprecations and attempts to push the great dog away but Admiral Jellicoe was adamant and, when Joss refused to seize him round the neck and be towed safely to shore, the Admiral merely pushed him with his great bulk until he was beached on the hard. Hattie, helpless with laughter, had come to meet them and the Admiral, looking tremendously pleased with himself, had bounded out, shaken himself all over her and pranced off to find a well-earned breakfast.

Hattie was still grinning at the memory when Joss reached *Westering* and, raising a hand to him, she turned away to take the Admiral for a walk up the track that led over the wooded hill to the boatyard. She liked Joss. He was ex-Army and their service backgrounds meant that they had certain things in common but she'd learned more about him from Toby than from Joss himself. She knew that he'd come outside at the end of his short-service commission and had decided to buy an old boat and do it up before setting off on an extended voyage. She guessed that he was in his late twenties and she liked his quiet competence and air of independence.

Hattie whistled quietly to herself as she followed the Admiral up the track. She was beginning to feel very much at home. Her cottage was quite comfortable and she could see that the mill was going to be delightful when it was finished. The surrounding countryside was breathtakingly beautiful and, although she had no desire to take up boating, she'd begun to take a great interest in the wildlife of the creek. Here Toby was very useful. He knew all the birds and their habits and was lending her books so that she could further her knowledge. He was more relaxed than Joss, more open, and Hattie found his company very restful. It was difficult to imagine him as he'd been in London and Hattie could sympathise with his desire to put the stress and fast-living behind him. Over a bottle of wine one evening he'd told her about Ruth and how she felt and about the impending divorce. Hattie listened but reserved her judgement. One of the things she'd learned during her career was that every story has two sides and, whilst showing sympathy for his own feelings, she decided that she'd like to meet Ruth.

She'd already met Georgia. At sixteen she was a rather heavily built girl with a faintly sulky, secretive air and, after a friendly greeting, Hattie had left her much to herself. She could sense the girl summing her up and was rather amused by the adult air she assumed. She was very possessive of Toby, whilst attempting to display indifference, and Hattie wondered just how much the divorce would affect her. Then, the next afternoon, Toby had appeared with a young woman he'd invited to tea. He'd brought her up to show her the mill and Hattie chatted with them on the hard, rather intrigued. She was obviously not an old friend and Hattie wondered whether Toby had decided to strike out on his own and how Georgia would take it.

Having reached the entrance to the boatyard, Hattie called to the Admiral and turned back to the mill. Sarah was coming to

23

lunch and Hattie had to get back to do some shopping. She loved her trips to Dartmouth and looked forward to a stroll along the embankment and a cup of coffee at one of the cafés. Despite Joss's teasing she was beginning to adapt very well to this quieter, slower life and had begun to feel that she was on a never-ending holiday.

Sarah, seeing how much Hattie was achieving and how happy she was, felt a strange pang of envy. This was absurd, she told herself. She had no desire whatever to live in a pair of old cottages whilst renovating a mill with no one but a huge dog, two young men and an assortment of wildfowl for company. Yet Hattie seemed so content, so single-minded. She ate, slept, came and went as she chose and, moreover, her emotions were so painlessly whole and intact. Sarah, who had trained herself to live with Nick's infidelities, found that particularly enviable; yet she knew she couldn't bear to live without him. From the first moment she'd met him, she'd adored him and her passion had remained unchanged during the ensuing fourteen years. But how hard it had been! She remembered each act of unfaithfulness and still burned with jealousy. Oddly, each occasion had merely served to make her desire him more and, though she knew she was making a rod for her own back, she never punished him or withdrew her love. In her heart she knew that Nick had married her for her money and connections but he had come to love her and he always came back to her. He was hers.

Sarah, listening to Hattie's plans over lunch, pushed away those disloyal feelings of envy. She knew that one day Nick would tire of playing the field and she would have him to herself. When that happened all the self-discipline she'd imposed upon herself over the years would have paid off. She smiled at Hattie with very real affection, remembering her kindness when she, Sarah, had first met her all those years ago. She was her only true friend, the only one who knew about Nick's behaviour and the pain it caused. Others might suspect but no one knew the real truth; only Hattie. Nick was very discreet, choosing his partners with care and finishing each relationship with great tact, making quite certain that his reputation remained unsullied. He was known as the best litigation lawyer in the West Country and he had no intention of rocking any boats. Sarah's money and contacts had helped to put him where he was and supported his expensive tastes, and she knew that he would never risk losing them for a mere love affair. Of course, she could have used her money as a weapon, she could have made conditions, but she'd always shrunk from the knowledge that she'd bought him. By various means she could persuade herself that his peccadilloes meant nothing, that they were only to be expected of such a handsome and successful man, and that she was the only woman that he really loved.

'I have a feeling that you're not concentrating.' Hattie's voice broke into her thoughts. 'I'm probably boring you to death. You must forgive me. It's all rather gone to my head. How are things with you? Nick behaving himself?'

Hattie was the only person who could have asked that question without it being offensive and Sarah nodded.

'No problems at the moment. Not for a while, actually. And you're not boring me. I think it's all very exciting. You look remarkably well on it.'

'I feel wonderful,' said Hattie simply. 'After thirty-odd years of working to rigid timetables it's sheer bliss to do exactly as I please. I keep thinking that I shall wake up one morning to find the holiday's over and I'm back on the wards.'

'And you're not lonely?'

'Good grief, no! There's Joss on his boat and Toby down the creek and the boatyard people. Not to mention Mr Crabtree. It's quite a little community. And when I start letting my cottages it'll be busier still.'

'But you will be careful, won't you? You'll interview people thoroughly and take references?'

'Don't fuss!' said Hattie good-naturedly. 'Admiral Jellicoe is the test. If they love him, they're in!'

Sarah looked at the Admiral, who was sitting looking hopefully at the plates with his huge head nearly on a level with Hattie's shoulder, and shook her head.

'You're spoiling him to death,' she said severely. 'I can see that. It's what comes of living alone. You treat him as if he were a person.'

'He *is* a person!' exclaimed Hattie indignantly. 'Aren't you, Jellicoe?'

She put an arm around his neck and he licked her ear affectionately and leaned heavily against her chair, moving her several inches across the floor. Sarah laughed.

'You're both hopeless,' she said. 'Come on. Let's get the washing-up done. I haven't seen all these places you've told me about yet. The orchard and the hard and the wonderful walk in the woods. I want to see it all before I go. I've promised Nick a blow-by-blow account.'

Hattie put the leftovers into the Admiral's bowl and began to stack the plates together.

'You shall have a guided tour,' she said. 'But I'm hoping Nick's going to come over to see it all for himself.'

'Of course he will. Now that you're settled in.' Sarah picked up a tea cloth. 'Just tell us when. But I couldn't resist a quick dash over as soon as we got back from holiday. Just to make sure you're OK.'

'It's lovely to see you. I can't tell you how comforting it is to know that you're just away across the moor. No, leave all that.' She took the tea cloth from Sarah's hands. 'I'll wash up when you've gone. Come and see my orchard. Trees and trees of lovely Bramleys. I'll be eating apple pie all winter long.'

With the Admiral at their heels they strolled out into the sultry June afternoon and Hattie experienced the great thrill of ownership as she showed her round and outlined her plans. They wandered out on to the hard and took the track that led up to the road through the woods. At its highest point, before it dropped away again to the boatyard, Sarah caught her breath at the view laid out before her. From here she could see the mouth of the creek, widening out into the River Dart. The water shivered and dazzled in the sunshine and white sails danced and swooped like gulls' wings over the river. As they stood gazing out they heard the unmistakable sound of a steam engine running through Long Wood on the further shore.

'Courtesy of our local steam railway preservation society.' Hattie grinned at Sarah's surprised face. 'Like living in another world, isn't it? I couldn't believe it the first time I heard it.'

'It's all quite beautiful. I almost envy you,' said Sarah as they turned back.

'Rubbish!' said Hattie. 'You'd be bored stiff in five minutes without all your committees and charities and dinner parties. But I hope you'll come and see me now and then.'

When she'd waved Sarah off, Hattie went to find Mr Crabtree.

'It occurs to me,' she said, perching on the edge of an old tea-chest in what would one day be her sitting room, 'that when I start letting the cottages I might need someone to help me out. Cleaning and so on, especially if I do holiday lets. Do you know anyone who might be prepared to come and lend a hand?'

Mr Crabtree rubbed a calloused hand over his bristly chin and delved into his overall pocket for his tin of tobacco. Slowly he rolled himself a cigarette whilst Hattie sat peaceably watching him. She'd grown used to the long silences he required for deep thinking and merely used the time to relax.

'Holiday lets're nuthin' but trouble,' he observed. 'People in an' out every fortnight, breakin' things 'n' damagin' the furniture. Yew'll be worryin' about the bookin's 'n' gettin' cancellations 'n' redecoratin' every five minutes. 'Tisn't never worth the bother of it all.'

'Oh,' said Hattie, somewhat disconcerted.

'Doun'ee take my word fer it.' He tucked the spent match tidily back in its matchbox. 'Anyone round 'ere'll tell'ee the same.'

'Perhaps you're right.' Hattie rose from her tea-chest, aware that there was nothing else to be achieved at the moment. 'You're getting on splendidly. It's beginning to look lovely.'

This was true; Mr Crabtree was a craftsman. He nodded an acknowledgement of her appreciation, stubbed out his cigarette carefully and prepared to resume work, casting a thoughtful glance at his flask.

'I expect you'd like a cup of tea,' said Hattie, interpreting the glance correctly. 'I know I would. Shan't be long.'

She went across the yard and began to wash up the lunch things whilst she waited for the kettle to boil. As she worked, she thought about Sarah. The more she saw of the married state, the less she regretted not marrying. Certainly Nick and Sarah's marriage was not a good example of wedded bliss but she'd never yet witnessed a good enough relationship to make her change her mind. As far as she could judge there seemed to be two types of *modus vivendi*; either a manipulative battle was carried on between the two protagonists, each of whom attempted to prey on the guilt of the other; or a peaceable union was maintained by one of the partners being prepared to give way on a permanent basis to the other.

Neither would have suited Hattie. She suspected that she might have reacted differently if she'd ever fallen so completely in love as Sarah had but she was inclined to think that, even at the height of her love affair, she'd never truly known what it was like to love and be loved. Perhaps if she'd had the child . . .

The kettle boiled and Hattie hung out the tea cloth and began to make the tea.

Chapter Four

Across the creek from Fisherman's Cottage, a small inlet was carved out beneath a steep, densely wooded promontory. Here, lying in almost permanent shadow, an old fishing boat was berthed. The *Abigail* had been converted some time ago and now had very spacious living quarters. Locally she was known as an unlucky boat and, some years before, she'd been brought round to the creek, moored in the inlet and forgotten. Quite recently a young man had been seen on board. Toby described him as a hippy – long-haired, heavily bearded, scruffily dressed – who made no attempt to venture out into the creek, approaching the *Abigail* from the landward side by walking down through the woods from the lane above where his motorbike was hidden away under the trees. Since the *Abigail* was supported by wooden legs which kept her upright when the tide went down, living aboard was perfectly comfortable and a long gangplank stretching from the stern to the foreshore made sure that she was always accessible at any stage of the tide.

After a few weeks, Joss rowed round to make acquaintance with her new owner and to have a closer look at *Abigail*. There was smoke coming from the chimney stack and Joss stopped rowing, leaned on his oars and hailed her.

'Ahoy there, *Abigail*! Anybody aboard?'

Silence. The tide was high and he paddled a little closer, suddenly aware of being watched from one of the portholes. He pretended not to see and rowed a short distance away before giving another shout. 'Anyone at home?'

There was a movement and a figure appeared in the companion-way. Joss shipped his oars, caught at a mooring rope and raised a hand. The young man came to the taffrail and stared down at him. 'What d'you want?'

Joss ignored the unpromising greeting. 'Just came to say hello. We're neighbours. I live aboard *Westering*, the ketch moored further up the creek. I'm Joss Sullivan.'

'Joss . . . ?'

'Short for Jocelyn.' Joss wondered whether *Abigail*'s owner had been drinking. He seemed unsteady in his movements and his speech was slow and very slightly slurred. 'Are you living aboard? You must have plenty of room.'

'Yeah.' The young man nodded and began to smile a little. 'Wanna come and have a look?'

'Thanks.' Suddenly Joss knew that he didn't want to go aboard and was regretting the impulse that had sent him rowing round. He hesitated. 'Just for a moment then.'

He made the painter fast and swung himself over the rail. The young man watched him, still smiling rather slyly. His hair was matted, his clothes stained and his bare feet were filthy. Joss repressed his instinctive antipathy and smiled.

'Been on board long?'

'Month or two. On and off.' He gestured to the companionway. 'Got some beer if you want it.'

Joss followed him down and his eyes grew wide at the scene below. The galley was full of empty tins and unwashed crockery, the stove was black with grease and grime and, although there were cabins fore and aft, it was obvious that this unsavoury owner was sleeping in the main cabin on a mattress pulled close to the woodburning stove. The mattress was piled with blankets and clothes, empty beer cans rolled unheeded into every corner and Joss found that he was holding his breath against the gut-turning stench that assailed his nostrils. The young man was still watching him with that unnerving smile and Joss wondered if he were perhaps slightly deranged. He felt a sharp sense of danger and looked him firmly in the eye.

'I won't stop now, thanks,' he said. 'This was simply a friendly call to say that I'm just up the creek if you need anything. Sorry, I didn't catch your name?'

'It's Evan,' he said, after a pause. 'Evan 'elp us!'

He began to laugh, a kind of high-pitched giggle, and Joss forced himself to laugh with him at the feeble joke.

'Quite. Very amusing.' He turned and went back up the companionway, gulping down the sweet fresh air for a moment before Evan joined him. 'Don't you find it a bit gloomy over on this side? Ever thought of moving her across the creek? You only get the sun in the height of summer, don't you? The trees block it out almost completely.'

'I don't mind.' Evan didn't take his eyes from Joss's face.

'Well . . .' Joss hesitated. 'I'd better get back. See you again.'

He swung himself down into the dinghy, cast off the painter and began to row away whilst Evan watched him from the deck. With a little shock Joss realised that someone else was watching him from below, a dark shadow beyond the porthole; that another person had been present all the time in the cabin up for'ard. Repressing a shiver, Joss pulled strongly for the creek and tried not to be melodramatic. Evan had probably got a girl down there and she didn't want to be seen, which was perfectly reasonable. Although Joss, being a sailing man, wouldn't have wanted the *Abigail* he found himself irritated by the fact that she was in such a disgusting state. She was so roomy and comfortable and could be made quite delightful. It was clear that Evan was not interested in her as a boat but simply as somewhere to slum.

Toby was fiddling in his boathouse across from the entrance to the inlet and Joss hailed him with relief.

'Been visiting?' Toby bent down to hold the dinghy. 'What's he like?'

'Pretty peculiar.' Joss grimaced distastefully. 'And the boat stinks. It's a real hole below. She could be a lovely boat but he's just using her as a dosshouse. I think he's got a woman on board.'

Toby raised his eyebrows. 'Lucky devil,' he said lightly. 'Want a drink? I'm just going to make myself some supper.'

'No . . .' began Joss and then changed his mind. 'OK. Anything to get the taste out of my mouth.'

'That bad?' asked Toby as they walked up the lawn together.

'There was a beastly smell,' Joss told him. 'Dirt and bad food and something else . . .'

'What sort of something else?'

'A sweetish smell. Sort of acrid.'

They looked at each other.

'Drugs?' suggested Toby. 'Smoking cannabis?'

'I wondered,' admitted Joss. 'He looked half-witted but sly. Anyway, I shall steer clear of him. Better keep an eye on Georgia when she comes down for the holidays.'

'Mmm.' Toby sounded preoccupied as he took the beer from the fridge.

'Isn't she coming?'

'Oh, yes. She's coming.'

After Joss had gone rowing back up the creek, Toby poured

31

himself another beer and wandered back outside. The sun was dipping behind the trees beyond the mill and he sat down on the wooden bench and stared out over the water. The problem was he simply couldn't get Miggy out of his mind. In those few days they'd spent together he'd fallen in love with her and he'd been miserable ever since she'd gone back to London. He'd told himself that it was foolish for a man of nearly forty to feel like a boy of seventeen in the throes of love but somehow it didn't help. In those early moments of madness he'd even invited her to tea and introduced her to Georgia. He grimaced a little as he remembered his daughter's reaction.

Georgia had been shocked to see her father in their home with a woman other than her mother. Her alarm had taken the form of unfriendly superciliousness. She monopolised Toby and had attempted to make Miggy feel thoroughly unwelcome. If Miggy noticed – and she must have done – she ignored it completely and kept the visit on fairly formal lines. She certainly gave Georgia no grounds for anxiety but Toby knew that his daughter was no fool. She'd never seen him with a young woman to whom he was obviously attracted. Much though he had tried to hide it, Toby knew that his feelings for Miggy had shown through his carefully schooled expression and he felt anxious and irritated by turns. After all, he'd been by himself for some while now and if Ruth chose to divorce him then he had every right to seek another relationship. Surely Georgia was old enough to accept that!

Toby leaned forward, resting his elbows on his knees. He watched the heron fishing on the further bank as the tide ebbed, but his thoughts were far away. Their time together had been too short to find out as much about Miggy as he longed to know but he guessed that things were not well within her marriage. He had no intention of causing trouble but he was determined not to miss his chance. He'd told her that he was coming to London for a few days and cautiously, but not necessarily reluctantly, she agreed to meet him. They'd been delighted to see each other again and he'd known then, quite surely, that Miggy felt as he did.

It had been a strange and magical sensation to know that the deep attraction was mutual and, very soon, he'd elicited the fact that she wasn't happy with Stephen. He hardly knew how to proceed. He sensed that they were both frightened at the speed at which their emotions were rushing away with them and, quite suddenly, he'd held out his hand to her as they sat on a bench beside the Serpentine, both locked separately in helpless fear.

After a moment she'd taken his hand and it was as if they'd passed beyond a barrier and were released from that paralysing impotence, able once more to take charge of their own lives. Toby knew exactly what he wanted but was unable to put it into words. It seemed far too early to tell Miggy how he really felt and it was only when he was back in Devon that he was seized with the dreadful thought that she might imagine that he was hoping for an affair with her.

Now, six weeks on, Toby sighed with impatience and drove his fingers through his dark floppy hair. It was unbearable to be so far away from her, to have no control. He had to leave it to her to telephone and he chafed with frustration and fear. She was going to come down with Daisy as soon as the school holidays started and Toby was living for that moment. He'd been praying that it would be before Georgia arrived for the long summer holiday and was deeply relieved to hear that she was going to France first with Ruth. He needed to be alone with Miggy and have time to get to know Daisy. They'd talked about her a great deal. It seemed that Stephen's temper frayed very easily if there was a hitch in the smooth, ordered running of his life and, on these occasions, Miggy felt inadequate and guilty and Daisy, it seemed, didn't help.

'Does she resent Stephen?' he'd asked, basely hoping to hear that they didn't get on.

'She doesn't resent Stephen,' she'd answered at last. 'She's not really that sort of child. They're just so different. Stephen's so . . . well, so absolutely down the middle and Daisy's sort of odd.'

'Odd?' asked Toby at last, when it seemed that Miggy felt that this was explanation enough.

Miggy glanced at him and then frowned. 'She's not what Stephen considers normal,' she said sadly.

Toby felt his heart give a little tock of selfish anxiety. He already had visions of Miggy leaving Stephen and moving into Fisherman's Cottage but an abnormal child was something of a setback.

'Whatever do you mean?' He kept his voice as casual as possible.

'It's difficult for me to understand,' admitted Miggy. 'She seems fine to me. But she's a very imaginative child and it throws Stephen. She talks to herself and invents people. You know? It's a kind of game but they seem very real to her. She lives in another world and Stephen thinks it's unhealthy.'

She'd sighed and Toby had taken her hand and held it tightly.

'It sounds perfectly normal to me,' he said reassuringly, and she'd smiled at him gratefully.

Remembering, Toby felt a yearning to hold her in his arms. When he was with her, he had no anxieties at all but now fear sometimes engulfed him and he wondered if he were quite mad. Could it really be possible to feel like this about someone you'd known for such a short time? Supposing he'd got it all wrong and that was just a passing madness? Even as he thought it, he rejected it. He loved her. It was as simple as that; and he intended to have her.

Toby finished his beer, glanced at his watch and got to his feet. Miggy sometimes telephoned about this time and he liked to be within earshot. He wondered whether this evening she'd tell him when she and Daisy would be coming down and the thought sent him hurrying up to the cottage.

Joss sat on his cabin roof, enjoying the last of the evening. He'd been glad to get back to *Westering* after his visit to *Abigail*. Even with the muddle that was necessary when a boat was being restored, she looked so clean and respectable after Evan's mess. *Westering* was a coble, built on the north-east coast some fifty years before. Being nearly flat-bottomed she was ideal for estuary cruising, resting quite happily on the mud and drawing only two feet of water. Joss had bought her very cheaply and, by doing as much as he could himself, hoped to restore her to her former glory whilst keeping within his budget.

He was well aware that his family considered it odd that he should want to waste two or three years of his life sitting on an old boat in a backwater but Joss had patiently explained to his disappointed mother that there was plenty of time to take up a respectable career once he'd got the wanderlust out of his system.

'Surely five years in the Army did that?' she'd asked plaintively.

Joss had explained that it wasn't the same thing at all and she'd turned to his sister – sensibly married to a stockbroker – for comfort. Joss had returned to Dartmouth, relieved to get away as usual. He sat in the stillness of the evening and felt his failure like a bitter taste in his mouth. How did you explain to your mother and your sister that a year in Northern Ireland had shattered your nerve and destroyed your confidence? How would they react if he told them that the sight of his sergeant with his leg

34

blown off and the screams of two young soldiers trapped beneath a burning truck still haunted his dreams and could bring tears of rage and pain to his eyes? Or that loud, sudden noises brought him out in a cold sweat of fear? How many times must he go over the scene of the ambush before he finally accepted that he hadn't been responsible? His father had died a general, unmoved by the horrors of war or the death of his companions, and it was necessary to come to terms with the fact that he wasn't the man his father had imagined his son to be.

The swifts screamed as they swooped above him and he saw Hattie emerge from the mill to take the Admiral for a last potter up the lane. The sight of the short brisk figure made him feel strangely comforted and he looked about him, relaxing in the peaceful atmosphere. The tide was out now, although *Westering* was still afloat in the deep-water channel, and a sickle moon hung over the mouth of the creek. Joss was visited by a healing sensation of calm and, returning Hattie's salute, went below for a nightcap before turning in.

Miggy decided to make one more trip to Devon alone before taking Daisy down. This time she stayed with Jo and David and, unable to keep her feelings bottled up any longer, told them the whole story. David, who disliked Stephen and was very fond of Toby, encouraged her to finish with Stephen and move down. Jo was more cautious. She considered Miggy and Stephen to be quite unsuited but she was afraid that Miggy was taking everything far too quickly. David pointed out that she and Toby were both old enough and sensible enough to know their own minds and Jo gave Miggy a quick kiss and told her that she only wanted her to be happy.

By the time Toby arrived to take Miggy out to supper, she was feeling calmer but, as soon as he entered the house, she was seized with a paralysing shyness. Now that Jo and David knew, the whole relationship took on another aspect. It had been an exciting and romantic secret, something to be hugged to the heart. Now she saw it through the eyes of others and suspected that it probably looked very different; grubby, perhaps, and rather sordid. Her temperament didn't take easily to lying or deceiving and she suddenly realised that David was looking at her and Toby rather speculatively. Miggy guessed that he was wondering if they were sleeping together and a wave of humiliation washed over her. She found herself resenting Toby, who was chatting easily to Jo, and almost wished that she'd stayed in London. She felt cheap and foolish and it wasn't until she and Toby were alone that she was able to think about him clearly again. So far they'd skirted round any talk of a future together, although it had been implicit in their conversations, and even now Miggy didn't know what Toby had in mind and she longed for the courage to ask him.

Toby, on his arrival at the cottage at Dittisham, took one look at her expressive face and knew exactly what she was feeling and thinking. He got her away as quickly as he could and drove her to Taylor's, where they had dinner sitting at the table in the bay window overlooking the boat-float. Neither of them had the least idea of what they ate but Toby kept the atmosphere light, talking amusingly and making her laugh. Miggy gradually relaxed but they were both aware of underlying currents of suppressed emotion and when Toby touched her hand she started violently and blushed. They looked at each other for a very long moment. Toby smiled as reassuringly as he could.

'Let's go somewhere and talk,' he suggested, and she followed him downstairs and back to the car.

Toby drove out on the cliff road toward Torcross and parked his Austin Healey in the deserted car park by the monument. They sat for some minutes in silence, staring out across the sea to Start Point, nervousness having rendered them both speechless. The day had been fine but the evening was cool and, although she'd protested earlier when Toby suggested they put the hood up, Miggy shivered a little. He took an old rug from behind his seat and wrapped her in it. It was salt-stained and threadbare but clean and she smiled gratefully as she huddled in its warmth. The smile gave him the courage to speak and, rejecting all attempts at tact, he asked the question uppermost in his mind.

'Have you . . . ?' He hesitated and then spoke quickly. 'Have you ever thought of leaving Stephen?' He felt her stiffen beside him and knew that he must put his cards on the table. 'I know it seems quite unbelievable,' he said, taking her hand and holding it tightly. 'But I love you. I realise we've only known each other a short while but I just knew it at once. I've never ever really felt like this before but it's as if I've waited all my life for you. I know it sounds improbably sentimental and like a B-movie but I can't help it.'

He stopped and the silence went on and on as the dusk flowed round them and the beam from the lighthouse on Start Point swept the dark horizon.

'I want to marry you,' he said flatly.

'But I'm married already,' said Miggy unhappily, and he put his arm round her and drew her close.

'Do you think Stephen would let you go?' he asked. 'If you wanted to?'

'It's all so quick,' said Miggy, trembling at this strange new love. 'I've thought of leaving him. That's why I came away on my own in May. He makes me feel so inadequate all the time and guilty about Daisy, and life's so miserable and humiliating. But this is all too quick.'

'It doesn't have to be.' Toby felt a surge of power and happiness. 'I don't want to rush you. You've got to be sure. It's just that I'm absolutely sure, you see, and I wanted you to know.'

She looked at him then and he bent and kissed her very gently for the first time and she stopped trembling and hugged him closely.

'I don't know what to do,' she said, and she pushed the coppery tendrils of hair back from her face and wrapped the rug about her again.

'Could you tell Stephen?' he asked. 'Do you think you could manage to do it? Would you like me to talk to him . . . ?'

'No,' she said quickly. 'No, no. I must do it on my own, my own way. I need to think it through. And there's Daisy.'

Toby thought of Ruth and Georgia. How would they take it if Miggy and Daisy suddenly moved in with him?

'I'm longing to meet Daisy,' he said bravely. 'And if you come to me, she comes too. No question.'

'Oh, I couldn't leave her,' said Miggy at once. 'I simply couldn't. She's mine. Oh hell! This is all too much.'

'It's not really. Not if we go a step at a time and don't panic. Once we're sure how we feel things will fall into place naturally. My marriage is already finished and I've been on my own for two years. If you feel you can face telling Stephen, you can move down as soon as you like. We may not be able to marry at once but that wouldn't bother me if it doesn't bother you.'

'I think it *would* bother me,' she answered honestly. 'Mainly, probably, because of Daisy. I couldn't bear for her to think we were just . . . well, shacking up together. It's got to be real. Permanent.'

'It would be,' he reassured her. 'As soon as we could. Or do you mean you'd want to wait until everything had gone through?'

He looked at her anxiously; that could take months.

'I don't know.' Her eyes were fixed on the sea. 'I need time.'

'You can have time. Only I'm afraid that when you get back you'll forget me. Or be persuaded against it.'

She looked at him again. 'Oh no, I shan't,' she said. 'And Stephen doesn't really want me any more. But it'll be hard . . .'

He kissed her again, passionately this time, as if he were attempting to imprint himself on her.

Chapter Five

Hattie drove round Dartmouth for the second time, saw a car pulling out from the kerb in Higher Street and parked in the empty space with relief. In the middle of August, with the town preparing for the Regatta, it was madness to hope for a parking place after nine o'clock in the morning. Nevertheless, with Nick and Sarah coming to lunch on Sunday she needed to stock up. Even with the town full of tourists, it was still a novelty to pass through the narrow streets where quaint old houses with beautiful carvings squeezed together, the overhanging upper storeys jutting out, almost touching their neighbours across the way. Hanging baskets with cascading flowers splashed bright pools of colour into the shadowy alleyways and the dark interior of St Saviour's church, glimpsed through its wide open door, looked cool and welcoming.

The smell of warm new bread and the aroma of fresh coffee assailed Hattie's nostrils as she strolled along Foss Street, her shopping temporarily forgotten and she promised herself a snack once she'd completed her purchases. She passed through Avenue Gardens and leaned for a while on the railing, looking down at the river. It was busy now with the pleasure steamers that plied upriver, between Dartmouth and Totnes, or out to sea for trips along the coast to Torbay. Hattie wandered on, looking out to sea, beyond the river's mouth where the castle stood beneath the hill known as Gallant's Bower and the small stone church of St Petrox sheltered in its lee.

Reluctantly, Hattie turned back into the town, digging for her shopping list in the pocket of her old sailcloth skirt. As she walked beside the boat-float, she thought she saw someone she recognised and wrinkled her brow in an effort to cudgel her memory. The woman was tall and slender with coppery short curls. A small girl in shorts and an aertex shirt stood beside her, holding her hand, and they both wore the same expression of anxious anticipation. Even as she wondered, Hattie saw the woman's face lighten and she glimpsed Toby's tall, lean figure, threading his way through the milling tourists as he came hurrying across to meet them. Of course! It was the woman that he'd brought down to the hard. Hattie watched them meet; the woman drawing back from Toby's instinctive attempted embrace whilst glancing warningly at the unsuspecting child. Toby, acknowledging her unspoken reproof, smiled quickly and bent down to offer the little girl his hand. She shook it warmly, beaming up at him, and Hattie felt their almost palpable relief.

Realising that she was spying she skirted the boat-float and crossed the road to Cundells, taking care that the little group shouldn't see her.

Miggy's stomach churned madly and her icy hand held tightly to Daisy's warm one. What on earth was she doing here, standing by this tiny harbour of bobbing boats, meeting a man she hardly knew? In the weeks since she'd met Toby she'd swung between elation and despair, hardly daring to believe what she felt to be true; that she'd fallen in love with him and wanted to spend the rest of her life with him. While they were together she'd been so happy; comfortable but excited and nervous, too. Away from him she'd hung on grimly to those memories, especially when she contemplated the positively terrifying fact of divorcing Stephen.

Despite the conviction that he'd be only too pleased to see the back of her and Daisy, she was beginning to wonder if this was quite true. She'd begun the proceedings by telling him that, during her time in Devon, she'd decided that it might be best for both of them if they separated. To her dismay he refused to take her seriously. He didn't even look alarmed. He reacted as though she were Daisy's age and behaving rather foolishly, not even deserving the compliment of rational discussion. Later, she'd brought the subject up again and this time he'd been rather impatient. Her telephone conversations with Toby sustained her but, during the long hours between, she found her courage and conviction slipping away. When she imagined spending the rest of her life as a shadow in the large house in Chelsea, however, her resolve was strengthened again and she was determined to follow her instinct and get out.

The turning point was, whilst in the downstairs loo, she overheard Stephen talking about Daisy to a close friend and colleague.

'Mad as a hatter,' she heard him say in his well-bred drawl.

40

'Potty as they come. I shall insist on boarding school as soon as she's old enough. The whole thing was a ghastly mistake, I don't mind telling you, but I'm not a man to evade his responsibilities or go back on his word.'

'Well, we tried to warn you at the time. Susan was terribly worried about it,' Miggy heard the friend murmur. 'Not really your type, is she?'

'I know, old man. Don't rub it in. Never mind. We get along . . .'

Their voices faded as they passed into the garden and Miggy remained hidden, tense with rage and humiliation. Very well, then. If he felt like that, she and Daisy would go. She imagined the house without Daisy, banished to some far-off school, and a sense of desolation swept over her. Without further hesitation she went to the telephone and booked a week for the two of them at a tiny hotel near Dartmouth. She would take Daisy to meet Toby and, if she still felt the same when she saw him again, she would take the plunge.

So here she was in Dartmouth with Daisy beaming up at Toby and asking if they could go sailing in his boat and Toby was beaming back and saying of course they could. Miggy looked at them both and felt weak with love and longing. Could she be so lucky as to have found a man who would love both of them as they needed to be loved?

'I like this place,' said Daisy, staring round with shining eyes. 'I love it, actually.'

Ever since she'd known she was coming for a holiday here she'd been reading her Arthur Ransome books and, in her imagination, the Walkers and Blacketts and the Callums thronged the stone steps that led down to the boats bobbing on the water below. Toby was watching the bright little face with its dreamy honey-brown eyes.

'You must come and see my cottage on the creek,' he said recklessly. 'You can meet Joss who lives on a boat and there's Hattie at the mill with her huge black dog, the Admiral, and I've got a little dinghy which you could learn to row . . .'

He glanced at Miggy, wondering if he'd gone too far but she was smiling at the expression of bliss on Daisy's face.

'I think I've made a conquest,' he murmured as they made their way to his car.

'It's nothing to do with you,' said Miggy firmly. 'It's the dog and the dinghy that's done it.'

Toby unlocked the car, almost overcome with happiness. He, too, had been wondering what his reaction would be when he saw Miggy again but, the moment he'd seen her anxiously scanning the passers-by, his heart had turned over in his breast and he was convinced anew that she was absolutely right for him. The child, in her old shorts and sandshoes, was very like Miggy to look at and her air of intense, expectant excitement was delightful to him. It was with absolute confidence that he'd approached them, determined that they could be happy together.

As the days passed he had no reason to review his feelings. All three of them had lived with strain and pressure and were acquainted with loneliness, and they seized these magic days and lived them to the full. Daisy certainly couldn't remember when she'd ever been so happy. For both her and the Admiral it was love at first sight and the characters that peopled her imagination roamed freely at her side as she explored the woods and rowed the short distance she was allowed in the little dinghy. After a few days, Toby paid their bill at the hotel and they moved to the cottage so that they could have more freedom. On the day before they were to return to London, Daisy went to tea with Hattie and the Admiral and for the first time Miggy and Toby were completely alone. This put a strange constraint upon their behaviour. For the whole week they'd been easy and natural but now Miggy avoided Toby's eyes and, when he caught her hand, she stood rigid.
    'Look.' He pulled her to him and held her closely. 'We want to be together, don't we? We know that now.' He tilted her face up. 'Don't we?' She nodded. 'Then I think we ought to get the next bit over with quickly. No!' He shook his head, vexed with himself. 'Oh hell! I'm just afraid it will get out of proportion, you see. Look, I love you and I want to marry you. But first of all, d'you think we could just go to bed?'
    Miggy gave a great sigh. 'I thought you were never going to ask!' she said. 'Don't just stand there talking. Daisy will be back soon and I don't want to rush it!'

'So how are you going to tell Ruth?' Joss joined Toby in *Westering*'s cockpit and handed him a glass of a beer. 'She'll have a fit.'
    'I don't see why she should,' said Toby. 'She's the one pressing for a divorce.'
    Joss laughed and shook his head. 'I think you'll find that has nothing to do with it. Women always like to have their cake and

eat it as far as I can see. She might want to be free but she'll be very upset if she thinks you're not going to remain available.'

'What do you know about it?' countered Toby. 'Single chap like you!' But his heart sank a little. 'As long as Georgia doesn't suffer there shouldn't be a problem.'

'You don't think you're taking the whole thing a bit too fast?' suggested Joss. 'You hardly know her, after all.'

'I knew you'd say that.' Toby swallowed some beer.

'So will Ruth. It *is* sudden, you've got to admit.'

'I fully expect that everyone will think I'm quite mad. I'm prepared for that.' Toby ran his fingers through his heavy dark hair and gazed across the creek. 'I can't hope that anyone will understand how I feel.'

'Oh, they'll understand how you feel all right,' said Joss. 'They'll just be surprised on your acting on it so promptly and so . . . well, so irrevocably.'

'How d'you mean, irrevocably?'

'Well . . .' Joss hesitated. He knew he was being a wet blanket but he was fond of Toby and didn't want to see him made any more unhappy than he'd been after Ruth left. 'Moving her in and so on. Bit drastic, isn't it? Couldn't you get to know her a bit better first?'

'With her in London and me down here? And what about Daisy?'

'Why can't they rent a cottage or something? Miggy could get a job and you'd have the time to really get to know each other.'

'I don't need any more time.' Toby finished his beer and set the glass down. 'I just know.'

'Is this how you felt when you met Ruth?' Joss guessed he was wasting his time but he was determined to do what he could to stop Toby making a terrible mistake.

'It's funny you should ask that.' Toby stuck his feet up on the opposite seat and crossed his ankles. 'I've been thinking about that. We were very young. Twenty-five-ish. Ruth's a bit younger. I'd been pushed into the bank by my father – the chairman was a friend of his – and I hadn't really wanted to do it but I found I was good at it. I was making money and life was fun and our friends were getting married and buying little flats and it seemed the thing to do.' He smiled at Joss's expression, aware of the fact that Joss would never do anything merely because it seemed the thing to do. 'We were the "beautiful people", going to the new nightclubs and dashing over to St Tropez and we were all swept along on the tide of the Swinging Sixties. Ruth was beautiful and sexy and fun and I thought myself very lucky.'

'But you weren't in love with her?' asked Joss when Toby seemed to have come to a halt.

'I'm not sure I thought about it,' he answered at last. 'It just happened. It was as if we could see ourselves playing these glamorous parts. Dancing the night away, running along beaches in the moonlight, picnicking on salmon and champagne, doing a ton down the M1 in an E-type. And then Georgia came along. Even when we decided to go for the good life down here I suspect that it was part of the image. The cottage in the country, weekends rushing down from London and so on. But for me it was real. And that's what I felt when I met Miggy. That it was real. For the first time.'

'D'you think that's why Ruth went back? Because she couldn't keep the image up down here?'

Toby thought about it and when he answered he hoped he didn't sound too disloyal. 'I think that was part of it. It was fine all the time our friends were visiting and envying us and we could play our host role. But there were too many long wet weeks in between. And I changed. Like she said, I was ambitious, successful, very London. Now I look like one of the local fishermen and drone on about the birds and so on. It was hard on her.'

'But you didn't love her enough to give all this up and go back with her?'

'No,' said Toby flatly. 'No, I didn't. The play was over and I wanted to settle down to boring old real life. Which means that I didn't really love her after all, I suppose.'

'And you think that it'll be different with Miggy?'

'I *know* it here.' Toby struck his breast. 'But when I think about it here –' he struck his brow – 'I'm scared to death!'

Joss burst out laughing. 'I think you're both crazy,' he said, 'so it'll probably be a great success. Stay and have some supper. I've got some spaghetti on the go.'

'Thanks. If you're sure you've got enough.'

Toby laced his fingers behind his head and tried to put his thoughts in some sort of order. Listening to Joss moving about in the galley below, his eyes fixed unseeingly on the hard, he wondered how he would broach the subject of Miggy and Daisy to Georgia. She was starting at Canford School in the sixth form in the autumn and he hoped that a new school – not to mention all the boys – would distract her attention from him. Toby uncrossed his long legs and crossed his arms instead in an attempt to quell the sinking sensation in the pit of his stomach. If only they could all just get on with it. He must have absolute faith in what he felt was right and not be deterred by well-meaning friends or his own private terrors. Just because his marriage to Ruth had failed didn't mean that he was incapable of having a successful relationship. He wondered how much he should tell Ruth; how much was necessary for her to know. She'd told him nothing so far about her own relationships and he never questioned Georgia.

Toby took a deep steadying breath. Georgia would be down in a few days and he would tell her all about Miggy and Daisy and go from there. One step at a time was the way to play it.

Chapter Six

The Admiral lay out on the slip in the warm September sunshine. As far as he was concerned, life was very satisfactory. The move from the small cottage in Hampshire with its tiny overstocked garden – where his efforts at landscaping had gone completely unappreciated – to this roomy house with its perfect surroundings of wood and water left nothing to be desired. Here, people appreciated his worth . . . Well, most people. It was true that Joss was lacking in certain areas of sensitivity but others, namely Miggy and Daisy, more than made up for it. The Admiral stretched luxuriously, rolled over and sat up. He felt a little peckish. He stared out over the creek where Daisy was rowing Toby's dinghy and decided that Mr Crabtree should have the benefit of his company. Apart from the biscuits in Mr Crabtree's pockets, the large cool kitchen – where the Admiral spent most of his sleeping hours – held a certain appeal as the day grew warmer. He hauled himself to his feet and padded across the yard and in through the open doorway of the mill.

As he vanished into the shadowy hallway, Sarah's car was just pulling in and Hattie came out of the cottage to meet her. Sarah pecked her on the cheek and collected several parcels from the back seat of the car.

'Nick sent you a bottle,' she said, 'and sends his love, of course. Honestly, Hattie!' She stood for a moment, parcels clasped to her chest, regarding her friend with amusement. 'Have you been near a hairdresser since you moved down? You look positively shaggy!'

'Haven't had time,' replied Hattie cheerfully. 'Too much to do. Come and have a drink while I organise some lunch. How are things?'

'Fine.' Sarah settled herself at the table.

Hattie searched for her corkscrew and dealt with the wine. 'All well?'

'Absolutely. So come on! I'm dying to hear the latest.' Sarah was fascinated by the small group of people who lived by the creek. 'Has this Miggy woman arrived?'

'She has indeed.' Hattie felt a strange sense of irritation to hear Miggy so described. It was quite amazing how quickly she'd been accepted into the community. 'I can quite see why Toby fell for her. She's charming. And Daisy's a poppet.'

'Well.' Sarah sipped at her wine and grimaced a little at Hattie's enthusiasm. 'They've obviously bowled you over.'

'I haven't got your reservations,' said Hattie honestly. 'If two people want to live together that's fine by me. I don't feel the moral implications are any of my business.'

'Well they ought to be.' Sarah's voice was sharp. 'If everyone took that attitude standards would disappear altogether.'

'If you take that argument to its logical conclusion then I admit that you're quite right. As it is, if Miggy wants to leave a man who doesn't love her and is making her unhappy—'

'You've only got her word for it,' interrupted Sarah.

'I appreciate that.' Hattie was beginning to lose patience. 'If she was happy with him, however, I doubt she'd want to come and live with Toby.'

'You make it sound that the pursuit of happiness is all that matters. Young women today have no staying power,' said Sarah, and Hattie stood up to continue her preparations for lunch. She knew Sarah's views on young women by heart. 'They give up at the first obstacle. Relationships have to be worked at. Girls want everything on a plate these days.'

Hattie washed a lettuce and wondered if Sarah would lose her antipathy to young women if Nick settled down and stopped pursuing them. There was another aspect, too, of Sarah's prejudice. Hattie knew quite well that each time Sarah heard of a woman leaving an erring husband, she felt that her own efforts were being belittled, that she might be regarded as a fool for carrying on in the face of his infidelities. Hattie's irritation died and her affection for Sarah and sympathy for her situation made her want to make her happy.

'D'you remember that anaesthetist at *Haslar* who had a passion for you?' she asked. 'What was his name? Matthew something, wasn't it?'

'Good heavens! That was hundreds of years ago.' But Sarah looked pleased at the memory and Hattie felt relieved.

'He used to follow you about and we all used to joke about how he'd love to send you to sleep with a prick . . . !'

They both burst out laughing.

'Honestly!' Sarah looked quite flushed.

'Those were the days.' Hattie topped up their glasses. 'Drink up. I'll take you over to the mill after lunch and you can see the progress. I should be in well before Christmas. I can hardly believe it.'

Miggy stood at the end of the lawn and watched Daisy rowing with great aplomb up the creek. There was no question that Daisy was happy. Even Georgia had not been able to spoil her joy in her surroundings. It was evident to Miggy that Daisy had cared very little for Stephen and that the prospect of never seeing him again bothered her not at all. Hardly any explanation had been required as to why Miggy was leaving him. It was as though the two years with Stephen had been an unfortunate incident which could be forgotten.

After all, thought Miggy, returning Daisy's wave, he isn't her father and he barely acknowledged her existence except to criticise her. Why should she miss him? And why on earth did I marry him?

Fear clutched her heart. She must have imagined herself in love or she never would have married him, so might it be possible that she could be making the same mistake with Toby? She could still hardly believe that she'd taken this drastic step; packing only the essentials for herself and Daisy and catching the train to Devon.

'We haven't got very much,' she'd told Toby when he'd arrived at Totnes station and seen their pathetic amount of luggage. 'I couldn't bring anything that was Stephen's. We've brought Patrick's books and a few clothes and Daisy's toys.'

Daisy beamed up at him. A large unwieldy teddy bear was tucked under her arm and she carried a small suitcase.

'We don't need much,' she assured him. 'How's Admiral Jellicoe?'

'Can't wait to see you again,' he told her. 'You're the only person who will go swimming with him.'

He took Miggy's cases from her and smiled reassuringly. She smiled back but her eyes were frightened.

'I've had to leave a note,' she said anxiously.

Toby nodded and waited until Daisy was ahead before he answered her.

'He still wouldn't believe you were leaving?'

She shook her bright head. 'I don't think he could contemplate the idea of my leaving him for another man. I'd rather we could have had it out properly. I've left him my solicitor's address like you said.'

Toby longed to drop the cases and hug her. He felt her panic rising as they went out to the car and she realised anew that she'd cut all her connections with the past. He bundled the luggage into the back, put Daisy in the car and took Miggy by the shoulders.

'It's going to be fine,' he told her firmly. 'It's right. You know that really if you'd just stop panicking.' He kissed her briefly. 'Come on. We're going home.'

Miggy, standing at the edge of the creek, tucked her hands into the sleeves of her jersey. It certainly felt like home, no question about that. Ruth, apparently, had taken quite a lot of furniture back to London with her and Toby had bought his own things so that the house had a rather masculine appeal and didn't feel too much like another woman's domain. When she considered it calmly she knew that she was doing no harm to Ruth, who had already left Toby and had asked for a divorce, and she felt absolutely certain that Stephen had never really loved her and, when the dust had settled, the only thing which would be hurt was his pride. Somehow she felt that her own happiness – and Daisy's – was in the balance and that it would be foolish, if not tragic, not to seize this chance.

Daisy was rowing back now, chin on shoulder, face intent. How quickly she'd accepted the situation! Miggy shook her head. Stephen had always said that Daisy didn't live in this world and he was probably right. So many things seemed to go right over her head and she was perfectly prepared to accept Toby as the man her mother loved and wanted to be with. Miggy had carefully explained the necessity of waiting for a divorce before she could marry Toby and that a great many people would consider that it was wrong for them to live with Toby until the divorce had happened and they could marry properly. When Daisy had appeared indifferent to the views of these people, Miggy had been obliged to point out that it could cause embarrassment for her at school.

'I've got Stephen's surname,' she explained. 'You've got Patrick's and Toby's got his own. It's a bit muddly. I've explained to the headmistress that Toby and I are going to be married as soon as it's possible but some of the children might . . . well, they might question you about it, you see.'

'That's OK,' said Daisy comfortably. 'You and I had different names at my last school, too.'

'Yes, but I was married to Stephen. The church disapproves of a man and woman living together if they're not married. It's called living in sin. Until our divorces come through Toby and I will be living in sin.'

Daisy looked at Miggy's worried face and put an arm round her. 'Is it really very bad?'

'There have to be rules and regulations or society would fall apart,' said Miggy at last. 'And once you start breaking the rules for one person then the rot sets in and lots of damage can be done. I'd rather be married to Toby and I shall be as soon as it's possible but I suppose we should live separately until we can be. It just seems rather silly. I want to be here with him.'

'So do I,' said Daisy at once. 'Is that why Georgia doesn't like us? Because we're living in sin?'

'I don't think Georgia dislikes us,' said Miggy carefully. 'It's just that she's never had to share her father with anyone before and it's a bit of a shock for her. We mustn't get in the way of their relationship. We'll have plenty of time with Toby when Georgia goes back to London.'

'She'll be gone soon,' said Daisy. 'She's got to get ready for school. She's going to a new one, too, so she's got to have lots of new things.'

Her eyes still on Daisy, Miggy thought about Georgia. She remembered the expression on her face when Toby had introduced them and how her heart had hammered with fear when she looked into the dark hostile eyes. Georgia obviously regarded it as rather disgusting that her father should want to marry again and she regarded them both with a scarcely veiled contempt. Miggy had suggested that she and Toby should have separate rooms until Georgia went but Toby said they must start as they meant to go on. As far as he was concerned they were exactly the same as any married couple and that's how it was going to be.

Nevertheless, Miggy was aware of Georgia watching them and found it quite impossible to be natural and easy with Toby. If he slipped his arm about her or showed any sign of affection she felt nervous and embarrassed and begged him to almost ignore her whilst Georgia was with them. He'd reluctantly agreed that his daughter needed time to adapt and had made a great fuss of her. Miggy knew that sixteen was an awkward age for a girl but at least she would soon be grown up and this stage of adjustment might not be too painful.

There had been a tiny breakthrough a few days before Georgia

51

had gone back to London. Toby had been needed at the boatyard and so had been unable to take them all to Totnes. It was market day and Miggy and Daisy were looking forward to seeing the ancient town on its busiest day of the week.

'It needn't stop you from going,' he said. 'I'll give you the directions. Or . . .' He hesitated and glanced at Georgia, who was eating her supper and taking no part in the discussion. 'Maybe Georgia might like to show you round. Totnes is one of her favourite places. She knows it like the back of her hand. What about it, Georgia?'

Georgia looked up and met Miggy's green eyes and Daisy's brown ones fixed on her face. She hesitated for a moment, various blighting remarks passing through her mind.

'I'd be so grateful if you think you could spare us the time.' Miggy's voice was gentle. 'I know it's silly but I'm not used to all these narrow lanes or Toby's car yet. I'm sure I should get hopelessly lost.'

There was another silence. Georgia was aware of a heady sense of power, shot through with a tiny thread of shame at her behaviour thus far. Daisy's eyes looked beseechingly into hers and she heard her own voice with something of surprise.

'We could go up by river,' she said casually. 'We could get one of the river boats from Dartmouth and then you wouldn't have to worry about driving or parking. It gets very busy on market day in the holidays. It's fun going up on the river. Then we can wander round the town and come back by boat after lunch.' She shrugged. 'If you want.'

'It sounds wonderful,' said Miggy, refusing to meet Toby's exultant eye but looking only at Georgia.

'And I can see the castle,' said Daisy.

'I'll drop you all into Dartmouth,' said Toby, 'and then you can phone me from Totnes and I'll meet you from the boat when it returns. It will depend on the tides, of course. Let's hope they fit in.'

And, of course, they had. It was one of those magic days when everything worked as it should. Away from Toby, Georgia was more relaxed and Miggy took care to let her see that it was her party. They had lunch at The Brioche and Miggy insisted on buying her a pretty Indian cotton scarf at Salago as a thank you present. The huge open market teemed with stalls displaying all kinds of wares: home-grown produce, cakes and bread, second-hand books and clothes and the Indian garments that were still so popular. Miggy was enchanted and Georgia enjoyed being the benefactress – as it were – of the treat.

Back at home, the gloom soon descended but Miggy felt heartened. She took the happy day as a good sign for the future and was content to let progress take its natural course. Now all she wanted was to get Daisy settled happily into her new school and to be able to relax with Toby. Since Georgia had returned to London they'd been tremendously happy. Could it be possible that this was how it would be? Surely it was almost too easy!

She watched Daisy row along to the boathouse and turned as she heard Toby's voice. He'd come out of the house and she went up the lawn to greet him.

'What is it?' He looked strained and her heart lurched with fright. 'What's wrong?'

'It's Ruth.' He took her hand. 'She's just telephoned. I wondered why she'd never replied to my letter explaining . . . everything. But it seems that she wanted to hear what Georgia had to say about it all and then get her off to school without any fuss.' He shook his head, looking puzzled, and Miggy watched him anxiously, hardly daring to speak. 'She says she's shocked and hurt at my behaviour and she's coming down for a few days. She'll be here tomorrow afternoon.'

Chapter Seven

Joss paid no further visits to the *Abigail*. Apart from the fact that he was working hard to do as much as he could on *Westering* before the winter closed in, he had no desire to renew acquaintance with Evan. Occasionally, on damp chilly days, smoke could be seen coming from the chimney but there was no other sign of life. On still evenings the roar of a motorbike's engine could be heard high up in the dense woodland and Joss guessed that it was Evan's but gave no further thought to him. He couldn't shake off the eerie sensation he'd experienced below in the filthy cabin nor the shock when he remembered the silent spectator, hidden in the fore cabin. Memories of bleak streets, graffiti-covered walls and blank windows had made his heart race and the fear of an unseen enemy bathed him in the familiar cold sweat which had enveloped him as he'd rowed quickly away.

In case Toby was too taken up with Miggy to remember their conversation about Evan, Joss had taken it upon himself to warn Georgia, afraid that she might be at that rebellious age when to be warned off someone or something was enough to make her instantly resolve to take an interest. Georgia, however, was repelled by his description of the grubby Evan and his sordid living quarters and was far too fastidious to wish to investigate, even as a protest against the arrival of Miggy and Daisy. Joss was relieved. Despite her puppy fat and a tendency to scowl, she was an attractive girl and Joss found her interesting company on the rare occasions when she managed to forget herself sufficiently to behave normally.

He expected Daisy simply to do as she was told and was alarmed when he saw that the idea of a mystery boat with an unpleasant young man living aboard merely acted as fuel to her overactive imagination.

'Just stay away from him,' he ordered her at last when she'd speculated on whether he could be a smuggler or a mad scientist or whether there might be a kidnapped person tied up in one of the cabins. 'Don't go anywhere near the *Abigail* or I'll tell Toby to take the dinghy away from you.'

Daisy made a face at his back. 'Don't get in a bate,' she said. 'May I come with you on your maiden voyage?'

'No,' answered Joss shortly. 'I shall be gone for months. Years probably.'

'But you'll give her a little trial run first, won't you?' she asked cajolingly. 'Couldn't I come on that? I could be the cabin boy.'

'Just go away, Daisy, and let me get on,' he said. 'There simply isn't room down here for both of us while I'm working. Go away.'

Daisy made another face and left him to it. She liked Joss but she felt his vision and sense of adventure were limited and she couldn't bear the waste. From *Westering*'s deck she saw the Admiral pottering on the hard and dropping down into the dinghy she cast off and began to pull for the shore. Hattie, seeing her approach, waited on the slipway.

'We're off for a walk,' she said as Daisy clambered out. 'Want to come?'

'Yes, please.' Daisy put her arms round the Admiral's huge neck and hugged him, burying her face in his fur. 'Miggy says may she come and see you later?'

'Of course she may. Have you always called your mother by her name?'

'I think so.' Daisy frowned a little. 'It seemed such a nice name when I was small. And so many people were called Mummy.'

'Sounds reasonable.' Hattie thrust her hands in her jacket pocket and wondered how things were going at the cottage. They all knew that Ruth was expected. 'Will you be coming with Miggy later?'

'Yes, please. Toby and Ruth will have things to talk about on their own.'

'Would you like a picnic to take into the woods? I'll make a chocolate cake.'

'My favourite.' Daisy ran ahead calling to the Admiral and Hattie followed more slowly, speculating on Ruth's arrival and hoping that she wasn't going to cause trouble.

After a great deal of careful consideration Ruth had decided to spend the Friday night with a friend in Dartmouth and arrived at the cottage after lunch on Saturday. By this time both Toby and Miggy were so nervous that they could scarcely communicate.

'She has no right at all to be shocked and hurt,' repeated Toby for the hundredth time, striding up and down the kitchen. 'She left me. She asked for the divorce. It's quite irrational. Joss must be right after all.'

'Joss?' Miggy stood leaning against the dresser, feeling his fear.

'Joss foretold this. He said that she might have been the one to go but she'd still want to have me on a string. I didn't believe him. I mean, what on earth for?' Toby opened his hands in an appeal for enlightenment. 'She's got her own life now. When she asked for the divorce and refused to consider a reconciliation we decided that she should have the London flat. The two properties are roughly the same value. She took all her things. And some of mine! Why should she want to change her mind now?'

Miggy was silent. Although it was irrational she hated the phrase 'refused to consider a reconciliation'. It meant that Toby had wanted Ruth back, hadn't been pleased to see her go. Supposing he decided that, if she wanted to come back after all, he ought to give it a second try? Perhaps he still loved her, deep down, and had just been hurt and she, Miggy, was a sort of second best. She pushed her fists into the pockets of her long denim pinafore dress that she wore over a simple white T-shirt and could find nothing to say. Toby glanced up at her and came swiftly to her side.

'This isn't going to make any difference to us,' he said. He took her by the upper arms and shook her slightly. 'Miggy! Listen to me. I love you. The other's all over, I promise.'

They leaped apart as the back door was pushed open and Ruth stood in the kitchen doorway. Her glance went immediately to Miggy, standing stiff and straight in front of the Welsh dresser, swept over her and passed on to Toby, who'd moved to stand by the table.

'Hello, darling,' she said and, going to him, kissed him lightly on the cheek.

His hands instinctively lifted to hold her and then fell to his sides.

'Hello, Ruth. This is something of a surprise. Miggy, this is Ruth.'

'Hi.' Ruth made no attempt to move towards Miggy but merely nodded to her across the kitchen.

There was a silence whilst Miggy took in Ruth's ash-fair long hair, her London outfit and her slim but shapely form. She felt shapeless and dowdy by comparison and her confidence plummeted still further.

Toby was unprepared for the shock of seeing Ruth here in the flesh with Miggy in the same room. He was having to fight the feeling that Ruth actually still retained rights over him and he realised that, after all, more than eighteen years of marriage couldn't simply be wiped out leaving complete indifference behind. Ruth sensed his uncertainty and took swift advantage. She'd known all along that it would be Miggy who would be the most disadvantaged. She, Ruth, was still Toby's lawful wife; Miggy simply his mistress who had abandoned her husband and brought her small child to live with a married man.

'Well.' Ruth laughed a little and shook her head. 'You were a bit quick off the mark, weren't you, darling? I couldn't believe you'd move someone in so quickly. Poor Georgia. Did you think about her feelings at all?'

'Hardly quick, was it? You left two years ago, remember?'

'And only a few weeks ago you were in London begging me to come back.'

'A few weeks . . . ?' Toby caught himself up. He was letting Ruth lay all the traps and then walking into them. Miggy's face was deathly pale under her bright hair and he went to stand beside her. 'I refuse to let this become a slanging match. When you asked for a divorce I hadn't met Miggy. I thought it was sensible to keep the marriage going for Georgia's sake.'

'Only for that?' Ruth raised her eyebrows and slipped him a provocative little smile. 'That's not how it sounded in London.'

'Maybe not—' he began, but Ruth moved forward, taking out a cigarette before dropping her bag on the table.

'Got a light, darling?' she asked, and he automatically reached for the matches and she made the lighting an intimate little affair before shaking back her hair and looking at Miggy as she exhaled the smoke. 'Would you mind leaving me and my husband alone for a moment?'

Dumbly Miggy turned to go but Toby reached her before she gained the door and put his arm round her. He smiled down at her, still holding her, and some measure of confidence returned to warm her. 'I want you to stay,' he said quietly.

She smiled at him, aware of Ruth's watchful eyes. It had already been agreed that she should leave them to discuss things on their own and she knew that Toby felt her fear and was unhappy about her.

'Don't worry,' she said, and was able to receive his kiss without feeling ashamed. 'I'm going to see Hattie. I'll be back soon.'

She went out without looking at Ruth and there was a little silence.

'So what was all that about?' asked Toby.

'All what?' Ruth perched on the edge of the table, taking care to show a great deal of slender leg.

'I simply don't understand you.' Toby dropped into a chair, resisting the urge to seize one of Ruth's cigarettes. He hadn't smoked for three years and he had no intention of weakening at this crucial moment. 'You left me two years ago, you've refused to come back, you want a divorce. What on earth is this little drama about?'

'How long have you known her?' She answered his question with another.

'Four months. I told you in my letter.'

'I don't believe you.'

Toby stared at her. 'I've known her for four months. What's the matter with you, Ruth? Look.' He shook his head. 'I know I may be naïve, the good old gullible male, but would you just explain what's going on here? You have no rights any more to burst in here and start questioning me about my private life. We're nearly divorced and we've got our own lives. I don't come rushing up to London to find out what you're up to with Alan.'

She flushed and he saw that his thrust had gone home and his assumptions were correct.

'I think you agreed so readily to the divorce because you'd been having an affair with this woman and you saw your chance to be free without having to admit to anything. I feel cheated and betrayed. You didn't say a word, just left all the dirty work to me and let me feel that it was me making all the running.'

He stared at her open-mouthed and then pulled himself together.

'You're mad,' he said at last. 'I've known Miggy for four months and please remember that when you wrote and told me about the divorce – which, by the way, was six months ago not a few weeks! – I came straight to London and asked you to reconsider. Joss was right, after all.'

'Joss?' She got off the table and stubbed her cigarette out on a small china dish on the draining board. 'What's he got to do with it?'

'When I told him about Miggy he said that you'd fight it. That you wanted your freedom but you'd want to keep me on a string as well. I simply didn't believe him but I can't think of any other explanation for your amazing behaviour.'

'So it's all over the creek. Discussing me with anyone who will listen and playing the poor abandoned male. Well, I've changed my mind. I don't want a divorce.'

Toby put his elbow on the table and rested his head in his hand. He massaged his forehead with his fingers and finally looked at her.

'I can only imagine that this is dog in the manger with a vengeance,' he said quietly. 'I'm afraid it's immaterial to me what you want. I waited for two years hoping that you'd come back and now it's all over. I want to marry Miggy. Whatever you do or don't do nothing will change that.'

Ruth watched him. She had been unprepared for her feeling of fury when she saw Miggy standing motionless by the dresser: her dresser, dammit!

'You haven't forgotten that this house is still in our joint names?'

'We agreed that you should have the flat in London,' he said quickly. 'Both properties are of equal value. We agreed—'

'I've changed my mind. This is my home. You can't just throw me out.'

'Ruth, please.' He bit his lip and tried to take control of the situation. 'I can see that this has all come as a shock. Shall we try to stay calm and discuss things rationally? Naturally we shall need to take legal advice but I promise you I have no intention of letting you suffer financially. Surely you believe that. You and Georgia will be looked after. As for this being your home, you've hardly been inside the door for over two years.'

'I think I might want to change that.'

Toby closed his eyes for a moment. 'Supposing you tell me in words of one syllable exactly what it is that you want?' he said after a moment.

'I think we've both been too hasty,' she said. She shook back her hair again and came to the table. 'I think I'd like to try a reconciliation after all.'

'I'm sure she doesn't mean it.'

Toby held Miggy's hands tightly between his own whilst Hattie poured drinks in silence. He'd been so overwrought that he'd told them both the whole story the minute he'd arrived in Hattie's kitchen to find Miggy. Ruth had returned to her friend in

Dartmouth and Toby raced down to the mill and had startled both the women with his recital. He felt anxious and confused. Miggy seemed withdrawn and cool, watching him warily, and he longed to take her in his arms.

Miggy was suffering from similar sensations. A Ruth in the flesh was a very different proposition from a Ruth in London and, now that Miggy had seen her, she couldn't prevent herself from picturing her and Toby together in the intimate situations that eighteen years of marriage must produce and finding, to her horror, that she felt jealous and insecure. Could she really compete with someone like Ruth? Toby might protest that he was passionately in love with her, Miggy, but so had Stephen in the early days. Miggy stood stiffly, unresponsive in Toby's embrace.

Hattie watched them. She felt inadequate; distressed by the complications of their relationship and deeply thankful that she'd never been torn apart by the destructive emotions that love called forth.

'Drink up.' She pushed a glass of brandy into Toby's hand. 'Let's not panic. Legally she doesn't stand a chance. She left you and has stayed away all these years. Keep things in proportion.'

'I know that.' Toby released Miggy and swallowed half the measure. 'It's just so damned unfair. She's done exactly as she pleased all these years and now she's trying to rot my life up. Why?'

Hattie exchanged a glance with Miggy. They'd already discussed it all before his arrival. Hattie was dying to know what was going on, Miggy had been completely knocked off balance and the mixture was fatal. Within a few minutes they'd been nattering together like old friends.

'I think Joss has the right of it,' said Hattie when it seemed that Miggy was incapable of speech. 'It's one thing playing the field in London when your husband is sitting complacently in Devon keeping your home warm for you and quite another when he ups and takes you at your word and gets a life of his own. Perhaps the mention of divorce frightened off the boyfriend.'

Toby stared at her, struck by this new idea, and Hattie wondered how it was that apparently intelligent men could be so naïve when it came to analysing the emotions. She and Miggy had already discussed this possibility exhaustively.

'Good Lord!' he said.

'Has she gone?' asked Miggy.

'Yes. Yes, she's gone back to Dartmouth,' Toby assured her. 'Don't worry about that.'

'What I meant was, has she really gone? Or is she going to keep popping in? Or might she move herself back in permanently?'

'She can't do that,' said Toby at once, but he sounded uncertain. He couldn't remember the legal situation when it came to the matrimonial home. Would she really go that far? 'I'm sure she's gone. She's got her job to consider, after all.'

'Perhaps she's given it up,' said Miggy. She was feeling a little more confident now she saw that Toby made no effort to defend Ruth or show any desire for her company. 'Has she got a key to the cottage?'

'Oh hell!' exclaimed Toby. 'Surely she wouldn't just keep turning up! I can't believe that! Oh, damn and blast!'

'How did you leave it with her?' asked Hattie. She gave Miggy's arm a little squeeze. 'Don't worry. I'll lend you the Admiral. He'll see her off!'

Miggy tried to smile. 'I don't want her turning up and upsetting Daisy,' she said. 'I won't have Daisy made to feel we're doing something rather horrid and grubby. Perhaps we should go away till we've sorted things out.'

'No!' said Toby strongly. 'You're not going anywhere. You belong here with me. Both of you.'

'Still.' Hattie was thoughtful. 'It's not a bad idea. Just till we know she's off the premises, as it were.'

'What difference does it make?' demanded Toby in distress. 'Miggy's been living at the cottage. Georgia would bear witness to that. What's the point of her moving out now?'

'I'm not thinking of it legally,' said Hattie. 'Just from the most sensible point of view. If there's no one to make scenes to Ruth'll probably go quicker, if you see what I mean.'

Miggy and Toby stared at each other. He looked so miserable that she went to him and slipped her arm round him.

'Hattie's got a point,' she said gently. 'And I simply won't have Daisy upset. Just till we know she's gone and we can take advice.'

He shut his eyes for a moment and then nodded. 'I suppose so. But where shall you go? Oh honestly! It's too much!'

'They'll stay here of course,' said Hattie comfortably. 'Don't be so daft! Where else would they go? We can all squeeze in for a day or two. We'll tell Daisy that Ruth and you have to wind things up and it's better to be right out of the way till it's all done.'

'Oh, Hattie.' Miggy hugged her. 'Could we really?'

'That'd be great, Hattie.' Toby sounded deeply relieved. 'I shan't mind so much if they're just up here with you. I'll get it sorted as quickly as I can.'

'I'll phone Nick,' said Hattie. 'Now that's settled and we can have a breather I'll ask his advice. He's a lawyer friend of mine. He'll tell us what's what. Now, go and take the Admiral for a soothing walk in the woods and find that child and I'll get some supper going. Give me half an hour. Go on. Push off. I've got things to do.'

Chapter Eight

At the end of October Hattie moved into the mill. There were a few odds and ends to finish but the main body of the work was completed and she simply refused to wait any longer. She was delighted with the results of Mr Crabtree's labours and most especially with her drawing room – light and spacious, with a huge woodburning stove built on the central circular millstone on which the grain had once been ground. This ceramic stove had glass doors on both sides so that she could sit at either end of the room and still watch the flames. French doors opened out on to the terrace that looked south over the stream and down the creek, and the room reached right up through the first floor to the roof itself where the rafter beams were exposed. On the end wall, a wrought-iron circular staircase led up to a balustraded gallery. Up here Hattie put her mother's Georgian bureau and a small bookcase whilst in the drawing room below she placed a collection of deep cushiony sofas and armchairs on the huge square rugs which covered the polished oak floor.

She was determined not to furnish her new home too hastily but to collect things carefully and thoughtfully. She had the basic requirements, the rest could grow together naturally. There was a large kitchen with an oil-fired Esse that heated the water as well as radiators in the bathroom and the two bedrooms. Her bedroom also faced south and was enormous. It was really two rooms knocked into one but Hattie loved large rooms and, since there still remained a spare bedroom for guests, she could see no reason why she shouldn't indulge herself. She bought a king-sized bed which she loaded with cushions and quilts so that it resembled a nest more than a bed. A bookcase dominated one wall whilst opposite, her mother's mahogany bow-fronted chest sat comfortably beside a tall Victorian wardrobe.

Hattie was planning her house-warming party when Joss appeared in the kitchen. She looked up from her list and nodded to him as he sat in one of the Windsor chairs which, along with the

65

large refectory table, she'd discovered at the Jolly Pedlars in Dartmouth.

'How're things with you?' she asked. Her moving in had kept her so busy that she was out of touch. 'Everything OK?'

'It looks as if we're in for some equinoctial gales,' he said. 'The forecast's not at all good. I was thinking that I might batten *Westering* down and move ashore, if it's OK with you?'

'Perfectly OK. The cottage isn't too comfortable, I'm afraid. It's got hardly any furniture left in it but there are enough bits and pieces for you to manage with.'

'I promise you it'll seem palatial after being on a boat,' said Joss feelingly. 'Thanks. I'll ferry some things across, then.'

'Will it be that bad right up a creek like this?' she asked him. 'Won't we be protected?'

'Well, it won't be like being out at sea but it'll be pretty wild. It's one of the highest springs of the year tonight and it can get very rough.' He smiled a little at her expression. 'Don't be surprised if the water comes over your quay.'

'Heavens!' She stared at him anxiously. 'Am I likely to be flooded?'

He shook his head and got to his feet. 'The mill's never been flooded to my knowledge. I'd better get going. The wind's getting up already.'

When he'd gone, Hattie sat and listened. He was quite right. It moaned and wailed round the mill and the Admiral appeared, paced round restlessly for a while and then stretched out on the slate floor behind her. Presently she went out on to the quay. Joss was fiddling with *Westering*'s mooring ropes and checking round the deck making sure everything was secure. The tide was out but a line of flotsam and jetsam along the hard and the slipway showed how much higher the water had risen above its usual level. The wind was strong and gusty and it roared through the trees on the hills surrounding the creek. The heavy, grey, bulging clouds were leaking a fitful drizzle and Hattie shivered.

The glorious autumn weather had come to an abrupt end and she felt quite relieved to see Joss rowing the dinghy, piled with his belongings, across to the hard. She went to help him unload and between them they carried his things into the cottage Hattie had so recently vacated. The Admiral came out to investigate and proceeded to get in everyone's way until Hattie said that she'd take him inside and put the kettle on whilst Joss got sorted out.

'Come over when you're ready,' she told him and, with the

66

Admiral padding beside her, went into the kitchen just in time to snatch up the telephone receiver before Sarah rang off in despair.

'I wondered where you were,' she told Hattie. 'It seems there's a gale warning and Nick thought you ought to know.'

'It's very kind of him,' said Hattie, 'but even now we're battening down the hatches and preparing for the worst.'

'Oh. Well, that's OK then. I hope you'll be all right.'

'Of course I shall be. If it looks as if we're going to flood up I'll hang out of my bedroom window and Joss can rescue me in his dinghy.'

'Honestly, Hattie, it's no joke. It can be terrible at this time of the year down here.'

'Real *Mill on the Floss* stuff,' sighed Hattie contentedly. 'You'll find me in Joss's arms floating down the river to Dartmouth like Maggie and Tom.'

'Oh shut up!' said Sarah crossly. 'Just look after yourself, that's all. Give me a buzz in the morning.'

'I'll be fine. Bless you for phoning.'

Hattie grinned to herself as she went to make the tea. Somehow the drama of the approaching storm made her feel all the more part of her new environment and she wondered how Daisy was enjoying it.

At that moment, Miggy was driving Daisy back from school through the narrow lanes. The abundant summer foliage had died back but, in the hedges, the bright berries of the hawthorn and black bryony glowed amongst the brown dry leaves and clusters of hazelnuts. The black clouds scudding from the west parted momentarily to release a dazzle of brilliant sunlight which gleamed on a field of golden stubble and touched the hills with flame. A flock of starlings swept low across the landscape and scattered before the gale. The trees crouching crabbed and bent above the high banks creaked in the rising wind and the whole countryside seemed to be full of movement and life.

Miggy felt stirred and excited. She was not used to being so exposed to the elements and felt a fierce enjoyment of this unleashed power thrum in her blood. The last few weeks she'd been happier than she could remember – even with Patrick – and she felt as if she were a whole new person; young and alive, loved and valued. She'd been overwhelmingly relieved to find that Ruth's plots could come to nothing. Nick had driven over with Sarah on the Sunday after Ruth's visit to the cottage and had gone through the legal situation very carefully with Toby. Miggy had stayed out of it but it seemed that, with all that had gone before, Toby was well within his rights to serve an injunction on Ruth to keep her out of the cottage and, should it be necessary, had grounds to divorce her for desertion or even adultery.

Toby had written a long and carefully worded letter to her in London and since then there had been silence. They guessed that Ruth was taking advice and, when the silence became prolonged, they felt fairly safe that she'd been advised that she had no grounds on which to base her demands. Nevertheless, Miggy still felt a little anxious. She had a presentiment that Ruth would not give up so easily and she knew that Toby was upset by the whole business. He would prefer to keep the relationship on an amicable basis not least because of Georgia.

Miggy turned into the lane that led down to the creek and drove past the mill and the hard.

'Joss has come ashore,' said Daisy. 'Look. He's pulled his dinghy right up. Much further than usual. I hope it doesn't get washed away.'

'I'm sure he knows what he's doing.' Miggy looked at *Westering*, bleak and bare as she rode at her moorings on the rising tide, and felt relieved to know that Joss was tucked up in Hattie's cottage. 'Let's go and see if Toby's back from the boatyard. No going out after tea, Daisy. Promise?'

'I promise,' said Daisy, who thought that Joss was very poor-spirited to go ashore with such an exciting night forecast. Grown-ups were really very dull. 'I wonder if that man on the *Abigail* is on board or whether he's gone ashore, too.'

'He'll be perfectly safe right up there,' said Miggy, parking the car. 'Make sure you haven't left anything out that might get blown away and then come and have tea.'

As the weather worsened and high tide approached, the wind veered to the east and the violent gusts which battered against the mill and screamed round *Westering* were equal to gale conditions.

On *Abigail* Evan lay on his pile of mattresses and listened to the storm. He'd already come to the conclusion that living on the boat through the winter would be no fun. He'd made no attempt to work on her and she was in a poor way with her blistering paint and rusting fittings. Her seams needed recaulking and at each tide muddy water forced its way into the bilges, seeping out as she was left high and dry but leaving a residue of smelly mud behind. The deck needed paying and was now leaking in several places. He'd had to move his pile of mattresses after one very wet spell in the summer and the whole boat smelled dank, and there was a chill atmosphere that was very depressing.

Evan shivered and huddled more deeply into his blankets. He'd forgotten to fetch any firewood for the stove and he was out of paraffin. As the rain poured down and new leaks began to appear Evan got up to make himself a hot drink. The fire was nearly out and he cursed himself for forgetting to lay in supplies. By the time he'd made his coffee there was a regular drip of water on his bedding which he half-heartedly tried to pull away before giving up and going to crouch near the stove. The sensible thing would be to move into the fo'c'sle and sleep there. The small cabin was at least dry and soon the fire would be out anyway. Evan instinctively shivered and pulled an old coat over his shoulders. From the beginning he'd had a strange feeling about that cabin. Sometimes he'd even imagined that someone was in there; waiting, watching him. It was an eerie sensation and strong enough for him actually to go to take a look on more than one occasion. There had been other noises, too; footsteps pounding overhead, hoarse cries and a soft, heavy thudding noise, like a body falling.

He drank some coffee and laughed to himself. Mad! He must be going quite mad! There had never been anyone else but himself on the boat since he'd bought her for practically nothing from a yacht brokerage upcountry. The locals wouldn't have anything to do with her, he knew that now. He'd put it down to superstition and old wives' tales but now he wasn't so sure. It didn't help that she was moored in such gloomy surroundings but it had suited him quite well. The *Abigail* was his hideaway. Nobody knew where he went, nobody could find him, nobody could question him, demand money that he'd borrowed. He was safe.

Evan glanced at the door that separated the cabin from the fo'c'sle. Was that a noise? His last remaining paraffin lamp was beginning to gutter and he felt a wave of pure terror. He felt quite certain that someone was there, beyond the flimsy bulkhead, waiting. He swallowed some more coffee, fighting back the irrational fear that threatened to possess him. If only he had a smoke! He set down his mug and ran his hands over his face, his eyes darting – despite himself – to the door to the fo'c'sle. He'd get out! As soon as the storm was over he'd leave this bloody boat and this gloomy creek and get out. He'd pull himself together, go back upcountry, get himself a job.

A gust of new violence struck the *Abigail* and Evan gave a stifled cry of fear. The door up forward had swung open revealing the black interior of the little cabin and for one fearful moment Evan braced himself. The boat began to surge as the waves created by the strength of the gale pushed her into the shore. She was brought up short by her head warps and surged back only to be snubbed by her stern warps. She began to roll and pitch. Evan, his eyes still fixed on the pitchy darkness of the fo'c'sle, slowly became aware of a rhythmic muffled booming which resonated through the hull and struck even more terror to his heart. He found himself listening for the noise, counting the seconds between each one, his breath coming in short frightened gasps.

All at once he knew he could bear it no longer. Keeping his eyes on the door, he stood up, dragging on his leather jacket and backing towards the companionway. He knew that he must get out. Somehow he must get ashore and back to civilisation. He climbed quickly into the deckhouse and lunged out on deck into the black night almost as if he were being pursued. The sheer force of the wind knocked him to his knees and he gasped and snatched at the handrail, hanging on for dear life, stunned by the noise. The gale unleashed yet more frenzied violence which snapped the *Abigail*'s bow warps and drove her towards the beach whilst the trees swayed and moaned above her.

The rain lashed down, soaking Evan in moments, and the wind screamed in the rigging whilst the water boiled round the boat and the waves crashed against the shore. Gaining his feet and clutching desperately at the handrails on the deck house, Evan staggered as the wind buffeted him backwards, snatching his breath. He lost his balance and, screaming with terror, was carried into the path of the heavy boom which had broken free from its inadequate fastening and was swinging as the boat rolled, striking now the shrouds to port, now the starboard shrouds. His feet skidded on the slippery deck as the boom struck him full in the face, smashing him back into the bulwarks. He slipped down, the blood from his shattered skull streaming along the deck and mingling with the torrential rain which beat on his sodden crumpled body.

The next morning Hattie emerged cautiously from the mill accompanied by the Admiral, who had slept undisturbed through the storm. Hattie had watched most of it from her bedroom window and was heavy-eyed with lack of sleep. She'd dozed towards daybreak and then come downstairs to find that the electricity was cut off. Thanking heaven for the Esse, she boiled a kettle and went to see if Joss was awake. There was no reply to her banging and she wandered out on to the quay, the Admiral bounding ahead.

The gale had blown itself out and the creek lay still and placid beneath a pale blue-rinsed sky. The debris from last night's tide lay high on the hard, and branches and leaves, torn from the trees, were scattered along the foreshore. Two swans glided silently up the channel and Hattie stood in the silence of the morning and marvelled at the complexities of nature. Joss's dinghy was already tied up alongside *Westering*, although there was no sign of him, and she turned back to the house hoping that no disasters had occurred.

She was eating her breakfast when he appeared and she raised her eyebrows interrogatively at him.

'Nothing amiss,' he said cheerfully. 'Taken in a bit of water, but nothing too serious. I checked with Toby. They're all fine but he says it looks as if the *Abigail*'s gone aground and lost one of her legs. Could be the gale moved her a bit and the leg's gone down on some soft mud. No good going over with the tide coming in. We'll need to see the damage. Do I smell coffee?'

'You do.' Hattie jerked her head towards the percolator. 'Help yourself and top mine up while you're there. What a night!'

'Fun, wasn't it?' Joss grinned. 'I'm dreading Daisy's strictures on my cowardice. She thought it was chicken of me to come ashore.'

'So do I,' said Hattie, spreading honey on her toast. 'And you a soldier. Ah well. We can't all be in the Navy, of course. Some of us have to settle for second best. Now a sailor would have been out there, braving the elements . . .'

'I'm sure he would,' agreed Joss, entering this familiar battle with his usual enjoyment. 'Only someone daft enough to join the Royal Navy would be daft enough to stay out in those conditions. You know what the Admiralty Interview Board says, don't you? "Only half-wits need apply. We like to supply the other half in our own time and in our own way!"'

'Oh, well . . .' began Hattie, and paused as the telephone rang. 'That'll be Sarah. She'll be thinking you and I are doing a Tom and Maggie Tulliver.'

'A what? Joss stared at her, perplexed.

'Yes, well there you are,' sighed Hattie as she picked up the receiver. 'I'd quite forgotten. If you join the Navy you have to be able to read!'

Chapter Nine

It was Bert Crabtree who told them the history of the *Abigail*. The shock of Evan's death reverberated round the creek although, as Joss pointed out, since it was obviously an accident none of them need feel guilty that they'd ignored their strange and solitary neighbour. Only Bert shook his head doubtfully at this. He was finishing off the major repairs to the second cottage and had come in for his elevenses to find Hattie with Joss and Miggy discussing Evan's death.

''Tweren't no accident,' he said helping himself liberally to sugar. 'Unlucky boat. That's what she is.'

Pressed to elucidate he settled himself comfortably at the table and told them how, from the beginning, misfortune, death and violence had followed in the *Abigail*'s wake. On her final trip as a fishing boat she'd developed engine trouble and had been obliged to put in at Plymouth. Two of the crew elected to find their way back home overland but the captain remained on board with the mate whilst repairs were carried out. Meanwhile, the captain decided to pursue a long-standing dalliance with a young married woman, making her way to her small cottage near the Barbican. Having spent a pleasant last evening with her he made his way back to the boat unaware that the girl's jealous husband, having suspected his wife's betrayal and spied on them, had preceded him to the *Abigail* and hidden himself in the forecastle to wait his chance for revenge.

The captain and the mate, who shared the after cabin, had sailed halfway round to Dartmouth before the stowaway made his presence known. In the ensuing struggle the captain was stabbed, fell overboard and drowned. The mate, when he intervened, was thrown against the winch, breaking his back in the process. The jealous husband, determined to escape rather than be brought to justice, tried to lower the rowing boat. During the struggle the *Abigail* had turned broadside to the waves and the boom – which was used as a derrick to launch the small boat – with the rowing

73

boat now attached was swinging wildly as she rolled. The husband, who was no sailor, lost his balance and his head was stove in by the boom with its cumbersome burden.

There was a little silence when Bert finished his tale.

'If they were all killed how do we know what happened?' asked the cynical Joss.

'Who said they were all killed?' countered Bert. 'The mate didden die. Left a cripple, 'e were. Found 'im when they saw 'er driftin' and towed 'er in. None of the fishermen would look at 'er after that. Someone from upcountry bought 'er eventually but 'e 'ad money problems and then 'is wife died sudden like and 'e never finished doin' 'er up.'

There was another silence whilst Bert noisily drank his cooling coffee.

'Odd, isn't it?' asked Miggy at last. 'Odd that he had his head bashed in, too.'

Hattie made a sceptical face and Joss rolled his eyes disbelievingly.

'Amazing how these stories get started,' he said when Bert had returned to his work. 'You'll probably hear a hundred different versions with very convenient twists. Take no notice.'

Nevertheless, he remembered how he'd seen the shadowy figure watching him from the fo'c'sle and felt an icy shiver down his spine.

'For God's sake don't tell Daisy,' warned Hattie, clearing up the mugs. 'She'll be fascinated.'

'Heavens, no!' Miggy shuddered. 'It gives me the creeps, true or not. I wonder what will happen to the *Abigail* now?'

'Somebody else will buy her and do her up and she'll be a lovely boat,' said Joss. 'I don't believe a word of it!'

Miggy wandered thoughtfully back to the cottage, still distressed by Bert's story and Evan's death. Presently, however, her mind returned to her own problems. She'd been right in believing that Ruth's apparent acceptance of the situation was too good to be true. She'd written a letter to Toby telling him that Georgia would be coming down for Christmas and, just to show that there was no ill will, she would like to accompany her. She hoped that he would accept this olive branch in the spirit in which she extended it. It was important – she added – for Georgia's sake that they all behaved in a civilised and friendly manner.

Toby had been dismayed but prepared to make allowances and,

to Miggy's horror, seemed perfectly happy to go along with Ruth's suggestion.

'But, Toby,' cried Miggy, feeling equal parts of fear and anger, 'it's our very first Christmas together. It'll be a disaster!'

'Nonsense, darling,' said Toby uneasily. 'Why should it be? I'm sure Ruth's accepted the situation and I have to think about Georgia. I don't want to put her nose out of joint.'

'Of course not. But I thought you said that Georgia never comes for Christmas. You told me that she always spends it in London with Ruth and comes down to you for the New Year. On her own.'

Toby glanced at her. There was no mistaking the tone of those last three words. Miggy's face was set, her eyes bleak and he went to her and put an arm round her.

'Look,' he said, 'I don't want Ruth here for Christmas any more than you do. You must know that. I can't imagine why Georgia should suddenly change her mind and want to come but I can hardly tell her that she can't, can I?'

Now, as Miggy crossed the lawn and went into the cottage, she remembered how she'd longed to point out that it was more likely to be Ruth who had changed Georgia's mind for her. It seemed very unlikely that a girl of nearly seventeen would choose to spend Christmas on a creek in a quiet backwater when she could be in London. With a tremendous effort, Miggy had resisted the urge to tell Toby that she didn't trust Ruth for a second. She'd begun to realise what pressures second marriages were heir to. She could see how people carried the hang-ups from their earlier failed relationships with them and how they affected their attitudes and behaviour.

Miggy went into the kitchen and began to think about lunch but her thoughts preoccupied her and she sat down at the table and brooded. Her marriage with Stephen hadn't posed these problems. He'd never been married before and Patrick was dead. Apart from which, the twenty-five-year-old Patrick – fresh from the Slade and determined to be the new William Blake – was a very different proposition to the successful, wealthy, thirty-five-year-old Stephen. They inhabited such different worlds that comparisons would have been ludicrous. When Toby had described his young life with Ruth and their group of trendy jet-setters, however, she'd felt a pang of understanding, remembering her own early years with Patrick and their friends. They'd rented attic rooms or basements, lived on curry and coffee and shared their aspirations with other like-minded, poverty-stricken students.

Miggy, her chin cupped in her hands, remembered the magic of those days. She wondered how she and Patrick would have coped, thinking of his jubilation as he set out on his scooter for his first commissioned job; a mural in a coffee bar in Soho.

'This is just a beginning!' he'd cried as he ran down the three flights of steps from their tiny attic rooms, having kissed her and Daisy an enthusiastic farewell. 'Just you wait and see!'

But it had been the end. A passing car had tipped the handlebar of his aged scooter and he'd swerved and been crushed by a bus. Miggy felt the hot tears pricking her eyes and a lump constricting her throat. How desperate she'd been! How lonely! Only Daisy had kept her going through those dreadful days; Daisy and the support of those friends who, despite their penury, helped out till she found a job and shared Daisy round between them all so she could work the hours required to support them both. Later, Stephen had discouraged these friendships and, although Miggy had staunchly refused to abandon her friends, they'd gradually drifted away. Stephen and his house in Chelsea had overawed them and Miggy began to lose touch with them.

Why had she married Stephen? Was it because he was so absolutely unlike Patrick that there could be no comparisons? Or was it the overwhelming temptation of his wealth; the thought of being able to give up the dreary little jobs and actually spend time with Daisy in beautiful, peaceful surroundings? Of course, she'd imagined herself in love with him. She'd met him after a few weeks in her first really good job in the little art gallery and he'd been invited to an exhibition. She'd been giving out programmes and carrying round glasses of wine and he'd joked with her and flirted a little and, after five years of struggling with no time for herself, it was all rather exciting and glamorous. She'd been flattered by his attention and the affair had swirled delightfully along, quite out of control.

'Real King Cophetua and the beggar maid stuff,' muttered Miggy, getting up with a sigh. 'At least he's agreed to a nice easy divorce.'

She'd never imagined it would be otherwise. It was only to be expected that, once she and Daisy were gone, his friends would cluster round and tell him that he was lucky to see the back of them. Toby had insisted that they should take nothing from Stephen, and Miggy was only too happy to agree.

'After all,' said Toby, 'fair's fair. You've left him to live with me and Daisy's not his child. I really don't see how we can expect him to continue to support either of you.'

Stephen, who had been about to write a letter containing these very sentiments, was too relieved not to have to fight his point to make any further difficulties and the whole relationship ended quite painlessly. Ruth, however, was another matter. The problem lay in Toby's innate niceness. Although he'd stuck his heels in and refused to go back to London, he nevertheless felt terribly guilty about it. He knew that this was the nub of the failure of his marriage with Ruth and now, having found Miggy, felt required to make tremendous efforts to see that Ruth and Georgia were as happy as he was.

Miggy banged the fridge door shut and poured herself some wine. How could you tell someone they were too nice? Added to which, his good-natured generosity made her feel an utter cow! Toby, blissfully happy and grateful in his love for Miggy – and hers for him – would never understand why she couldn't just accept that Ruth and Georgia were around and make the best of it. Surely, he'd pleaded when he saw how upset she was by Ruth's suggestion, surely their happiness was great enough to encompass a few other people along the way?

'No it bloody isn't!' muttered Miggy rebelliously after a second swallow at her wine. 'It's just not that simple. I know it isn't!'

She knew instinctively that Ruth was out to wreck the relationship but how could she say so to Toby? Miggy felt vulnerable. She knew that Toby loved her but they weren't married and Daisy was not his child. There had been no more talk of the divorce and, when she mentioned it, Toby became very uptight.

'I was pretty brutal to her, you know,' he said, 'and that letter Nick and I wrote put it all on the line. I think we've got to give her time to adjust. I'll discuss it with her at Christmas.'

'I'll believe that when I see it!' said Miggy now, topping up her glass.

'Talking to yourself?' asked Toby from behind her. 'Dear, dear! That's bad!'

Miggy gave a squawk of surprise, spilled her wine and then hugged him tightly as he slipped his arms round her and kissed her.

'Believe what when you see it?' he murmured in her ear.

'Nothing,' she said hastily. 'Just something Hattie was saying earlier. Are you home for lunch? Like a drink?'

'Just a quickie,' he said, continuing to kiss her.

'Oh good. My feelings entirely.' Miggy put her glass down and led him firmly out of the kitchen and upstairs. She grinned at his expression. 'You've heard the old saying, haven't you?' she asked as they fell together on to the bed. 'You're getting old when a quickie before lunch means a drink.'

Sarah, driving back from a charity lunch in Plymouth, switched on her windscreen wipers against the late November rain and wondered how she could persuade Hattie to come to them for Christmas. She'd been adamant that she was going to stay at the mill.

'I'm going to have a Christmas Eve party,' she'd told Sarah, 'and Miggy's invited me to Christmas lunch. I hope that you and Nick will come to my party, though.'

Sarah had grumbled that she could see that Hattie was putting her new friends first but Hattie merely grinned affectionately and told her not to be an old fool. She was prepared to admit to herself that she was being a little foolish, surprised at how jealous she'd felt to see Hattie settling in so happily, not really needing her at all. Of course, she was pleased for her, but still . . . And Nick had said that certainly they must go to Hattie's Christmas Eve party.

Out of habit Sarah mentally reviewed the guest list for attractive young women.

Only that Miggy, she thought as she drove through Crapstone, and she's not Nick's type at all.

A familiar fear clutched her heart. How did she really know what Nick's type was? When they were together it was the sophisticated, well-informed girls he seemed to be drawn to, enjoying intelligent conversation and beauty at the same time. Miggy was certainly not sophisticated, nor did she seem possessed of any marked intelligence, thought Sarah waspishly, and shook her head disapprovingly. Whatever Hattie might say, the girl had no right to abandon her husband simply because she'd met someone else she preferred. And what sort of example was it to the child?

Sarah relaxed a little. At least she'd be able to enjoy the party without fearing that Nick would meet someone that would set him off on one of his affairs. It was months now since Nick had been involved with another woman. She invariably knew. His pattern of behaviour always changed slightly and always in the same way. This, given that he was such a clever man, was really rather stupid.

Sarah felt a flash of contempt for Nick's weaknesses, which was almost immediately swallowed in her overwhelming love for him. They'd spent an idyllic two weeks at the little retreat in the Shropshire hills which they'd bought a year before. Though rustic and isolated, it was charming and Sarah had made it comfortable, warm, welcoming, though it would be no place to stay in the winter. It had been perfect for the late September days and Sarah had been so happy she'd wanted never to leave it. Their friends would have found it difficult to recognise Nick; casual, easy and loving in these wild surroundings. They'd walked on the hills, had dinner at The Bear in Ludlow, talked endlessly – and made love.

Sarah's lips trembled into a smile as she turned into the drive. It had been so magical, so perfect, just the two of them together and no terrors that he might be involved with another woman. He'd made love to her often and she'd felt young again and pretty and desirable. Oh, it had been so wonderful! Sarah parked the car and went indoors. She was beginning to dare to believe that Nick had come to the end of his long protracted youth and might be settling down at last. If only she could be enough; enough to satisfy all his needs and be to him what he'd always been to her.

She went into the kitchen to make herself a cup of tea and decided to telephone Hattie whilst the kettle boiled.

'Nick says Christmas Eve will be fine,' she told her. 'Do you know enough people for a party?'

'It won't be very big,' said Hattie. 'Put that down at once, Jellicoe! Sorry. Yes. You and Nick. Toby and Miggy. Joss. Toby's partner at the boatyard, Jerry, and his girlfriend. Oh and Toby's estranged wife, Ruth. And Georgia if she wants to come which probably means Daisy, too, if Miggy doesn't want her left alone. She can watch television upstairs or something.'

'Sounds an odd mix.' Sarah's peace of mind was evaporating. She'd already heard that Ruth was very pretty – and obviously unattached. 'Bit embarrassing for everybody, the estranged wife coming, isn't it?'

'Very,' said Hattie cheerfully. 'That's why I thought a party might help the ship along. And that's why I'm going to Christmas lunch with them. Poor Miggy's terrified.'

'Well, I think it's a bit much,' said poor Sarah, who now had an estranged wife, a seventeen-year-old girl and a partner's girlfriend to worry about. 'Honestly, Hattie—'

'Must dash,' said Hattie unrepentantly. 'The Admiral's just

carried my shopping bag outside and it's still got the sausages in it. We'll talk again soon. Thanks for phoning.'

The line went dead and Sarah banged the receiver down with an exclamation of irritation. Really, Hattie was just like an irresponsible child these days! Sarah made her tea, thought about the party with something like despair and tried to pull herself together. It was quite unlikely that this Ruth and Nick would hit it off. And, anyway, didn't she live in London? Sarah felt her spirits rising a little. Of course! That would almost certainly put paid to anything happening on that front and removed the daughter as a threat, too. Perhaps, after all, it wouldn't be too bad. For a brief moment, Sarah considered buying something new to wear and discounted it almost at once. Her clothes were expensive, classic and in keeping with her age, and she certainly didn't need anything new. And never, never would she descend to attempting to compete with those elegant young women. She'd seen women in their fifties, thin to starvation point, wearing mini-skirts, their hair bleached, make-up caking in the lines and wrinkles! Never would she be one of them, mutton dressed as lamb with a vengeance.

Sarah poured herself a second cup of tea. She must have confidence that Nick was settling down and that her own personality would keep him by her side. After all, there had never been the least suggestion that he might want to leave her. She pushed the thought of her bank balance and the beautiful things she'd given him resolutely away. Nick loved her; that fortnight in Shropshire had certainly proved that. She must hold on to those memories and be patient.

Chapter Ten

Christmas was just as bad as Miggy feared. From the beginning it was apparent to her that Ruth was using Georgia as a pawn and, what's more, that the girl was resenting it a little. It was she who threw the first spanner in the works by refusing to go to Hattie's party, saying that she'd already made arrangements to visit a friend in Dartmouth. Ruth began to frown, saw Toby watching her and smiled quickly.

'Well, if that's what you want . . .' She looked helplessly at him. 'She doesn't change, does she? She always knew her own mind from day one. Do you remember . . . ?'

It was the first in a whole series of 'do you remembers' which effectively excluded Miggy and Daisy and drew Toby back into their shared past. Miggy fumed silently, Ruth exulted slyly and Toby desperately tried to maintain an amicable balance between them. To begin with, however, there wasn't much time for reminiscences. As soon as Georgia's evening had been organised, Daisy begged to be left alone at the cottage. Secretly, she'd always wanted to be on her own at night in a house, to find out what it was like to frighten herself silly, and this seemed a good opportunity. For once, she was not to be coerced and it was Hattie, to whom Miggy had telephoned in despair, who solved the problem.

'Jellicoe can look after her,' she said at once. 'He'll be a pain here, anyway, with all the goodies laid out. He's very good about not taking food but with his head now well above the table top it's a terrible temptation for him. Tell Toby to come and get him.'

Daisy was perfectly happy with this arrangement and so was Miggy. The Admiral was a friendly animal but he barked a deep terrifying bark at the least noise – as well as being the size of a small pony – and she knew that no one would get near Daisy whilst he was at hand. So it was that finally Miggy set out along the hard with Toby. Ruth had already set out for Dartmouth, cross that Toby had gone off to get the Admiral just when she'd hoped to succeed in her attempt to make him take Georgia to her friend's

81

house. The party set the scene for the whole Christmas, with Ruth playing a rather wistful 'I'm all alone in the world' role which aroused Sarah's sympathy, Nick's interest, Joss's amusement and Miggy's wrath. Even Toby wasn't taken in although he was too soft-hearted to do much about it.

Christmas Day was a nightmare as far as Miggy was concerned, with Ruth's 'do you remembers' and her ability to create the impression that the cottage was still her home. She talked about past Christmases, invited Toby to discuss mutual friends and managed to be girlish and gay and charming. Miggy greeted Hattie and Joss with deep relief at lunchtime, feeling as though she'd already lived through weeks of Christmas. Since Hattie and Joss were quite unreceptive to Ruth's wiles, lunch passed fairly peacefully but, by the evening, Miggy felt she might scream at the top of her voice if she heard Ruth call Toby 'darling' one more time. She still had visions of them twined together – happy, in love – and if Toby so much as smiled at Ruth she felt quite murderous.

When they went to bed she and Toby had a row in low fierce whispers until, terrified that Toby might fling off downstairs and Ruth might hear and follow him, Miggy caught at her common sense and apologised in a small voice, sitting on the very edge of the bed with her back to him. He caught her and pulled her to him and she felt her need of him overtake her jealousy and all was well again until the next afternoon when Ruth suggested she and Toby went through the old photographs together so that they could share them out.

'Let her get on with it,' advised Hattie when Miggy dropped in on her after a long solitary walk through the woods, unable to bear another squeal of 'oh darling, just look at my hat' and 'you always fancied me in that dress'. 'She's only deceiving herself. Toby may be bearing with it but he's not going to be taken in after all these years.'

'I wish I could believe that,' said Miggy, stroking the Admiral who was sitting heavily on her feet, and allowing himself to be hugged whilst she let off steam. 'He's so bloody patient with her!'

'Poor old Toby.' Hattie shook her head. 'He's rather between the devil and the deep blue sea, isn't he? What are you scared of?'

Miggy raised her cheek from the Admiral's coat and looked at her in surprise. 'How d'you mean?'

Hattie shrugged. 'You're obviously frightened about something.

D'you think he doesn't really love you after all and wants her back?'

'Well,' said Miggy breathlessly, taken aback at having her terrors put so baldly into words, 'now you mention it . . . Yes, I suppose I am.'

'Then you're a twit,' said Hattie kindly. 'Anyone can see he adores you. Don't be so wet. And don't let her get away with it. Carry the war into her camp. Ask her why she left the creek. Or how long she's known her boss. Unsettle her. If you can't ignore her, engage her in battle.'

'Bless you, Hattie.' Miggy stood up to go and dropped a kiss on Hattie's cheek. 'You're terrific!'

'Pooey!' said Hattie. 'And the next time you go for a long walk, come and fetch Jellicoe first! It's too damp for me out there today and now he's been deprived of a good hour's exercise!'

Miggy went back to the cottage and into the sitting room. Toby was reading but smiled at her as she came in. He looked anxious and she smiled at him reassuringly. Ruth, sitting unnecessarily close to him on the sofa, raised her eyebrows at her as if she were the intruder.

'What's your husband doing this Christmas?' she asked as Miggy picked up a book and prepared to sit opposite.

'I've no idea.' Miggy remained on her feet. 'I may be old-fashioned but I believe that if you've walked out on your husband then you have no rights to interest yourself in his life afterwards. In my book that's bad taste.'

The colour mounted in Ruth's cheeks. 'What would you know about bad taste?' she asked viciously. 'Bringing a young child to live with a man you're not married to and exposing her to gossip. Moving into another woman's house and living on her husband . . .'

'That'll do, Ruth.' Toby flung his O'Brien to one side and got up. 'That's more than enough. Remember that you invited yourself this Christmas and for Georgia's sake we agreed. *We* agreed, Ruth. Miggy and I. This is her home not yours and I'm suggesting that you leave it at the earliest possible moment. Georgia can go back to London on the train.'

'We agreed that for Georgia's sake—'

'Exactly.' Toby cut her short. 'For Georgia's sake. Georgia's already told me that it was your idea to come down instead of sending her at New Year and I honestly can't imagine that she's getting much benefit from all this back-biting. Christmas is almost over and I suggest you pack your bags and set off first thing tomorrow morning. Joss has invited Miggy and me out to supper in Dartmouth so you've got all evening to get your things together.'

He went out. There was silence whilst Miggy wondered whether to follow him but decided instead to sit down with her book. Before Ruth could speak Daisy came in and flung herself on the sofa. Ruth looked at her in distaste and got up.

'Georgia's in my room if you want her,' said Daisy. 'Listening to my Captain Beaky tape. She says she's bored rigid.'

Ruth went out without a word and Miggy smiled at Daisy. 'Enjoyed your Christmas?' she asked, hoping that she hadn't noticed Ruth's coldness.

'OK. I like it better on our own. D'you think Toby would take me out sailing tomorrow if I ask him?'

'I'm sure he would,' said Miggy, getting to her feet. 'Let's go and find him, shall we?'

Hattie walked along the foreshore on New Year's Eve and felt a great sense of satisfaction and achievement. The thin, flat disc of a moon, like a very old silver coin, hung in a frosty sky, its reflection shivering into shining fragments as the tide washed in slowly over the mud. The Admiral, running ahead, put up a duck and its outraged, comical quacking echoed round the creek. Hattie glanced across to the cottage where she would be going later for a drink to welcome in the New Year. Things seemed to have settled down there again with Ruth's departure and she hoped that there would be no more disturbances. She'd wondered whether Nick might take an interest in Ruth. He'd certainly talked to her at the Christmas Eve party but that was only to be expected since Nick always talked to the prettiest woman at any gathering. With Sarah present, however, he'd made no attempt to be other than pleasantly friendly and she couldn't believe that he'd pursue Ruth to London.

Hattie had nearly reached the corner of the smaller creek where *Abigail* was berthed. Between them, Joss and Toby had moved her on to her moorings and she was upright again and back on her legs, waiting there now, dark and deserted. Hattie shivered a little and turned back, calling to the Admiral. Despite her natural good sense, she felt a twinge of unease at the thought of the old boat and the remembrance of Evan's awful accident. It had been the one black cloud on the otherwise clear sky of the past months.

She put the memory away from her and thought of her own plans. The second cottage would be ready for a tenant by early spring and she dwelled pleasurably on how she would advertise and who might reply.

She took a turn round the orchard beside the mill pond, whose weed-covered surface glowed greenly in the unearthly moonlight, and she touched the old lichened branches of the bare apple trees. She remembered how she had first seen the orchard with its carpet of daffodils and, later, with the trees covered by a foaming mass of pink and white blossom, and longed for the spring to come again. As she crossed the rickety little bridge over the stream she thought of Sarah's strictures. Although she laughed Sarah's fears away, the idea of choosing a reliable friendly tenant was a little daunting. The problem with small communities was that it was vitally important that everyone pulled together. Perhaps, as well as having to pass the Admiral Jellicoe test, prospective tenants should be vetted by Toby and Joss as well.

She'd just settled the Admiral when Joss arrived.

'All ready?' he asked. 'I've promised Daisy I'll let off a maroon at midnight. She's being allowed to stay up to see the New Year in.'

'We'll have the coastguard round,' warned Hattie. 'And then what will you do?'

'I know the coastguards who patrol this guard,' said Joss imperturbably. 'I sail with a couple of them. Anyway, one maroon gets the lifeboat, not the coastguard. I doubt they'll see us from Salcombe and come surging round.'

Hattie laughed as they set out together. 'Why on earth did you join the Army?' she asked. 'Wouldn't the Navy have you? You seem so much more a sailor than soldier.'

'Family tradition,' said Joss non-committally. 'My father's regiment and so on. Very strong on tradition, my family. They had a fit when I came outside and moved on to *Westering*.'

Hattie glanced up at him as he strode beside her. 'I imagine they don't approve of your plans for sailing round the world single-handed or whatever?'

'Correct,' he answered shortly.

She sought for something to say to lighten the tension but they were already crossing the lawn to the cottage and the door opened and Miggy and Toby and Daisy came streaming out to meet them.

★   ★   ★

'Here's to us, my love.' Nick raised a glass to Sarah as she sat, bundled in shawls, on the sofa in their drawing room. 'With thanks for another year together and best wishes for the next one.'

'Oh darling, I'm sorry to be such a wet blanket.' She raised her glass to him and sipped. 'What a time to get the flu!'

'You couldn't help it.' He tucked a slipping shawl round her tenderly. 'Don't be silly.'

'I know how you enjoy the Hope-Latymers' parties.' She smiled at him. 'I'm glad you didn't go without me, after all.'

'It never occurred to me to go without you. That was your silly idea. We shall see the New Year in together as we've always done.'

'Oh, Nick.' She held his hand tightly and blinked back threatening tears. 'I hope we always shall.' She sneezed violently, blew her nose and felt feeble and ill.

'And why shouldn't we?' He bent his head so that his hazel eyes twinkled into her streaming ones. 'Are you planning to leave me?'

At this quite ludicrous suggestion she simply shook her head, dismissing the idea as unworthy even of reply, and he smiled and slipped an arm round her so that she rested back against him. 'I love you,' she said weakly, and thought that she might burst into tears after all.

He put his glass on a low table and pulled her gently round to face him.

'Oh, don't look at me,' she cried quite involuntarily. 'I look so awful. So plain.'

She scrubbed at her face with her handkerchief and attempted to pull away but he held her firmly and turned her face up. She closed her eyes tightly and then opened them and looked at him.

'I love you,' he said quietly. 'I love you, Sarah. That never changes in spite of . . . how things might seem sometimes.'

She realised that she was holding her breath. Never had they discussed Nick's affairs. They'd always behaved as though they simply didn't exist. Sarah knew a moment of terror. Was he going to start admitting to his affairs and telling her about them? She knew that she simply couldn't bear it.

'I know,' she said quickly. 'I know it. Take no notice of me. I'm feeling weepy and middle-aged and silly.'

'Remember Shropshire?' he asked, and her face changed and she clung to him.

'Oh, Nick. It was perfect,' she whispered.

'So it was,' he agreed. 'Perfect. I've had a thought. I don't think I can bother to wait to see the New Year in. Shall we go to bed and remember Shropshire together?'

'Oh, Nick,' she said again and he kissed her briefly and pulled her to her feet.

'Go on up,' he said. 'I'll finish down here and be right behind you. Take your glass.'

He watched her go, smiling at her as she glanced back, and then, whistling tunelessly to himself, tidied up and put the guard across the fire. He stood for a moment, staring down at the flames, and then turned away and followed her upstairs.

The moon sailed high above the creek; a breathless moment before the tide turned. *Westering* rocked gently at her moorings and, up in the woods, a vixen barked. The trees leaned black above the shallows, a breath of wind disturbed the surface of the water and the dark shadows on the *Abigail*'s deck looked like patches of dried blood. The moon slipped away behind the trees, the tide turned and, in the east, a spectral lightening of the sky heralded the new year.

Chapter Eleven

The year passed quickly – or so it seemed to Hattie. During March, Joss moved back on to *Westering*. He'd spent many of the dry early spring days aboard and, although he knew there was plenty of wet cold weather yet to come, he wanted to be back in his own quarters. He knew that he could always use the cottage as a bolt hole if the need arose and it was good to be afloat again; to feel the keel lifting under the swell of the tide and hear the wind singing in the shrouds.

Hattie, meanwhile, was preparing for her first tenant. The second cottage was swept and garnished and waiting, and Bert Crabtree began work on the first cottage which Joss had just vacated. Everyone wanted to give advice about the wording of the advertisement and warn her about possible problems and Nick dealt with the subject of leases at great length. It was, therefore, with a mixture of relief and disappointment that in May she received a letter from an old nursing friend, newly retired, who was looking for a billet while she waited for the little bungalow she was buying to be built.

Naturally, it was good to be able to help out an old friend – especially one who wouldn't quibble at the rent – nevertheless the simple transaction removed some of the excitement.

'Never mind,' said Miggy consolingly, when she heard the news. 'Perhaps it's a good thing. You can practise being a landlord on someone you know for a bit. Then you'll learn all the pitfalls.'

'That's true enough.' Hattie made a face. 'And Monica's a nice sensible woman. She won't be any trouble.'

Miggy burst out laughing. 'That sounded terribly damning, Hattie,' she said. 'That bad, is she?'

'No, no.' Hattie pulled herself together but she grinned a bit. 'She's a very good friend. Just . . . well, just the least bit dull, let's say.'

'What were you hoping for? A couple of pop stars? Prince

89

Andrew phoning up to say that he found his cabin at the naval college too small?'

'Oh, shut up,' said Hattie good-naturedly. 'Get back to your work. Standing around here gossiping and wasting my time. How's Toby?'

'OK.' Miggy's face clouded a little. 'Bit of a problem with Georgia.'

'Oh dear. Now what? I thought everything had quietened down since Christmas.'

Miggy perched sideways on the little wall that edged Hattie's quay and stared down into the water.

'It has. Rather too much, that's the trouble. Georgia's not a very good correspondent, which is perfectly reasonable at her age, but she didn't come down for half term and then she didn't come for Easter either. Ruth wrote and said she'd gone ski-ing with some school friends. Toby was very disappointed.'

'Ah.' Hattie stuck her hands in the pockets of her old tweed jacket and pursed her lips. 'Well, I suppose it's the obvious thing for Ruth to try next.'

'How d'you mean?' Miggy looked up at her.

Hattie shrugged. 'Well, trying to come between you and Toby didn't work so she's going to punish him by making it difficult for him to see Georgia.'

'You think that's what it is? Toby thinks she may have turned Georgia against him.'

'Rubbish!' said Hattie impatiently. 'That girl's got a mind of her own. If she'd been younger she'd have made trouble for you. As it is, it was pure luck that she was just going away to school and taking an interest in boys. Gave her something else to think about.'

'Well, I agree with that. She was difficult to begin with but at Christmas I felt that she didn't really care too much. She was more interested in being with her friends.'

'Of course she was. And that's how it should be. I suspect that Ruth is making it difficult for her to come down and – to be brutally honest – Georgia's probably not too bothered about it. Let's face it! She's used to doing without her father.'

'I think you're right.' Miggy stood up and pushed back her curls. 'The problem is that Toby's hurt and I don't know what to do about it.'

'I'm sure if he gives it rational thought he'll understand how the mind of a seventeen-year-old girl works. Very tunnel vision. Clothes and boys and jollies. She'll be down in the summer.'

Miggy smiled at her gratefully. 'Bless you, Hattie. You always help me to think straight.'

'Pooey!' Hattie turned away towards the mill.

'I'll get back. See you.'

Miggy strolled along the hard enjoying the warmth of the early May sunshine on her face. The thing that worried her more than Georgia's apparent defection was the fact that there was still no mention of a divorce. Toby had assured her – after discussions with Nick – that, if Ruth decided to halt the proceedings she'd initiated, then he could proceed to divorce her on the grounds of either adultery or desertion.

Miggy crossed the lawn and sat down on the bench. A solitary shelduck patrolled a stretch of water near the nest where his mate was sitting on a clutch of eggs. Presently the drake waddled out on to the newly exposed mud and began to patter with his red webbed feet. Toby had told her that they did this in order to bring prey to the surface and she watched the dark green head with its bright red bill that poked at intervals into the mud. She loved the creek as much as Toby did, fascinated by its natural life. Soon she would have been here for a whole year and could begin to look for the things she'd become familiar with as each season passed. Further down the creek the swans had built their enormous nest high above the water line and Toby had taken her by boat to see the heronry, on the banks of the Dart on the way up to Totnes, where the females could just be spied, sitting on their unwieldy, twiggy nests.

And that's one of my problems, she thought. I feel broody.

It hadn't occurred to her that she would feel such a longing to bear Toby's child. She'd never felt the least inclination to have a child by Stephen and he had made it clear that Daisy was quite enough as far as he was concerned. It was surprising that such an ambitious man shouldn't want his own children but he'd told her very early in the relationship that he had no desire to be a father and, later, Miggy wondered whether he'd realised that he'd be such an indifferent parent that he'd wisely decided to follow his instincts.

Perhaps Daisy had put him off completely! Miggy smiled to herself. One of the great joys of her relationship with Toby was the great affection which Toby and Daisy shared. It was such a relief and she was immensely grateful to him for taking Patrick's child to his heart. Her gratitude was such that she felt ashamed to find that, when Toby was obviously missing Georgia and worrying about her, she felt slightly put out because he didn't regard her and Daisy as sufficient. She was shocked that she could have such unworthy emotions and suffered great guilt but she couldn't quite help wishing that Georgia and Ruth could vanish out of the picture altogether. Perhaps it would be different if Georgia could come to accept her and Daisy as her father's new family and then her anxieties might cease.

Miggy sighed a little and shook her head. She suspected that she wouldn't feel quite secure until she and Toby were married and that, along with her broodiness, was the thing that occupied most of her thoughts. Would Toby be prepared to start divorce proceedings against Ruth? Really Ruth was being very clever. Miggy suspected that, until he was certain of Georgia's continuing love, Toby would be unwilling to start divorcing her mother for adultery. He knew very well how easily Ruth could guide Georgia's life, even if she couldn't control her mind, and Miggy sensed – and sympathised with – his dilemma. The point was, as far as she was concerned, she simply didn't feel able to contemplate becoming pregnant unless she and Toby were married. Despite his unwavering love for her, she simply wasn't prepared to take the chance. It was bad enough living with him as his mistress. She hated signing her name in shops or giving it on the telephone and dealing with the confusion that arose. Perhaps it was old-fashioned and foolish of her but it was the way she was made.

Miggy glanced at her watch and got up. It was time to fetch Daisy from school. Thank God her child was so easy-going, so unmindful of the world, or she might be hurt or damaged by the pattern her life had followed so far. In fact, she seemed to thrive on it. Miggy drove up the lane, her cares scattered temporarily by the now familiar yet ever new delight created by the drifts of bluebells growing in the hedges. Soon trails of dog rose and honeysuckle would be seen amongst the leaves which were bursting open and softly covering the black twigs with misty tender green. She slowed the car to let a rabbit hop across the lane and her worries receded and joy swamped her senses. She was so lucky, so very lucky.

But still, she thought as she paused at the top of the lane to wait for a tractor, I would so love to have a baby.

Westering, with Joss at the helm, motored gently down the creek. He'd have preferred to bend the brown canvas sails on to the tall bare poles and sail down but it simply wasn't worth it for the short journey round to Dartmouth. She'd been taking a lot of water and it was time to put her on the grid by the embankment and have a good look underneath. He was rather dreading the result of his examination and had already formed the resolve that, should work be required which he was unable to undertake, he would ask Toby if she could be slipped at the boatyard and the repairs carried out in return for his labours. He hoped that the boatyard was busy enough to need him and sighed as he saw his departure being delayed for some considerable time.

It was wonderful to be moving again; to feel the water creaming under the keel and the breeze fanning his cheeks. He'd known from the beginning that restoring *Westering* would be a long job. Although he'd picked her up at a very reasonable price there was very little spare cash left and he knew he'd have to do nearly all the work himself. Now he must simply hope that Toby was prepared to do a quid pro quo.

He turned her out into the river and chugged downstream, passing the entrance to Old Mill creek and Sandquay with Britannia Royal Naval College on the hill above. He watched some midshipmen in the college cutters practising coming alongside and thought of Hattie. During the winter months ashore, he'd spent many of the long evenings in the mill's kitchen and, encouraged by Hattie's common sense and humour, he'd begun to talk of his experiences in Northern Ireland. Unable just yet to be totally honest with her, he'd attributed his nightmares and guilt to a fellow officer; a good friend whose experiences still coloured his life and destroyed his confidence. Hattie listened thoughtfully, showing neither derision nor disgust at this unmanly behaviour.

'I can quite understand it,' she'd said. 'Terrorist warfare is so difficult to deal with. Not knowing who your enemy is, unable to trust even small children. You're not even allowed to fight back. Absolutely terrifying. There's bound to be an aftereffect. The sad thing is that these mental wounds don't show and get little or no treatment.'

When Joss, heartened by this attitude, muttered that a soldier should be able to cope with fear and bloodshed without feeling squeamish Hattie's response was unequivocal.

'I think far too many people have become indifferent to suffering,' she said at once. 'We see it on the television and read about it daily in the newspapers so we've become immune. Personally, I prefer a man who is compassionate enough to care about other people's pain. And when it comes to the men you're serving with, it must be so. Or should be!'

Joss had felt a tremendous relief. Slowly, a measure of self-worth was returning and he knew now that he'd be sad to leave the creek. He'd become part of the small community and he wondered how he'd feel when he finally set sail and said goodbye to them all; Hattie and that wretched Jellicoe; Miggy and that pest Daisy; Toby and his chums at the boatyard.

Keeping an eye on the Higher Ferry as it set off across the river, Joss thought about his own people and his face hardened a little. He heard regularly from his sister; reproachful little missives reminding him of how hurt his mother was at his indifference to her unhappiness, of situations becoming vacant where strings might easily be pulled on his behalf, of how disappointed his father would have been had he been alive. His sister made it clear that he should be prepared to redress the balance of his father's demise by giving up his Bohemian lifestyle and taking up a career which could restore their pride in him. Joss went at intervals to see them but the intervals were getting longer and longer. He felt deeply guilty that he'd failed them all but knew instinctively that he was not ready to cope with their demands. In any case, his sister would have been offended to have her position as their mother's chief prop usurped; he knew that. No point in wasting his life; pouring it out as a useless oblation on the ground for some non-existent god. When he had come to terms with himself he would be able to be of use to them and until then their paths must continue to lie apart.

Joss approached the grid, watched by interested spectators on the embankment above, and prepared for the tricky manoeuvre of putting *Westering* in exactly the right position. He cleared his mind of his worries, as he had learned to do in the Army, and concentrated on the job in hand.

It was Daisy who noticed that there were people once more aboard the *Abigail*. The cottage looked almost directly into the small creek and her bedroom window now sported a telescope through which she surveyed the comings and goings along the water.

'D'you think they're coming to live on it?' she asked, slipping into her chair at the kitchen table, whilst Toby and Miggy exchanged uneasy glances. 'May I row over and say hello?'

'No!' they said in unison and she stared at them in surprise.

'It's not a funny man on his own this time,' she said. 'It's a man and a woman.'

'Even so,' said Miggy quickly, 'let's leave it for a bit. They're probably just having a look over her. Surely we'd have heard if they'd bought her. We can't just burst in on them.'

Daisy shrugged, baffled as usual by this odd code that grown-ups adhered to, and poured ketchup liberally over her pizza. 'OK. I'll keep an eye on them, though. If they have moved on board it's only polite to go and welcome them. You have to be polite to people when they're new. Make them feel at home.'

'I don't notice this unselfish high-mindedness where Monica's concerned,' observed Toby with a tiny wink at Miggy. 'You don't seem too bothered about whether she feels at home.'

Daisy made a face. 'She's a bit boring,' she admitted. 'Drones on about how lucky I am to be living here. Anyway, she's got Hattie.'

'Wouldn't you have heard if someone had bought *Abigail*?' asked Miggy when Daisy had finished and asked to be excused. 'Surely we'd have seen them being shown over her?'

'It's possible someone's bought her sight unseen.' Toby looked thoughtful. 'They may consult us if they want something done. But we won't be able to keep Daisy away indefinitely. They'll be bound to want to be friendly. We can't tell them they've bought an unlucky boat and we're all scared to death to go near her.'

'I realise that.' Miggy bit her lip. 'Oh, Toby, I've got a horrid feeling about that boat.'

Toby reached across the table and took her hand. 'We mustn't get carried away,' he said gently. 'I'm sure it's all just a lot of rumours.'

She shook her head. 'I've tried to believe that but I just have this funny sort of dread when I think about her.'

Toby gave her hand another squeeze and released it.

'I'll make some coffee,' he said.

As he filled the kettle he recalled his great delight and relief at receiving a letter from Georgia saying that she'd be down for several weeks of the summer holiday. He intended to talk seriously to her about the divorce then. He'd decided that she was old enough to understand the situation but he wanted her to hear it from his own lips and not some twisted version from Ruth. Once he'd explained it all to her, then he would go ahead and divorce Ruth. Until then he didn't want to mention it to Miggy lest some misunderstanding should cloud their relationship. Toby had never known such happiness and he was determined to protect it.

'Coffee,' he said and bent to kiss her. 'Don't worry. We'll keep an eye on Daisy and if necessary think of some way to keep her off the *Abigail*.'

She smiled up at him and nodded.

'I know I'm being daft,' she said. 'Any chance of an hour off? We could take the boat down the river. Blow away the cobwebs.'

'Brilliant idea.' He was delighted to be able to please her. 'Get Daisy organised and I'll phone Jerry and tell him I'm taking the afternoon off.'

Chapter Twelve

The summer drew on and no more was seen or heard of the couple aboard the *Abigail*. None of the local yacht brokers knew anything about them and it was concluded that the couple had been members of Evan's family who had either decided to let her rot or put her with an upcountry brokerage. Miggy felt that anyone considering buying the *Abigail* should be warned about her history but the others were more cautious. Even Hattie couldn't be totally persuaded that a prospective buyer should hear the old stories but each of them felt secretly relieved that they were not required to take a decision either way and therefore no responsibility need be shouldered.

Hattie experienced an even deeper sense of relief when Monica told her that the building of her bungalow was so well up to schedule that she could move into it some weeks before Christmas. Feeling guilty at the light-heartedness with which she approached her friend's departure Hattie was most convincing in her assurances that Monica would be sorely missed. So convincing was she that Monica began to wonder whether or not she should stay on in the cottage until the New Year, after all, and Hattie was obliged to backtrack hastily. Monica's rather damping presence brought home to Hattie the importance of the right tenants in her cottages and she felt even more apprehensive than latterly. The close company of her friend had proved a very mixed blessing.

Miggy, on the other hand, had found Georgia's visit much easier than she could have imagined. There was no doubt that a year in the sixth form of a boys' public school had been exactly what was required to turn Georgia from an overweight sulky adolescent to a pretty slim outgoing young woman.

'I can't believe it,' Toby said to Miggy a dozen times a day. 'It's a complete metamorphosis.'

'She's got a boyfriend,' Miggy told him. 'One Justin Dangerfield. He's head of almost everything as far as I can tell. It's lovely to hear her talk about him. I'd love to meet him.'

It seemed that they were soon to have this opportunity. Georgia was gratified at Miggy's interest in her life. She didn't pry or criticise or advise; she just listened, exactly as though Georgia were a contemporary. The girl was flattered by this approach – not one that she was used to with Ruth – and began to relax completely and enjoy herself. Miggy suggested that Georgia should have driving lessons and from that moment on they were fast friends. After a few lessons, Miggy bravely allowed Georgia to drive her through the quieter lanes and even to Totnes on market days.

'She's really very good,' she assured a nervous Toby, who had terrible visions of two-thirds of his beloved family being killed in an accident. 'She has a natural flair for it.'

Once in Totnes they explored the market thoroughly, had coffee at one of the charming old cafés and always finished up in Salago. Georgia could spend hours in this delightful shop and was generally dragged away only because the car would be over-parked if they didn't hurry. Towards the end of the first week, after a telephone call from the much discussed Justin Dangerfield, she asked rather off-handedly whether it would be a problem in any way if he visited the cottage.

'Not a bit. Fine by me,' said Toby easily, with a quick glance at Miggy. 'Why not?'

Miggy nodded. She had just poured pre-dinner drinks and pushed a glass of wine across the table to Georgia. 'Great idea. When's he coming down?'

'Well, anytime really.' Georgia looked as casual as she could and took a grateful gulp of wine. She knew Ruth would have a fit if she could see Miggy generously dispensing alcohol. 'He lives in Dorset so he can be down in a couple of hours. He's passed his driving test and he's allowed to borrow his mum's car.'

'Well, you fix it up how you like, sweetheart.' Toby smiled at her. 'He can stay over if he wants to.' He looked at Miggy again. 'That's not a problem, is it?'

'Not at all. It will take two minutes to make up the spare room bed.' She raised her eyebrows at Georgia. 'Want to phone him back and arrange it?'

When she'd gone Toby held out his arms to Miggy and they hugged happily. He had no reservations now of talking to Georgia about the divorce. He knew that not only was she mature enough to cope with it, she was also kindly enough disposed towards them to make it easy for him. He decided, after a great deal of reflection, to approach the matter after Justin's visit. In the first place she'd be more likely to concentrate; in the second, she might be even more receptive. He felt a little guilty about this manipulative approach but decided that it was the most sensible.

Justin's visit was a tremendous success. He was a tall dark boy with an easy air and pleasant manners, and Miggy and Daisy were quite bowled over by him. Once again, Georgia was delighted by Miggy's attitude which was to imply admiration that Georgia had found herself such a dishy man and to treat Justin as another adult. This was by no means contrived. Miggy treated people of all ages simply as other human beings. As far as she was concerned, age didn't really come into relationships, which made her an easy if unusual companion. Justin was properly deferential towards Toby, who took it in his stride but told Miggy afterwards that it made him feel at least a hundred.

The two young people were very sweet to Daisy – who was learning to sail a small dinghy that was for sale at the boatyard – even taking her with them on one or two of their expeditions. Daisy, however, felt the company of young lovers to be a little cloying and most of the time pursued her own interests. The few days of Justin's stay passed quickly and, when he'd gone, Toby – his heart lurching and hammering – took Georgia off for a stroll in the woods and explained his dilemma.

'It could be quite simple and painless,' he told her. 'We've been separated for three years and we both want a divorce. At least, I thought we did. There need be no mud-slinging or name-calling. But Mum seems to have backed off and I don't know what to do.'

They strolled slowly forward, Georgia gazing straight ahead. 'Mum's jealous of Miggy,' she said at last. 'And Alan seems to have cooled off a bit.'

'Ah.' Toby gave a sigh and nodded. 'I wondered about Alan, I must admit. I simply can't understand the jealousy bit. She left me, after all.'

'That's a bit simplistic, Dad.' Georgia looked at him compassionately and Toby was struck anew by her sudden maturity. 'I think she liked the idea of you sitting down here still being faithful and all that. You know? She might get fed up and have other men but she likes to think you've still got a passion for her. Makes her feel good.'

Toby looked baffled and Georgia laughed and squeezed his arm. After a moment he laughed with her. 'Women!' he said. 'How do you think she'll react if I write and tell her that I'm starting divorce proceedings?' He prayed that she wouldn't ask him on what grounds. Even with this new open relationship he didn't feel equal to discussing adultery with his daughter.

'Blow a gasket, I should think.' Georgia sounded almost indifferent. 'But you'll have to, won't you? It's not fair to keep Miggy hanging about. It's not a very nice situation for her, is it?'

'No, it isn't.' He felt almost faint with relief at her acceptance of this fact. 'OK then. I just wanted you to know. You may have to face the music, after all.'

'Don't worry about me. I can handle Mum. I hope it's not too awful, though. For any of us.'

When Georgia returned to London, Toby told Miggy his decision and saw the joy and relief sweep across her face. Once more, guilt assailed him. Even he hadn't realised how much it meant to her.

'Soon,' he told her. 'It'll all be over soon.'

In September Toby had a letter from Georgia who was back at school.

'When your letter came,' she wrote, 'Mum was very quiet. I guessed what was in it and prepared myself to try to back you up if necessary but she hasn't mentioned anything to me at all. Luckily it was just before I came back to school so I'm glad to be out of it really . . .'

A few weeks later, Ruth launched a final attack. She telephoned one evening when Toby was in the bath and Miggy spoke to her.

'I understand you had a boy staying this summer when Georgia was with you,' she said without greeting or preamble. 'You know exactly how I feel about your morals but did you really think it was quite right to have two young people under the same roof, letting them go off together alone?'

'Are you serious?' demanded Miggy, when she'd got her breath back.

'Perfectly serious. Did it occur to you to find out anything about this boy first? Had you any idea what his reputation might be like?'

'No,' said Miggy slowly. 'No it didn't. I suppose I trusted Georgia's opinion of him.'

'Oh, honestly!' Ruth gave a snort of disgust. 'A seventeen-year-old girl in the first throes of infatuation? Well, I wouldn't expect much else from you but I certainly imagined her father would have more intelligence and anxiety for her wellbeing.'

Miggy clutched the receiver tighter. 'Is Georgia OK?'

'Bit late to worry about that now, isn't it? I'd like to speak to my husband.'

'Who is it?'

Toby's quiet voice in her ear made Miggy jump and he looked with surprise at her flushed cheeks and bright angry eyes. 'It's Ruth,' she whispered furiously, holding the receiver tightly to her chest so that Ruth shouldn't hear. 'She's cross because we had Justin here with Georgia and she's making all sorts of vile suggestions!'

Toby took the receiver from her clasp and spoke calmly. 'Hello, Ruth. How are you? What's all this about Georgia?'

'Oh, at last. Really, Toby! I could hardly believe my ears when Jackie Sutherland told me that Justin Dangerfield had been staying with you in the summer. Miggy told me that you made no enquiries about him, just took Georgia's word for him. Honestly! Living with Miggy hasn't improved your moral standards!'

'You think my morals were safer when I lived with a wife who flirted with every presentable male, had an affair with her boss and was continuously in debt?' There was a dangerous silence and Toby spoke again. 'Do I gather from this diatribe that something's wrong? Has this young man, whom I found quite delightful, got some sort of dreadful reputation?'

'As it happens, yes. He's a terrible flirt, drinks too much and he's always rushing about to parties.'

'Sounds a fairly normal eighteen-year-old,' mused Toby. 'There must be some sensible reason for this outburst, Ruth? Is Georgia pregnant?'

He heard Ruth gasp and gave Miggy a tiny wink when she turned to stare at him anxiously.

'If she were pregnant,' said Ruth viciously, 'it would be entirely your fault.'

'No, no.' Toby began to laugh. 'Not entirely. Incest isn't one of my vices. Come on, Ruth. None of this is making the least impression. I've just had a letter from Georgia, who is obviously very well and happy, and if Justin is a dangerous libertine I'm not the judge I thought I was. He and Georgia spent no more time alone together than any other young couple of their age. They had Daisy with them most of the time, too. We enjoyed having him here. He was well-mannered, sweet with Georgia and fun to have around. Perhaps Miggy's influence encouraged him to show us his better side.'

'Bastard!'

The line went dead and Toby's face changed. He looked angry and Miggy watched him, hardly daring to speak.

'It's OK.' He smiled at her but with some difficulty and she went to him and he slipped his arm round her.

'What was all that about?'

'Ruth having one last try. She's had my letter and she's going to have to back down and let it all happen quietly. This is the only way left to hurt us.'

'But is Georgia OK?'

'Of course she is.' Toby was thoughtful. 'We may have to get used to a few of these but if we get what we want in the end it will have been worth it.'

'I feel very guilty. We ought to have checked Justin out. Georgia's still very young, I suppose.'

'She's seventeen,' said Toby impatiently. 'Soon she'll be able to vote. I refuse to question and harass her. Much more likely to make her do something reckless I should think. You should trust people until they prove themselves unworthy of it.'

'It's a nice idea.' Miggy still looked troubled. 'She made it sound as if we wouldn't care what happened to her.'

'Of course. That's part of the strategy. To keep wrong-footing us. Well, it won't work. I love Georgia just as much as she does and I'm just as concerned for her welfare. Don't look so upset. Damn and blast Ruth!'

She smiled at him. She loved him so much it hurt and she hated Ruth for upsetting him and trying to undermine his affection for his daughter. Part of her, however, had thrilled to his words 'she's going to have to back down'. It seemed that the divorce would go through after all, otherwise Ruth wouldn't be using such oblique tactics.

Westering spent most of the summer on the boatyard's slip and by the time she was back at her mooring it was time once more to be battening down the hatches for the winter. Because of the unforeseen repairs, Joss was now well behind schedule and had to ask Hattie if he might use one of her cottages again. Monica had gone and both cottages were ready for occupation but Joss felt rather guilty about taking one of them.

'I can't afford the rent you'd get for a winter let,' he told her frankly. 'I've got a contract with one of the yachting magazines to do monthly articles about renovating a boat and getting her ready for a voyage. It's not much money and I could manage a bit more than last year but you could get much more.'

'Let's see how it goes,' said Hattie. 'I don't want to do winter lets really. Bert has frightened me silly about it all. I want nice long-term tenants. Not a lot of coming and going. I shall advertise again now Monica's gone and Number One is ready but I might not get any replies. Move in anyway and we'll play it by ear.'

'But what about the rent?'

Hattie shrugged. 'You can pay what you paid last year.'

'But I was working on the other cottage last year in lieu of most of the rent,' protested Joss. 'It was peanuts. I shall feel guilty.'

'No you won't.' Hattie smiled at him with great guile and sweetness. 'I've got other plans for you this winter. There's a lot of work to be done in the orchard and I want to clean out the mill pond.'

Joss burst out laughing. 'I take it all back. You're a worse slave-driver than a sergeant I knew at Sandhurst. And that's saying something. He was an old whatsit, he was! I remember when I first arrived I addressed him as "sir" in my fear and ignorance. "Don't call me sir, lad!" he bellowed. "I *work* for a living!"'

They laughed together and swapped a few like anecdotes until the Admiral strolled in and sat heavily against the dresser. Hattie went to sort out his lunch and Joss disappeared outside to start preparing *Westering* for the long winter. Hattie pottered about mentally reviewing the year. After all the excitment of buying the mill and moving in, this year had almost been an anticlimax. Having Monica hadn't really been a good idea – although how she could have refused her she hardly knew – but now both cottages were ready and she hoped that next year would see more activity. She really couldn't decide what sort of tenants she would prefer and knew that, in the end, it would probably be taken out of her hands.

She put the Admiral's food bowl on the floor and he sat staring at it mournfully as was his wont. He sighed deeply and rolled an eye at Hattie reproachfully.

'It's a perfectly good lunch!' she said crossly. 'I refuse to feel guilty about it.'

His tail thumped the floor a little as she bustled round, heating her soup and toasting some bread, until he got up suddenly and ate his whole meal with a hearty appetite and every evidence of enjoyment.

'You're an old fraud,' she told him and, pushing the saucepan to the back of the Esse, went to answer the telephone.

It was Sarah. Hattie hadn't heard much from her and Nick since their annual autumn trip to Shropshire and she settled comfortably at the table for a good long chat. Sarah's voice was light and happy and Hattie caught herself smiling too, infected by Sarah's high spirits. They'd had another wonderful holiday and Nick was fine and she was so busy . . .

Hattie let her talk on, well aware of the reason for her happiness. It was so long now since Nick had misbehaved himself that Sarah was daring to believe that his infidelity was a thing of the past and she could relax at last and feel secure. They made arrangements to meet and Hattie hung up and went back to her soup stirring. Joss put his head in at the door.

'Sorry to disturb you again. Did I leave my cap behind?'

They both glanced round the kitchen until their eyes alighted on the Admiral who, wedged between the table and the dresser, was chewing ravenously on Joss's cap.

'I shall kill him,' muttered Joss, retrieving the rather battered-looking article after a bit of a tussle.

The Admiral, who'd rather enjoyed the game, settled back and put his head on his paws whilst Hattie snatched the cap from Joss, brushed it with her sleeve and handed it back.

'No harm done,' she said briskly. 'Shouldn't leave things lying about.'

Joss sucked in his cheeks, his eyes fixed pointedly on a rather large tear in the tweed, and jammed it on his head.

'Looks lovely.' Hattie grinned at him. 'Want some lunch?'

'No, thank you.'

Joss marched out with an air of dignified reproach and Hattie sat down to her solitary lunch, still grinning. She'd noticed the change in him during the last months. She suspected that his confidence was returning and, with it, his self-esteem. It had taken her a few seconds only to realise that this friend he talked of, who still suffered from nightmares and guilt since his tour in Northern Ireland, didn't exist and that it was Joss who was trying to come to terms with the shock of watching his comrades die. Gradually, carefully, she'd been able to ease his pain, without letting him suspect that she knew the truth, and their friendship had deepened and strengthened. It would be a sad day when Joss left the creek on his voyage.

Chapter Thirteen

Miggy came out of the doctor's surgery in Victoria Road and walked back to the car, parked on the embankment. The April day was cold and sleety rain swirled out of a leaden sky. She passed along beside the boat-float and crossed the road to pause for a moment beside the car. The wind whipped the sullen grey water into little white-crested waves and the passengers crossing to Kingswear on the ferry huddled below in the shelter of the cabin. Miggy was remembering how she'd met Toby nearly two years before in the Royal Castle; that strange feeling that she'd known him for years, accompanied by a breathless excitement. How frightened she'd been, back in London, that she might be making a terrible mistake; how terrified when she'd taken the final plunge and she and Daisy had stood together by the boat-float waiting to meet him again!

Miggy gave a huge contented sigh and climbed into the car. She shook the sleet from her bright hair and stared at herself in the driving mirror, tilting it a little so that she could see her gleaming eyes and flushed cheeks. The miracle had happened and she was pregnant. The divorce had come through just before Christmas and she and Toby had been married at once, quietly in a register office, with Hattie and Joss, Daisy and Georgia in attendance. Afterwards there was a simple celebration at the Royal Castle and then they'd all gone back home to the creek.

Home! thought Miggy. Now she could safely think of it as home. She and Toby had hugged and hugged and danced round the kitchen whilst Daisy carefully produced the bottle of champagne which Hattie had secretly given her lest the day should go flat on them once the excitement was over. Miggy smiled as she remembered how the flying cork had knocked a cup from the dresser and Daisy had become tipsy on the champagne and how, much later, she – Miggy – and Toby had gone to bed and made love as though it were the first time; or the last!

And now she was pregnant. An October baby; a warm golden

mellow month to have a baby and all the summer ahead to relax at last and savour her good fortune. Miggy negotiated the boat-float and headed for home, wondering how Toby would react to the news. No mention had been made of a baby. She'd imagined that he was sensitive enough to guess that, until she felt secure, she wouldn't take the chance but he might simply have assumed that one daughter and one step-daughter were enough. She felt a tiny twinge of anxiety. She should have discussed it with him, of course. He might not want to enter into all the traumas of fatherhood again, after all he was nearly forty-two against her thirty-four. Eight years might make all the difference.

By the time she reached the hard she'd convinced herself that Toby wouldn't want another child and had already visualised the expression of quickly disguised horror that would appear on his face when she told him. She crossed the lawn, let herself in and went straight to the fridge to pour herself a drink. How on earth could she have taken such a momentous decision without consulting him?

'Ah!' Toby was in the doorway smiling at her. 'You're back.' He looked at her more closely. 'Are you OK?'

'Mmm.' She nodded, hardly daring to trust her voice. She took another sip at her wine and he came right into the kitchen, coming close to her and peering at her quizzically. 'Honestly I am!'

'No you're not,' he said flatly. 'What's wrong? Spit it out.'

'I'm pregnant.' She said it quickly, holding her glass in both hands and staring at him over the rim. 'Due in October. I should have asked you first.'

'Oh, Miggy, how fantastic.' He shut his eyes for a moment and his smile was perfectly, blissfully unforced and genuine. 'That's brilliant. Oh darling, how wonderful. One of yours, one of mine, one of ours!'

'Oh, Toby.' She put her glass down, weak with relief, and put out her hands to him. 'I had a sudden terror that you might not want any more children. I should have talked it over with you.'

'Rubbish!' He held her hands tightly. 'You instinctively knew I'd want more. I always wanted lots of children. I was terribly sad that Ruth refused to have any more. It's fantastic news.'

'How do you think Georgia will take it? Girls can be a bit odd at that age about this sort of thing.'

'She'll be thrilled,' said Toby robustly. 'So will Daisy. Let's just hope she won't want to teach him to swim or sail or something before he can walk.'

'What if it's another girl?'

'Three daughters.' Toby grinned and gave her a kiss. 'Four women in one house! Let joy be unconfined! Come on. Get your coat on. We're going along to tell Hattie. She can be godmother and Joss can be godfather. The first creekside baby, Miggy! Whatever sex it is, it's going to be very special!'

Sarah drove slowly across the moor. The gorse was in full flower and new shoots of bracken, growing like tiny trees from the dark peaty earth, were a bright fresh green. The stunted thorn was massed with blossom and the issues and pools, replenished by weeks of heavy rain, sparkled in the warm late May sunshine. Lambs huddled close at their mothers' flanks and rain shadows chased each other across the rocky outcrops of the high tors.

Sarah drove on, eyes inward-looking, unseeing of the beauty. She knew with heart-wrenching, gut-sickening certainty that Nick was having an affair. This time it was doubly, trebly, agonising. She'd been so sure, so sure . . . Sarah pressed her lips tightly together and swallowed. How could he? When they'd been so happy for so long! It had been the longest truly happy time she'd ever had with him. She'd allowed herself to be lulled by his loving, caring behaviour, longing to believe that he was ready to settle down at last.

At Christmas she'd known the faintest breath of anxiety. They'd been invited to Abby and William Hope-Latymer's party and this year, with no flu to prevent them, they'd gone along. Oddly, it was the fact that Nick seemed unaffected by the presence of the extraordinarily beautiful Cassandra Wivenhoe that had surprised her. Cass was exactly the sort of woman that Nick was unable to resist, yet he barely spoke to her. It alerted Sarah's suspicion but, when there were no signs of the usual clandestine meetings or guarded behaviour, she'd dismissed the idea and, indeed, counted it as confirmation of her growing belief that Nick was changing. But lately, to her horror, the old pattern had started to repeat itself; unexpected meetings in the evenings, extended business lunches, occasional weekends with clients.

Sarah never bothered to check; she'd been too humiliated by discovering painful truths in their early years together. Better to accept the lies and pretend to believe them. It saved both their faces and allowed a certain degree of dignity to be maintained. This time, however, she doubted if she could bear it. She wondered if it were Cass. This was always her first thought; who is she? How old

is she? What does she look like? She'd already cudgelled her brain
and remembered that last autumn Nick had spent the weekend
with William Hope-Latymer, sorting out a boundary dispute or
some such thing. She wondered now if he'd met Cass – who lived
in the same village with her naval officer husband – during that
weekend. If he had, she was prepared to swear that he'd made no
attempt to follow it up. Perhaps he'd been fighting the attraction
and, when he'd met her again at the party, his feelings had been
too strong for him.

She gave a tiny dry sob of pain and humiliation and wished
she'd never seen Cass. Her imagination now would give her no
peace. Yet Cass had seemed indifferent to Nick, too, although
a mutual friend had disclosed that Cass had a reputation as a
flirt and was known to have had several affairs within the naval
circles the Wivenhoes inhabited. Their assumed indifference at the
party told its own story. In her heart, Sarah knew. Some sixth sense
warned her that Nick and Cass were lovers and her happiness and
peace were shattered.

Why do I go on loving him? she asked herself as she passed
through Ivybridge and headed for Dartmouth.

Some dark unwelcome voice told her that it was because it
was the only area within their lives together in which Nick
remained in control and that some requirement within her for
a dominant assertive male responded to his callous behaviour.
Her wealth removed the need for him to support them and
she was far too bossy to allow him a say in the running of
the house or her own social life. Only in this one way did
Nick continue to disregard her power and gratify his own needs
and some tiny part of her was cowed by it and worse – and
she shrank from this realisation – was excited by it. It was
a dark, rather sick excitement but it was strong enough for
her to be unable to resist him even when she knew he was
deceiving her.

Yet she'd been so happy during this last year. As Sarah skirted
Totnes and plunged into the lanes around Ashprington she felt
another uprush of misery. She was quite certain that, if only Nick
could resist these affairs, they could be very content together. She
pulled into the mill's yard and switched off the engine. Dressed in
a scruffy and ancient Guernsey and an even shabbier tweed skirt,
Hattie was grooming the Admiral who lay stretched out obligingly
on his side so that she could comb out the tangles underneath his
broad frame.

'It's a shame he loves the water so much,' puffed Hattie as Sarah approached. 'It's hell getting the knots out!'

She glanced at Sarah and immediately stood upright, the Admiral's grooming forgotten.

'Hello.' Sarah kissed her old friend and offered a bunch of garden flowers. 'How are you?'

'How are you? That's more to the point. You look fagged out.' Her concern gave way to understanding. 'Oh, Sarah. It's not Nick? Is he . . . ?'

'I think so.' They went towards the house together.

The Admiral stretched languidly and rolled upright. The biscuit he always had after a grooming was not forthcoming and he suspected that he'd been neglected. He snapped idly and unsuccessfully at a passing fly. With Bert Crabtree no longer working at the mill, his supply of treats had dried up considerably. The Admiral yawned and brooded on life. The human race was divided into two sorts, suckers and non-suckers. Joss was certainly one of the unsympathetic latter group. Miggy, now . . . The Admiral got up and cocked his ears in case he'd been remembered, straining to hear the familiar sound of the biscuit tin being opened and feet hurrying out to him. Silence. Then voices, sniffling noises, chair legs being scraped back, more voices . . . One of those days! The Admiral sighed and set off purposefully in the direction of Fisherman's Cottage.

'Sorry.' Sarah mopped at her red eyes. 'I didn't mean to come and drain down all over you.'

'Pooey,' said Hattie and topped up Sarah's glass. 'That's what I'm here for. I'm just so sorry . . .'

'Let's forget it for the moment.' Sarah sat up straighter and some of her briskness returned. 'I was a fool to be lulled into a false sense of security. Actually, I've got a message for you from Nick about your cottage.'

Hattie raised her eyebrows and sat down opposite. 'Really?'

'He's got a tenant for you if you want him. It's a young chap called James Barrington. He's just finished his law qualification and he's starting his articles at a practice in Dartmouth. He did his holiday placement at Murchison, Marriott and Nick helped to place him with the firm in Dartmouth. He's looking for a cottage to rent for the two years. He told Nick he'd rather be out where he can do some sailing and be a bit independent.'

'He sounds positively heaven-sent.' Hattie stared at her, Sarah's problems momentarily forgotten. 'Have you met him?'

'I have actually. He was at John Marriott's sixtieth birthday party last summer. He's an extremely nice boy. Twenty-two-ish. Easy and unaffected. I think he'd fit in here very well.'

'Well, that's fantastic.' Hattie raised her glass. 'I'll drink to it. So far nobody suitable has turned up. A couple with three screaming kids, one of whom kicked the Admiral, and a middle-aged man whose wife's left him and who's out of work and made me feel distinctly uneasy. And a young naval couple who've been offered married quarters in the college and have decided to take them after all. It's much harder than I thought.'

'Well, when you live just across the yard it's more important, isn't it?' Sarah passed a piece of paper across the table. 'This is his telephone number. Nick didn't give him yours in case you didn't want to follow it up.'

Hattie took the paper and hesitated. 'Do you mind if I do it straight away? I'd hate to miss such a desirable tenant!'

Sarah laughed. 'Carry on,' she said. 'Oh, and Nick said to say that his parents are well off so you don't have to fear the rent falling into arrears.'

From the deck of *Westering*, Joss watched the Admiral's brisk progress along the hard, saw him approach Miggy, who was gardening, and smiled as they went indoors together. Briefly, he envied Toby. The cottage was lovely and Miggy was sweet; even Daisy and Georgia were tolerable as far as offspring went. And now there was the new child on its way. Sitting in the cockpit with his cup of coffee, Joss tried to picture himself in Toby's role. He shook his head. It seemed that he wasn't cut out for it. He enjoyed sex but had no desire to settle down and increase the population of an already over-burdened world. He also realised that, until he was cured of his nightmares, he had no intention of risking himself in a relationship. What self-respecting woman would be prepared to stay with a man who woke up yelling his head off and drenched in sweat? There was no doubt that he was beginning to see an end to this crippling weakness but it would be some time yet before he took any chances. He'd been rather taken with a girlfriend of Miggy's who'd been for a brief visit to the creek but he'd kept his feelings well concealed. Once he wouldn't have hesitated to follow it up but Hester had returned to London and Joss had deliberately put her out of his mind. He stared up at *Westering*'s tall masts and imagined the sails bellying out as she ran before the wind. That was much more like it!

Joss finished his coffee, saw Daisy wander out on to the lawn and slipped hastily below. He had no time to take her sailing or to let her sit on *Westering* chattering to him. All last summer, whilst *Westering* was being slipped and when there was very little to do in the boatyard, Joss had been teaching Daisy to sail. With characteristic generosity, Toby insisted that Joss should be paid for these lessons and deducted them from the bill which was mounting on *Westering*. Joss was touched and put his whole heart into teaching Daisy as much as he could. She was very able and adored it but now the sailing boat had been sold and Daisy was at a loose end. She still rowed herself about in the dinghy but the sailing had whetted her appetite and, at intervals, Joss stepped the mast in his own dinghy and took her down the creek and out into the Dart.

He was surprised that Toby hadn't bought the boat for her but Miggy told him that, since in the main she'd be sailing alone, they thought she was still a little too young to have her own sailing boat and Joss agreed wholeheartedly. The idea of Daisy sailing off, with no one to curb her imagination or quell her wild ideas, was quite alarming. Nevertheless Joss was too much of a sailor himself not to feel in sympathy with her. He put his mug in the sink and decided to take her out for an evening sail if he got through his tasks.

Daisy sat on the bench and stared down the creek. The Admiral, having had his biscuit, came to lean against her legs and she ruffled his soft black coat.

'I wish I had my own boat,' she told him and he pricked his ears as he listened to her voice. 'I've got a whole week of half term and no sailing.'

She looked longingly towards *Westering* but knew better than to disturb Joss while he was working. Miggy came out and watched the small figure sympathetically. It was no use offering Daisy a trip into Dartmouth or Totnes. Shops bored her rigid and it was still too cold for swimming. She wandered down the lawn and sat beside her on the bench.

'How about a trip to Torcross?' she suggested. 'We could go for a walk along the beach and then have tea at the Sea Breezes. Or would you like to go to Dartmouth or Totnes? You choose.'

'Torcross,' said Daisy at once. 'Can Jellicoe come?'

'I'll ask Hattie,' said Miggy, getting up. 'I'll give her a call and if she says yes, he can come.'

She went into the house and Daisy continued to sit on the bench staring out over the creek watching a cormorant perched on a buoy in the channel, his black wings outstretched to dry in the cold breeze. She was deeply happy. The news of the coming baby had added to her sense of security. It put the final seal on her instinctive feeling that she had come home and was now where she belonged. The happiness of Miggy and Toby washed into her own life and held her safe and the baby was exactly right to make the whole thing complete.

Daisy stroked the Admiral's ears and rubbed her face in his fur and he wagged his tail and aimed a lick at her cheek. Her only unfulfilled ambition at present was to have her own sailing boat and even that lack couldn't really destroy her satisfaction. A cloud hovered over the sun and Daisy's eye fell on the *Abigail*, lying dark and gloomy at her mooring. She shivered suddenly, feeling a moment's unease, and was glad to hear Miggy calling to her. Jumping from the bench she ran quickly to meet her.

Chapter Fourteen

James Barrington drove his second-hand Citroën Dyane jauntily through the narrow Devon lanes. James, born and raised in Dorset, was no stranger to high hedges, restricted visibility and inadequate passing places. Nevertheless, the recently purchased car was very precious to him and, despite the jauntiness, he kept a wary eye on possible damage to her paintwork. His mother had advised an introductory visit to Miss Wetherall at the mill before he committed himself to renting her cottage but refused his offer to come along for the ride and see for herself. She realised that James felt it incumbent upon himself to allay her motherly anxieties and, though she appreciated his offer, she suspected that he would prefer to take this step alone.

She was right. James was secretly relieved that she hadn't taken him up on his offer, enjoying this feeling of being out in the adult world at last; the owner of a car and a Mirror dinghy, in possession of a job and soon to be a householder. James, who had also been raised in the Anglican faith, his father being a country parson, sang a tuneful snatch of the Te Deum and peered at a signpost that was all but obliterated by cow parsley and convolvulus: 'Abbot's Mill Creek 2 Miles.' He swung the wheel and headed down the narrow lane. The tall grasses and luxuriant summer growth leaned out to brush the car on each side and, as he slowed, he was aware of the scent of honeysuckle.

He rounded a bend, caught his breath and braked abruptly. Far below, the creek lay mysterious and still, its steep wooded banks clothed in a patchwork of green, the fields above – golden with standing corn or dotted with grazing sheep – swelling gently against the misty horizon. A soft haze, diffused with glowing sunlight, smudged the distant view but he could see a small sailing boat tacking its way up the river making the most of the gentle breeze and, his heart beating with a sudden excitement, James let in the clutch and followed the winding lane down to the head of the creek.

Hattie, who'd been on the watch for him, came out to greet him, liking the look of him as he stepped from the car, his face bright with enthusiasm. He was not over-tall but well-built and his throat and arms were brown against the cream open-necked cotton shirt with its rolled-up sleeves. His dark blond hair, cut short at back and sides but longer on top, flopped rather engagingly over his forehead and he thrust his fingers through it before shaking hands with her.

'Are you by any chance Miss Wetherall?' he asked and, when she nodded, he introduced himself and looked around with delight. 'This is a terrific place. Are those the cottages?'

Hattie smiled; his enthusiasm was rather like Daisy's. 'They are. Do you want to view first or have some coffee first?'

'Oh, view first,' said James at once. He caught himself up, wondering if such excitement was in keeping with his new responsibilities. 'That is . . . it's up to you, of course. Whichever is most convenient.' But his eye wandered wistfully to the pair of whitewashed cottages tucked beneath the golden thatch.

'View first, then,' said Hattie briskly. 'We can talk terms while we have our coffee.' She led the way, still talking. 'They're both identical. One big living room and one sizeable kitchen downstairs. Two bedrooms and bathroom up. Plenty big enough for a bachelor . . .'

James cast an appreciative glance round at the mill with its quay and followed her inside.

'Looks like Hattie's new tenant's arrived,' said Joss. 'Ready about.'

Daisy ducked beneath the boom and peered across to the hard. Hattie's round short figure was accompanied by a leaner, taller one and Daisy could see her gesticulating as she showed her companion the surroundings.

'Concentrate.' Joss's voice recalled her attention and she paid out the sheet so that the jib filled gently and they swept gracefully across the creek.

Hattie raised her hand to them and they waved back, too far away to shout. The young man waved too and Daisy felt an instant liking for him, appreciating his friendliness.

'Jellicoe's the test,' she murmured, bracing a little as a stronger breeze came pattering across the water. 'That's what Hattie says.'

Joss kept his eyes on the cat's-paws dimpling the surface. 'Of course it's quite impossible for anyone who can't cope with that great brute to be a decent honest upright person!' he said sarcastically. 'Here it comes! Hold her steady.'

'I wonder if Jellicoe will like him,' wondered Daisy anxiously, having taken an unexplained liking to Hattie's putative tenant.

'Or even,' Joss's tone was more heavily sarcastic, 'whether he will like Jellicoe! Not nearly so important, of course! Ready about.'

'Coffee?' Hattie pushed the kettle on to the Esse's hotplate.

'Please.' James couldn't prevent a happy smile from spreading itself over his face. 'This is just fantastic. I can hardly believe my luck. I just love the cottage. And a place to keep my boat.' His sigh was one of unalloyed bliss and Hattie smiled to herself. 'How far are we from Dartmouth would you say?'

'Oh.' Hattie screwed up her nose. 'Difficult to say, milewise. The lanes are so winding. Ten minutes, timewise. Blast! I forgot to get the milk out.'

James looked at her questioningly and she answered his look without thinking. 'Admiral Jellicoe's asleep in the larder and he's the very devil to wake up.'

James's face took on a careful expression; polite interest accompanied by an attempt at sympathy with which to cover his concern. 'Ah,' he said non-committally.

Hattie burst out laughing. 'Ah well,' she said, 'I'd've had to wake him. He's my final test. You've passed all the others!'

James looked puzzled as Hattie leaned heavily against the larder door, which barely budged. 'Out you come, Jellicoe,' she said. 'Wake up and come and meet James Barrington.'

She watched his face as the Admiral, yawning and stretching, slowly emerged from the cool of the larder. He sat for a moment, exhausted by such a major effort and sighed at the injustices of life. James stared at him in delighted incredulity.

'Wow!' he breathed. 'Oh, I don't believe it!' He crossed the kitchen and crouched before the huge dog, their heads at equal level. 'Hello, old chap,' he said softly and stroked the heavy head. 'Oh boy! You're a real beauty, aren't you?'

The Admiral rolled an eye at Hattie, checking that she was taking note of this well-deserved adulation, yawned again and thumped his tail languidly.

James burst out laughing. 'He's magnificent,' he said. 'What did you call him? Admiral Jellicoe? What breed is he?'

115

'He's a Newfoundland.' Hattie seized her opportunity to fetch the milk. 'He's three.'

James shook his head in disbelief at the size of him and rocked on his heels when the Admiral laid a heavy paw across his knee.

'Hi, there,' he said, and shook the great paw gently. 'Hi there, Jelly baby.'

With James settled at Number One Mill Cottages, Hattie concentrated on her search for a tenant for the second cottage. She now knew how many people wanted to claim you for a friend once you lived in a place as beautiful as the South Hams and she could have filled the cottage over and over again with holiday-makers. Unfortunately, most of these so-called friends would have been quite hurt if she'd asked for rent whilst they stayed and she was obliged to harden her heart against them, inviting only her closest friends who stayed with her in the mill. She'd begun to despair of finding someone as totally suitable as James when Miggy strolled down to the mill one morning, a few weeks after James had moved in, to ask if Hattie would consider letting the second cottage to an old chum Hester Strange.

'I think she'd fit in terribly well,' said Miggy. 'You remember her? She came down for a long weekend in the autumn. Fair and very pretty. And Ned's a sweetie. She asked me to ask if you'd consider her. I hope you will. She's had a bit of a tough time, to be honest.'

Hester had been made pregnant by her New Zealander boyfriend, Phil Strange, at the end of her second term at art school. He was in England to escape the domination of a very strong-willed mother and was working as a representative for a company who sold agro-chemicals when he and Hester married. His family were farmers and when his father died there was tremendous pressure on Phil to return home. By this time he'd already been regularly unfaithful to Hester and he'd finally returned to New Zealand with their elder son, Jeremy, then five years old. Phil had continued to support Hester, and the baby that was born after his departure, but Hester had now divorced him and was selling the house they'd bought together. Although she'd have some money from her share of the sale of the property tucked away, her intention was to find a job and try to start a new life for herself and her second son.

Hattie, touched by this rather bleak little potted history, remembered Hester very well. She'd seemed friendly, ready to join in, adaptable, and Hattie could think of no reason why she should refuse her request. It would answer her own problem wonderfully well and she began to see that her tenants might always arrive through friends. She told Miggy that she'd be very happy to have Hester at Number Two Mill Cottages and, shortly afterwards, she received a letter from her. Hester was simply waiting for the house to sell and, anxious that Hattie might let the cottage to someone else meanwhile, assured her that there was a lot of interest in the property but that she couldn't just walk out. Would Hattie like a deposit, she asked, as a gesture of her sincerity?

Hattie wrote back at once saying that the cottage would be waiting for her but perhaps she might like to come for a weekend to look over it and agree the rent. No deposit would be required, as she intended to let it for a few weeks during the summer to several people who would gladly pay for a summer holiday in such an idyllic spot but, as soon as she received an offer for the house, she must let Hattie know. Hester agreed at once and arranged to come down to stay with Miggy later in the summer. Hattie heaved a great sigh of relief at the thought of two long-term tenants, put her problems behind her and turned her attention to Sarah.

Daisy fell properly in love with James at their second meeting. He moved into his cottage three days after the summer holidays started and Daisy, on her way to the mill in search of the Admiral, stopped short when she saw him putting his dinghy on one of the mill's moorings. James, in his old jeans and a sweatshirt, immediately guessed her identity. He straightened up and smiled at her.

'Hi. Am I right in thinking that you're Daisy? I'm James Barrington.'

She came on slowly, nodded and blushed suddenly. 'Hello,' she said a little breathlessly, staring at him entranced and feeling inexplicably and unusually shy. 'Is that your boat?'

'It is.' He looked proud and Daisy felt a surge of identification with his pride.

'She's really nice,' she said sincerely – and enviously. 'I'd love a Mirror dinghy but Miggy says I'm too young.'

James was silent, unwilling to be drawn into family politics, and continued to fiddle with mooring ropes. She looked so wistful, however, that he smiled at her again. 'If your parents agree, I'll take you for a sail later,' he suggested. 'Miggy's your mum, isn't she? Do you want to ask her? Or,' caution raised its head, 'perhaps I should introduce myself?'

'Come and meet her,' said Daisy instantly. 'She's finding

117

the heat a bit much so she's sitting in the summerhouse. Do come!'

'OK.' James took one last look at his boat and set off with Daisy along the hard. 'This is a terrific place, isn't it? I wish I'd lived in a place like this when I was a kid.'

'Terrific!' agreed Daisy fervently skipping to keep up with his energetic strides. 'I love it.'

He followed her through the gap in the hedge on to the lawn and approached the summerhouse. Hattie had briefed him thoroughly on the identity and history of the small creekside community, nevertheless James stopped abruptly as he came face to face with Miggy. She'd been reading but, hearing their voices, had cast the book aside and was waiting expectantly. Now in her seventh month, she'd taken to wearing loose, ankle-length dresses in soft spriggy cottons. Her face glowed with health and contentment and her bright hair was longer and flaked across her brow and curled round her creamy throat. She half sat, half lay on a low reclining chair in the shadowy summerhouse, her green eyes smiling consideringly up at him and he stared back at her speechlessly.

'This is James,' Daisy was telling her. 'He's got a Mirror dinghy and he says he'll take me sailing if you'll say it's OK.'

'Hello, James.' She pulled herself upright and held out her hand. 'I'm Miggy Dakers.'

'Yes.' His throat was oddly dry. 'How d'you do?'

'We've all been longing to meet you, of course. Sit down for a moment. Or are you busy settling in?'

'No, not really.' He sat down in an old Lloyd Loom basketwork chair, unable to take his eyes from her. 'I haven't got too much in the way of belongings.'

'But you have a boat?'

James laughed and suddenly everything was a little easier. 'I have a boat,' he agreed. 'And I'd be very willing to take Daisy out if you're happy about it. I've done masses of sailing at school. I was at Allhallows on the Devon coast so I've had lots of experience.'

'Please, Miggy,' begged Daisy. 'We won't go out of the creek.'

'Well, perhaps not to begin with, anyway.' Miggy smiled at James. 'Have you sailed on the Dart before?'

James shook his head. 'Joss is going to take me out on the river, show me around and so on. Meanwhile, Daisy and I will stick to the creek.'

'You must come and meet Toby,' Miggy told him. 'Come and have some supper this evening.'

'Oh yes!' cried Daisy. 'We'll have a sail and be back in time for supper. The tide will be just right. Please?'

'Well.' James looked pleasantly overwhelmed. 'Thanks. I'd love to. I start work on Monday so I want to get some sailing in . . .'

'That's settled then.' Miggy prepared to rise and James hastened to help her to her feet. Her hand was cool in his. 'Shall we have a cup of tea and then the tide should be just about right?'

They went up the lawn together, Daisy hurrying ahead and James tried to keep from staring at Miggy. She moved with an indolent grace that enchanted him and he thought that he'd never seen such a lovely and delightful woman ever before. Miggy, unaware of the feelings she'd aroused, was wondering about supper and whether her invitation had been somewhat rash. Never mind! She could always wander along to the mill if stocks were a bit low. Hattie always kept the larder full enough to feed the Navy should it come steaming up the creek.

'Isn't Hattie wonderful?' she asked, continuing to follow her own train of thought.

'Fantastic,' agreed James. 'And what about Admiral Jellicoe? I couldn't believe my eyes when I saw him!'

They made the tea, chatting companionably whilst Daisy skittered to and fro, and then carried it back to the summerhouse to drink in the shade. Daisy, however, kept her eyes firmly on the tide and rose inexorably when she judged the moment right.

'Time for our sail,' she told James and he rose reluctantly, glad in the knowledge that he would be back again before too long.

Chapter Fifteen

As it happened, none of the residents of Abbot's Mill Creek saw the couple arrive at the *Abigail* one hot, still afternoon towards the end of August. The relentless sun dazzled on the turgid water and no breath stirred amongst the dark shadows of the trees. Apart from a lone seagull, swooping low over *Westering* with a harsh evocative call, and the heron, alert and motionless in the shallows, the creek was deserted. Miggy was taking an afternoon rest on her bed and Toby was at the boatyard. Joss was shopping in Dartmouth, Daisy was up in the woods with the Admiral, whilst Hattie was sitting in the orchard, frankly and naturally asleep – head tipped back, newspaper scattered across her ample chest – snoring contentedly. So it was that the couple motored round from Dartmouth in a small open launch and went aboard the *Abigail* without being noticed, and it was two hours later, when the launch tied up at the little quay and the couple came ashore, that Hattie realised that she had new neighbours.

She'd woken with a dry throat and a raging headache, the sun beating down on her unprotected face, no longer in the shade she'd sought earlier. Gathering up her belongings, she went indoors for a much-needed cup of tea and she was enjoying a second cup – and beginning to feel a little less grumpy – when she heard the launch's engine and voices calling to each other. They were already ashore by the time she got outside, standing on the quay and looking about them. They beamed at her as she appeared and came to introduce themselves whilst enthusing about the mill, the creek and the River Dart generally.

Hattie felt her headache returning and her grumpiness with it. They were such a hearty, determined pair that they threatened to overwhelm her but she realised that she was being silly and tried to pull herself together a little. It was at this point she grasped the fact that they were not just the type of summer visitor who came sailing – or motoring – up the creek and decided to drop the hook and stay an hour or so. She'd already developed a certain antipathy to some of these holiday-makers who strolled about on her quay – despite the notices which declared it to be private – and whose children played noisy games on the hard but she tried to remain good-tempered and polite. Now, however, as she took in the content of their duet, her jaw dropped and she stared at this jolly, loud-voiced couple with something like horror. She spoke without thinking.

'*Bought* the *Abigail*? Did you say you've *bought* her? Oh dear!'

Janice Parker smiled at her indulgently. 'Now we know all about it,' she said soothingly. 'Several of the locals have told us about its past.' She laughed and shook her head. 'Well, we said, didn't we, Brian, what old boat hasn't got a pretty chequered history? Superstitious nonsense but what can you expect from people like that?' She paused and looked with some concern at Hattie. 'Are you a local?'

Hattie felt exasperation returning. Unless you spoke like some comic yokel on the television, no tourist ever believed you might be a local.

'I was born near Exeter,' she answered crisply.

Janice and Brian Parker exchanged glances.

'Of course, we have to accept that most legends have a grain of truth in them . . .' began Brian didactically.

'Would you like a cup of tea?' Hattie wasn't interested in a lecture on folklore. 'I've just made some. Come on in.'

'Oh. That's kind. We must take our boots off. Brian! Your boots!'

'Oh, don't worry, for goodness' sake.' Hattie glanced at the spotless yellow sailing wellies and wondered what Joss's reaction would be. 'But if you'd like to take off your Mae Wests, you'll probably be more comfortable.'

'We'll be fine,' said Janice, clinging to her life jacket and staring round the kitchen. 'What a lovely home you have, Hattie.'

Hattie sucked in her cheeks to prevent some ill-advised remark from slipping between her teeth. She felt an absurd and unreasonable irritation at being called 'Hattie' so familiarly by this barely known woman and sought to calm herself. She poured two mugs of tea and put them on the table with the sugar bowl.

'Help yourselves,' she began and jumped violently as Janice, her eyes staring at a point beyond Hattie's shoulder, screamed loudly.

'Oh my God! Oh, Brian!'

Hattie turned quickly to see the Admiral in the doorway, accompanied by Daisy.

'Oooh!' Janice gave another scream and the Admiral cocked his ears, puzzled. 'Whatever is it?'

'It's a dog,' said Hattie crossly. 'My dog, in fact. He won't hurt you.'

'Don't let him near me,' beseeched Janice. 'I can't abide dogs. Oooh!'

She scrambled from her chair and backed further round the table as the Admiral, his tail waving cautiously, came forward to examine this strange phenomenon more closely.

'Keep still, Janice!' admonished Brian. 'He won't bite you if you keep still!'

'He won't bite you anyway!' said Daisy, affronted by this slur on the Admiral's manners. 'Not while you're Hattie's guests.'

Her disgusted gaze fell on the yellow wellies and their life jackets and she looked at Hattie, her eyebrows lifted. Hattie gave her a tiny wink.

'Janice and Brian Parker,' she said, introducing them. 'This is Daisy who lives along the creek. And this is Admiral Jellicoe.'

'He looks like a bear,' said Janice fearfully.

'They've bought the *Abigail*,' Hattie told Daisy, who opened her eyes in amazement and gave the Parkers another more penetrating stare. 'Are you moving on board straight away?'

'That's right.' Brian relaxed visibly as the Admiral, bored by such foolish behaviour, barged into the larder. The door slammed behind him as he flopped down behind it. 'It needs a fair bit doing to it but we're looking forward to the challenge. Aren't we, Janice?'

'Her,' muttered Daisy. 'Boats are hers not its.'

'Yes, indeed.' Janice too had regained a certain amount of composure although she couldn't resist a question. 'Does he roam free round here?' She jerked her head towards the larder door. 'The dog, I mean.'

'Oh, yes,' said Hattie quickly, delighted to find some method of deterring these new neighbours from just dropping in. She felt in her bones that Janice was a dropper-in. 'He's always out and about. He's an excellent guard dog.'

'Where have you come from?' asked Daisy, as the Parkers digested this unwelcome information. She looked again at their yellow footwear and the life jackets. 'Did you come over from *Abigail* dressed like that?'

'That's right, dear.' Janice smiled condescendingly. 'You can't be too safe on the water, can you, Brian? I expect you know that, dear, living by a river. You have to respect the water.'

'Have you owned a boat before?' Hattie spoke quickly before Daisy could reply.

'Well, no.' Brian shook his head 'Only narrow boats on holiday so far. But the *Abigail*'s only a glorified houseboat really, isn't it?'

'Brian's been overworking,' Janice explained quickly. 'So we decided to take a bit of time off. We've rented out our little home in the Midlands and we're going to be water gypsies.'

The Parkers exchanged a glance whilst Hattie and Daisy gazed at them in awe.

'What . . . what fun,' said Hattie faintly. 'Isn't she in rather a bad way?'

'Well, that was reflected in the price,' admitted Brian judiciously, 'although we insisted that it was cleaned up inside.'

'Below,' corrected Daisy, under her breath.

'Brian'll have it looking lovely in a trice.' Janice smiled encouragingly at him. 'Ever so good with his hands, he is, aren't you, dear?'

Hattie swallowed back a nervous desire to burst into hysterical shrieks and had a coughing fit instead.

'Sorry,' she gasped as she choked. 'So sorry! Oh hell and damnation!'

The Parkers exchanged another glance and simultaneously rose to their feet.

'We must be on our way,' said Janice, looking nervously at the larder door lest the Admiral should emerge. 'Thanks for the tea. You must come over when we've settled in a bit.'

They hurried out and Daisy and Hattie followed them to the launch and watched them down the creek.

'Dear God!' said Hattie with great feeling.

'Wait till Joss sees them, that's all,' declared Daisy with a certain satisfaction. 'He'll have a fit. Honestly! Poor old Jellicoe!'

'He'll see 'em off.' Hattie grinned at her. 'Come and have some tea. I need to regain my strength after that visitation.'

'Well . . .' Daisy hesitated and looked at the watch Toby had given her for her birthday. She held her wrist to her ear. 'What d'you make it?' she asked anxiously.

Hattie consulted the large, man's wristwatch which she always wore. 'Quarter past five,' she announced. 'Got to go home?'

'No . . .' Still she hesitated. 'James is going to take me sailing when he gets back,' she said at last. 'The tide will be just right. I'll wait for him here.'

Hattie shrugged. 'Suit yourself but he's never home much before six. Plenty of time for some orange juice and a piece of cake. We'll hear the car.'

'OK.' Daisy gave in.

She was back on the hard promptly by quarter to six and was still sitting on the slip at twenty past when the Citroën jolted down the lane. A few minutes later James appeared, hastily dragging on an old sweatshirt.

'Oh, James!' Her voice was plaintive. 'You're late. We'll only just catch the tide.'

'Can't help it.' He stooped to tie the lace of his plimsoll. 'They've kept me at it all day long.'

'Messrs Whinge, Whinge, Bellyache and Moan.' She repeated the comic name he'd given the legal practice and he grinned at her.

'Shoulder to the wheel, nose to the grindstone. Never mind, I'm here now! Come on. Let's get going!'

Sarah stood at her bedroom window watching the sunset. Although the sun had long since vanished, a crimson sky, streaked with gold, still flamed in the west. In the darkening sky to the east a huge apricot moon rose with a slow stateliness above the horizon and long shadows stretched stealthily across the silvery grass. Sarah felt her misery welling up inside her. It swelled in her breast and she felt the hot tears forcing themselves into her eyes. All through the summer Nick had pursued his affair with Cass Wivenhoe despite Sarah's desperate prayers that, with four children home for the summer holidays, Cass would find it impossible to get away. In the light of such difficulties Sarah had hoped that their passion might fade.

Instead, it appeared that these pressures were adding fuel to the flames. Nick was moody and quiet, preoccupied and distant, and Sarah recognised the signs of a serious attachment. No quick passing fling, this. She leaned forward a little so that her head rested against the cool glass. Now that Nick had resumed his old ways, she almost wished she'd never known that long happy spell during which she'd convinced herself that he'd changed, grown up at last. Somehow it was crueller, more difficult to come to terms with, than she'd ever known and she began to wonder how she would survive it. To her own amazement she was managing to preserve a calm exterior which belied the conflicting emotions which raged in her breast.

Nick seemed to notice nothing at all. He was courteous, kindly – and utterly remote. He told her that he had several difficult cases that required a great deal of thought and concentration, shutting himself in his study, early and late. He'd taken to sleeping in his dressing room, so as not to disturb her when he finally retired to bed, and she despised herself for the longing she felt for him and the loneliness that lacerated her as she lay alone in the cool linen sheets.

Sarah felt the tears trickling down her cheeks but was too tired, too miserable to brush them away.

I love him, she thought. I love him so much. And the tears ran faster and she wept unrestrainedly. She was frightened. Having seen Cass's beauty, imagining her entwined with Nick, she wondered how she could ever hope to win him back. There had been something different about this affair and she felt cold with fear when she contemplated a future without him. After all, he really didn't need her money. Supposing . . . ?

Sarah wiped blindly at her tears and tried to control her morbid thoughts. It was extraordinarily unlikely that Cass would abandon four children and her husband yet there was something added this time, something that had been missing during Nick's other affairs. At some moments she would swear that he was actually suffering, missing Cass, longing to be with her. She remembered her certainty that Nick had met Cass some months before the affair started and now believed that, even then, Nick had feared to become involved; had been so frightened by the strength of his feelings that he'd deliberately refused to pursue Cass. If it were true it was apparent that those feelings had become too strong for him.

Sarah turned away from the window and stared at herself in the looking-glass which hung on the wall above the mahogany chest of drawers. Involuntarily, she grimaced at herself; at the drawn lined face, the cropped grey hair, the sagging jawline. For a brief moment she saw Cass's lovely face etched beside her own reflection and she burst into sobs, sinking on to the foot of the bed and covering her face with her hands.

The telephone bell made her start and, giving herself a moment to calm down, she leaned across the bed and lifted the receiver.

'Hello, my love. Good day?'

She composed herself quickly 'Nick. Yes. A very good day, thank you. An excellent meeting, lots of support.'

'That's wonderful. Not so wonderful this end, I fear. A few

things have cropped up with this nightmare of a case. John and I are still at the office and we're going to have a session together. No idea what time I'll be home.'

'I must admit I was beginning to worry about you. Shall you have eaten?'

There was a fractional pause. 'Yes. Oh, yes. We'll go to the pub and pick up something there. Don't worry about that.'

'Fine. See you later then.'

'Don't wait up. 'Night, my love.'

Sarah replaced the receiver carefully and sat quite still, her hands in her lap. The fiery glow in the western sky had quite disappeared now and soft moonlight began to flood into the room. Still Sarah sat on, fighting a losing battle. Presently she stood up stiffly and made her way downstairs. She went into the tiny room she used as a study and took an address book from her bureau. She opened it at the letter M and, after another moment of internal struggle, dialled a number. It rang for some time but, before she could begin to hope too much, she heard a click and a testy voice spoke in her ear.

'Marriott here.'

Sarah gently replaced the receiver and stood looking at it for some moments. Knowing that she was breaking all the rules she'd so carefully set herself, she found the directory and looked up the Ws. She dialled another number and waited. Presently a young voice announced the number.

'Hello.' She spoke rapidly. 'Could I speak to Mrs Wivenhoe, please?'

'She's not here. At least . . . Hang on a sec.' The receiver was obviously being clutched to a chest and she heard the voice shouting. 'Charlotte! Char! Has Ma gone yet? Right. Hello?' The voice was back in her ear. 'Sorry. She went out about half an hour ago. A friend phoned unexpectedly. Can I take a message?'

'No, no. I'll try in the morning. Thank you.'

So that was that. Frustrated, miserable, cross with herself for breaking her unwritten rules, she went into the kitchen and poured herself a very stiff gin and tonic. She carried it to the door and stood staring out into the moonlit evening. She wondered where they were and tried not to imagine them together; sipping her drink as calmly as she could, wondering how Nick would react if she were to confront him. She knew she never would, that she would do anything to keep him. She fastened her mind on the prospect of their approaching holiday in Shropshire. At least she had this, something to look forward to, maybe an opportunity to win him back. She remembered the last two magical holidays at their tiny retreat and a warmth stole round her heart and lifted her spirits a fraction. She simply mustn't give in. Maybe this would be his very last fling; the final passion of an Indian summer.

Chapter Sixteen

October was a gentle month with quiet warm days, hazy with golden sunshine, and chill nights during which the mist wreathed and smoked along the waters of the creek and lay knee-deep in the valley behind the mill.

'We feel certain that the baby'll be another girl,' said Miggy as she sat in Hattie's kitchen one afternoon watching her make a stew. 'Toby insists we stick to flower names but I wonder if the time's come to break the mould. My mind's a blank.'

'Oh, you mustn't do that,' said James, who had a day off to work on a case at home but had gravitated to the mill's kitchen when he saw Miggy pass the window. 'It's such a fun idea. Names are so important. Look at old Jellicoe. Can you possibly imagine him called anything else? What do you say, Jelly baby?'

'Don't call him that!' said Hattie out of habit, chopping meat, watched by an unusually vigilant Admiral. 'What would *you* call her, then? Assuming it's a her.'

'Well.' James hesitated and looked a little shyly at Miggy. 'If she had hair the same colour as you or Daisy I think you should call her Marigold.'

'Heavens!' Miggy began to laugh, saw that he looked rather hurt and decided to take him seriously. 'You don't think it might be gilding the lily?'

'No,' he answered firmly. 'It's a wonderful colour!'

Miggy smiled at him, becoming aware of his private passion for her. 'We'll give it consideration,' she told him. 'Hattie's going to be godmother.'

'Poor little worm,' sighed Hattie, dealing with some carrots at high speed. She was godmother to a dozen of her friends' children, well aware that in some oblique way their mothers felt they were making up to her for her childless state. 'I never go to church and haven't got a clue what godmothers should do.'

'Are you an atheist?' James pretended to look shocked.

'Certainly not!' she said indignantly. 'I just don't believe in putting God into little boxes and attaching dogma to Him, that's all. He's too big for all that.'

'You'll make a wonderful godmother,' said Miggy, and sighed a little. 'I must admit I shall be glad to get on with it now. Janice came over yesterday afternoon and I felt exhausted when she'd gone.'

'You don't have to be on the point of giving birth to find Janice Parker exhausting,' rejoined Hattie tartly, banging a lid on the casserole and putting it in the bottom oven. 'Thank God for Jellicoe! That's what I say. She never comes near the mill.'

'Joss calls them the Nosy Parkers,' said James. 'He says they're always dropping in on him to have a look at *Westering* and take notes. Drives him mad.'

'They *are* inquisitive,' agreed Miggy slowly, 'but, to be honest, I can't help feeling sorry for them.'

'You feel sorry for everybody,' said Hattie accusingly, but she smiled at her. 'I feel sorry for them, too. Must be ghastly to be them!'

'Brian's got a problem,' said Miggy, rather as though she were breaking a confidence.

Hattie opened her mouth to observe that, having met Janice, she knew this already, saw Miggy's expression and closed it again.

'How d'you mean?' James looked at the shadows under Miggy's eyes and worried that she was too frail for her huge burden. 'What sort of problem?'

'He drinks,' said Miggy rapidly. 'Don't say anything. He has spasmodic drinking benders and he botched some exam papers and got the push from his Poly. That's why they've come away. To let things die down for a bit.'

'Oh, honestly,' said Hattie crossly. 'Why did you have to tell me? You've spoiled it all now. I've really enjoyed having a good bitch about the Nosy Parkers and now I'll have to feel guilty! Hell and damnation!'

Miggy and James burst out laughing but Miggy sobered fairly quickly.

'It's awful, really,' she said. 'She was rather pathetic when she told me. Pretended that it was because he'd been under tremendous strain. She says he's so brilliant they work him too hard.'

'Oh, pooey!' said Hattie impatiently. 'If he's that brilliant he'd be an Oxford don or something.'

'I suppose she's bound to defend him, though, isn't she?' asked Miggy anxiously. 'I know I would if it were Toby.'

Hattie looked at her and her expression softened. She saw that James was gazing at her, too, with undisguised love and she thanked God that she'd never been exposed to the conflicting emotions of infatuation.

'I expect you're right,' she sighed, and then brightened a little. 'Shall we have a drink? I think I need one!'

'But is the sun over the yardarm?' James winked at Miggy and Hattie aimed a good-natured cuff at his head. 'Ouch!'

'Get the glasses out,' she told him. 'And be quick or you shall have no stew tonight.'

After James had walked Miggy back to the cottage, Hattie brooded on the Parkers. She wondered how they'd cope during the long dank Devon winter in their gloomy little creek and whether she should make some effort to be more friendly. Feeling cross at having to worry about them she pulled on her jacket, dragged the reluctant Admiral out of the larder and set off for a walk through the woods.

Janice Parker, huddling in the large cabin, was realising how different living aboard was going to be with the winter approaching. Already there was no sign of the sun in their creek and it was, somehow, doubly depressing to see the sun shining on the shore opposite whilst they were plunged deep in shadow. There was a dank chill air about the place and, just occasionally, she felt that there was a brooding presence with them on the *Abigail*, especially at night when they went to bed in the fo'c'sle cabin. She never let these feelings show. It was difficult enough to keep Brian's spirits up without being moody herself; bright and cheerful was the only way to cope.

She stirred herself, wished she'd gone to Dartmouth with Brian and was seized with a sudden nameless fear. She glanced instinctively behind her at the open door into the forward cabin and thought she saw a shadow move. The sensation of isolation and extreme gloom was sharpened to an impression of danger and she stood up quickly. She was aware of an overwhelming need to look into their sleeping quarters and assure herself that nothing was amiss and this need propelled her to the door. A quick glance round showed her that all was well but, as she slammed the door behind her with a gasp of relief, she experienced an even sharper desire to get off the boat. She remembered that she'd promised to fetch wood for the fire while the tide was out and, pulling on her anorak and her boots, she climbed down the ladder and began to walk along the foreshore.

Joss lay on his day bunk enjoying an after-lunch cigarette. *Westering*'s centreboard divided the main cabin in half and Joss used the port side as a snug with comfortable upholstered benches and a flap table, whilst the starboard side – which was also a passage to his sleeping quarters in the fore cabin – had a full-length bunk. Here he could stretch out, looking past the galley and up through the hatch.

He drew slowly on his cigarette – an expensive luxury these days – and thought about Hester Strange. When he'd gone to the cottage for supper and seen her again he'd felt the same attraction that he'd experienced when he first met her. Despite a few amorous adventures, Joss had contrived – like Hattie – to remain heart-whole and this experience had come as a shock. He didn't want it, he told himself. He was perfectly happy as he was, free, untethered by responsibility, in full control of his life. Nevertheless, her face, almost austere in repose beneath the thick fair fringe – the slatey blue eyes behind round granny spectacles, the delicate lips – remained firmly etched on his mind. Her small son, Edwin – nicknamed Ned – was absurdly like her; the same thick fringe and blond mop, the same grey-blue eyes and delicate colouring. His spectacles had been National Health horn-rims and he looked like a young, earnest, rather vulnerable owl.

Joss realised that he was looking forward to their arrival at the creek. Hester's sale had fallen through and, although she had another buyer, the move to the mill cottage must be inevitably delayed by at least a month. She was anxious lest Hattie should give her up as a bad job but Hattie liked the look of Hester and Ned, and promised to hold on a little longer. Miggy had given Joss a briefer rundown of their history than she'd disclosed to Hattie. Hester had been at art college with Miggy and Patrick but had become pregnant in her second term and married her lover. He'd cheated on her almost from the beginning and on many occasions Hester had been on the point of leaving him. Ned had been a last-ditch effort to save the relationship – a failure as it turned out – and now Hester's former husband had returned to his home in New Zealand with the eldest child.

'The man must be mad,' Joss had muttered incautiously and, seeing Miggy's quick glance, had retired into his shell. He had no intention of becoming an object of interest in the creek or a butt for

Hattie's derision. He rather wished he'd spent less time ridiculing the lovesick or deriding marriage as an outmoded institution but it was too late now.

He took a last lungful of smoke and stubbed out his cigarette in an ashtray on the bunk beside him. As he did so he felt the familiar bump as a boat came alongside and his heart sank. He wasn't in the mood for visitors and, since Toby was at the boatyard, Daisy was at school and James at his office, it could only mean one thing. He slid off the bunk, climbed the companionway steps and stared down into Janice Parker's expectant face.

'Hello,' she said with an eager hopefulness. 'I'm just going across to the hard to meet Brian and I thought I might just have a word.'

He nodded unenthusiastically and caught the painter as she scrambled aboard. They'd bought a delightful little dinghy for rowing inexpertly about the creek, keeping the launch for trips further afield, and Joss gave it an envious glance as he fastened the painter. Janice had plonked herself down on the bench that ran round the cockpit and Joss sighed inwardly.

'Like some coffee?' he asked with a continuing lack of enthusiasm but Janice shook her head.

'Brian'll be here in a minute,' she said. 'Thanks all the same. I just wondered . . . I know it's all a lot of nonsense really but I was just wondering about the *Abigail*. You know? Those rumours and so on. What exactly was the story?'

'She's got a reputation as an unlucky boat,' said Joss indifferently. 'Just the usual thing, I imagine. Most old boats have violence and bad luck in their history as you said yourself.'

'But there was something recent, wasn't there?' She watched him closely and the irritation she always inspired rose in his breast.

'A man was killed on her a couple of years back,' he said callously and immediately regretted it when he saw the horror in her eyes.

'Killed?' She almost whispered it and he cursed under his breath.

'It was an accident,' he said impatiently. 'It was a terrible night. Gale force. He came up on deck and was knocked out by the boom. Cracked his skull. Nothing sinister about it. Could happen to anybody.'

'I see.' Janice looked relieved. 'Yes, I see. We met some people in the Dartmouth Arms and they were saying—'

'People like to make a good story out of it,' Joss interrupted her. He had no desire to pick over the bones of Evan's death or watch

133

her ghoulish interest in a version of Bert Crabtree's story. 'Take no notice. Ah!' He sighed with relief. 'Here comes Brian.'

The Parkers kept their car on the hard and rowed their provisions across; not for them the long walk down through the woods that Evan had preferred. Janice was already on her feet and preparing to depart and Joss assisted her down the ladder.

'Thanks,' she said to him when she was settled in the dinghy and unshipping the oars. 'You've relieved my mind a bit, I must say.'

'That's fine.'

Joss raised his hand and blew out his lips as she rowed away. He didn't quite know why the Parkers should irritate him as much as they did but somehow he felt edgy now, not wanting to settle down to the jobs he had to do. Although he was preparing to spend his first winter on *Westering* there was still plenty of work to be done if he wanted to be away by the end of next summer. Nevertheless he felt restless. The evenings were drawing in apace and he wondered just how long they would seem once the boat was battened down for the night; not quite the same as being in the cottage, with Hattie to drop in on across the yard if he felt bored. He knew that *Westering* would be cramped and dark during the short wet days of winter but, if he couldn't cope on a creek only yards from his friends, how on earth would he cope with months at sea?

Joss went below and stared round. There were a million small tasks waiting to be done but he found himself thinking of Hester and remembering Hattie saying that, if the weather was really bad, he could always use James's spare bedroom. He smiled a little as he recalled the way James had pursed his lips and shaken his head doubtfully.

'Subletting,' he'd said thoughtfully. 'That'd be in direct contravention to the lease. Of course, if you made it worth my while . . .'

Joss wandered back on deck. The Parkers were hurrying to and fro loading the dinghy and he saw Miggy driving away to collect Daisy from school. With it dark by seven, only rarely now was Daisy to be seen waiting on the hard for James to take her sailing after work, although they still went out at weekends. Joss felt a rare sensation of melancholy and an unusual need for company. The Parkers were in the dinghy now and heading back to the *Abigail* but Joss disappeared below. He might feel in the mood for a chat but not with the Parkers. With an effort he overcame his low spirits and settled down to work.

★   ★   ★

Miggy, driving home with Daisy through the lanes, remembered how she'd felt a year ago wondering whether Toby would ever be able to divorce Ruth and how Georgia would react. Georgia, now in her first term at Durham University, had been far less trouble than Miggy had feared and had taken the news of the coming baby with commendable restraint. She'd stayed in the summer as usual but, much to Miggy's relief, was too full of excitement about her approaching life as a student to worry unduly about having a half-brother or sister. She'd told them that Ruth had a new boyfriend who was in advertising, which was a different sort of relief, and that she was thinking of changing her job.

Miggy sighed with satisfaction and looked with pleasure at the countryside she was beginning to know so well. The colour was dying from the sky and the soft autumnal tones were chalky and sombre as the mist crept over the quiet land. She glanced at Daisy sitting silently beside her and took one hand from the wheel to touch her knee for a second.

'Are you OK?'

Daisy nodded, still staring ahead, and Miggy guessed that she missed her evening sailing with James. Her passion for him had in no way abated and Miggy had been tenderly amused to see Daisy's relief when James had barely given Georgia a second glance.

'James thinks we ought to call the baby Marigold if it's a girl. What d'you say to that?'

'Because of our hair,' said Daisy at once. 'He told me that's what I should have been called.'

'Oh.' Miggy thought about this. 'Well then. You don't think it rubs the hair in a bit?'

'No,' said Daisy scornfully. 'It's a good name.'

'That's settled then,' said Miggy guessing that if James had suggested calling the baby Hellebore or Stinkwort, Daisy would have probably agreed to it.

'I wondered if you'd meet me today.' Having been interrupted from her reverie Daisy was disposed to talk. 'I thought you might have started the baby.'

'No sign yet,' said Miggy cheerfully, turning into the lane to the creek. 'It's bound to be a girl. Women always keep you waiting.'

'Did I?'

'You certainly did. Nearly three weeks.'

'You won't be able to get behind the wheel soon,' observed Daisy, and patted the lump affectionately.

'It's not easy,' admitted Miggy. 'I may let Toby fetch you from now on, just in case.'

As she parked the car, she saw Joss standing in *Westering*'s cockpit watching some ducks swimming purposefully towards the mill. There was something unusually despondent about the set of his shoulders and she hailed him.

'Come and have a drink later,' she shouted. 'Stay to supper.'

Even from that distance she could see his expression lighten and she returned his cheerful wave of acceptance whilst wondering what might have depressed the usually imperturbable Joss. She locked the car and followed Daisy through the hedge, suddenly thankful to see the lights gleaming out through the uncurtained windows and to find Toby in the kitchen making tea.

Chapter Seventeen

One morning, while the good weather still held, Sarah wandered into the garden feeling listless and tired. Although the sun shone, the sparkle was gone from the air and there was a sultry heaviness. An earlier bright blowy day had brought down some leaves and she fetched the rake and began to sweep them into a pile. Her movements were slow and desultory and presently she abandoned her task and sat down on the garden seat, the rake propped beside her. She was deciding whether to have an early lunch, simply because it was something to do, when she heard the telephone begin to ring.

Feeling a strange presentiment of fear, she hurried into the house and picked up the receiver.

'Sarah, it's Nick.'

'Yes.' She took a deep breath. 'Hello. What's wrong?'

'Bit of a problem's come up. I'd like to come home and discuss it with you. Will you be around? Are you in to lunch today?'

'Yes.' Terror made it difficult to breathe but she was too well trained to question him. 'Yes, I'll be here.'

'I'll be straight out.'

The line went dead and, after a moment, Sarah replaced the receiver and went back into the garden. She was still sitting on the seat when Nick drove in, parked his car and walked across the grass. He sat down beside her and took her hands in his. She stared at his hands, imagining them in other circumstances, and waited for him to tell her that he wanted to leave her for Cass Wivenhoe.

'I have a confession to make,' he said, and his voice was composed and calm. 'It's all rather sordid, I fear, so I'm hoping that you'll be generous and understanding although there's no reason why you should be.' His grasp tightened a little. 'Since early spring I've been having an affair with Cass Wivenhoe. It started as just a silly fling but it's got rather out of control I'm afraid and I need your help.'

137

She couldn't look at him. Surely he didn't expect that she would give him up quite so easily, simply because he requested her to do so? She looked away from him out over the garden, knowing he was marshalling his thoughts and composing phrases in his head.

'I'm going to ask you to do something that you'll find unforgivable, Sarah. Cass has become impossible. She's taken the whole thing much too seriously and she's causing trouble. I want you to go and see her.'

She looked at him then, staring at him incredulously, ideas whirling as she reassessed the situation.

'Go and *see* her?'

It was Nick's turn to look away, though he still held her unresponsive hands.

'I've thought it over very carefully. She simply won't take no for an answer and she's beginning to make a nuisance of herself at the office.'

Sarah felt a tiny stab of contempt. Of course, the sanctity of the office and Nick's reputation must remain untarnished. Hypocrite! she thought, yet she felt an overwhelming – if shaming – relief. He was still hers. Nevertheless, she felt angry that he'd taken her loyalty so much for granted and had no intention of making it easy for him.

'But why should I see her? I hardly know her.' Her voice was cool.

'I know that.' He paused, biting his lip, still unable to meet her eye. 'Believe me, I've thought it through very carefully.'

I bet you have! thought Sarah, determined not be rushed or pushed into anything from a misplaced sense of gratitude or relief.

Nick stood up, stuck his hands in his pockets and moved away. She watched as he stood staring at the grass at his feet. Presently he returned and sat down beside her.

'Look,' he said, 'I can't think of any other way round this. I've got to ask you. If you went to her and told her that I've asked you to see her, that she's wasting her time . . .' He swallowed and looked at Sarah. 'That she's just one of several.'

She stared back at him. 'Well, that's true so far,' she said, and he looked down so that he should not see contempt – or the pain – in her eyes.

'She may not think so.' His voice was quiet and she bent towards him.

'What else is there?' she asked sharply.

'I said certain things . . . Oh,' he shook his head and flung out his hands, 'as one does in these situations—'

'Does one?' she interrupted bitingly, and he was silent.

'Go on,' she said at last. 'What else was so different this time that Cass Wivenhoe should think she's special?'

'I took her to Shropshire,' he said. 'To the cottage.'

The blood seemed to sing in her ears and the garden blurred and swung before her shocked eyes. Her heart pounded and she clasped her icy hands together.

'It was unforgivable,' he said rapidly. 'I was mad. It was the weekend you went to visit your mother. I . . . I have no excuses, I can only throw myself on your long-suffering patience. Oh, Sarah, I promise—'

'No!' She stood up, willing herself to remain upright, though her knees shook and her head still reeled. 'No promises! So you want me to go to Cass Wivenhoe and tell her that you take all your grubby little amours to our very special place where we've been so happy . . .'

She began to weep and he leaped up and took her by the arms.

'Don't touch me!' she screamed. 'How could you!' She put her hands over her eyes. 'How could you take her there and . . . Oh God!'

He pushed her forcibly down on the seat and thrust his handkerchief into her hands.

'I'm sorrier than you'll ever believe. Why should you believe it? Or anything that I say to you ever again?' He sighed heavily and, unbelievably, she actually detected a tinge of self-pity. 'I'm an unutterable fool and I know I've ruined everything . . .'

'Yes!' she shouted, her face close to his. 'Everything! Just don't expect sympathy as well!'

He sat back and she wiped her streaming eyes and tried to choke back the sobs that shook her, furious that – even now – part of her mind was already preparing for this terrible interview, accepting that she must support him.

'Go on,' she said at last. 'What else must I say?'

She heard him swallow but when he spoke his voice was dispassionate as though he were briefing a clerk. 'I suggest that the thing that will deter Cass is for her to be classed as one of many, a passing whim. You should imply that you knew about the affair and that I took her to the cottage, and . . .' he paused fractionally, 'to The Bear. The fact that we've discussed it will strengthen the point that she means nothing to me. If . . .' he hesitated again. 'If you could possibly bring yourself to treat the whole thing lightly, as a kind of . . . joke. I'm sorry!' he cried as she gave an involuntary gasp of pain. 'Please try to forgive me, Sarah. It's simply the only way that will stop her.' He took her hand and she let it lie, limp and unresponsive in his grasp. 'I love you,' he said. 'Unbelievable though it might sound. I do love you.'

She was incapable of a response and they sat for some while in absolute silence.

'Very well,' she said at last. 'I'll go this afternoon. Do you want lunch? I shall have a cup of coffee. I couldn't face anything else.'

'I'll make the coffee,' he said quickly, glad of something to do, to take the opportunity to be away from her and relax for a moment.

Sarah nodded, knowing exactly what he was thinking and despising him and herself in equal measure. But what choice did she have? To let Cass ruin Nick's reputation and make their marriage a laughing stock? To leave him? She knew that neither option was acceptable and, if that were so, Nick was right and this was the only way out.

Later, still dressed in her old navy cords and Guernsey with a scarf knotted at her throat, Sarah drove across the moor, through Dousland and Meavy and so to the rectory where the Wivenhoes lived. She drove slowly up the drive between the rhododendron bushes and caught her breath sharply as she saw Cass standing on the lawn. She, too, had been raking up leaves and was leaning on her rake watching a golden retriever plunging into the pile and tossing the leaves into the air, so that Sarah had the time to observe her slim voluptuous grace, the thick golden hair, the lovely face. As she heard the car Cass turned her head, the smile fading from her lips, her expression changing to disbelieving horror as Sarah came towards her across the lawn.

Afterwards Sarah drove away, mouth dry, hands shaking, and instinctively headed for the mill. She knew that she couldn't go home, to sit and wait for Nick's return; to see the anxious eager expression that he would attempt, unsuccessfully, to hide; to report the conversation and Cass's reaction. She'd done his dirty work for him and needed time to recover. She knew that she would be unable to hide her contempt and she must restore her self-respect and remind herself of her love for him before she dared to face him. As she drove, the scene on the rectory lawn re-enacted itself in her

head and she heard her own voice – light, easy, assured – and Cass's
– desperate, shocked, disbelieving – echoing on and on . . .

'. . . Nick's got a problem . . . very difficult, my dear . . .
doesn't want to see you any more . . . in most cases it all ends
quietly . . .'

'Most cases?'

'. . . weren't the first . . . won't be the last . . . all quite harmless
. . . thought you understood . . . after all, you do have a certain
reputation yourself.'

'I don't believe you . . . Nick wouldn't . . . You're bluffing!'

'Oh, my dear . . . have to be brutal . . . told me he'd taken you
to our little place in Shropshire . . . sure you went to The Bear . . .
takes them all there . . .'

'I don't believe this!'

'. . . been into the office . . . very foolish . . . he'd never leave
me . . . private income . . . my family . . . luxuries . . . a very selfish
man, vain too . . .'

'He sent you to me?'

'. . . he's a weak character . . . looks to me to help him out . . .
used to his little distractions.'

'But how can you live like that? I just can't understand?'

'Can't you, Cass? How does Tom manage?'

There had been a dreadful silence then. At last Cass had
struggled to her feet and asked her to go.

'Tell Nick he has nothing to fear . . . I shall never speak to
him again.'

'. . . hope we shall be able to remain friends . . . good many
mutual acquaintances . . . imagine you wouldn't like any gossip
. . . I must be off. Goodbye.'

Sarah realised that she was clutching the wheel with numb
fingers, her shoulders rigid. She pulled on to the edge of the moor
and set herself to relax. The dreadful thing was that, during the
appalling scene, she'd felt a genuine pity for Cass. It was apparent
that Nick had led her to believe that she was much, much more
than another flirtation. She saw the shock and pain in Cass's face
but had driven herself on, convincing Cass, making her believe
the unbelievable.

Sarah stared out unseeingly across the moor, unconsciously
massaging her stiff hands, flexing her fingers. The enormity of the
whole affair burst upon her; the cruelty of being asked to confront
her husband's mistress, the necessity to lie and support him in his
infidelity. Sarah dropped her head into her hands, too exhausted

by her ordeal even to be able to weep. Could it be possible that she would ever be able to pick up the threads of her life and her marriage and carry on? She thought of Nick and, feeling nothing but despising, contempt and dislike, experienced a shock of terror. Was it possible that, this time, he really had gone too far and killed her love for him?

She sat aghast before such a thought. Even during the lowest moments of their relationship, she'd never questioned her love for him; always certain that it was deathless. Perhaps it wasn't true; perhaps even her stubborn, determined passion had its limitations. She recalled Cass's face and her cry, 'I don't believe this!' and had known a mad impulse to take her in her arms and cry, 'Neither do I!'

'But if I stop loving him,' she murmured, 'what else is there left to me?'

She was filled with a desolate loneliness and, starting the engine, drove on, following the well-known path that led to Hattie.

Dusk was falling as she pulled into the mill yard and she climbed out slowly, feeling old and ill. She stood for a moment, unable to summon sufficient energy to carry her to the door but, as she stood, the front door opened and Hattie was framed in the friendly light that streamed out from the hall.

'Sarah?' she heard her ask, puzzled. 'Is that you? What's up? Are you OK?'

At the sound of her voice Sarah began to weep and Hattie came forward then and, putting an arm about her, drew her gently inside.

Nick paused in his pacing and glanced for the hundredth time at his watch. He'd come home, sick with apprehension, to find a dark and empty house with no sign of Sarah and no note. He was desperate to know whether she'd seen Cass and how the interview had gone and felt a strange mixture of relief and frustration when he realised that his anxiety must be further prolonged. He'd poured himself a stiff Scotch, lit the drawing-room fire and tried to relax. It was impossible. Dark thoughts began to edge into his mind. Supposing Cass had painted a graphic picture of their affair? He imagined them screaming at each other, coming to blows even . . . Worse! Nick grimaced at the thought, perhaps they'd discussed him, affected a friendship, compared notes . . . !

He gave an involuntary exclamation of distaste and humiliation and got up as though to drive the unwelcome pictures away with physical activity. He'd poured himself another drink and gone into the kitchen. Despite his fears, he felt hungry and he looked into the fridge to see what might have been for supper. Nothing was obviously prepared so he cut himself some cheese and took some biscuits, eating them standing by the kitchen table, his eyes on the clock. What could have happened to her? He refused to contemplate anything of a melodramatic nature. Sarah simply wasn't the type, no matter how upset she might be. Nick kept his thoughts turned firmly away from the enormity of what he had demanded of her and concentrated on practicalities. She might have had an accident, of course. It was only to be expected that she'd been overwrought, not concentrating on her driving.

Nick hesitated in his pacing. He could telephone the local hospitals to see if any accident cases had been brought in but it might prove embarrassing . . . He finished his drink abruptly and did what he'd meant to do since he'd first arrived home and found Sarah gone. He went into her study, checked in her address book and telephoned the mill.

Hattie's voice was self-possessed as usual and Nick writhed a little as he asked the question, keeping his own voice as light and casual as he could.

'Good evening, Hattie. Is Sarah with you, by any chance? I think we got our wires crossed earlier and I'm not certain when to expect her home.'

'Hello, Nick. Yes, she's here. She's going to stay the night. She's not feeling too well.'

'Oh, I'm sorry.' He sounded properly concerned. 'Could I have a word?'

'She says she's not feeling up to it.' Hattie sounded regretful but Nick gritted his teeth lightly together, humiliated in the knowledge that Sarah would have told her everything.

'I see.' He allowed himself to sound very slightly put out.

'She says not to worry. Apparently she's achieved what she set out to do this afternoon and you can relax. OK? Make sense to you?'

'Perfectly, thank you.' His tone was cold now. In truth he considered Sarah's disloyalty with Hattie far worse than his own with Cass. Hattie, after all, was their friend and Sarah had no right to discuss such a personal thing with her without his permission. 'Perhaps she might be up to phoning me in the morning? Good night.'

He replaced the receiver abruptly, able now to submerge some of his own guilt in his disapproval at Sarah's behaviour. Nick poured himself a third drink, took it into the sitting room and picked up the newspaper. Obviously all was well and he could relax, and when Sarah returned he would make it all up to her. The problem was that women were likely to get things so terribly out of proportion. He sighed, feeling rather sorry for himself, sat down stretching out his legs to the fire and immersed himself in the newspaper.

Chapter Eighteen

Miggy was relieved to see that Sarah had returned home when she and Toby delivered Daisy to the mill on their way to the hospital. It had been a long-standing arrangement that Daisy should stay with Hattie if the baby should show signs of arrival late in the day but Miggy, knowing that Sarah disapproved of her for leaving Stephen, was glad that she'd gone that morning. A distant thunder rumbled round the creek and stabs of lightning were sighted out to sea and, by the time Hattie and Daisy were ready to settle down for the night, the rain was falling in torrents and they could barely see across the creek.

Hattie tucked Daisy up in the small bedroom and wondered how the Parkers were faring. One thing was certain; having heard of Evan's fate it was unlikely that either of them would venture up on deck during the storm. She went back downstairs and began to lock up for the night. She'd allowed Daisy to stay up fairly late and decided that there was no harm in an early night for herself. Admiral Jellicoe – who seemed to enjoy storms and would happily sit in the pouring rain – came in rather reluctantly and settled down as usual with his night-time biscuit. Hattie gathered up her glass of water, her book and her spectacles, switched off the lights and went slowly upstairs and into her bedroom.

The large room looked welcoming and cosy. Part of this was due to the fact that Mr Crabtree, under Hattie's instructions, had reopened the fireplace and, during the winter, a log fire burned in the grate right through the night. It was lit at about nine o'clock so that by bedtime it was burning cheerfully and the room was warm.

'I agree it's a luxury,' she said unrepentantly to the envious Miggy. 'In fact it's positively decadent! But you can't imagine the joy of lying in bed and watching the shadows on the ceiling! Takes me back to my childhood.'

Hattie pottered comfortably, pausing occasionally when a stronger gust than usual smote the sturdy walls. She pulled back the brown velvet curtains and peered out over the creek, wishing that Joss was tucked up in the cottage but she could see lights gleaming from the portholes and knew that he was quite safe. She'd begun to accept the painful fact that Joss aroused the maternal tendencies which the abortion had denied her and she was determined not to become a nuisance to him. Hattie dropped the curtain and, having arrayed herself in one of her long, roomy nightshirts intended for large, tall men, she went to sit in the rocking chair by the fire. This was one of her happiest times of the day; the room lit by a bedside lamp, the firelight leaping on the cream walls and the friendly hiss and crackle of the logs. The dark wood gleamed, casting back golden reflections, and Hattie's chair creaked quietly as she rocked gently and turned the pages of her book. Behind her the huge bed, massed with quilts and cushions, waited invitingly and the china figures on the top of the chest seemed to come alive and move in the light of the flickering flames.

A more powerful gust than usual struck at the mill. It howled round the house, which seemed to shudder beneath its impact as it flung the rain at the window, and screamed in the chimney. Hattie bent to reach for another log and paused as the door opened and a gold head appeared.

'Are you all right, Hattie?' asked Daisy anxiously. 'I thought I'd make sure you weren't nervous. Oh!' She caught herself up with the involuntary exclamation. 'How cosy it is in here!'

'Can't you sleep?' Hattie edged her footstool across. 'Come and sit by the fire. Noisy old night, isn't it?'

Daisy sat on the stool and stretched her thin hands to the flames. Hattie's room looked magical, like something out of a fairy story, and Hattie herself, in the long blue nightshirt with a crimson shawl round her shoulders, looked a different person. It was unexpected and Daisy liked it. She stood up after a bit and began to prowl round, examining the room. The bed looked enormous, not like a bed at all but more like some giant colourful nest. She fingered the china figures on the chest and finally paused before the bookshelves, peering at the titles in the dim light.

'Gosh!' she said in awe. 'You've got *Alice* and *Pooh* and Beatrix Potter!'

'Certainly!' returned Hattie crisply. 'They're very old books now. Never mind. They read just as well, if not better.'

'*Naughty Sophia*,' read Daisy, '*The Singing Cake, The Midnight Folk, Five Children and It, The Secret Travellers*. You've got lots of books, Hattie.'

'Too many really.' Hattie sighed. 'But I can't bear to part with a single one. Like some cocoa?'

'Ooh yes!' Daisy's eyes shone. 'Could we have a midnight feast up here by the fire?'

'Why not?' Hattie hauled herself out of the chair and thrust her feet into sheepskin slippers. 'I'll go and forage.'

'Shall I help?'

'No,' said Hattie, who didn't want the Admiral disturbed. 'You stay here in the warm and keep the home fires burning.'

When she'd gone, Daisy tried out the rocking chair for a while and then carefully placed a log from the wicker basket on the fire. She was standing at the window, watching the rain stream down the glass and catching glimpses of *Westering* riding out the storm when Hattie returned.

They sat companionably before the fire, eating chocolate biscuits and drinking cocoa and finally, when Daisy's head had drooped once or twice, Hattie announced that it was time for bed. She saw Daisy's wistful expression and hadn't the heart to make her spend the noisy night alone in a strange bed.

'Come on then,' she said to Daisy's delight. 'Plenty of room for a little one in here.'

Before she could change her mind, Daisy scrambled amongst the quilts and pillows of the glorious bed and snuggled blissfully down. Hattie made up the fire, put the guard round and climbed into bed, turning out the light.

'Sweet dreams,' she said, propping herself about with cushions. She pulled a quilt around her and shut her eyes but Daisy lay awake, feeling as if she were floating, and watched the flames dancing on the ceiling. The shadows stretched and shifted, mesmerising her, and presently her eyelids drooped and she slept.

The gale raged for three days before it blew itself out. By this time there were several trees down across the foreshore where various pieces of wreckage had been washed up. The Parkers emerged looking pale and subdued. They'd been quite unprepared for the ferocity of such weather, wondering why on earth they'd ever thought that life afloat would be fun.

Joss, on the other hand, was in good spirits. *Westering* had stood the storm very well and, although it had shown up several weaknesses, on the whole he was satisfied.

Miggy came home with the baby, Marigold, and life slowly settled back to normal. Toby was delighted with his new daughter, writing at once to Georgia not only to tell her the news but also to reassure her – should it be necessary – that she was his firstborn and any amount of new babies would never oust her from that position. If Georgia was in need of that reassurance it certainly wasn't apparent in her letter, which was full of congratulations. A few days later, however, he received a letter from Ruth. He opened it with anxiety and read it with surprise. She congratulated him on his new daughter, asked after Miggy and observed, with a certain wistfulness, how much she'd like to visit them all. She was surprised, she wrote, at how lonely she was these days and regretted many of her earlier decisions. She knew that it was too late now to put the clock back but she hoped they'd consider allowing her to visit for a few days. She'd so love to see Georgia's new half-sister.

Toby read the letter through again with mounting alarm. It seemed so extraordinarily unlike Ruth. He felt unequal to showing it to Miggy just yet, knowing that her first feeling would be suspicion and her second one fear, but he couldn't quite dismiss it out of hand. He read it a third time with growing sympathy. After all, he'd been so lucky. He had a whole new family, as well as Georgia, whilst Ruth had very little. She explained in her letter that the new job had failed to materialise and he guessed – reading between the lines – that her new affair was over.

During the next few days Toby brooded. He had a weakness for wanting to see everybody happy and he spent hours wondering how this might be achieved. There was no harm, after all, in Ruth being a friend. Surely he and Miggy had so much love between them that a little might be spared for Ruth. There was no need for a relationship that had begun with love to end in bitterness. Something prevented him, however, from voicing these views to Miggy. Each time he saw her, pale but radiant after the protracted birth, he felt a strange inability to show her the letter or tell her his hopes. So the weeks passed and still he came to no decision.

It was when Georgia wrote, asking if she might spend the New Year with them that Toby saw an opportunity to deal with the problem Ruth presented. He wrote to Georgia, urging her to come for as long as she wished and suggesting – in passing – that Ruth might like to come for a day or two. A few days later Georgia telephoned.

'Hi, Dad,' she said. 'Got your letter, thanks. Are you serious about Mum and New Year?'

'Well,' Toby glanced through the open door and then pushed

it to with his foot, 'I had a very nice letter from her about the baby. She said she was lonely and would love to come down for a few days.'

'Well, it's up to you.' Georgia sounded sceptical. 'She's a bit down at the moment but I don't want any problems springing up again. Not with the new baby and things.'

'I'm sure Ruth knows the score. I was brutal enough last time, heaven knows!'

'OK.' He could almost see her shrug. 'But keep it short.'

A little later he broached the subject with Miggy.

'Oh, not Ruth, too!' She stared at him in alarm. 'Why on earth does she want to come?'

'I think she feels badly about her behaviour and she'd love to see the baby.'

'Oh hell!' Miggy looked so upset that Toby felt a twinge of fear.

'Do you really feel that strongly about it?' he asked.

'Of course I do!' she cried. 'She's been absolutely vile to me from the beginning. She's a troublemaker and I don't trust her an inch.'

She glanced at him and immediately regretted her words. He looked bleak and sad and she tried to push down her resentment and be more generous.

'I don't blame you,' he was saying. 'I just hoped all that bitterness might be done away with. It would be nicer for Georgia if we could all be pleasant to one another. I don't want her to have her nose put out of joint.'

Miggy swallowed her exasperation, remembering how much more difficult Georgia could have been. It couldn't have been easy for her to accept Miggy and Daisy and now Marigold.

'Neither do I,' she said. 'Of course I don't. But I can't see where Ruth comes in. Still,' she shrugged and looked resigned, 'if Georgia wants her along there's nothing to be done, I suppose.'

Toby hesitated. Now was the moment to say that it was nothing to do with Georgia and that Ruth had invited herself but it seemed easier to let it stay as it was and the moment passed.

Christmas approached. To Daisy's disappointment James was going home to Dorset but Hattie and Joss were invited to the cottage for Christmas lunch and Miggy began to feel worried about the Parkers.

'I feel dreadful at leaving them out,' she said to Toby. 'I really

149

don't want them but we can't leave them all on their own over there, can we?'

He put his arms round her and hugged her. 'Let them come,' he said. 'We can't ignore them. Just for lunch. Joss and Hattie will help it along. It's Christmas, after all.'

The Parkers were pathetically pleased to be asked. They were both quieter than formerly and even Hattie was able to regard them with equanimity. The lunch passed off very well but Miggy was relieved when it was all over.

'I wish you were around for New Year,' she told Hattie as they washed up together. 'I'm dreading it.'

'Mmm. Well, watch out.' Hattie looked dubious. 'I'm off to Sarah and Nick's and I can't put that off but just keep an eye on her.'

When Ruth and Georgia arrived, however, it seemed that no such precautions were necessary. Ruth was quiet, well-behaved, very much the guest. She cooed flatteringly over the baby and had brought Daisy a pair of much longed for roller skates as a belated Christmas present. Miggy detected Georgia's hand here but was disarmed by Daisy's shining eyes. Toby was delighted that his family – old and new – could be so civilised and made Ruth very welcome. When they were alone, whilst Miggy was attending to Marigold, Ruth very prettily proffered her gratitude.

'It was so sweet of you to let me come,' she said, sitting on the edge of the kitchen table whilst he made after-lunch tea and coffee. 'You know, I really miss you.'

'Oh, Ruth.' He tried not to feel moved or flattered. 'I'm sorry it went wrong.'

'I know.' She watched his back, remembering things. 'I was a fool.'

'Let's not talk about it. Do you still take sugar?'

'I'm afraid so.' She gave a throaty chuckle. 'You know me. All the vices, I'm afraid.'

He sensed danger and tried to lead the conversation to safer ground. 'I was sorry that the job fell through.'

'Oh well.' She glanced round the kitchen. 'How familiar this feels. Just like old times, isn't it? Me perched on the table, you making tea. God! I really do miss you!'

'Ruth,' he said warningly. 'Please don't.'

'Don't you miss me even the tiniest bit?' She slipped off the table and went to him, putting her hands on his sleeve. 'Oh, darling, I'm sure you do. You've been so sweet to me. You used to fancy me rotten. Couldn't get enough. Surely it can't all be gone?' He was so still that she thought she'd won and she moved a hand across his stomach, her breath coming quickly. 'I've wanted you all weekend. Oh, Toby, it needn't change anything here. You could always come up to London now and then. Just for old times' sake.'

'I don't like the sound of that!' Miggy was standing in the doorway, her chin high.

Toby jerked round but Ruth stayed beside him, eyebrows raised. She guessed that Miggy had heard only the last sentence and she spoke quickly before Toby could move.

'I was saying how sweet it was of Toby to invite me for old times' sake,' she said smoothly. 'Forgive and forget. That was always your motto, wasn't it, darling?'

'Not always.' Toby shook off her hand and went to Miggy. 'Nothing to worry about. Marigold OK?'

'She's fine. What's this about you inviting Ruth? You said that Georgia asked if she could come.'

'Oh, darling.' Ruth chuckled. 'We've been caught out.'

Miggy stared at Toby and he cursed himself for not sticking absolutely to the truth. How stupid he'd been to think he could trust Ruth! How naïve to think that love could conquer all.

'Ruth wrote asking to come,' he said starkly. 'She sounded miserable and lonely and when I checked with Georgia it seemed that it would be a good idea to try getting together again with the past firmly behind us. I was a fool to think it could work.'

'Oh, darling, no.' Ruth tried one last throw. 'Jealousy's a terrible disease . . .'

'Forget it, Ruth.' Toby turned his back and smiled at Miggy and after a moment, with some reluctance, she smiled back. 'I've made you some tea,' he told her. 'Shall we take it up and talk to our new baby for a bit?'

Ruth watched them go, her face dark, and made no effort to look less forbidding when Georgia appeared.

'Is this my coffee?' she asked and then saw Ruth's expression. 'What's up?'

'Nothing.' Ruth shrugged. 'Just good old boredom. Nothing changes here after all.'

'Why should it? Come on, Mum. Forget it. Drink your coffee and we'll go and see Sue. You remember her, don't you? She was at St Margaret's with me. You always got on well with her mum. No good sitting about brooding.'

Upstairs, Toby put an arm round Miggy as she stared down at the sleeping Marigold.

'I was wrong,' he said. 'Quite wrong. Stupid, too. Never again. Honest!'

Miggy smiled a little, all her former fears revived despite her new-found security. She looked down at the baby and felt a measure of calm returning.

'Promise?' she said at last, and put her arms round him as he began to kiss her.

Chapter Nineteen

Brian Parker watched Janice climb down into the launch, start the engine and set off across the creek to Fisherman's Cottage. She was having a day out with Miggy; a look at the shops and lunch in Totnes and then on to the Cider Press at Dartington for tea. She raised her hand to him, her expression a mixture of suppressed excitement at the prospect of a day away from the boat and anxiety for him, left all alone. Brian waved back, delighted to see her go. He'd had no idea how claustrophobic it could be to live in such cramped surroundings with her. They simply couldn't get away from each other. He knew that the *Abigail* was a very big boat compared with others that people lived on but he simply didn't know how they managed it and survived without committing murder.

He watched Janice edge the boat into Toby's boathouse and glanced round the creek. As usual it was a misty dull day, although not actually raining, and he felt the depression that had been his almost constant companion for the last year clamp down on his spirits. He knew that it was unfair to blame Janice for things that were rooted in his own inadequacy but did she have to be quite so determinedly cheerful, quite so bracing! If only she could see that sometimes he'd have preferred it if she'd burst into tears or lost her temper. God knows, there were enough irritations attached to living aboard to test the patience of a saint! Brian looked up at the cliff of trees that seemed to tower over the boat. So heavily wooded was the promontory that, even with the branches stark and bare, the dense mass blocked the light and effectively hid what little sun there was during these dank February days.

Brian stifled an exclamation and went below. Here it was so dark that the paraffin lamps had to be kept burning all day but, whilst on *Westering* this gave a jolly, cosy appearance to Joss's living quarters, on the *Abigail* it just seemed to add to the gloom. Brian thought of their bright roomy bungalow with its well-kept garden and felt like weeping. Why had a few weeks' holiday in a narrow boat on the waterways of the Midlands made them feel that it would be fun to be water gypsies? Brian stared listlessly round the galley. He knew that there were all sorts of things he could do to make the boat more habitable but he could never summon up the energy. He remembered how he'd worked on the bungalow, loving every minute of it, always finding some new task, never happier than when he was improving it.

He abandoned the idea of a cup of tea and wandered into the saloon. After all, whose fault was it that they weren't living happily in their bungalow? He'd been very ready to agree to let it to friends and come away from the whispers and nudges. Janice was confident that it needed only a year or so for the gossip to die down but what then? Brian threw a few pieces of damp wood on the sullen smoking fire and felt another urge to burst into tears. How cruel life was to him, how ready to deal out retribution! Thousands of people had done far worse than he had without being punished so drastically. He wondered if he'd ever find another job and how long their savings would last. The rent from the bungalow helped, of course, and their lifestyle was a cheap one. The *Abigail* had seemed such a bargain and, at the beginning, he'd seen how comfortable she could be with a certain amount of tender loving care. Toby had suggested she be towed to a more cheerful mooring – she had no engine – but, as yet, they'd been unable to find a suitable place for her where they'd be allowed to live aboard.

Brian perched for a moment beside the fire. There was plenty to occupy him during Janice's absence but, as usual, he felt that debilitating lassitude creeping over him. There was something about the boat that sapped his will, something brooding and unhappy. Janice had laughed cheerily when he mentioned it rather tentatively.

'Imagination, love,' she said, archly soothing, as though he were six years old. 'All those rumours preying on your mind. Someone had an accident here, that's all. It could have happened to anyone. Now, no miseries. You know miseries aren't allowed on the good ship *Abigail*. You must put it out of your mind.'

Nevertheless, he was certain that she felt it sometimes. He'd come upon her quietly and seen her sitting, chin on hand, face bleak, watching, listening. He'd woken suddenly one night, convinced that someone was standing beside their bunk and, on another occasion, had heard footsteps running overhead on the deck, hoarse shouts and the dull thud of something falling. When he told her, he saw the fear in her own face before she could control herself although, almost immediately, the bright cheery mask was back in place. Sometimes it would have been good to see her frightened, if only to have an opportunity to comfort and encourage her rather than it being always the other way round.

Brian got up, went into the forward cabin and flung himself on their bunk. He put his hands behind his head and stared at the bulkhead. Nobody had warned them about condensation that kept their bedding damp or how tiresome it was to have to row across a wet windy creek every time they ran out of bread. They'd given up trying to have fresh milk and settled for the powdered variety, and he got so sick of mould everywhere; on clothes and food and any kind of upholstery. Yet again Brian fought to hold back the sobs that threatened to bubble up from his hot, resentful, unhappy heart. A tiny thought flickered at the back of his mind and he swallowed once or twice and licked his lips. He had a secret. On this godforsaken, cramped, floating hell he'd managed to keep a secret from Janice's prying, darting, ever-vigilant eyes.

Brian's fingers crisped towards his palms and he shut his eyes tightly. During the Christmas festivities he'd pinched a bottle of Scotch from Toby's drinks table. There'd been so many bottles clustered together and then that awful Hattie from the mill had plonked another one down and said 'just a little something to see the New Year in', or some such rubbish, and no one had taken much notice. No one except Brian. When everyone was seeing them off he'd gone back – said he'd forgotten something – and slipped the bottle into the inside pocket of his coat. Joss was leaving too, and Hattie, and there was all that silly affected kissing and hugging that he found quite insufferable so that he was able to get down into the launch without anyone being the wiser. And now that bottle was hidden right at the back of his locker, wrapped in his summer shirts.

Brian sniggered quietly to himself. Janice hadn't suspected a thing. How closely she watched when they shopped together, how busily she unpacked for him if he went alone! She'd made quite certain that no drop of alcohol had been smuggled aboard and, when they dined out, she saw to it that he had no extra glassful.

'God dammit!' he screamed suddenly as a surge of pure hatred shot through him. He crashed both fists down on the blankets. 'Damn it! Damn it!'

He screamed and sobbed and was dimly aware not only of his own hatred but of other impulses of angry energy that formed a miasma around him and filled the cabin. He stumbled from the bunk and fell to his knees, groping to the very back of the locker. For one terrible moment he couldn't find the bottle and scrabbled violently, his breath short, muttering imprecations, his face contorted with effort and fear. The interfering cow had found it and taken it away! But no! But no! His urgent questing fingers made contact with smooth cool glass and he gave a triumphant cry and drew it forth, weak with relief, cradling it to his chest. The shock had been such that he unscrewed the cap at once and took a little sip; a small one to be savoured, rolled over the tongue, worshipped almost. He fell back on the bunk, exhausted from his outburst, and took a second sip. The smooth, rich, golden liquid seemed to be filling his veins; soothing his anger, comforting and calming. Brian pulled the pillows into a heap and leaned back, stretching out again along the bunk, the bottle held between his hands. He would have just one more sip, perhaps two, just enough to restore his spirits and encourage him to do some work. He must ration it very carefully against other days when he might be left so blissfully alone.

'The thing is,' said Janice, stirring and stirring her tea, 'that I don't like him to think I'm worried. It rubs it in, doesn't it? So I have to keep jolly all the time.'

Miggy watched the spoon going round and round, dragged her gaze away and looked into Janice's anxious face. 'That must be quite exhausting,' she said. 'Surely you can allow yourself a moment of ordinary human reaction from time to time?'

'No.' Janice shook her head. 'You don't know Brian. He gets very low, given the opportunity. I said to myself at the very beginning, "Janice," I said, "it's up to you, my girl." Can't allow any cracks to show.'

'It sounds a bit lonely,' ventured Miggy. 'And exhausting.'

'I do get tired,' admitted Janice. She drank some tea and beamed at Miggy. 'I've enjoyed today ever so much. It's really done me good.'

'We must do it again sometime.' Miggy smiled back, hiding her own exhaustion. Janice had talked non-stop since her arrival at the back door. 'You'll feel better now that spring's on its way.'

'It hasn't been like we thought.' Janice sighed a little and made a face. 'Had a real romantic view of it, we did. It's just he's so miserable all the time. There's ever such a lot he could do but he just mopes about.'

'It's very tiring living with someone who's depressed. I don't know how you cope, stuck over there all on your own with no one else to talk to.'

'We walk a lot.' Janice felt a great deal better. Just talking about it all had put her problems back into proportion and given her the courage to carry on. 'Gets us off the boat. And it'll be better when the spring comes. You're quite right about that.'

'You really must try to find a better mooring.' Miggy reached for the teapot. 'It would make so much difference if you could see the sun now and again. Another cup?'

'Why not? May as well be hung for a sheep as a lamb. Thanks. I expect you're enjoying a break from the baby?'

No, thought Miggy. No I am not. I'm tired and bored and would much rather be with Marigold.

She smiled. 'It's been fun,' she said. 'But I mustn't be too late getting back. Poor Hattie will be worn out. She's not used to babies.'

'I can't stand that dog of hers.' Janice shuddered. 'Great brute. Terrified to go up to the car I am sometimes. I don't think it should be allowed to roam free like that.'

'Jellicoe won't hurt you,' said Miggy, trying to sound sympathetic.

'People always say that about their dogs, till they bite someone. D'you fancy another apricot slice? Let's be devils, shall we?'

Brian snored a little, struggled into wakefulness and settled himself more comfortably. He was deeply at peace, content, relaxed. He heard a noise and came more fully awake, raising his fuddled head and straining his ears. Nothing. He fell back on the pillow and yawned widely, the almost empty bottle still clutched in his hands. Presently he opened his eyes. There it was again; the sound of feet hurrying on the deck above his head, shouts, a heavy thud. Brian frowned a little, attempted to rise and groaned, wondering if he could be bothered. He was simply too tired. He raised the bottle to peer at the inch or so of liquid at the bottom and smiled to himself. Before he could finish the last of the whisky he heard the noise again. There must be someone up on deck; more than one person. There were the cries again and the thud as though someone had fallen.

Brian swung his legs off the bunk and got painfully to his feet. Who on earth could be on the *Abigail* at this time of a dull wet February day? Whoever it was, they were a damned nuisance and he intended to give them a piece of his mind. A clear terrifying thought catapulted into his dazed brain. Perhaps Janice had returned! He stood up quickly, cracking his head on a beam, and, cursing softly, lurched into the saloon. Surely it couldn't be that late? Still clutching the bottle he went to the bottom of the companionway ladder and stared up into the wheelhouse. He thought he saw a shadow move and he began to climb clumsily up the ladder, still holding the bottle, his head reeling. The ladder gave a little, dislodging from its loose fixing as he swayed and jerked his way up. He was nearly at the top when it swung loose. He lost his balance and, trying to save himself and the bottle, pitched backwards into the saloon below.

'I've enjoyed it ever so much,' said Janice for the tenth time as she clambered into the launch. 'I can't thank you enough. We'll do it again soon, won't we?'

'Soon,' promised Miggy, her heart sinking. 'Of course we will. If Brian doesn't mind.'

'Glad to see the back of me for a bit,' said Janice cheerily. ''Bye then.'

She waved to Miggy and set off across the creek. Secretly she'd been rather anxious all day that Brian might get fed up with being alone and take himself off to Dartmouth. She'd managed to put this thought to the back of her mind fairly successfully, so taken up was she with her outing and Miggy's sympathetic response to her problems, but now she found that the anxiety was a very real and frightening one. Brian had been so low of late, especially since Christmas, and she wondered if she'd been foolish to leave him to his own devices. As the launch chugged across the creek she strained her eyes to see the car. It was parked exactly as it had been this morning. Surely, if he'd been out there would be some little difference.

Knowing that she was clutching at straws, Janice brought the launch alongside with only a few bumps and fastened the painter. Her anxiety increased when there was no sign of Brian coming out to help her on board or ask about her day.

'Hello there,' she shouted as she gained the deck. 'I'm back.'

The door to the deckhouse was open and she went in, calling again as she reached the companionway ladder.

'Brian! Are you there, love?'

It was only as she prepared to descend that she noticed the

ladder swinging loose and, almost at the same moment, saw the crumpled form below her.

'Oh my God!'

It was barely a whisper. Brian lay on his back at the bottom of the ladder, his legs twisted beneath him. She felt a great surge of panic accompanied by a distinct desire to get off the boat as quickly as she could. She fought them both back and called to him urgently. His eyes opened slowly and she gasped with relief.

'Oh, Brian. What happened? Are you badly hurt?'

'It's my back.' His lips hardly moved and she strained to hear him. 'I can't move, Jan.'

'Oh, Brian.' She gave a little sob. 'Hang on, love. I'll go for help.'

'Jan!' He tried to move and gasped with pain. 'Don't leave me on my own. Don't leave me, Jan!'

'Oh, love. I've got to. You need help. I'll only be a minute. I'll phone from Miggy's and then I'll come straight back. Oh, love.'

Tears streamed down her face as she fled back through the wheelhouse and untied the painter with clumsy trembling hands. It was terrible to leave him alone and in pain and, as she almost slid down the ladder into the launch, she wondered if she should have stopped long enough to make him comfortable or give him a painkiller. As she started the engine she comforted herself that she might well do more harm than good and that he needed proper medical attention. How long had he lain there, helpless and in pain, in that creepy atmosphere that seemed to pervade the boat? He'd sounded truly frightened when he begged her not to leave him.

Janice gave a tiny sob as she headed back across the creek. She shouldn't have left him alone. He'd always had a strange feeling about the *Abigail* and now it seemed he was right. There was some kind of evil presence, she'd been aware of it herself although she'd always denied it. And now there was something else; something that lurked on the edge of her memory; a smell she'd noticed as she'd kneeled, peering down into the saloon. It was only as she raced across the lawn and hammered on Miggy's door that she recognised it as the smell of whisky.

159

Chapter Twenty

Before Hester and Ned moved into Number Two Mill Cottages, the Parkers were back in their bungalow in the Midlands.

'Thank God it's a bungalow,' said Hattie. 'It'll be easier for the wheelchair.'

'I still can't take it in.' Miggy hadn't recovered from the shock. 'Fancy breaking his back just falling down the ladder. Oh, Hattie, it's awful. Janice says it's because he was drunk but I just know it's something to do with that boat. D'you remember Bert Crabtree telling us that the mate broke his back and was crippled?'

'Pooey!' said Hattie, but her tone lacked confidence. 'Sheer coincidence!'

'Twice?' Miggy arched her brows. 'Evan and now Brian. Janice insists it was the whisky and that everything else was imagination because they were so depressed. What's so terrible is that Toby's sure it was his whisky. D'you remember you gave us a bottle at Christmas? Toby could never find it and now he thinks Brian took it. Anyway, they're trying to sell the boat. They need the money desperately and Janice has asked us not to tell people about *Abigail*'s history.'

Hattie was silent; torn between agreeing that it was all superstition anyway and feeling shocked that they wanted to keep the tragedies hushed up simply to make some money.

'I doubt that the local brokerages will take her on anyway,' she said at last. 'With luck it won't be any of our business. I wish someone would tow the damn thing down the creek and sink her out in the river.'

'That's not a bad idea.' Miggy looked thoughtful. 'Anyway, don't say anything to Hester. It's such a gloomy start to her new life down here.'

'She'll be in for Easter.' Hattie brightened up a little. 'I began to think she'd never get here.'

Hester's arrival was exactly what was needed to stop people

161

brooding on the Parkers' problems. She, too, was tremendously relieved to think she and Ned had made it at last.

'And here we are,' she said, hugging Miggy tightly at the end of the first day. 'Oh, it's wonderful to see you and know you're just down the creek.'

'It's going to be such fun to have you here. I can't believe it.' Miggy looked round the sitting room where several tea-chests stood, waiting to be unpacked. 'You're nearly organised.'

'I wouldn't have been without your help.' Hester sank into the nearest armchair and strained her hands back through the thick heavy fringe. 'I'm exhausted!'

'I'm not surprised. You had a very early start. Sure you don't want a bed for the night?'

Hester shook her head. 'Thanks all the same. It's going to feel very odd after all these years in London. I've been living in the same house ever since I was married. Do you realise I was only nineteen?'

'Heavens! I suppose you were.' Miggy thought about the past years. 'Isn't it weird, Hes? Patrick dead, Phil in New Zealand. Me with a new daughter.'

Hester rested her head back on the chair and closed her eyes. 'Toby's lovely,' she said. 'I really envy you.'

'Oh, Hester . . .'

'No, no. Ignore me.' She sat up and grinned at Miggy. 'I intend to eschew all self-pity. Where's Ned?'

'With Hattie and the Admiral,' said Miggy promptly. 'He's completely bowled over by Jellicoe.'

'Physically or emotionally?' asked Hester. 'I've never seen such a huge animal. He makes two of Ned.'

'He won't hurt him. Why don't you have a bath and an early night? We'll carry on in the morning. Soon have you straight.'

'Sounds good to me.' Hester yawned widely. 'I'll find Ned and then follow your excellent advice.'

When Ned was tucked up in his new bedroom, however, Hester found it difficult to leave the quay. The April day had been bright and blowy and now, though the wind had dropped, it was still cold. A small flock of dunlin was running before the tide, which was creeping in over the mud, and a robin was singing in Hattie's orchard. Hester wrapped the large shawl more firmly round her and wandered out on to the deserted hard. The peace was almost unnerving to one who had lived in London for twelve years, and she shivered in the chill evening air. Slowly she became aware of a gentle plashing and presently she saw Joss rowing slowly and peacefully up the creek. She watched the water rippling away from the dipping oars, marvelled at how effortlessly the boat moved and saw him hesitate fractionally when he glanced back across his shoulder and saw her leaning on the wall.

As he came abreast with *Westering* he raised a hand to her. 'Welcome to Abbot's Mill Creek.' His voice carried easily across the water.

'Thank you.'

There was a short silence whilst Joss kept the dinghy steady. He glanced at her and saw that she was watching him as she leaned on the wall.

'Care for a trip across the creek?'

'Heavens!' She sounded surprised but pleased. 'I've never been in a boat before.'

Joss rowed along to the slip. 'Never been in a boat!' he said. 'Disgraceful. Think what you've missed.'

'Now, if I ask you if it's really as nice as all that, you can go on being Ratty and tell me that there's nothing like messing about in boats.'

She continued to lean on the wall regarding him with a mischievous smile until he'd jumped ashore.

'Come on then, Moly,' he said. 'We'd better start your education. I'm sure you've done enough spring-cleaning for today.'

She laughed as she went down the slip. 'Just a very quick one, then. Ned might wake and wonder where he is.'

Joss handed her carefully into the dinghy, pushed off and climbed in, settling himself at the oars. 'He'll be able to see us from his bedroom window,' he said. 'Moving in OK?'

Hester nodded and hugged herself in the shawl. 'It's wonderful,' she said dreamily. 'We love the cottage. And what about you? Are you off on your voyage this summer?'

'Difficult to say,' said Joss evasively. 'Still got a lot to do. It'll be a bit of a push to get away before the bad weather starts.'

Hester gazed round at the stillness and the beauty. 'Won't you miss it all quite dreadfully?' she asked.

'Yes,' said Joss, after a moment or two. 'Yes, I think I probably shall.'

The evening was cold enough for Sarah to light the drawing-room fire and now she sat opposite Nick, pretending to read her library book. Since her confrontation with Cass in the autumn it was as if her emotions had been stilled, set like a fly in amber. When she'd returned home from the mill, constraint on both sides kept them at a distance from each other. Sarah knew exactly how Nick felt about her flight to the mill, her refusal to talk to him when he telephoned and her disloyalty in telling Hattie what had happened. In her view, however, he had no right to either resentment or self-pity and his cool and slightly wounded attitude had no effect on her.

Sarah, realising that she'd read the same paragraph three times, turned the page. Nick, immersed in *The Times*, cleared his throat. She looked round the familiar room with its elegant pieces, expensive hangings and rugs, original watercolours and cool colour schemes. Her workbox with the latest tapestry on its frame stood on a low stool by her chair whilst Nick's journals and books were piled tidily on the small table beside his larger armchair. The result was restful, though there was nothing cosy about it, and the room pleased her. She looked upon it as an achievement – a perfect marriage of wealth and good taste – but this evening she caught herself wondering how different it might have been if they'd had children. Would Nick have strayed quite so often? Might children have held him when she couldn't? She thought of sticky fingers on the covers, muddy shoes on the chairs, toys strewn across the floor and shook her head. She knew deep down that she was not cut out for motherhood. Nick had answered all her needs, fulfilled all her requirements and she needed no one else. Even now, with this unspoken barrier between them, she regretted nothing.

Nick turned a page of his newspaper and shook out the sheets. Sarah stared at the newsprint, imagining his face behind it, trying to will a measure of feeling into the indifference that held her. When he realised that his hurt disapproval was not moving her to make efforts to dispel it, he'd become anxious. By then it was too late. The ice had already chilled the searing rage and resentment that had sent her to Hattie, sealing in her pain, and she was unresponsive to his anxiety. The only time she'd shown any emotion was when she told him that she'd put the cottage in Shropshire up for sale.

'But why?' He'd asked the question before he was overcome by confusion.

'*Why*?' Sarah stared at him incredulously. 'You actually ask me *why*?'

He'd flushed a dark unbecoming red and she'd continued to stare at him, a look of contempt that he'd never seen before curling her lips. He knew at once that this was not the time for bravado.

164

'I'm sorry,' he said. 'It was a stupid, insensitive question.'

'Yes it was.' Still she stared at him. 'Did you really imagine that I'd be able to go there again?'

There was a kind of amused disdain in her voice which was far more worrying than anger and Nick felt the stirrings of real fear. Could it be possible that this time he'd really gone too far? Dwelling on her indiscretions with Hattie had helped to keep thoughts of his own shocking behaviour well to the back of his conscious mind but now he was obliged to think of the enormity of his request. To save his reputation he'd been more than ready to sacrifice Sarah's finer feelings but surely she should realise that they were working as a team here; that it had been for the benefit of both of them that the affair had to be stopped.

'I realise,' he began, hesitated and then rushed on, 'I realise how very much I've hurt you . . .'

'Do you?' Her voice still held that extremely unpleasant note. 'Do you, really, Nick?' She laughed a little. 'I wonder.'

He glanced at her and felt almost frightened by the glitter in her steely grey eyes.

'I was thinking about us,' he pleaded, abruptly shedding his pride. 'Can't you understand that? Nothing must be allowed to come between us.'

She laughed then and, once again, it had the ring of genuine amusement that chilled him. 'And what were you thinking about when you made love to Cass at our cottage? In our bed? You didn't consider it to be the sort of thing that might come between us?'

He flushed again but still she stared at him, refusing to let him off the hook.

'Please.' He closed his eyes for a second as though overcome by the indelicacy of her question and she gave a derisive snort.

'Grow up, Nick, why don't you?' she said contemptuously and he looked at her in amazement, unable to believe his ears. 'I've had enough!' she cried, answering that look. 'D'you understand? Enough of your philanderings and lyings and cheatings. I've turned a blind eye all these years and now you've made me look at you, fair and square. *You* made me look, Nick, and I don't like what I see.'

'But, Sarah, please.' Fear showed in his face and for once in his life he forgot himself completely. 'Don't be like this, please. I know I've behaved badly but it got out of hand. It's you I want, you know that, the others mean nothing.'

She gave an exclamation of distaste and turned away from him.

Thoroughly frightened now, he went after her and seized her arm. 'Stop!' he cried. 'Listen to me. Give me a chance to explain.'

'I'm not interested.' She jerked her arm free. 'Don't worry, I'm not going to leave you or make a fuss. I just don't want to think about you at all at the moment.'

'Don't you love me any more?' He still looked frightened.

'No,' she said indifferently, after a moment. 'No, I don't think I do.' And she'd walked out, leaving him staring after her.

Now, sitting by the fire, her library book abandoned, she wondered if it were true. Such callous indifference to her feelings, his assumption that her love for him would forgive him anything, had come as a terrible shock to her. It had shattered her self-deception beyond repair and she could no longer close her eyes to his weaknesses. Did she still love him? For a moment a sense of loneliness overwhelmed her. They continued to live together, sharing the house but very little else. By an unspoken agreement Nick now slept in his dressing room and mealtimes were conducted as though they were two strangers sharing a table at a hotel. Sarah stared into the flames. Did she really want to go on like this month after month? She remembered that happy period of time before Nick met Cass and felt a terrible pang of longing. Could it be possible that, having had such a severe lesson, Nick might now be ready to settle down? And, if so, did she care any longer? She thought again of those idyllic months and felt that weakening loneliness stir within her.

She raised her head to look at him and found that he'd lowered the paper and was watching her. He looked so unhappy that she stretched out a hand to him without thinking. He cast his newspaper aside and reached for her, slipping from his chair so that he was kneeling beside her. He bent his head over her hand, holding it against his cheek and she raised her other hand and lightly touched his hair.

'Forgive me, Sarah. Please forgive me,' he said rapidly without looking at her. 'I've been such a bloody fool but I swear that I never will be again. I've been so lonely, Sarah.'

He looked up at her and she saw there were tears in his eyes. Part of her seemed to be standing back, watching cynically, warning her, but another part, the lonely, weak, hungry part, smiled at him and nodded and suffered him to put his arms round her.

Hattie read Sarah's letter with cynicism mingled with sympathy, understanding why Sarah had chosen to write instead of telephoning as usual. Now that the place in Shropshire had sold – Sarah wrote – they were thinking of buying a holiday cottage on the north coast of Devon and were going off for a couple of weeks to have a look round and see what was on the market . . .

Hattie finished the letter and shrugged. Well, after all, why not? Sarah would never leave Nick so why not bury the past and get on with it? She'd noticed a placatory, wistful touch, almost as if Sarah needed Hattie's approval – she was well aware that Sarah expected her to despise her for giving in – but Hattie could see no point in them living in misery for the rest of their time together. Nick hadn't changed. It was simply that Sarah had been forced to confront the truth about him. Maybe, when the shock was over, she'd find that very little had changed. If a second honeymoon in Lynton – or wherever it was – gave them a new *modus vivendi* then good luck to it! Hattie gathered the sheets together and stuffed them back in the envelope. She'd telephone later and tell her not to be a silly moo and to have a wonderful time. All this fuss about a simple biological urge!

Thank goodness, thought Hattie, finishing her breakfast, thank goodness that I know nothing about love!

Chapter Twenty-One

James drove out of Dartmouth on a hot June afternoon and headed for home. He could hardly believe that he'd been living in the mill cottage for nearly a year now and yet, sometimes, he felt as if he'd been there all his life. His romantic passion for Miggy remained unchanged. She was his ideal of the perfect woman, pretty, funny, gentle. During the months that she'd been pregnant he'd had several long chats with her in the summerhouse on the long sloping lawn and she'd told him about her life with Patrick and the difficult years after his death. He'd read between the lines about her time with Stephen and recognised the strength that lay behind her vulnerable appearance. The few girls that he'd met since could in no way measure up to this illusion of perfection but James was quite content with his life as it was for the present.

It was rather like living in an extended family and he was fond of all of them. Hattie and Joss had been preoccupied of late with the war in the Falklands and had spent hours listening to news bulletins, scouring the newspapers and discussing it endlessly. He sensed that they were both rather disappointed when a ceasefire was agreed – although they had been distressed by the loss of lives – and their on-going wrangle regarding the superiority of Navy over Army and vice versa had been temporarily shelved during the months of the war.

James turned off at the Sportsman's Arms and thought about Hester. It was nice to have a neighbour, especially a friend of Miggy's, and he was already fond of the small solemn Ned. He'd taken him sailing several times, with Daisy keeping a firm eye on him, but he was a rather nervous little boy and James always waited now for Ned to ask if he could join them rather than suggesting it himself. He feared that he might feel obliged to accept and James wasn't at all certain that Ned was particularly keen. Daisy was still a constant companion. Since it never occurred to James that a girl of thirteen could imagine herself in love with a young man of twenty-three he felt no strain or embarrassment in her company.

She was straightforward and unaffected and, if he thought about it at all, he simply guessed that her predilection for his company was because he was the one nearest to her in age and – even more likely in his view – he owned a Mirror dinghy.

Any romance in the creek was definitely between Joss and Hester, in James's opinion. They were being extremely cautious but James had his suspicions. When Joss announced that *Westering* wouldn't be ready to sail before the bad weather set in, James felt they were confirmed. Joss had looked extremely self-conscious when Hattie pulled his leg about it.

'You've had enough time to *build* a boat by now!' she'd cried. 'What more can you possibly do to her?'

And when Joss had muttered about various jobs still needing to be done and wanting her to be in first-class condition, she'd made a rude derisive noise.

'Pooey!' she'd said. 'You're like a finicky old man with that boat. If you clean and polish her any more there won't be any wood left. Still, it merely backs up the old saying: "The Navy rules the world, the Army cleans it." We'd all be talking German by now if it'd been left to you lot.'

Nevertheless, James knew that Hattie would hate it when Joss left and he knew that Joss knew it, too. Underneath all the bickering and leg-pulling he sensed a deep strong affection and he'd sometimes wondered whether Joss would ever leave the creek at all. Now that Hester had arrived on the scene his doubts were even stronger and he could imagine how very hard it would be for Joss to sail away. James sometimes wondered how he'd feel when he had to go himself.

He swung the car into the lane that led down to the creek, slowing in readiness for the view that never failed to give him a thrill of pleasure, and then sped on down to the head of the creek. He pulled into the mill yard, dashed into his cottage and, within a few minutes, was hurrying out on to the hard clad in shorts and T-shirt, his suit and tie flung anyhow across his bed.

She was waiting patiently as usual, watching the tide. Her face lit up when she saw him but her voice was reproachful.

'I thought you were never coming. Hurry up! The tide's just on the turn.'

'Couldn't help it! Messrs Whinge, Whinge, Bellyache and Moan have kept me at it all day long.'

'I know. Shoulder to the wheel.'

'You're so right. Nose to the grindstone. But I'm here now.'

As they sailed down the creek they waved to Miggy, walking on the lawn with Marigold in her arms, and he wondered what it must feel like to be going home to a pretty loving wife and a baby with copper-coloured curls.

Hester stared at herself in the looking-glass. She strained her fringe back from her face, sucked in her cheeks and wondered what she'd look like with different spectacles. She felt edgy and dissatisfied with her appearance. Since her arrival at the creek she'd put on weight and, although she wasn't fat, she felt conscious today of those few extra pounds. She fetched a huge sigh, wandered over to the bedroom window and stared out at *Westering*. It had been the happiest summer she could ever remember. She'd forgotten that it was possible to be relaxed and at peace with herself. The dark times were behind her now and she was deeply thankful that she'd had the courage to make a new start. So she mustn't, simply mustn't, get involved again with anyone just yet. She wasn't ready for another commitment however tempting it might be. Hester sighed and then brightened as she saw Miggy coming across the quay.

Hurrying down, she flung open the door and went to meet her.

'Hi!' Miggy slipped an arm round her and gave her a quick hug. 'I wondered if you were feeling at a loose end with Ned starting back to school this morning?'

'I am feeling a bit mizzy.' Hester wrinkled her nose. 'I always miss Ned, especially at the end of the long summer holiday, but actually I think it's just one of those days anyway. How on earth are you going to cope with Daisy away all week?'

'It'll be very strange.' Miggy followed Hester into the kitchen and perched at the table. 'It's only weekly boarding but she wants to go and Georgia was very happy there. I shall miss her dreadfully, of course, but it'll probably be good for all of us.'

Hester frowned as she filled the kettle. 'You make it sound as if there's a problem.'

'Not a problem,' said Miggy slowly. 'But second marriages are always difficult, I suspect. You have all the hang-ups from the first one for a start.'

'I suppose that's true.' Hester sat down opposite. 'But you and Toby seem so happy.'

'We are,' agreed Miggy. 'But that doesn't mean that we don't have to work at it. I'm conscious that Daisy's not really his daughter and have to be rational and reasonable when he seems to put Georgia's interests before hers. And I find I can't forget what he says drove him mad about Ruth and try not to do the same things. And vice versa, of course.'

'Heavens!' Hester made a face. 'Sounds more complicated than I imagined.'

'You have to think about it. After all, you don't want to make the same mistakes you made the first time round.'

'But surely Toby doesn't find Daisy difficult? They seem so fond of each other.'

'Oh, they are. But having a girl of thirteen around can be . . .' Miggy hesitated. 'Distracting,' she said at last. 'We have very little privacy.'

Hester shrugged. 'That must be true of every married couple with growing children,' she protested.

'I'm sure it is,' said Miggy quickly. 'But it's less stressful if both of you are the child's parents. Daisy had a very hard time with Stephen and I can get quite neurotic about her and Toby not getting on. I worry if she cheeks him or if he gets cross with her although I know it can't be avoided.'

'But that happens all the time in all families,' said Hester consolingly.

'I know. But you see where there's a blood tie there's a different atmosphere. The step-parent can always deny responsibility for the inherited genes which make the child difficult or whatever. And the child can resent being controlled by someone who has no rights to tell him or her what to do. There's no recognition, if you see what I mean.'

'I had no idea there was so much to it.' Hester got up to make coffee. 'Poor Miggy. Sounds horribly complicated.'

'I'm incredibly lucky,' said Miggy at once. 'Toby's been terrific and Daisy's a sweetie. All I'm saying is, it's there. You have to watch for it. Make sure everything's balanced out fairly.'

'And that's why Daisy's going off to St Margaret's?'

'Daisy's going because she wants to,' said Miggy firmly. 'For her it's the Enid Blytons and all her other books coming true. And I'm not going to dissuade her because I think it will be very good for Toby and me to have some time together alone. I know there's Marigold but she's too young to be that sort of problem.'

'Well, it'll be very nice to have some time to yourselves.' Hester pushed a mug of coffee towards her.

'Yes, it will,' said Miggy frankly. 'Remember I've never been alone with Toby. Most couples have several years together before the children come along and plenty of years to cement the relationship before they're getting to the intrusive age. Toby and I have nothing to fall back on. No shared past. When we're with other people and the past is talked about, our anecdotes and memories are all related to other partners.'

'That must be rather bleak.' Hester looked at her compassionately. 'I've never thought about it before.'

'I hate it,' admitted Miggy. 'I feel insecure thinking that Toby had all those years and I wasn't part of them. And that's what I mean. Second marriages are fraught with difficulties that aren't present in the first relationship.'

'And is Ruth off your back now?'

'Yes, I think so. And Georgia's no problem. We've been terribly lucky. It will be interesting to see how Marigold grows up. So.' Miggy swallowed some coffee. 'Tell me about the job.'

'I've been lucky too. It's in a café and antique shop owned by a woman who has just split from her husband. She can't really manage on her own although her daughter helps out after school, at weekends and at holidays. It means I can do nine thirty till three so it'll fit in with getting Ned to and from school. No weekends, no holidays.'

'That really is terrific luck.'

'I just hope I'll be able to cope.'

'An antique shop and café in one,' mused Miggy. 'Rather a good idea.'

'I said I'd studied Art and Design but never mentioned that I had to give it up because I was pregnant with Jeremy. She was quite impressed.'

'Have you heard from them?' Miggy glanced quickly at Hester and saw her face change.

'Not recently,' she said shortly. 'They're both OK and that's the end of it as far as I'm concerned.'

There was an awkward silence.

'Sorry, Hes,' said Miggy. 'Tactless of me.'

'Never mind.'

'I must be off.' Miggy stood up. 'Toby's looking after Marigold but I mustn't stay too long. Like to come back for some lunch?'

'I won't, thanks. I want to get things well and truly up together before I start work on Monday. It'll be a bit of a shock to begin with.'

'OK. You know where we are if you feel low.'

'Thanks.'

Miggy set off along the hard and Hester watched her for a moment before turning back to the cottage. The Admiral strolled out of Hattie's front door and sat down, leaning against the door post, and Hester smiled at the sight of him; he looked so enormous and so comforting.

'Hello, Jelly baby,' she murmured, using James's name for him.

She sat down on the doorstep beside him and put an arm round his massive neck. He sighed deeply and she leaned against his great bulk, feeling comforted by him as usual. She was cross with herself for being touchy and remorseful for snapping at Miggy. The familiar guilt rose up to confront her and she felt that she might burst into tears. If only she could be free of the dreadful torment of guilt! Even Miggy didn't know the full extent of her shameful secret but Hester often wondered whether, if she were able to share it, confession might dispel the guilt a little. She could never share it! She took off her spectacles and rubbed her face in the Admiral's coat, hugging him fiercely, and he sat like a rock and licked her cheek comfortingly.

She didn't notice Joss till he was almost beside her and she stared up at him blindly, fumbling for her spectacles again.

'All this passion in broad daylight,' he said lightly. 'What a shameless flirt that dog is!'

Hester smiled a little shakily and hauled herself upright. 'He's blissful,' she said, copying his light tone. 'I wish I had one just exactly like him.'

'God forbid,' said Joss in horror. 'The creek simply isn't big enough for two monsters like Jellicoe!'

'And who is taking my dog's name in vain?' demanded Hattie, appearing from the hall. She'd seen Hester with the Admiral but guessed that she wanted to be alone. 'And what do you two want? You look like some sort of deputation standing on my doorstep.'

'I'm just off to Dartmouth,' said Joss, looking faintly embarrassed and attempting a casual air. 'I wondered if anyone needed anything?'

'Are you both going?' demanded Hattie with artless cunning. 'I might trust Hester to get me one or two things.'

'Well, actually . . .' Hester flushed brightly.

'Fine. I'll make a little list. That's very kind. Shan't be a sec.'

She hurried inside and Hester looked at Joss.

'Splendid,' he said, smiling at her. 'We'll have a sandwich at the Castle.'

'Oh.' She looked confused and rather shy. 'OK then. I'll get my bag.'

She vanished through her own front door and Joss was alone when Hattie returned with her list.

'You're an interfering old whatsit,' he told her.

'Well, honestly,' grumbled Hattie. 'All this pussyfooting about. That's the trouble with you Army types. So worried about your stiff upper lips you've forgotten what to do with them!'

'I shall ignore that extremely vulgar remark,' he said, folding up her list and putting it in his pocket. 'And I'll ask you to mind your own business in future.'

'All I can say is it's a bit pathetic when a pretty young woman has to sit hugging a dog because the young men round here are so wet. And furthermore—'

'Shut up, Hattie!' muttered Joss wrathfully as Hester emerged, 'or I'll murder you and throw your body in the creek.'

'Pooey!' said Hattie contemptuously. 'When you're big enough you'll be too old.' She beamed at Hester. 'Don't hurry back. Enjoy yourselves.'

They crossed the quay to Joss's car and he opened the door for her and gave her a little smile. Hester smiled back but she felt shaky inside and tried to pull herself together. They were both silent; Joss considering and rejecting various remarks, Hester tongue-tied with her foolish shyness. The easiness of their earlier days together had mysteriously slipped away and they were both conscious of the proximity of the other.

'It's so beautiful,' murmured Hester at last, taking refuge in banality. 'After London, it's just like being on a perpetual holiday.'

'I can believe that.' Joss thought quickly. 'Have you ever been round the coast to Torcross?'

Hester frowned a little. 'I think Miggy took us there,' she said. 'We went on a coastal road and the views were magnificent. We could see across to some lighthouse.'

'Like to do it again? We could get the shopping done quickly and go right out to Start Point. That's the lighthouse.'

'It sounds fun,' said Hester lightly. 'Why not? But I must be back in time for Ned.'

'Don't worry about that. We can pick him up on the way back. I promise we won't be late for him.'

175

'He panics, you see.' Her voice was suddenly anxious and her eyes were vulnerable behind the round granny spectacles. 'I can't seem to help him out of it.'

Joss felt a strange and most uncharacteristic urge to stop the car, throw his arms round her and ask her to let him look after both of them for the rest of their lives. Instead, he grasped the wheel firmly.

'He'll grow out of it,' he said confidently. 'Let him come to new experiences in his own good time but encourage him to try new things.'

Hester glanced at him gratefully, made as if to speak and changed her mind. She settled back comfortably in her seat instead and the silence this time was relaxed and companionable.

Chapter Twenty-Two

Toby strolled home from the boatyard through the wood, feeling deeply content with his lot. Much as he loved Daisy, the few days each week in which he now had Miggy to himself were very precious and he was enjoying watching Marigold grow without having to worry in case anyone was feeling left out. Like Miggy, he was aware of the strains of second relationships and, although he'd accepted that there was no way in which Ruth could be drawn back into the fold, he very much wanted to keep the four females attached to his establishment as happy as they could possibly be. He knew that both Hattie and Joss considered him an old softy but he had an inbuilt desire to make people happy and with Miggy and the girls he believed he was achieving just that.

At the point where the road was highest he paused to look down over the creek. The autumn day was misty and the ebbing tide receded gently from the foreshore where a few handsome oystercatchers searched for food, preceded by a flock of dunlin who probed the mud with sensitive bills. *Westering* floated motionless on her mooring, her mirrored reflection barely disturbed in the pewter-coloured water. How odd the creek would look without the ketch moored out in the deep water channel.

Some association of ideas caused Toby to look out across the creek to the *Abigail*, just visible, still standing on her legs. The Parkers had asked them to keep an eye on her until she was sold but neither Toby nor Joss was particularly keen to go aboard. There had been no sign of any interest and Toby wished that she'd sink at her mooring or that something would happen to prevent anyone else buying her. He watched the heron's slow, lazy flight upstream before continuing his walk back to the cottage, thinking now how extremely satisfying it would be if Joss and Hester made a match of it. They could settle in Number Two Mill Cottages and become a permanent part of the community.

'And what about Joss's voyage?' Miggy had asked when Toby divulged his plans for them.

'He could do shorter trips,' said Toby. 'Hester could go with him. After all, he'll have to settle down one day.'

'What an old matchmaker you are,' she'd teased him. 'You've got James earmarked for Georgia, now it's Joss and Hester. What about Daisy? Or Hattie for that matter?'

'I'm not worried about Hattie,' he'd told her quite seriously. 'Hattie won't go away. I'd just like to keep everyone here, that's all.'

She'd laughed at him, but not unkindly, and he accepted the fact that he had mother hen tendencies, preferring to keep his chicks under his wing if possible. Georgia had flown the nest, of course, but she returned regularly and had started to bring friends with her. Toby liked that. She'd been down for Regatta week and he'd piled them all into the Lysander and motored round to Dartmouth to watch the fireworks. There had been a kind of magic in being on the river in the dark with all the little boats dressed overall for the occasion as well as the Guardship, moored out in the channel, blazing with lights. Miggy and Georgia had prepared a picnic and Toby had opened some champagne and they'd eaten in the semi-darkness, ooh-ing and aah-ing as the fireworks burst and exploded high above. The embankment was packed with revellers and it was fun to call across to other boats and drink mugs of hot coffee as the evening grew cold.

Georgia had come to sit beside him as they motored back whilst Miggy went to check that Marigold was happy, tucked up on the bunk below.

'That was great, Dad,' she'd said and he'd grinned at her as her hair blew across her glowing cheeks. 'It was really good!' And she'd put her arm round him and hugged him tightly.

Remembering, Toby felt a glow of pleasure and was still smiling when he entered the kitchen and found Miggy leafing through a cookery book.

'You look happy!' She smiled back at him. 'I didn't expect you so early. Ready for lunch?'

'Well . . .' He pretended to hesitate. 'I remember you telling me once something about quickies before lunch. And I'm not so old yet that I mean a drink.' He raised his eyebrows at her and she laughed as he slipped his arms about her and pulled her up from her chair.

Sarah was ironing. Although the November morning was dank and drear the morning room was cheerful enough, with a coal fire

178

burning brightly in the small Victorian grate and the cherry glow of the velvet curtains reflecting warmly from the cream-painted walls. Sarah, who had an unexpected passion for the songs from the great musicals of the forties and fifties, was playing her record of *Oklahoma* but had long since ceased to listen to the well-known tunes. As she lifted one of Nick's shirts from the ironing board and hung it carefully on a hanger, her mind was far away. She took another shirt from the pile in the laundry basket and spread it out. As the iron swished softly to and fro, with little sizzles of water hissing as she pressed down hard on the creases, Sarah brooded.

The terrible truth was that her old love for Nick refused to be resurrected. The new cottage had, as yet, come to nothing although they'd gone to look at several places. The holiday was intended to be just what was needed to restore the old harmony between them but it simply hadn't succeeded. It was as if, since the confrontation with Cass, something essential to her relationship with Nick had died. She remembered the weeks of numbness that had followed and how she'd decided that something must be done about it. The idea of the cottage had been a lifeline which they both imagined would draw them back to the quiet waters of their previous existence until that frightful October day.

Sarah smoothed the cotton shirt over the board and topped up the iron with water from a small jug. The idea hadn't worked out. She'd gone with Nick across to the north coast, ready to look at cottages, determined to make a new start, and then, on the second or probably third morning whilst she was sitting in the warm May sunshine on the terrace of the small hotel, she'd realised that she couldn't be bothered. It occurred to her that she was indifferent where once she'd been anxious: uninterested in how he felt or what he did. Even the realisation wasn't much of a shock.

I've had enough, she found herself thinking. He's pushed me too far and I've had it.

She watched him coming back along the narrow street, a sheaf of house particulars in his hand, and discovered that she was completely unmoved by him. Hitherto she'd always felt a thrill of pride and love when she beheld his tall elegant figure and striking good looks. His grey hair was still thick, his figure was lean and upright and he dressed in expensively casual clothes, attracting attention wherever he went. This morning, however, as he came towards her, waving the papers and looking quite boyish in his enthusiasm, she'd felt a deadening sense of boredom. Whatever it was that had kept her tied to him, dependent on his love, anguished by his betrayals, was dead. She watched him with newly opened, cynical eyes and could hardly make the effort to return his wave.

What a fraud he is, she thought. He's continually playing a part. Oh, I can't be bothered!

She watched as a woman coming out of a shop bumped into him, feeling a mild contempt for his exaggerated bow of apology and his need for the stranger to find him attractive, even for that brief moment in time. He grimaced comically at Sarah as the woman went on her way – laughing at his antics and quick words – inviting her complicity, shrugging at the tiresome necessity to respond to the demands of others.

What an ass he is, she thought dispassionately and deliberately poured the last of the coffee into her cup so that there was none left when he arrived, slightly breathless, at the table.

Now, Sarah hung up the shirt and dragged a corduroy skirt from the pile, her mind still on the holiday. As they'd sat at the table, reading through the details from the estate agents, she'd decided to do nothing about her revelation until the holiday was over. She needed time to think. None of the houses had been quite suitable although, in a different frame of mind, she might have been more flexible. As it was they returned home with Nick feeling disappointed, believing that the purchase of a cottage would have been the answer to everything. He was well aware that, despite the softening on Sarah's part, things were far from right and she knew that he was beginning to lose patience.

Perfectly reasonable, thought Sarah, turning the skirt inside out and pulling it on to the board. It's more than a year now. I've simply got to make a decision.

The difficulty was, what should the decision be? There were several options. She could throw Nick out – after all, she had plenty of grounds for divorce. She could sell up, move right away and make a new life somewhere else. Or they could continue as they were. Depending on her mood, all three options held certain attractions. Sometimes, the idea of a completely new life was rather exciting; after all, Hattie had done it, coming out of a career and doing something quite different. On the other hand, she would hate to give up her charities and committees and leave her friends. The easiest option was to do nothing, simply carry on as they were, but Sarah knew that it couldn't remain an option for ever. It wasn't fair to either of them.

Sarah hung up the skirt, switched off the iron and went out to the kitchen to make some coffee. The real problem was that she was too old to have to take such drastic decisions. She was over fifty and the cold voice of common sense told her that she should be sensible. The telephone rang and she picked up the receiver, still holding the jar of coffee in her other hand. It was Nick.

'Sarah. Something's come up. I'm going to be a bit late tonight. This wretched client can't get in till seven o'clock and I simply must see him today.'

Sarah stood quite still, staring at the label on the jar, reading the brand name several times. 'Sorry. I was miles away. Right. Will you have eaten?'

'Oh, I think so.' He sounded easy, faintly indifferent to the idea of food, bored by the prospect of this tiresome client. 'Don't worry about me. You carry on.'

'I will,' she said. 'I'll do that. See you later.'

She replaced the receiver, still staring at the jar of coffee. She knew that tone in his voice, the ready excuses, the attempt to deceive.

'You bastard!' she said aloud. 'You bloody bastard.'

The telephone rang again and she snatched up the receiver.

'Sarah? It's John Marriott here. Are you well?'

'I'm very well, John.' Sarah summoned all her self-control. 'And you?'

'Quite well, my dear, thank you.' The voice that could sound testy if caught unawares was full of charm. 'I was hoping that you and Nick might come to my rescue tonight.'

'I'd be delighted to help, John. What is it?'

'Some friends have just rung up. They're down for two days and have asked me to meet them. The easiest thing is to take them out to dinner. I don't cope too well with entertaining since Margaret died and I was hoping that you and Nick could come along to help spread the load, as it were. I thought it was sensible to check with you rather than him.'

'I'd be delighted to come, John,' said Sarah at once. 'Nick can't, I'm afraid. He's just rung to say that he's got to meet a client. I can't understand why Nick's clients need to see him after office hours so often.'

There was a tiny silence whilst Sarah balled her hand into a fist and shook it exultantly at the absent Nick.

Get out of that, you bastard! she mouthed silently and hastily composed herself as John murmured tactful remarks about awkward clients.

'Never mind,' she said sweetly to him – she was very fond of

John – 'I'm quite used to it. But if I can be of any use to you, I should love to come. I get a bit lonely here on my own in the evenings.'

'I'd be delighted if you'd join us,' he said quickly. 'I'll collect you, shall I?'

'No, no. I'll drive myself in. You don't want to have to come right out here. What time shall I arrive?'

'Come and have a sherry with me first,' he said. 'That would be quite delightful. I don't have to tell you the way.'

'I'll be there at seven,' Sarah promised and hung up.

And that's dropped Nick right in it with the senior partner, she thought grimly.

She made her coffee and, ignoring the rest of the ironing, went upstairs to look out something attractive to wear for dinner that evening.

It was a very pleasant evening. John's friends were easy to talk to, the food was delicious and Sarah enjoyed herself. Later, when Sarah and John arrived back at his tall elegant town house overlooking the park John invited her in for some more coffee and she accepted readily. He made her comfortable by the fire, refusing to let her help him, and disappeared to the kitchen. Sarah stretched out her legs and lay back in the chair, feeling oddly youthful and daring. There was a heady sense of freedom in acting as she had this evening; going out to dinner with a man other than Nick, even if it were only dear old John whom she'd known for years. Sarah's eyes rested on a silver-framed photograph of Margaret – John's dead wife – which stood with others on a low table.

Sarah smiled at Margaret and Margaret smiled back; the rather fixed, gentle smile that she'd smiled for years. She'd been a tireless worker for charity, sat on endless committees and had entertained John's friends, smiling that same, slightly absent, set smile that hardly touched her eyes. She'd been efficient, self-effacing and completely forgettable except, presumably, by John. Sarah tried to remember how long she'd been dead – three years, four? – and sat up as John came in with the tray.

'Sorry to take so long.'

There was a little fuss as a table was drawn up and the coffee set on it and poured and another little bustle when he realised that he'd forgotten the sugar but, presently, they sat companionably sipping and talking over the evening.

'I've really enjoyed myself,' declared Sarah, pouring herself some more coffee. 'It's been such fun. We must do it again.'

She knew how ambiguous her words were and waited for him to pick up the gauntlet. Staring at the flames, she felt light-hearted and faintly mischievous and – quite unexpectedly – remembered the passionate young anaesthetist at *Haslar*. John meanwhile was looking at his coffee cup and trying not to misunderstand her.

'It was a most enjoyable evening,' he agreed cautiously.

Sarah recalled that he'd been forty years a lawyer and decided to give him a little nudge.

'You must get very lonely, John.'

'Yes, I do.' He sighed rather heavily and then smiled at her quickly. 'Only to be expected.'

'I get lonely, too,' said Sarah boldly. 'Nick seems to have these spells quite frequently when he's out in the evening an awful lot and away at weekends, as well.'

The silence that followed was charged with both unease and expectation.

'Nick has a very heavy work load,' began John loyally but with a certain amount of awkwardness. 'It must be very difficult for you sometimes, my dear . . .'

'Oh, it is.' Sarah threw caution to the wind, hearing Nick's voice in her head and knowing exactly what form his work was taking at this moment. 'Especially when the work load consists of an attractive young woman.'

This time the silence had both an appalled and an exultant quality.

'This . . .' began John, swallowing nervously, 'this is very distressing.'

'For you or for me?' asked Sarah sweetly. 'I don't wish to distress you, John. I'd hate that. As for me, I'm way past the distressed stage.'

'Oh, my dear.' John looked sadly at her. 'I'm so sorry. I suppose I imagined you didn't know. You've always behaved so beautifully . . .'

'So stupidly!' said Sarah bitterly. 'I've let him get away with it for far too long until he's demoralised me and I feel ridiculous. It's all over, John.'

He stood his cup back in its saucer and moved the table to one side, stretching out a hand to her. He looked shocked and Sarah felt rather taken aback by her own outspokenness.

'I'm sorry,' she said as she took his hand. 'It's really not your problem. I don't know quite what came over me.'

'Nonsense.' He squeezed her hand. 'We're old friends. I'm honoured that you should choose me as a confidant.'

'Oh, John.' Sarah shook her head and tried to laugh, wondering how he would react if she told him that she'd seen him as a way of getting her own back on Nick. 'I simply don't know what to do.'

'Then do nothing drastic for the moment.' He still held her hand.

'Typical lawyer's advice,' she said lightly, but when she looked at him she was surprised to see a twinkle in his blue eyes.

'Perhaps,' he said, and she felt a twinge of excitement at a note of complicity in his voice. 'But I suggest a touch of sauce to make it more palatable.'

'Sauce?'

'What's good for the gander is good for the goose,' he said blandly, and she stared at him in amazement. 'How about dinner next week?'

'I'd . . . I'd like that very much.'

'Excellent.' He gave her hand a final squeeze and stood up. 'I'm going to make some fresh coffee and then I suggest we make a date.'

When he'd gone, Sarah flopped back in her chair with a gasp and met Margaret's long-suffering smile. A terrible suspicion seized her. Was that fixed smile and the endless charity work a cover-up and a distraction for difficulties within her own marriage to John? And what if it was? Sarah closed her eyes and stretched luxuriously, a smile on her lips that was neither fixed nor long-suffering but merely triumphant.

Chapter Twenty-Three

For Christmas, Daisy gave Ned a fishing rod. Ever since a trip out to sea in the Lysander, when Ned had been wedged beside the helmsman and given a line to catch mackerel, he'd had a passion for fishing. To his amazement and enormous pride, he'd caught four mackerel and had the thrill of seeing them cooked for supper and eaten with relish. The joy of it had overborne his fear of the water and he sat on *Westering* by the hour, with borrowed tackle, hoping to repeat his good luck.

Knowing Daisy's intention – and with his own plans to further – Joss bought and presented him with the little dinghy that the Parkers had owned. Ned was cautious with his gratitude and Hester frankly appalled.

'He can't row,' she protested, 'and he can't swim properly either.'

'He can learn to do both,' said Joss gently, with memories of a skinny, undersized Daisy manhandling Toby's much larger, heavier dinghy. 'He needn't go far and he can have someone with him. But it'll make him independent. He can go fishing on his own.'

He stared back at the two pairs of slatey blue eyes looking at him anxiously from behind round owly spectacle frames. Ned and Hester looked at each other.

'I needn't go far,' repeated Ned hopefully, thinking about the mackerel and swallowing his fear.

'He can tie up at the quay,' Joss pointed out, 'or on one of my mooring ropes. Daisy will go out with him at weekends and I'll teach him to row to start with.'

'He'll have to wear his life jacket,' said Hester firmly, retrieving what she could of her control over Ned's welfare.

'Of course he will,' said Joss cheerfully, winking at Ned. 'We'll only do very short bursts to begin with.'

So, as the spring drew on, Ned and Joss, or Ned and Daisy, could be seen rowing slowly to and fro in the little dinghy and, by Easter, Ned was taking short trips alone and could be seen, tying up in different places, blond mop bent over his fishing rod, waiting for a mackerel. He caught an eel and many crabs but the mackerel continued to elude him unless Toby or Joss took him out to sea. Joss was more than happy to take Hester and Ned out in *Westering*, hoping to get them used to her, trying to make headway in his relationship with Hester.

She eluded him as the mackerel eluded Ned yet he was quite certain that she cared for him and tried to discover what it was that held her back. In the end, he talked to Toby who tried to reassure him.

'Miggy says it's because she had such a terrible time with that first husband of hers. And now she's moved and got a new job. Like starting a new life, I suppose. Perhaps it's too quick for another relationship yet. I can see that, can't you?'

'Oh yes, I can understand it,' said Joss somewhat desperately, 'but I can't sit here for ever, waiting. I look such a twit. Everyone knows that I could have got away last summer with a bit of an effort. What will people say when I don't go this summer either? Anyway, I want to get going!'

'I know you do,' said Toby compassionately. He was probably the only person who realised just how much Joss had put into *Westering* in preparation for his long-awaited voyage. 'Not that you have to worry about what people say. It's no one's business except yours. And Hester's.'

Joss sighed deeply and rubbed his hands over his face. 'I don't know how to handle it,' he admitted. 'I've never been in this situation before. We get so far and then a barrier comes down. It's so bloody frustrating!'

Toby put a consoling arm about his shoulders. 'You've just got to hang in,' he said. 'You must give her time, if that's what she needs.'

'You and Miggy didn't need time,' muttered Joss bitterly. 'You just grabbed each other and got on with it. It's simply that she doesn't love me enough.'

Toby racked his brain for comforting words and, finding none, hugged Joss briefly and released him. 'You mustn't give up. You're absolutely right for each other. Everyone says so.'

'Yes, well. I can't say it helps having everyone sitting round watching,' said Joss ungratefully.

Toby chuckled a little. 'That's the price you have to pay for us all being so fond of you,' he said sympathetically. 'Tough, isn't it?'

'Hmph!' Joss was not to be comforted.

Later, Toby spoke to Miggy about Hester.

Miggy put down her knitting and looked worried. 'There's been something she's never told me,' she said thoughtfully. 'To begin with she didn't mind being pregnant. She was quite batty about Phil and she was thrilled when they got married. She simply didn't believe it when he started being unfaithful and then she was very unhappy. We'd started to move in different worlds then, although we always stayed in touch, but she became . . . oh, sort of evasive, difficult to pin down.'

'You think she was hiding something?' guessed Toby when Miggy lapsed into silence.

'I *did* feel that a bit.' Miggy cudgelled her memory. 'She never seemed to want me to visit her at home. It was always somewhere else, a shop or little café.' She shrugged.

Toby frowned, hands in pockets, shoulders hunched. 'I wish we could do something.' He jingled the change in his pocket. 'It'll be a tragedy if Joss feels obliged to sail away and leave her to it.'

'We simply mustn't interfere,' cautioned Miggy at once. 'Even if he goes, he'll probably come back fairly quickly. It's a pity that he's always taken such a cynical view of love. Talk about the biter bit!'

'Perhaps she'll confide in you,' said Toby hopefully.

'Maybe.' Miggy picked up her knitting. 'You can't force that sort of thing.'

Hester sat on the edge of the quay, legs dangling and watched Ned rowing himself across the water towards *Westering*. Every now and again he glanced proudly at her and she waved encouragingly. He waggled his fingers, still clutching the oars, and turned his head, chin on shoulder, so as to see where he was going. Hester felt swamped with love and terror for him. He was so small and vulnerable; top-heavy in his life jacket, his face clamped in a frown of concentration. She saw him reach *Westering*'s mooring lines, ship his oars carefully, and tie his painter with small clumsy fingers.

'Getting on well, isn't he?'

Hester glanced round at Hattie and nodded. Hattie looked at her thoughtfully and Hester turned back to watch Ned who, having tied the dinghy to *Westering*, was now fumbling with his fishing tackle.

'Children are so agonising,' she said fiercely and Hattie heard her swallow.

'Dreadful,' she agreed. 'Do you ever know a moment of pure peace?'

'Very seldom.' Hester tried to laugh. 'They're so terribly vulnerable. And you realise that you're vulnerable too and become afraid to take chances.'

'Is that why you're holding Joss off?'

'Oh, Hattie,' said Hester, after a long silence. 'That's a bit below the belt, isn't it?'

'I expect so,' said Hattie cheerfully. 'I never abide by the rules. Waste of time I call it. Don't see the point of all this pussyfooting.'

Hester sighed and got to her feet, sticking her hands in her jeans pockets. 'I don't suppose you do. But it's not quite that simple.'

'People always say that when they're too cowardly to make decisions,' said Hattie brutally.

'You're on Joss's side.' Hester decided to adopt Hattie's own tactics. 'You just want what he wants.'

'Only if it's right for him. And for you.'

'How can we know that?' Hester looked at her and Hattie saw the anguish in her eyes. 'I'm afraid!'

'But why?' Hattie shook her gently by the arm. 'By all accounts it wasn't your fault that your marriage failed. You got trapped into marriage with the wrong man. Doesn't mean you'll make the same mistake again.'

Hester stared straight before her and Hattie felt a wave of compunction.

'You're quite right,' she admitted. 'I'm an interfering old busy-body. I just can't bear waste, that's all. And Joss is stupid enough to go off on his ridiculous voyage merely to save his face.'

'I don't know what to do.' Hester looked so wretched that Hattie felt really guilty.

'Come and have a cup of tea and we'll talk about something else. Or shall I bring it out here so you can keep an eye on Ned?'

'No, he's OK.' She cast a quick glance at the small figure hunched over his rod. 'Thanks.'

She followed Hattie into the mill, stepping over the Admiral, who lay across the doorstep in a deep sleep. Hattie bustled about trying to lift the atmosphere by chatting lightly about his ability to sleep through anything but Hester wasn't listening.

'I have another son, you know,' she said abruptly and Hattie was silenced. 'He's twelve. You've probably heard that I became pregnant when I was barely nineteen and married Phil straight away.' She laughed a little, mirthlessly. 'I was secretly delighted. I adored Phil and I couldn't wait to be a wife and mother.' She wandered over to the sink and stared out across Hattie's geraniums to the hedge that bordered the lane. 'When I knew there were other women I felt sick. I coped with it very badly. Phil used to laugh about it, tell me about the women he went with. It turned him on.' She took off her spectacles and folded her arms across her breast, hunching her shoulders, gathering herself together. Hattie watched, transfixed; afraid to move and break the spell. 'I began mistreating Jeremy,' she said dully. 'I took it out on him. He looked very like Phil and I found I was just taking out all my hate and degradation on him. Before it could get too bad Phil's mother came and took him away.' She turned round to face Hattie who was shocked to see tears streaming down her face. 'I loved him, you see. I did love him. But I couldn't help myself. I used to scream and shout . . .' She shook her head and wiped her cheeks with her fingers.

'But you never touched Ned?'

Hester shook her head. 'It was all over by then. Phil's mother was always at him to go back home. She hated it that he'd married a British girl. She came over to see him and realised what was happening with Jeremy. She said that we must go straight back to New Zealand with her or she'd tell the police and have Jeremy taken away. I refused to go. I knew that it would be hell living under her thumb and anyway, Phil and I had nothing left.' She sniffed, rubbing her sleeve across her eyes. 'I didn't tell them I was pregnant.'

'You poor child,' said Hattie gently.

'I had to lie all the time. I couldn't bear for people to know about Jeremy so I could never invite people home. My parents knew. They had to when Phil took him back to New Zealand. His mother told them. My mother's never forgiven me. She thinks it's shameful that a mother can mistreat her own child, you see. She looks upon me as a kind of monster, I can see it in her eyes. I don't go home any more.'

Hester put her spectacles on whilst Hattie made the tea, allowing her time to pull herself together.

'I think it's important,' she said at last, pushing a mug of tea across the table towards Hester, who still leaned against the sink, 'that you learn to forgive yourself.'

'How can that be done?' Hester didn't move.

'Try to see what appalling stresses you were under. Make the allowances you'd make for others in your situation.'

Hester shook her head stubbornly. 'There can be no excuse for hitting a child. I know plenty of people do it but you hear the reactions too, don't you? On the bus, in cafés, in the school playground. "I don't know how a mother could do it!" they say.'

'That's because they're basically dishonest people,' said Hattie calmly. 'I know that many young mothers under enormous strain, mental or physical, have an urge to be violent and many succumb to it. Naturally they don't have the courage to own up to it publicly. A friend of mine told me that she always had to go out of the room leaving her baby to cry because she knew if she stayed she'd beat its head on the wall simply to shut it up.'

'But she didn't actually do it, did she?'

'Only because they were well enough off to get an *au pair* to take the strain. It always amazes me that the human race expects so much of its poor puny little self. Hubris, I call it. We're weak, foolish and frail yet we have such great ideals. Wonderful, of course, and essential but we don't have to punish ourselves for ever if we slip a little. Drink your tea.'

'Oh, Hattie.' Hester smiled weakly but her lips trembled. 'D'you think I haven't tried to rationalise my behaviour? D'you think I *want* to go through life hating myself?'

'Probably,' said Hattie cheerfully and Hester's head snapped up and she stared at her. Hattie nodded back. 'It can be easier sometimes to wallow in your comfortable familiar self-pity than to try a bit of straight thinking or forgiving yourself so that you can put past failures behind you and stop being a pain in the arse.'

Hester looked so shocked that Hattie was obliged to stare out the pain in her eyes so that she could continue to use the knife on the growth that was destroying Hester's life.

'Forgiving yourself means growing up and moving on. Knowing your weaknesses and turning them into strengths is a full-time job and very painful to boot. Much easier to hug your failures to you until the hatred of them turns into a kind of love and they grow until they block your sight and distort your vision. Self-honesty is an incredibly painful acquisition and the most wonderful asset you can have. But, my God, you have to work at it!'

Hester had turned quite white. She moved forward to the table and sat down as though she were drunk. Her heart was hammering so loud that she thought Hattie must hear it. She set her tea down and burst into tears. Flinging her arms out straight across the table and laying her head on them, she wept as though her heart must break. Hattie stood up and came round the table

190

to her. She stood beside her, stroking the blonde hair that spread across Hester's arms.

'Who was it,' she mused aloud, 'that said, "If you cannot forgive yourself you cannot hope to forgive others"? I'm sure that's true. Perhaps the time's come for you to give it a try. I'm going out to check on Ned. For goodness' sake drink that tea!'

Hattie went out and stood on the quay and stared at Ned as he sat in his little dinghy. Joss stood above him on *Westering*'s deck and she raised a hand in answer to his salute.

And who the hell d'you think you are, she asked herself grimly, preaching to people? Holding forth as if you know it all! You who've never been married or had a child. Or known love.

She gave a snort of self-disgust and, seeing the Admiral pottering on the hard, she called to him and set off up the lane through the woods.

A little while later, Hester came out of the mill. She stood uncertainly on the quay and Joss straightened up and watched her. She waved to him and then cupped her hands to her mouth.

'Would someone like to give me a lift over?'

She saw Ned's head come round and then tip back to look up at Joss and she heard the faint murmur of their voices. Ned waved and Joss climbed down the ladder, dropped into his own dinghy and was soon rowing to meet her. Up in the woods, Hattie watched Hester climb into the boat, settle herself in the stern and Joss row slowly back to *Westering*. With a sigh she turned away, put her hands into her pockets and plunged on through the trees, the Admiral running ahead.

'Dear God,' she muttered. 'Forgive me for an interfering old woman.'

Chapter Twenty-Four

In late June, Miggy drove through the deep lanes to collect Georgia from the station at Totnes. Her university term was finished and she'd decided to come early for her holiday this year. Miggy was pleased. It meant that Toby would have time with her before Daisy arrived home for the summer. She wondered how Georgia would get on with the twenty-month-old Marigold, strapped into her seat in the back, sucking her thumb peacefully as she stared out at the hedgerows. The powdery flowerets of the umbelliferae nodded at the car windows and hedges were twined and laced with honeysuckle and dog rose. Bees clambered clumsily into the speckled trumpets of the tall foxgloves and, through an open gate, Miggy caught a glimpse of a kestrel, hanging motionless in the milky blue sky, its glittering eye fixed on the swaying grasses in the field below.

How happy I am, she thought. How happy and how lucky.

She remembered, as she often did, how she'd met Toby in the Royal Castle and felt the usual twinge of fear as she realised how easily they might have missed each other. It didn't bear thinking about. No Marigold – Miggy glanced instinctively in the car mirror – and none of this deeply satisfying contentment. Daisy was settled and happy at school and – apart from her continuing, oddly determined love for James – growing up very satisfactorily.

Her thoughts swung to Joss and Hester. One morning, about a month before, Hester had telephoned and asked if Miggy would come and see her at the cottage. Puzzled at her rather odd tone, Miggy had waited for Toby to come back from the boatyard and set off. Hester was waiting for her. She had a strained look about her and had plunged without preamble into the terrible story of her marriage. Stunned with shock, Miggy had listened in complete silence until Hester had stopped speaking and then she'd gathered the stiff, unyielding form into her arms and hugged her until Hester had relaxed and hugged her in return so that she could barely breathe.

'I'm sorry I lied to you, Miggy,' she said more than once. 'I couldn't bear for people to know about Jeremy.'

And Miggy, who'd experienced exhaustion and frustration – especially when she'd been doing three jobs at once to support Daisy after Patrick's death – and who knew how easily the barrier between self-control and madness can be crossed, merely hugged her tighter.

'I *do* hear from him,' Hester said later, after the emotion was passed. 'But I think Phil's mother censors his letters and she'd certainly keep him turned against me. I think about him and what he must be like now. Seven years! I haven't seen him since he was five years old but I daren't suggest that he visits me. I can't bear the thought of him politely saying "no thanks".'

Miggy looked at her in horror. 'They had no right to take him,' she said. 'No right at all.'

'I know that now.' Hester nodded. 'But I was so afraid, you see. And I actually thought it would be better for him. He must have hated me. I hated myself.'

Miggy watched her, understanding more fully her terror that something might happen to Ned and her almost pathological fear for him. How frightful to know that your child was growing up somewhere beyond your knowledge! What a price to pay for cracking under strain and pressure that was simply too much to bear!

As she drove down the hill into Totnes and turned into the station, Miggy was conscious yet again of her own good fortune. At least, however, it seemed that Hester and Joss were moving forward now and Miggy could only assume that Hester had been able to tell him, too. She'd agreed to accompany Joss on a short cruise, taking Ned along with them, planning to be back in the creek for September.

As Miggy parked the car, the train pulled in. She got out quickly, scanning the passengers and saw Georgia walking up the platform, lugging her case. Miggy hurried to meet her.

'I can't believe that you're twenty,' she said to her, holding her at arm's length. 'It doesn't seem possible. You look terrific!'

Georgia grinned. 'I'm getting old,' she said, and bent to look through the window at her small half-sister.

'Hi,' she said, taking an old-fashioned rag doll with long dark plaits from her bag and passing it in through the window. Marigold took it, turning it over slowly and examining it solemnly.

'Dolly,' she said carefully, at last, and beamed at Georgia who ruffled her curls. Miggy, now in the driver's seat, leaned over to have a closer look. 'It's mine!' said Marigold firmly, clutching it to her chest possessively and Georgia laughed as she climbed into the front beside Miggy.

'Straight home?' she asked, starting the engine. 'Or tea in the town and a quick look at Salago first?'

Their eyes met and they grinned at each other.

'What d'you think?' said Georgia, settling back happily as Miggy turned left and headed towards the town.

James came out of Plymouth Crown Court, hesitated for a moment, and headed for Carwardine's. Plymouth was busy with shoppers and tourists and he hoped he'd find a seat. Inside, inhaling the evocative and mouthwatering scent of fresh coffee, he glanced round, his eyes accustoming themselves to the gloom after the bright day outside. Almost immediately, he recognised the senior partner of Murchison, Marriott. He was talking animatedly to a woman who was partly turned away from him but he glanced up for a moment and paused, frowning a little. James smiled at him.

'Good morning, sir,' he said. 'I'm James Barrington. I did my summer placements with your firm.' He looked at his companion and recognised Mrs Farley. 'Hello,' he said. 'How nice to see you.'

'How are you?' Sarah moved along for him and he sat down beside her. 'How are things at the creek?'

'Very good, thank you. I can't tell you how grateful I am for recommending me to Miss Wetherall.'

'I'm sure she's delighted to have you there. Give her my love and tell her I'm looking forward to seeing her on Thursday.'

'I will indeed.' James ordered some coffee and looked enquiringly at the other's empty cups.

'Not for me,' said John Marriott. 'I must get back.' He hesitated for a moment. 'Must be nearly finished with your articles, aren't you?'

'They're throwing me out in October.' James grimaced sadly. 'I've got a few interviews coming up but I shall be sad to leave Dartmouth.'

'A friend of mine in Oxford might be able to fit you in. Like me to have a word?'

'That would be brilliant.' James's face glowed. 'Thank you, sir.'

'Don't promise anything. I'll be in touch.' John Marriott got to his feet and looked at Sarah.

'See you soon.' She smiled at him conspiratorially and James didn't see the tiny wink she gave him. 'Thanks for the coffee.'

'It was a very great treat to meet you unexpectedly,' he said somewhat ponderously.

'So,' said Sarah, when he'd gone. 'I think I'll have another coffee, after all.'

She nodded to the waitress and James decided that she was enjoying some sort of secret joke. A tiny smile twitched at her lips and her eyes gleamed.

'You're looking very well,' he said before he could stop himself. 'Much younger,' and caught himself up with a flush of embarrassment.

Sarah burst out laughing and, relieved, James laughed with her.

'I didn't mean to be rude,' he assured her but she shook her head and tapped him on the arm.

'Never apologise for telling a woman she's looking good,' she said. 'Now, what are you up to in Plymouth?'

'Morning in court,' sighed James. 'Rather depressing.'

Sarah smiled at him and he had the odd feeling that, given the chance, he'd probably like her very much.

'Have you got to hurry back?' she asked.

'Not really.'

'Then let me treat you to lunch and you can tell me all the latest news from Abbot's Mill Creek.'

When he arrived back at the office, John put his head into Nick's rooms.

'How are you, Nick?'

'Well, John. Very well, thanks. And you?'

'Can't complain. Wanted to invite you and Sarah to the cottage for the weekend. Thinking of selling it at the end of the summer so I want to make the most of it.'

Nick feigned disappointment. 'Don't think I can, this weekend, John. What a damned shame. Got this blasted case . . .'

'I am sorry.' John pretended to hesitate. 'No good hoping Sarah would take pity on me, I suppose? Got the Anstruthers staying.' This was a couple that had returned to Scotland the day before. 'I find the entertaining a bit of a strain since Margaret died . . .'

He watched hope and relief dawn in Nick's eyes. 'Well, I don't see why not. Lovely change for her. She loves Salcombe and she's got quite hooked on the sailing. It's too boring for her when I'm closeted with work.'

'You work too hard, Nick.' John decided to push his luck. 'Surely you could take a few hours off and come over. Get in a bit of sailing yourself.'

Nick pursed his lips and shook his head regretfully.

'Not a chance, John. Thanks anyway. But if you'd like to phone Sarah . . .'

'I might just do that. If you've no objection.'

'Don't be silly. Delighted for her to have a bit of fun. Oh, regards to Sally and Mike.'

'To . . . ? Oh, of course.'

John went out and Nick shook his head tolerantly. Poor old buffer. Must be pushing sixty-five. Getting past it a bit. Couldn't even remember the names of his guests. Still, Nick thought, this would get him right off the hook, if only Sarah would go. There was no doubt that John had become much friendlier during the last nine months and Sarah's willingness to act as hostess for him nicely cemented the work he'd put in regarding his promotion to senior partner when John retired. A whole weekend . . . Nick pushed back his chair and went to the window. Staring out over the chimney pots of Plymouth he allowed himself a measure of self-pity. Sarah had changed, no doubt about it, and no one could blame him if he was obliged to look for a little comfort elsewhere.

Later in the afternoon, John telephoned Sarah. 'Swallowed it hook, line and sinker,' he said gleefully. 'You have official permission to spend the weekend with me.'

Sarah's chuckle sounded in his ear. 'You're a wicked old man,' she said. 'Margaret wouldn't like it!'

'Margaret's not going to get it,' he said daringly, and she gave a shout of laughter and hung up on him.

Still later, Nick made a telephone call. 'All's well, my darling. A weekend to ourselves. Sure you can borrow the flat?'

'No problem. How did you manage it?'

'Aha! Little girls shouldn't ask questions.'

'You're a very naughty boy and I'm sure your wife wouldn't like it.'

'My wife's not going to get it,' said Nick. 'See you on Friday.'

'What are you up to?' asked Hattie, looking at Sarah's bright eyes and noticing the spring in her step. 'James said you were looking very young and I can see what he means.'

'What a delightful boy he is,' said Sarah with a great deal of feeling. 'I'm sure he'll go far.'

'Oxford, by the sound of it,' said Hattie glumly. 'What with Joss and Hester going off and now James, it'll be very empty round here.'

Sarah forgot her own jolly plans and looked compassionately at her old friend. 'You've allowed yourself to get too attached to them,' she said sympathetically. 'But they'll be back. Well, Joss and Hester will. You said they're only going for the summer.'

'Yes, that's true.' Hattie sighed and frowned. 'I feel a bit down,' she admitted. 'A feeling of doom and gloom. Don't know why.'

'I'm sorry,' said Sarah inadequately. She felt guilty for feeling so bright when Hattie was so miserable.

'Never mind.' Hattie shook off the depression which threatened her. 'What have you been up to? How are things with you and Nick? I thought you said everything was over.'

'In a way it is. I told you, I just couldn't get the feeling back. No matter what I did, nothing worked. It was dead.'

'That's very sad,' said Hattie. 'It really is. You loved him so much.'

'I know.' Sarah stared at her, still surprised after all these months. 'It's rather frightening. One always feels that love should last for ever.'

Hattie snorted. 'Well, given that it so obviously doesn't, I can't imagine why one should think anything of the sort. Definitely a triumph of hope over experience as far as I can see. But in your case, your love had gone on so long and in the face of so much adversity that it came as a shock, I must admit.'

'To me too.' Sarah shrugged. 'It was the suddenness of it, I think.'

'Not,' said Hattie, 'that I don't think you had excellent reason to stop. In your place, I'd have stopped years before. And that business with that woman . . .' Hattie shook her head. 'Unbelievable!'

'I think that was the turning point.' Sarah's face was sombre as she remembered it.

'I'm not surprised. But you seem to have recovered, if you don't mind my saying so. All that stuff about buying another cottage and then deciding you were going to leave him . . .'

'I know. I changed my mind.'

'That much is clear to me,' said Hattie with faint sarcasm. 'What I want to know is – why?'

Sarah dithered and Hattie watched her with growing puzzlement. Sarah had always been so sensible, so moral, so proper, so ready to condemn those who fell short of her standards and here she was behaving like a probationer of eighteen.

'Sarah!' said Hattie in her commanding officer's voice. 'Pull yourself together. You've been hinting and blathering all day. What are you up to?'

'I'm having an affair with John Marriott,' blurted Sarah, and stared at Hattie in alarm. 'Oh hell! I wasn't going to tell you!'

'Why not?' cried Hattie indignantly. 'Hell and damnation! I'm your oldest friend and you weren't going to tell me when you performed your first truly human action?'

'Oh, Hattie!' Sarah began to laugh. 'I thought you'd think it shocking. He's sixty-three and I'm fifty-three . . .'

'Pooey!' said Hattie impatiently. 'What's that got to do with anything?'

'It's wonderful,' admitted Sarah blissfully. 'I feel like a whole new person.'

'And I take it Nick doesn't know?'

'Heavens no! He's got a fancy woman at the moment, so he thinks he's deceiving me without having a clue what John and I are up to.'

Hattie pushed her way into the larder, attempting to dislodge the slumbering Admiral, and seized a bottle.

'We must drink a toast,' she said. 'This moment must not pass unrecorded.'

Sarah found two glasses, giggling helplessly. 'What's the toast?' she asked.

'We're drinking to the splendid occasion of your finally becoming a fully paid-up member of the good old human race,' said Hattie. 'Here's to you, Sarah. Go for it, girl!'

They were still laughing when James put his head round the door.

'Hello.' He raised his eyebrows at the two of them sitting there with a nearly empty bottle on the table and grinned in sympathy. He recognised the results of a good old alcoholic binge when he saw them.

'Come and join us,' said Sarah, remembering what he'd said about her looks. 'We can always do with a young man.'

'Watch her,' warned Hattie. 'I'm going for another bottle

and if she lays a finger on you – scream! Jellicoe will rescue you.'

'I shall do nothing of the sort,' said James daringly, entering with alacrity into the spirit of the thing. 'I know a good thing when I see one. I should be so lucky.'

'Dear boy,' said Sarah, much moved. 'I shall make certain that you get that job in Oxford. Meanwhile we're going to get thoroughly pissed.'

'Good idea,' said James at once. 'Hang on. I'll get another glass.'

Later, with Sarah asleep in the spare room, Hattie marvelled at the change in her. She'd been so obsessed by Nick for the last twenty years that Hattie had almost forgotten that other happy side that she had to her character. How crushing love could be when it was unequally matched! Hattie opened the window wider to the warm night air and climbed contentedly into her huge nest.

Chapter Twenty-Five

A stillness hung over the creek. The water dazzled blindingly in the sun and a heat haze shimmered on the distant hills. Only the woods were dark and cool and Joss, rowing slowly down to the boatyard, was glad to rest his eyes on their green depths as a relief from the brightness of the water. The gentle plash of the oars and an echoing hammering from the boatyard were the only sounds on this hot afternoon; even the birds were silent.

As Joss rowed, he thought about Hester. He accepted that he'd mellowed in the last four years. With the arrival of Hattie and then Miggy, with Daisy and Marigold, the atmosphere in the creek had changed. Imperceptibly his desire to get away on *Westering*, to find pastures new, had altered and he suspected that he'd been trying to escape from himself. He felt surprisingly reluctant, now, to leave and was grateful that Hester and Ned were giving him the excuse for which he'd subconsciously been hoping. Not that he really needed an excuse to change his mind but it made it easier. Now, he could plan shorter trips, frequently returning to the creek and, perhaps, getting a job in Dartmouth.

He glanced at the *Abigail* – for once in full sunlight – as he rowed past the end of the small creek. In the glare of the midday sun she'd lost that brooding, sinister air and was merely an old, rotting boat which, before long, would be reduced to a hulk. Joss looked for Miggy as he drew level with the lawn but there was no sign of her. Of course, Toby's happiness had been part of the unsettling process. When Joss had first brought *Westering* up the creek Toby had been living a bachelor existence and the two of them had drifted into an easy friendship, with evenings at the pub and impromptu meals. He could remember almost resenting Miggy's arrival on the scene, certain that Toby would regret his hasty decision. He also recalled his own attempts to dissuade him and Toby's quiet assurance that Miggy was right for him.

Joss rested on his oars for a moment so that he could light a cigarette. He found that the idea of being permanently attached

201

to another person still caused enough anxiety to require a soothing drag. He stayed for some moments, inhaling deeply, still leaning on the oars. It was the top of the tide and the boat rocked gently, quite still, as if waiting for the water to start running out beneath the keel. Joss stared at the mill and wished that Hester hadn't told him about her other son. He'd been quite unable to repress an internal start of revulsion at the thought of her striking a small child – especially often enough to have the child removed from her care. Try as he would, he couldn't separate this picture from his image of her although she had no idea how he felt. It was there, like a tiny burr against the skin, and he found it hard to be quite so wholehearted in his love since she'd poured out her secret to him. Confession might well be good for the soul but it put a terrible pressure on the confidant.

Joss pitched his cigarette butt into the water and bent to his oars. Toby, he knew, would have no such problem if he were in his position. Toby possessed that greatness of soul which forgave unstintingly and looked for the percentage of good that even the most unlikely individual has buried within him. He could always lay himself alongside the suffering and weakness of others and identify and understand, and his love would encompass, encourage and uplift. Joss envied him but he was not like him. He knew that his own imagination was too narrow and his compassion too limited and he wished that she hadn't told him. Yet it was because of Hattie's compassion and imagination that he'd been able to free himself from his own burden of guilt. Surely he could do as much for Hester?

The tide had turned. Pulling more strongly now, Joss glanced over his shoulder and began to guide the dinghy in towards the boatyard slip.

At much the same time, Ned was standing at the school gate, staring anxiously at the arriving cars, his heart beating erratically. He was quite sure that he'd forgotten to tell his mother that school was finishing at lunchtime today and only a kind of desperate wishing for a miracle kept him standing there. As the remaining cars drew away, he felt the tears welling up into his eyes and his lips trembled. What should he do? The mother of one of his small friends paused beside him.

'Mummy late, Ned?'

He stared up at her gratefully. 'I think I forgot to give her the note,' he said, anxious as always of authority, unwilling to admit as much to his form mistress who might be cross. Ned couldn't bear for people to be cross; it screwed him up inside and made him feel ill. 'She'll be working, I expect.'

The kindly mother took pity on him. 'I can drive you home,' she offered, 'but will there be anyone there for you?'

'Oh, yes!' cried Ned with relief. 'Hattie will be there. And Joss.'

'Hop in, then.' She opened the door and he slid thankfully in and beamed at Richard who'd been waiting patiently.

'What a lovely place!' cried Richard's mother as she pulled in at the mill and saw the ducks dozing in the shade, heads under wings, and the two cottages squatting comfortably beneath the golden thatch. 'I haven't been down here for years. Of course the road doesn't go on, does it? I'll have to turn and go back the way we came. Sure you'll be OK?'

'Hattie's here,' said Ned, indicating the mill's door which stood wide open.

'Fine. Tell Mummy I'll pop in on her one day. 'Bye.'

They drove away, Richard waving from the window, and Ned stood looking round. The cottage was locked up and he had no key and James was at the office. He dropped his school bag and crossed to the mill.

'Hello, Hattie,' he called.

There was no reply and presently he ventured into the kitchen and peeped into the sitting room. Not even the Admiral was about and Ned wandered out on to the quay. The tide was well up, his little dinghy just afloat up on the hard, and he made a sudden decision. He would go fishing. He scrambled out of his socks and sandals, leaving them out of the tide's reach, and picked his way carefully to the dinghy. He untied the painter from its mooring and clambered in, pausing with one foot still in shallow water so as to be able to push her off as Joss had taught him. The boat floated out a little way and rocked gently whilst Ned put on his life belt, struggled with the tapes and checked his fishing gear in the little forward locker. He sat down on the centre thwart, fitted the oars into the rowlocks, and pulled slowly away from the shore, wondering where he should tie up.

There was no sign of life on *Westering* and he decided against using her mooring ropes. He was determined to catch something today and racked his brain to think of a place where he'd never fished from which might just prove lucky. He drew level with Miggy's deserted lawn and glanced idly round. The high prow of the *Abigail* caught his eye, her anchor chain stretching down into the water, and he began to feel excited. He could tie his painter to the anchor chain, fish from his boat and still be in sight of the cottage. Hester had made him promise that he must always stay in sight of one or other of the creekside dwellings and Ned studied the view from the *Abigail* carefully as he rowed towards her. He was looking straight across to the lawn and the summerhouse and Ned felt pleased with himself. Here was a whole new stretch to fish and it might prove lucky for him. How nice it would be to have some fresh mackerel for supper. He tied the painter carefully to the chain, most of which was coiled on the deck above him, and settled down in the stern. The tide began to run out, the sun beat hotly on his unprotected head and Ned began to feel weary, his arms holding the rod ached. The water gurgled under the keel and the trees whispered and rustled a little as a tiny breeze sprang up. The dinghy rocked soothingly and Ned's head nodded a little, his arms relaxed and presently he slept.

The Admiral heard Ned's voice echoing in the depths of his dreamless sleep, stirred and slowly stretched himself. He bounced the larder door open far enough to hook his paw around it and emerged into the kitchen which was warm and bright after the cool dim larder. He listened for a moment before padding into the hall. There was no sound. He strolled out into the mill yard, glanced disinterestedly at the ducks and padded on into the orchard. It was just as he'd suspected. Hattie lay asleep in her chair; head back, gently snoring, newspaper strewn around her. The Admiral surveyed her thoughtfully. A cold nose thrust into the neck or a wet tongue applied liberally to the face always had an effect. Often, however, it wasn't the effect he was seeking and he sighed heavily. These human beings made life so complicated. Anyway, it was Ned's voice he'd heard and Ned often carried interesting and tasty snacks in his pockets.

The Admiral withdrew from the orchard and followed Ned down to the hard. He was in time to see him pulling away in the dinghy and sat down to think things through. The idea of a snack still motivated him and he thought of Miggy and her unfailing hospitality. Pausing only to paddle a little at the edge of the tide, he set off towards this other source of underserved goodies.

Rowing against the tide, Joss headed back upstream. The boatyard had been able to supply the last of his requirements for the trip and they could be off, now, in less than a week. Joss's heart lifted at the thought of *Westering* sailing, running before the wind, rocking at evening anchorages in foreign ports. She was the perfect boat for coast hopping. He felt a sudden surge of excitement. It was time to stop worrying and holding back; time to make the commitment. He loved Hester, he was sure of it, and they were on the brink of a wonderful life together. All he had to do was to stretch out his hand and take it.

Joss fetched a deep breath and waved to Miggy, playing with Marigold and the Admiral on the lawn. He rowed on and had passed the entrance to the inlet when he heard a high-pitched cry and a strange crashing rattle followed by a splash. The Admiral started to bark and, as Miggy's screams echoed round the creek, he saw the huge dog leap from the lawn, flounder through the mud and plunge into the water, swimming strongly towards the mouth of the small creek.

Ned had wakened suddenly. Some noise had disturbed him; the sound of running feet, a cry, and a thud as though some heavy weight had fallen. Ned stared round him, frightened. The sun had moved behind the trees and the *Abigail* threw a long shadow across the dinghy. Ned's head ached, his throat was dry and he knew a sudden atavistic need for safety which sent him scrambling forward to undo the painter. Whilst he'd slept the tide had dropped and the dinghy's prow was lifted out of the water, held up by the painter stretched taut against Ned's knot which was now just beyond his reach.

His weight, dragging on the chain, loosened the rusty housing which broke away and the chain began to pile over the edge of the deck, gathering momentum and crashing on to the dinghy below. Ned managed one scream of terror before he was knocked from the boat, crushed beneath the chain's weight and dragged down into the water.

Miggy heard his scream and saw with paralysing horror the dinghy attached to the *Abigail*'s chain and the chain now pouring down on top of the small figure. Her scream and the Admiral's frenzied barking had an instantaneous effect on Joss, who came racing back, but the Admiral was quicker. Joss, rowing as fast as he could – following the Admiral and trying to make sense of Miggy's screams – saw the dinghy as he rounded the point and his heart lurched with sick terror. The Admiral was swimming round and round, plunging his head beneath the water but quite unable to deal with the weight of chain which pinned Ned down in the mud. Leaping from his dinghy Joss plunged into the water which was now barely five foot deep, diving beneath the surface to tear and drag the coiling, crushing weight from Ned's body. It had knocked him senseless and now pinned him by the arm and Joss, the blood singing in his ears, scrabbled at the chain until Ned was free of it.

As soon as Joss reached the *Abigail*, Miggy raced for the house, a weeping frightened Marigold clutched tightly in her arms. She dialled with trembling fingers and waited, half sobbing, until Hattie answered.

'Hattie!' Her voice was high with terror. 'Come quickly, Hattie! Ned's drowning. Joss is getting him out. Be quick!'

'Phone for an ambulance. I'm coming now.'

When she'd spoken to the emergency services and given them minute instructions on how to find the creek, Miggy slammed the telephone back on its rest and fled back on to the lawn. Joss had laid the small lifeless body in the little dinghy – his own had drifted away – and she watched him cut the painter free, leap in and start to pull for the shore, the Admiral swimming strongly beside him.

'Hattie's coming, Joss!' she screamed. 'She's coming here! Oh hurry!'

Rowing with quick strong strokes, grim face on shoulder, Joss sped across the water that divided the *Abigail* from the lawn. Still clutching the sobbing Marigold, Miggy strained to see the limp figure lying on the thwart.

'Oh, no,' she moaned. 'No. Please, God, don't let him be dead.'

Joss dragged the dinghy over the mud, seized Ned gently in his arms and scrambled up on to the lawn. As he fell to his knees beside the bruised inert figure, Hattie arrived.

'Get out of the way,' she said calmly, feeling carefully for broken bones, 'and keep his mouth and nose clear. Take that child away, Miggy. Get the kettle on and find some warm rugs. Joss stay with me and tell me exactly what happened.'

As she began her attempt to revive him Joss – his eyes fixed on Ned's bruised face – told her what he knew. She pumped the thin frail cage of bone whilst water trickled out of Ned's mouth and Joss crouched on his heels, arms crossed, his own lacerated hands clutched unconsciously beneath his armpits, watching breathlessly for signs of life. He had no idea how long they'd been there when Hester arrived beside them but, before he could move, she began screaming. He stared up at her as wild, desperate words, punctuated by gasping sobs, streamed out of her wide-stretched mouth; tears poured down her cheeks as she accused him.

'Oh Christ, he's dead! . . . It's all your fault . . . You would give him that bloody boat . . . you've killed him . . . Oh my God. I *hate* you. Oh why did I let you bully me? . . . Oh, Ned.'

She fell on her knees beside him and tried to pull Ned into her arms but Toby was there, dragging her away still screaming at Joss who stared at her, white-faced and shocked.

It was Miggy who heard the ambulance and ran out to guide them along the hard and, as they burst on to the lawn, Ned was suddenly and violently sick and Hester collapsed weeping into Toby's arms.

In the early hours of the morning Joss slipped into the mill. Hattie sat alone at the kitchen table playing patience. She glanced up at him and pushed the cards aside. Joss looked exhausted, his clothes were grubby and a familiar smell clung about him. Only later did Hattie identify it as paraffin.

'How is he?' he asked.

'Comfortable. They brought him home and he's tucked up in his own bed. He's bruised and exhausted and he'll need plenty of rest but he's alive and undamaged. Thanks to you.'

Joss shook his head quickly but didn't dwell on it. 'I'm off, Hattie.'

'I thought you might be.' Her calm voice disguised the stab of misery she suffered. 'Are you sure you must?'

'Quite sure. You heard what she said.'

'I heard the ravings of a momentarily deranged woman who arrived home to find her son drowned. Or so she thought.'

'She blamed me for giving him the dinghy and teaching him to row. She said it was all my fault. She told me she hated me and never wanted to see me again.'

Hattie shrugged. 'As I said, she was temporarily insane. She'll feel quite differently tomorrow.'

'Maybe. But I shan't. Anything between us would be quite impossible now, Hattie.'

'Oh, my dear boy . . .'

'Impossible, Hattie,' he repeated forcibly. 'Can you honestly see us setting out happily on *Westering* after this? A jolly family group? Do you seriously imagine that she'll let Ned go on a boat ever again? Do you think he'd *want* to?'

Hattie sighed and shook her head. 'Perhaps not. But it doesn't mean you have to go.'

'And what do you suggest?' he asked derisively. 'That I hang about on *Westering* waiting for her to overcome her hatred of me and his terror of boats?'

'Oh, Joss,' she pleaded, unable to sustain her calm any longer, 'this is your home, too. You shouldn't allow her to drive you away.'

'I was going anyway, you know that. I'll be back one day, Hattie. I promise you.'

She stared up at him and he saw the tears in her eyes.

'Ah, you daft old woman,' he said fiercely, dragging her into his arms and holding her tightly. 'Don't make it harder, for God's sake! Look after yourself. I'll be back. I'll come sailing up the creek one day, Hattie, home for good!'

'Promise?' She couldn't stop the tears flowing and he took her face in his hands and kissed it quickly, first one cheek then the other.

'Promise. One day.'

He turned away from her and put an envelope on the table. She swiped the tears from her eyes with the sleeve of her Guernsey.

'What's that?'

'Something I want you to do for me tomorrow. I'm going now before it gets light.' He bent to stroke the Admiral who, exhausted by his efforts, lay stretched out deeply asleep on the flagged floor. 'Look after her,' he muttered and straightened, pausing to look back from the door. 'I promise,' he repeated, in answer to her unspoken pleading, and was gone.

Hattie remained quite still for some moments. After a while, she switched off the lights and made her way slowly upstairs. She went into her bedroom and across to the window. There was no moon but she could see Joss in his dinghy, a shadow moving within the darker shadow of *Westering*. At last he seemed to have disappeared and she waited to see him aboard the ketch. There was no sign of him, however, and it was much later that she saw him again, still in the dinghy, paddling round to the stern. She watched him go aboard and presently heard the low hum of the engine and saw *Westering* move slowly down the channel.

When she could see him no longer she turned away and sank down in the rocking chair. He would be back; he'd promised. She thought of his pain and saw again his white, anguished face, staring up at Hester as she stood above him on Miggy's lawn and screamed her hatred at him. She imagined him alone at the helm, his life in ruins, his hopes smashed, torn with guilt. She began to weep again, rocking herself to and fro. Supposing he met someone else and decided never to return? He was a young man; how easy it would be for him to start another life elsewhere, the creek and its inhabitants fading into some half-forgotten memory. Oh, the cruelty of it; that he should have to leave amidst such misery when they'd all been so happy! What if he were to be ill, alone on board, far from land and uncared for? Supposing he were run down by a tanker on a dark moonless night and died, terrified and alone in the cold water? Pain and love tore at Hattie's heart and the great cry of agony from the Old Testament rang in her mind. *O my son Absalom, my son, my son Absalom! would God I had died for thee, O Absalom, my son, my son!*

Hattie bowed her head, desperate with misery, and, as the hot tears fell on her tightly gripped hands, she wondered how she'd imagined that she'd never known love.

Chapter Twenty-Six

Toby lay awake staring wide-eyed into the darkness. Miggy slept against his shoulder, worn out with the stress and shock of the day, and he held her closely whilst he re-examined the events of the afternoon. Miggy had telephoned to him at the boatyard after she'd summoned the ambulance, gabbling about Ned drowning and Joss saving him whilst Marigold howled deafeningly in the background. Abandoning his work, he'd raced back along the path to the cottage and come upon the ghastly spectacle: Ned, apparently lifeless, being worked on by Hattie: Joss, kneeling beside her, white as death: Miggy trying to quieten the distraught Marigold. Whilst she boiled kettles and found blankets, Miggy explained what she thought must have happened. Toby took Marigold and rocked her in his arms, listening in horror.

Into the midst of this, a distraught Hester had arrived. Having found the school closed and no Ned she'd raced home, seen his socks and shoes on the hard, the dinghy gone and no sign of him anywhere in the creek. Pausing only to listen to the bare facts, she'd fled out on to the lawn where the most appalling scene followed.

When Ned and Hester were in the ambulance and on their way to Dartmouth hospital, Joss had quite suddenly run away down the lawn, waded through the mud and flung himself into the water. For one terrible moment, Miggy confided later, she thought he was going to drown himself. She and Toby had hurried to the end of the lawn in time to see Joss swimming strongly after his dinghy, which was drifting down the creek. They watched him hook his arms over the stern, haul himself aboard and sit for a moment, head bent, the water streaming on to the thwarts. Presently he began to row back to *Westering* with slow long sweeps of the blades. He rowed past the lawn without glancing at them and took the dinghy alongside the ketch.

Later, Toby had rowed over to *Westering*. As he came alongside, Joss emerged to meet him and Toby swung himself aboard.

'Are you OK?' he asked, laying an arm along Joss's shoulders.

'As well as can be expected under the circumstances.' Joss's face was closed and haggard.

'You saved his life, Joss.' For some reason it sounded like a plea.

'Having risked it in the first place by giving him the boat.' It was evident that he intended to reject any form of comfort.

'Come on, old chap,' said Toby gently. 'She was out of her mind. She didn't mean it.'

'I think she did. Forget it, Toby. I'm slipping off in the morning, early. No point in hanging around. Give Miggy my love. And the girls.' He tried to turn away but Toby gripped his arm.

'For heaven's sake, Joss! Don't you think it's a bit drastic?'

'I should have gone earlier.' Joss shook himself free. 'Please just accept it, Toby. I'll be back sometime. When things have blown over. A year. Maybe two.'

'You'll say goodbye to Hattie, won't you?'

'For God's sake!' said Joss roughly. 'What d'you take me for? Of course I shall. I've got a few things to do first. Take care of yourself.'

They'd clasped hands and Toby had climbed back down into the dinghy and rowed away. Joss leaned against the rail and watched him go, lifting a hand when he reached the boathouse.

Now, Toby eased his arm from beneath the sleeping Miggy and peered to see his watch. He hoped to be up and about by the time Joss sailed in the morning but it was still only a quarter to three. Nearly high tide. Perhaps Joss would go down on the last of the ebb. Toby tried to settle himself for an hour's sleep. He was just dropping into an uneasy slumber when he realised that the room was becoming lighter. He jerked awake. Could he have possibly fallen asleep and missed Joss sailing? The glow grew brighter and he heard a strange rushing noise, like a mighty wind.

Fire! he thought and he slipped from bed and ran to the window. There was another roar and a sheet of flame licked up, lighting the room with an unearthly brightness.

'What is it?' cried Miggy from the bed. 'Oh, Toby, what is it?'

'It's the *Abigail*,' said Toby, his eyes on the leaping flames. 'She's on fire.'

Miggy joined him at the window and he put an arm about her.

'But how?' she whispered. 'My God! She's going up like a torch. How on earth has it happened? You don't think anyone's on board, do you?'

'No,' said Toby slowly. 'I don't. I'm going to phone Hattie. She'll see the flames but she won't know what it is.'

He went downstairs, hauling on his dressing gown, and dialled the mill.

'Hattie,' he said as soon as she answered. 'The *Abigail*'s on fire. You can probably see the flames.'

'And hear them,' she said. She sounded exhausted.

'Have you seen Joss?'

'Yes, I've seen him. He's gone. He sailed about half an hour ago.'

'I thought he might have done.' There was silence. 'Hattie? Should I phone the police?'

'No.' She sounded positive. 'Let her burn. Should have been done years ago.'

'That's what I thought. I'll come down in the morning and decide on our story just in case we get the authorities round.'

'Fair enough. 'Night, Toby.'

Hattie replaced the receiver and sat down at the kitchen table. She remembered the streaks on Joss's clothes and the smell of paraffin that had clung to him and wondered if he would now have enough left for his lamps or his cooking. Presently she reached out a hand and picked up the envelope Joss had left for her. She tore it open and drew out a sheet of paper. A cheque fluttered out with it and she twisted her head to look at it as it lay there on the table. It was made out to Janice Parker in the sum of six hundred pounds. Hattie shut her eyes for a second. That must represent the whole of Joss's savings, all that he'd earned working through the winter at the pub. She flattened out the sheet and read the crabbed writing.

Dear Hattie, *he'd written*,

By the time you open this you'll know what I've done. I wish to God I'd done it four years ago when Evan died and we all laughed at Bert Crabtree's story. Enclosed is the purchase price for the Parkers. Could you send it on to them? I don't see why they should suffer any more. If you get the police nosing round I suggest Toby says he saw some vagrants on board. Anyway, no one can do anything about it. I'm not going to press charges!

Take care. I shall think of you all and miss you more than you can possibly imagine.

God bless.

213

His signature was a scrawl. Hattie folded the letter carefully, put it back in the envelope and ripped the cheque across. She and Toby would buy what was left of the *Abigail*. Joss had paid a high enough price already.

Ned stirred and mumbled in his sleep. His dream seemed bound up in that earlier dream and he heard again the running feet, the cries and the sickening thud of something falling, only this time it was he who was falling; crashing down, felled by some unseen weight. He couldn't breathe, he was being held beneath the water which was filling his mouth and nose . . . He screamed, struggling to break free, and found himself in his own bed with his mother trying to hold him back on his pillow lest he should hurt himself.

'A dream,' he mumbled. 'I had a dream.'

'You're safe, quite safe,' she assured him, smoothing back his hair. 'Try to sleep. Good boy. It's all over now.'

She murmured on to him, soothing and gentle, but he was already slipping back into sleep although Hester continued to crouch beside him, holding his hand. Later the dream returned and now it seemed to be part of the glow that lit the room and the noisy rushing roar that filled his ears. The footsteps and the cries were louder and more urgent until, suddenly, they died away with the fire and there was silence and Ned drifted back into a deep dreamless sleep.

Hester stood by the window, watching the glow fade and merge with daybreak. *Westering* had gone and she knew that in that uncontrolled moment of terror and madness she'd destroyed her hope of happiness with Joss. She remembered the unforgivable things that she'd said and the tears coursed down her cheeks. That she should have spoken so to Joss who had been so kind to her, so patient and generous to Ned, seemed quite impossible now.

I am mad, thought Hester, leaning her hot forehead against the cool glass. Unhinged, unbalanced. With Jeremy and now with Joss.

She began to weep soundlessly again, feeling weak and exhausted, quite unable to form a sensible or hopeful thought. Seeing that Ned was deeply and peacefully asleep, she left his bedroom and went downstairs to make some tea. Presently, wrapped in her warm shawl, she went out on to the quay and leaned on the wall from where she had seen Joss rowing up the creek on her first day.

She heard his voice again.

'Welcome to Abbot's Mill Creek . . . Care for a trip . . . ? Never been in a boat . . . ? Come on then, Moly . . .'

She dropped her head in her hands. She remembered the heart-stopping shock of seeing Ned lying on the lawn; his hair plastered to his fragile skull, face as still as death, a livid weal across his cheek. She'd been certain that he was dead. He'd died because she'd been weak and given in to pressures that he should be allowed freedom, to take risks. An ungovernable rage filled her heart, swelling until it burst out of her mouth in violent, hate-filled, choking sentences. She'd tried to seize Ned's lifeless little body – Ned, who had been her responsibility and whom she had failed! – but had been pulled away. Then Ned had moved, been sick, and she realised with a wave of relief, which was so huge that her legs buckled beneath her, that he was actually still alive.

After that, things became a little hazy and a sense of lassitude and of seeing things as if they were at the wrong end of a telescope overtook her; the effect of the injection she'd been given. She hadn't taken the sedative they'd sent home with her. She'd wanted to remain awake and alert in case Ned should stir. The earlier injection, however, had slowed her reactions and it was only now that she realised what she had done. She'd smashed all hopes of a relationship with Joss and, what was worse, she'd driven him away.

Raising her head, she stared across the empty creek. Two swans were breasting up on the incoming tide; swans which Joss had always fed and who were as regular in their habits as the ducks that waddled along to the mill's back door for breakfast. This morning there was no Joss, no *Westering*, and, filled with an aching sense of loss, Hester put her head in her hands and wept. She started violently as an arm was laid across her shoulders and she turned to look into Hattie's tired, red-rimmed eyes.

'I'm so sorry,' she said despairingly, speaking directly to Hattie's own suffering. 'I was mad. I don't know what came over me.'

'Don't you?' Hattie gave her a little hug and then leaned on the wall beside her. 'I do. It's called love. Mother love. Probably the most powerful of all the emotions.'

'I thought he was dead,' sobbed Hester. 'And I knew I'd failed him as I failed Jeremy. I wanted to die.'

Hattie looked out over the silvery water, sweeping ineluctably across the shining mud. The acrid smell of burning hung in the sweet cool morning air and she remembered her own feelings when she'd imagined Joss dying alone at sea . . . *my son, my son Absalom! would God I had died for three, O Absalom, my son* . . . Hester had already lost one child. How must she have felt when she saw Ned lying on the lawn? At last Hattie could make a pretty good guess at the emotions which had overwhelmed her and she knew that she must put her own instinctive antagonism aside. Joss had been right when he said that he'd have left the creek anyway. She'd known in her heart that he would go one day and, if Hester hadn't arrived, it might have been last year. It was no good making Hester the scapegoat for Joss's need to come to terms with himself. Nor could she blame her for emotions that she, Hattie, was experiencing herself.

'I'll go away.' Hester had stopped weeping. 'I feel I've smashed everything. I'll go as soon as I can. As soon as Ned's well again.'

'Don't be foolish.' Hattie made a tremendous effort. 'Why should you go? You're among friends here.'

Hester looked at her and, for an uncanny moment, it was as if Joss were indeed Hattie's son and she spoke as she would to his mother.

'I do love him.'

'I know,' said Hattie gently.

'It was just . . .' Hester swallowed and shook her head. 'You see, I went against my instincts about the boat. I just didn't feel Ned was ready for it. He's never cared for the water much. But, somehow, Joss made me feel I was being an anxious sort of smothering mother and making Ned a mother's boy. I felt guilty, as if I might be harming Ned instead of just protecting him, so I gave in.'

'And I pushed you, too. Oh, yes I did. I told you that you were being cowardly and gave you a lecture on self-honesty. How easy it is to take note of other people's so-called faults and rush in to tell them what they should do about them.'

'You helped me enormously over Jeremy. For the first time since they took him away I've started to come to terms with it. I was beginning to think that I could start afresh. And now this!'

She burst into a new storm of tears and Hattie put an arm about her, accepting her own part in the sequence of events.

'Shall we just forgive each other for everything, real or imaginary?' she suggested at last. 'Let's begin again with the new situation we're both in. You must stay. At least for a while until you and Ned are both recovered. Miggy and Toby will perfectly understand your reactions yesterday and they both know that, sooner or later, Joss had to go off on *Westering*. There will be no recriminations and no blame. It was a frightful shock for you. There will be nothing but sympathy for you both. And love.'

'Oh, Hattie.'

'That's settled then. And now I need some coffee. Want some?'

'Oh, yes please. Hattie? Was that fire in the night the boat that Ned was tied up to yesterday?'

'Yes,' said Hattie after a moment. 'Yes, it was.'

'How did it happen? D'you think—'

'There have been vagrants seen on board,' said Hattie briskly. 'They've probably been dossing down and caught something alight.' She shrugged. 'You know how it is.'

'My God!' Hester looked horrified. 'You don't think they were on board?'

'Of course not,' said Hattie robustly. 'They haven't been seen for a day or two. Probably left something smouldering. If there had been anyone on board they'd have made a showing earlier with all the drama going on.'

'Yes, of course.' Hester's face cleared and then clouded again. 'I hope that Ned hasn't taken against the creek. I'm sure he'll never want to go near a boat again.'

'He doesn't have to if he doesn't want to. Let's not anticipate problems. I'm going to make that coffee.'

'I'll check on Ned and be right over.' Hester smiled awkwardly. 'Thanks, Hattie. For everything. Especially knowing how you feel . . .'

'Pooey!' said Hattie, in faint echo of her former self, and turned away across the quay.

Hester lingered a little, watching the swans. Joss's voice and her own echoed in her head.

'Won't you miss it all quite dreadfully?'

'Yes. Yes, I think I probably shall.'

She remembered the sadness in his voice and imagined him slipping away in the early morning, alone and carrying with him such appalling memories. He'd saved Ned's life; there was absolutely no question about it. But for his prompt action Ned would have drowned, yet she had screamed and accused him and driven him away.

'Forgive me, Joss,' she murmured. 'I was mad. Oh, Joss . . .'

The sun edged out above the trees on the eastern promontory and the water was washed crimson. The pall of smoke that hung above the hull of the *Abigail* was tweaked and shredded

217

by a light breeze and she could hear the seagulls screaming
down on the river. With a heavy heart she turned away from
the beauty, went back to the cottage and climbed the stairs
to Ned.

Chapter Twenty-Seven

Nick pottered in the kitchen preparing his breakfast which he always ate alone. He'd had to exercise a great deal of tact to persuade Sarah that he required neither a hearty meal nor company at that hour of the morning especially when she appeared, on the pretext of making herself some coffee, to make certain that he was eating properly.

'Men are no good at looking after themselves,' she'd been fond of saying – but fairly soon she stopped saying it. It was so patently obvious that Nick was very good indeed at looking after himself. He'd forestalled those early morning visits to the kitchen by carrying coffee up to her in bed and, although she protested, his gently smiling obstinacy soon won the day.

Nick put his two evenly sliced pieces of wholemeal bread into the toaster and poured boiling water into the cafetière which made exactly the two cups of coffee required to go with the toast. This was a happy time of the day for Nick. He enjoyed the aroma of the fresh coffee and the smell of toasting bread which he ate in absolute silence. He'd discovered when he was quite young that to read a newspaper or book, or to listen to the radio, whilst he was eating impaired the enjoyment of both activities: he found that he concentrated fully on neither and Nick liked to concentrate on what he enjoyed. He put the butter in its blue dish on the table and regarded the new jar of Cooper's Oxford Marmalade with anticipation. He took enormous pleasure in the small luxuries of life, extracting the utmost from each one and dwelling on it afterwards with something very like affection.

The toast popped up and Nick put the slices into the cream china toast rack and pressed down the plunger of his cafetière. He stood at the window, waiting for the toast to cool, gazing out into the misty garden. There was no question of being interrupted this morning. Sarah was staying at John Marriott's cottage in Salcombe with Hattie. Hattie, she'd announced, needed a bit of a change for a few days and John had kindly loaned the cottage. It meant that

219

the Admiral could go too. Nick had been surprised that Hattie should need a holiday. In his view her life was one long holiday. He'd opened his mouth to say as much, caught an odd glint in Sarah's eyes and had said nothing at all.

Nick sat down at the table with a sigh. There was no question but that Sarah had been very odd of late. He spread butter generously on to the crunchy brown toast, piled on marmalade and bit into the delicious combination. She'd been so odd, in fact, that he'd decided to put it down to the menopause except that, from what he'd heard, the menopause tended to make women gloomy and depressed or touchy and tearful; sometimes a combination of all four. Sarah was none of these things. Nick poured his coffee into the fragile Worcester cup – he hated mugs – put in some sugar and stirred thoughtfully. Far from it, Sarah was positively ebullient. She whirled about the place humming or singing snatches of song and looking a good ten years younger. She made light witty remarks, was hardly ever in and seemed quite uninterested in what he was doing.

This was the nub of it. Nick started on his second piece of toast and faced this fact. It had come as rather a shock to him when he discovered, fairly early on, that Sarah knew about his affairs. However careful and discreet he was, her sixth sense seemed to start operating immediately and he'd know that she suspected him. Of course, he gave her no proof and she never confronted him. Soon, he'd accepted the fact that she knew about his infidelities but would never reproach him. Looking back, he realised that he'd enjoyed this state of affairs. Although she never spoke about those other women, there was a shade of pain in her eyes when she looked at him and a clinging urgency in her lovemaking that he found deeply exciting. She'd made him feel that she accepted he was too special to be satisfied with her but was too much in love with him to withhold herself from him even when he was cheating on her. Often he'd made love to her having come straight from one of his mistresses and he'd known that she'd guessed but couldn't resist him. It had amused him and he'd felt a kind of tenderness for this flattering weakness in such a strong woman.

He finished his coffee thoughtfully. It was this aspect that was missing now; had been for some time. Nick grimaced to himself as he refilled his cup. He knew exactly when the change had begun. It had been after that wretched affair with Cass Wivenhoe. He still felt hurt at Sarah's quite extreme reaction to that most unfortunate incident. Surely she could see that it was because he had no intention of allowing anything to destroy their marriage that he'd asked her to help him! And then all that ridiculous business about selling the cottage in Shropshire! Nick exhaled noisily with a self-pitying sigh. He'd really liked that cottage. Moreover, she refused to consider buying another one. He'd put this down to her fear that it made it too easy for him to be unfaithful, which was flattering but damned inconvenient. The Shropshire cottage, miles from civilisation and with no nosy neighbours, had been a perfect rendezvous.

The trouble was – and this had certainly come as a surprise – without Sarah as a spectator, his affairs had lost a little of their edge. He hadn't realised how much the pain and the desperate lovemaking had added to their pleasure; her pleading face and clinging hands had been part of the excitement. Without these added ingredients the extramarital menu had become a little dull. In an effort to resurrect her jealousy he'd been almost flagrant with his last affair but she'd been quite indifferent; not even sulky, merely uninterested.

Nick swallowed the last of his coffee and sat for a moment staring straight ahead. He simply couldn't believe that Sarah was still reacting to the affair with Cass. No, it had to be the menopause. One of his reasons for deciding this to be the cause was that she was no longer interested in sex and he knew that this was another symptom, along with the moodiness. She'd as good as turned him out of her bedroom, making his dressing room extra comfortable and telling him that she slept so badly that she'd keep him awake.

As he piled his breakfast things on to the draining board Nick gave a snort of disbelief. She certainly didn't look tired: quite the contrary. He'd never seen her look so well nor so happy. He felt a surge of self-pity and frustration. It was too bad of her to be quite so indifferent to his needs and, when he'd decided to confront her with the fact that she seemed no longer to care as to whether he lived in the same house with her or not, she'd forestalled him by telling him that she was off to John's cottage for a few days with Hattie. There was plenty of food in the freezer, she told him, and she'd telephone to let him know when she would be coming back. She'd breezed off, humming in that extraordinarily irritating way, and he'd been left feeling more annoyed than ever.

As he checked his briefcase, Nick suddenly wondered if this behaviour was a ploy to pay him back and bring him to heel. Perhaps she thought that this would be more effective than the clinging anguish she'd displayed and she was probably waiting for him to react. He smiled to himself. Perhaps the time had come, after all, to settle down and stop playing the field and, certainly, Sarah was looking so young and attractive that it might not be a hardship. Satisfied that he'd got to the heart of the matter, Nick let himself out of the house and went whistling down the steps.

'I think it's disgraceful.' Hattie towelled her wet hair thoroughly. 'Telling Nick I'm staying with you here. I'd no idea you were such an accomplished liar.'

'I've had a good teacher.' Sarah grinned. 'Anyway, you are here, aren't you?'

'Only for the day,' said Hattie primly. 'What a delightful place it is!'

'Isn't it just?' Sarah flopped down on the towel beside her and began to anoint herself with suntan lotion. 'John always says the cottage is at Salcombe but this is Portlemouth actually.'

'Well, he's picked a perfect spot,' agreed Hattie. 'Out of the gate straight on to the beach. He's not really going to sell it, is he?'

'Not now,' said Sarah contentedly, stretching herself out on the towel. 'He sees its uses now.'

Hattie chuckled. 'You're a fraud,' she said. 'But I couldn't agree more. All this lovely golden sand and a boat a few yards away on its mooring.'

'I've resurrected my old passion for sailing,' said Sarah. 'John's boat's too big for me to handle alone unfortunately or we could go out after lunch.'

'It's rather fun to have Salcombe just across the water. It gives the place a continental feel.'

'We'll go over on the ferry for lunch in an hour or so. It's a smashing little town.'

Sarah closed her eyes against the warm September sunshine and let the sand trickle through her fingers and Hattie looked down at her affectionately.

'So Nick hasn't guessed?'

'Not a dicky bird.' Sarah snorted. 'He would consider it quite impossible for any woman to prefer an old buffer like John Marriott to a young virile chap like him. Wouldn't believe it if I told him.'

Hattie looked at the smiling face crowned by a floppy sunhat and was suddenly transported back some thirty years to the beach at Stokes Bay, discussing some good-looking young doctor, each egging the other on, and she felt a stab of pure nostalgia for those hopeful happy days.

'You look very well on it.'

Sarah opened her eyes and shot Hattie a look of pure mischief. 'You can't believe what it's like to be having a relationship where I don't have to feel grateful. Quite the reverse in fact. It's so . . . so *releasing*, if you can possibly understand what I mean.'

'Oh, I think I can probably just manage to.'

'Oh, Hattie.' Sarah sat up quickly. 'Did that sound patronising? I didn't mean to. It's just such an odd reversal.' She stared at her anxiously and then looked cunning. 'Anyway, I think you've got a much more lurid past than you admit to.'

'Oh, don't start on all that old stuff,' said Hattie good-naturedly. 'You can mind your own business about my past. Anyway, I'm much more interested in your present. Where's it all going to lead?'

'I've no idea.' Sarah turned to stare across the estuary to Salcombe. 'I don't care too much at the moment. I'm just enjoying myself.'

'Does John want you to leave Nick?' asked Hattie curiously.

'I shouldn't think so.' Sarah began to laugh. 'And I wouldn't want to, anyway. At least, I don't think so. I don't know what I want yet.'

Hattie shook her head. 'I don't understand. But I'm not sure I want to. And what will you do if Nick pays a flying visit and finds I'm not here?'

'I'll think of something,' said Sarah carelessly.

'You really have changed, haven't you?' said Hattie. 'Surely Nick's noticed that much?'

'Oh yes, of course he has.' Sarah became serious. 'But he's trying to decide why.'

'He must be out of his mind.'

'I can cope with that,' said Sarah curtly. 'It's his turn. And then some.'

'I couldn't agree more.' She decided to shelve the subject. 'I'm going in to get a shirt.'

As Hattie went into the cottage the telephone was ringing and she snatched up the receiver and said, 'Hello?' rather breathlessly.

'Oh, hello.' Nick sounded rather nonplussed. 'Is that you, Sarah?'

'No, it's Hattie. How are you, Nick?'

'I'm very well. So you've arrived. Enjoying yourself?'

'Wonderfully. We've just had a swim. Sarah's out on the beach.'

'And Admiral Jellicoe? Is he enjoying himself, too?'

Hattie hesitated. 'Jellicoe loves the water,' she said evasively. 'He's a keen swimmer.'

Nick chuckled. 'The mind boggles. I'm sure he'll have the place to himself.'

Hattie laughed obligingly. 'Very likely,' she agreed. 'Shall I fetch Sarah?'

'Oh.' He seemed taken aback. 'Oh, no, no. Not if she's sunbathing. Later will do. It's nothing important. Enjoy yourself.'

'Thanks. I will.'

Hattie slipped on her shirt and went back to the beach.

'Nick phoned,' she said. 'If you ask me, he's checking up.'

Sarah pretended to look impressed. 'You don't say so,' she said.

'You don't think it was gilding the lily to tell him that I was bringing Jellicoe?'

Sarah chuckled. 'I thought it added verisimilitude to an otherwise bald and unconvincing narrative,' she said.

'Artistic verisimilitude,' corrected Hattie. 'If you're going to quote, don't tamper with the text.'

'Oh, shut up,' said Sarah. 'What else did he say?'

'Nothing. Wished me a happy holiday. That's why I think he was checking up.'

Sarah rolled on to her stomach.

'Where is Jellicoe?' she asked idly.

'Miggy's got him for the day.'

'Has everyone recovered from all that frightful business?' Sarah sounded serious again. 'What a terrible thing. Is the child OK?'

'Ned's fine. Children are amazingly resilient. He's become a bit of a hero at school, which is very good for him. He's a very shy, nervous little boy and I hope this may bring him out of himself a bit. Everyone looks upon it as an adventure rather than a tragedy which is just the right attitude. We'll see.'

'And his mother? Hester, is it?'

'She's OK. Tends to be over-protective, which is only natural. She's back at work now the summer holiday's over. It's all settling down again.'

'I expect you're all missing Joss.'

'Yes,' said Hattie after a bit. 'Yes, we're all missing Joss.'

'Any news of him yet?'

'Just a postcard from somewhere down in France. He intends to spend the winter in the Mediterranean.'

'Lucky old Joss.' Sarah rolled on to her back, pulling her sunhat down over her eyes.

'Yes,' said Hattie after an even longer pause. 'Lucky old Joss.'

In his office Nick replaced his receiver and stared sightlessly at his leather-bound blotter. So that much was true at least. Hattie and that huge brute of hers were at John's cottage. It was only when he'd got into the car and set out for the office that the shocking idea had struck him that Sarah might be taking her scheme of teaching him a lesson even further than he'd first thought. As he'd driven across the moor, he'd wondered if it could be possible that she might be playing him at his own game. His immediate reaction was to laugh at the idea. Surely at fifty-three, she was much too old for it to be considered seriously! He remembered how young and happy she was looking and a horrid fear took him by the throat. Impossible! he told himself, but the fear grew and his first act upon reaching his rooms, having dealt with his post, was to telephone the cottage. His relief at hearing Hattie's voice was out of all proportion and he felt quite annoyed at his stupidity.

Nevertheless, he decided not to take any chances. Now he'd decided that he knew what she was playing at, he knew what to do. He would respond by acting the devoted husband. He'd buy her presents and book some tickets for the opera and gradually woo her back. Let her play hard to get if it gave her any fun! Nick smiled indulgently and relaxed. Dear old Sarah! It would be nice to have her back in her old role again and if it meant a bit of humble pie to eat – well, he could cope with that!

Relaxed and urbane once more, Nick opened the file on his desk and began to prepare for his meeting with the first client of the day.

Chapter Twenty-Eight

In October James left for Oxford, which, coming so soon after Joss's departure, made it very hard for the others to hide their sadness. James had fitted in so well and seemed so much part of the little community. He was sorry to be going, despite the excitement of the job in Oxford, and promised that he would be back. When he was rich, he told Hattie during his final week, he would rent one of the cottages on a permanent long let and come down for weekends and holidays. She'd entered into the spirit of the thing, unwilling to spoil what should be an exciting adventure for him by looking sad.

'Why not? Or you could start up your own practice in Dartmouth.'

'That's a brilliant idea.' He beamed at her. 'Or I could buy myself in with Whinge, Whinge, Bellyache and Moan.'

'That's it! Then you can move back in here permanently.'

James brooded thoughtfully. 'I don't think one cottage would be big enough for a wife and children.'

Hattie looked startled. 'Sorry. I hadn't got as far as a wife. How many children were you thinking of?'

'Oh several,' said James at once. 'I'd like a big family. It would be a wonderful place to bring children up in, wouldn't it? I could teach them to swim and sail.' He sighed with pleasure at the treats in store.

'You shall have both cottages,' she said magnanimously. 'We'll knock them into one.'

'It's a deal!'

'Daisy's going to miss you terribly,' said Hattie. 'We all are. You must stay in touch.'

'Of course I shall,' said James, with the confidence of the young, but when he'd gone Hattie shook her head a little. She knew how easy it was to forget people when life was full and exciting.

On his last day at the office James finished early and arrived back at the mill well before his usual time. He changed into his old clothes and went out to the hard. Daisy was sitting on the wall, waiting, but she found it difficult to muster a smile. This was to be their very last sail before James left and her heart was heavy and her throat ached with unshed tears.

'You made it,' she said, trying not to let her misery show.

'I promised, didn't I?' said James indignantly. 'Just time before the light goes!'

There was enough breeze to keep them both busy and distract them from their separate preoccupations but the fading light soon drove them off the water.

'I suppose you won't get much sailing in Oxford,' said Daisy, trying to keep her emotion under control as they pulled the boat up the hard.

'None at all!' said James, affecting cheerfulness. 'Shan't have a boat! That's why!'

'Won't have a boat?' Daisy stared at him, shocked, her own grief temporarily forgotten. A horrid thought struck her. 'You're not going to sell her?'

Her hands gripped the transom, as though she would prevent such sacrilege by force if need be, and James smiled at her.

'No, I'm not selling her. I'm leaving her here. For you.' They looked at each other and he raised his eyebrows teasingly at her speechless amazement. 'Don't you want her?'

Daisy opened her mouth to speak, closed it, swallowed and shook her head in disbelief. Tears filled her eyes and James felt awkward and a little shy.

'I've cleared it with Miggy,' he assured her. He wanted to tell her that Toby had insisted on giving him half the value of the boat – James had refused to take more – but he'd made him promise not to tell anyone. 'I want you to have her,' he said gently. 'Anyway, she belongs here, now. And when I come down there will be something here for me to sail in. But she's yours, really.'

'Ours,' said Daisy quickly, blinking back tears. 'We can share her and I'll look after her while you're away. You'll be back soon, then?'

'Of course I shall.' He began to stow the sails, glad of something to do. 'You'll probably want to put her in your boathouse over the winter. She needs a bit of attention.'

'I'll look after her,' Daisy assured him, happier now that she had something of his, something that would bring him back. 'Miggy says will you be over in the morning, before you go?'

'Definitely,' said James, glad to postpone a final farewell and feeling oddly desolate, unaware that a quiet supper arranged with Hattie was in fact a surprise party with everyone coming along to give him a good sendoff.

'See you in the morning then,' said Daisy, who was in on the secret. She hesitated and then went behind the wall where she'd hidden a small bag. 'I'll give you this now, though.'

She drew out an oblong object and gave it to him. It was a framed photograph. James peered at it in the dying light, trying to make out the subject. Outside the open door of the mill Hattie stood with the others grouped round her. James studied it closely. Miggy smiled out at him, Marigold in her arms. Toby and Joss stood together, grinning at some private joke, whilst Daisy sat on a small stool at the front, her arm round the Admiral's neck and looking very serious.

'Who took it?' he asked at last and his voice was unusually husky. He cleared his throat. 'It's terrific.'

'Hester took it. She said she hadn't been here long enough for you to want her in it and Ned was at school. Luckily we did it before Joss went.'

'It's brilliant. Was it your idea?'

'Mmm.' She gave an embarrassed nod. 'You can put it on your desk in Oxford. So you won't forget us.'

'I'll do that,' he promised, and gave her a sudden, awkward little hug.

She clung tightly to him for a second and then turned and ran away along the hard and James went slowly back to the cottage, clutching his photograph.

Hester was relieved to get back to work, thankful that her old job was still open to her. The tea-shop's owner made it clear that, from the beginning of the next summer holidays, her daughter would be employed there full time but, until then, Hester was welcome to work her old hours. She was grateful to be kept busy and tired, apart from the fact that she needed the money. As the winter wore on she slowly came to terms with the problems in her life, thinking things through carefully and rationally, trying to hold off guilt and self-pity.

Ned had recovered surprisingly quickly from his ordeal, thanks mainly to the positive attitude of those around him. Although he was still prone to nightmares, Hester could accept now that he would probably always be prone to nightmares. Ned was that sort of person. She understood fully what Miggy had meant when she talked about recognition within families. She remembered how her father, on his rare visits, had always been amused by Ned's finicky ways and attacks of anxiety.

'Just like David,' he'd said tolerantly. David was his younger brother who had won a scholarship to Winchester and another to Cambridge. 'Ned'll finish up an Oxford don, you'll see. He's a clever type. Just like David when he was a boy.'

Her father had recognised the traits and accepted them. Would Joss have been able to do the same? Hester thought about it. Joss had a tough streak – like Hattie – and she wondered whether she would have spent her life on a tightrope between the two of them; watering down Joss's toughness, bolstering up Ned's courage. She remembered Hattie and Joss in fits of laughter when Joss told a story about an Army motto 'Mind over Matter' stuck up over a barrack room for new recruits. 'We don't mind,' the sergeant had said to the new young soldier, 'and you don't matter!' She hadn't thought it funny at all – imagining the feelings of the new young recruit – and had felt oddly isolated from the other two who were so completely on the same wavelength. Surely one didn't have to be members of the same family to be able to understand others and be tolerant of their faults and failings! She'd said as much to Miggy.

'After all,' she'd protested, 'Toby seems to have no problems with Daisy.'

'Daisy and I are very alike,' said Miggy, after she'd thought about it for a bit. 'He sees me in her and Marigold in both of us. If Daisy had taken after Patrick things might have been very different. Or perhaps if she'd been a boy. I found Georgia very difficult to begin with. One of the problems is that it's so easy to feel excluded by the previous shared life. Families have private jokes and sayings. When they talk about things they've done and people they know, you have no share in it. It's easy to feel like a stranger within the camp.'

'But *you* don't feel like that, surely?' asked Hester, who envied Miggy much more than she ever showed.

'Not very often. At the beginning I did. It was the one thing Ruth always played on. The "d'you remember" bit. I found that very hard but I was much more insecure then. I feel we're a complete family now and although there are occasional ructions between Daisy and Toby I can accept that it's normal and not get hang-ups about it.'

'You know,' said Hester, after a long pause, 'I don't think Joss and I would have worked together.'

'I can see that it was easy to be carried away by the setting and the proximity,' agreed Miggy cautiously. 'It was all rather romantic.'

'It was more than that,' said Hester. 'We both wanted love. Someone of our own whom we could trust. I wasn't absolutely sure about it but I was too scared at missing out so I decided to grab it. I think Joss felt the same way.'

'Oh, Hester.'

'I know.' Hester laughed a little. 'It's silly really. But I sensed that same reservation in him that I felt in myself and Ned's accident was enough to crack it wide open. I still have nightmares about the things I said to him though.'

Miggy was silent, remembering Joss's white face.

'I know.' Hester was watching her. 'I know what you're thinking. I can't stay here, Miggy.'

'Oh, Hester!' cried Miggy. 'For heaven's sake . . . !'

'No, no.' Hester shook her head. 'We don't belong here. Not like the rest of you. That's why I feel so guilty about driving Joss away.'

'He was going anyway . . .'

'I wonder. If you ask me, Joss didn't want to go. Not on a great long voyage. I think I was part of Joss's reason to opt for a shorter trip but I think he was looking for an excuse. He belongs here and I think he'd just begun to realise it.'

'Then he'll be back. He needn't stay away for ever. Once he calms down—'

'I don't think he'll come back while Ned and I are here.'

'Oh, honestly, Hester.' Miggy looked anxiously upon her quiet stubbornness. 'Please don't do anything in a hurry.'

'No, I shan't do that.' Hester sighed. 'I had a telephone call from my father last night. My mother's got cancer. Not long to live, it seems. I'm going up to see her.'

'My God!' whispered Miggy. 'I'm sorry.'

'Well.' Hester lifted her hands helplessly and let them drop in her lap. 'She's refused to see me for years. Ever since I let Jeremy go. She was disgusted with me and furious that she didn't have him herself. She was so bitter and angry she could hardly bear me near her. It seems such a sad waste now. Will you look after Ned for a few days for me?'

'Of course I will but wouldn't she like to see him?'

'She's always refused to see him. She said that she had no intention of getting fond of another grandson who might be murdered by his evil and uncontrolled mother or stolen by his father's unprincipled family.'

Miggy stared at her in horror and Hester grimaced.

'There wasn't much I could say in defence. My father tried to make her change her mind but she was adamant. I'm only allowed to go now because she's so far gone that she probably won't know me. But at least I can see my father. I've missed him dreadfully.'

'I had no idea.'

'Why should you? You didn't even know about Jeremy until early this year. It's not the kind of thing you talk about but, thanks to Hattie and all of you, I've been able to shed the load and get it out of my system.'

'Go and see your father,' said Miggy gently. 'Take as long as you need together. Ned'll be quite safe with us.'

'I know that. Thanks. I might take you up on that offer. Dad and I have a lot of time to catch up on.'

She left for London the next morning and was still there three days later when her mother died. She telephoned to Miggy to tell her that she'd like to stay on for the funeral but would be back quite soon afterwards and that she'd agreed to take Ned up for Christmas.

'It's time he knew his grandfather properly,' she told Miggy. 'Dad's delighted. I'll have a word with Ned if he's around.'

Miggy passed the receiver over to Ned and went to find Toby, who was watching *Sesame Street* with a fascinated Marigold.

'She adores Bert and Ernie,' he told her. 'I must say that I do too. And I think Oscar the Grouch is fantastic. Marigold can't understand why he lives in a dustbin. What's up?'

'It's just that Hester's mother has died,' sighed Miggy, sinking down beside them on the sofa. 'She's staying on for the funeral. I do wish something would work out for her, Toby.'

'I think she's right about her and Joss,' said Toby, putting the mesmerised Marigold between them. 'When you really think about it, Joss isn't the sort for a ready-made family. He's had no experience of fatherhood and, from what he's told me, he's never had a long relationship with a woman. I think it would have all been too much of a shock. I feel guilty about it, too. I was matchmaking like mad, trying to keep everyone here in the creek.'

'We all were,' said Miggy comfortingly. 'And now Joss has gone. And James.'

'Poor old Daisy.' Toby glanced round to make sure she wasn't in earshot. 'She misses him terribly.'

'First love is agonising,' agreed Miggy. 'Especially when you're only fourteen.'

'And who were you in love with when you were fourteen?' enquired Toby.

'The bus driver on the school bus,' said Miggy promptly. 'We all vied over him and I was broken-hearted when he was moved to another route. After that it was the new doctor. I had every illness known to man until my mother guessed what was going on. There was something about the combination of his white coat and his stethoscope that was unbelievably sexy!'

'Not in front of the child, please!' said Toby, shocked. '"Confessions of a housewife". I think it's disgraceful. Naturally, I was pure until I married.'

They stopped laughing abruptly as Ned appeared and Miggy drew him down beside them on the sofa. Marigold immediately wriggled round to sit beside him – she adored Ned – and they leaned together happily, thumbs in, chuckling at Big Bird's antics.

'You can see she's started already,' complained Toby, nodding at Marigold whose free chubby hand rested on Ned's bare – unconscious – knee. 'Her passions have been unbridled since she was barely a year old. Benjamin Bunny, Tigger, Bert and Ernie, Oscar the Grouch. Now it's Ned's turn. Who next, I wonder?'

'I'd better check out the driver of the playschool minibus,' sighed Miggy. 'You simply can't be too careful. Shall we leave them to it and have a drink before lunch?'

'As long as it's not a quickie,' said Toby warningly. 'No more Saturday quickies for me, thanks very much, with Daisy bursting in unexpectedly and saying, "What on *earth* are you doing?" Jesus! I thought I'd never recover from that one. I'll stick to drink from now on!'

'I thought she was with Hattie,' chuckled Miggy. 'How was I to know that the Admiral wasn't well and Hattie had taken him to the vet?'

'I want no explanations and no excuses,' said Toby severely. 'I've obviously got to the age when a quickie before lunch is definitely a drink!'

They went out together and the two on the sofa lolled contentedly, happy in the other's company, absorbed in how many words begin with the letter T.

Chapter Twenty-Nine

Sarah gathered her fellow committee members with her eye, pushed back her chair and stood up. Still stunned by her final announcement that she intended to resign from the various committees she chaired – although assuring them that she would still be supporting those charities they represented – they hurried to collect their belongings. Still putting caps on pens and shuffling papers together, they talked in low voices, one eye on Sarah as she bade farewell to the treasurer whose dining room had been loaned for the meeting.

Once outside Sarah grinned to herself as she slid quickly into her car and drove away. It was only fair to leave the field clear for the gossip and speculation that would follow: nor would it be confined to who would be elected in her place! Sarah chuckled aloud, glanced in her driving mirror and pulled out to overtake a tractor. How she'd enjoyed their expressions of amazement! In her head she heard their gasps and little exclamations and imagined the conversation now taking place over the usual tea and biscuits.

'I'd never have believed it! She's always been so dedicated. We shall miss her!' (Joan: generous, kindly, a tireless co-worker.)

'Oh, I've seen it coming for a while now. Sarah's changed. Look at her hair and clothes. I've had my suspicions . . .' (Kitty: bitch of the first water, worker only for the greater glory of Kitty Watts, skilled delegator of boring time-consuming jobs.)

'Well, she's certainly done her stint. Only fair to give others the opportunity to show their mettle. I'm certainly not one to shrink from the responsibility.' (Janet: brisk, efficient, with a predatory eye on the president's chair and her name in a distant New Year Honours List.)

'Well, as long as no one looks at me! These are super buns, Pattie.' (Evie: wealthy, easy-going, bullied into joining, terrified of taking decisions, delighted to pour out large sums of money in lieu of taking any post that might require serious thought.)

'You know I can't help wondering . . .' significant pause as Kitty gathers the gossips round her whilst the others, the ones who do the real work, begin to plan for the future.

Sarah snorted contemptuously and pressed her foot down on the accelerator. Things were hotting up. She'd been surprised and amused to find Nick paying court to her as he'd once done all those years before: a bottle of her favourite scent, a delightful pen-and-ink sketch of a moorland scene, a white silk shirt. Nick never descended to the flowers and chocolates routine of lesser men. For her birthday he'd given her an envelope containing weekend reservations for two at the Savoy and two tickets for the opera at Covent Garden.

Sarah began to laugh as she remembered opening it. Nick had watched her, so obviously overwhelmed by his own generosity and ingenuity that she'd toyed with the idea of saying that she was booked up with friends for the weekend in question. Even better, she'd considered wondering aloud whom she might invite to go with her! She was still chuckling as she drove out on to the open moor, shrouded in thick February mist, and headed for home. What was he up to? she asked herself. Nick had never betrayed himself by buying guilt presents and, anyway, she was certain that he was not involved with another woman. Why then this assiduous courting? Was it possible that he suspected something, that he'd noticed the change in her?

Sarah stretched to glance at herself in the driving mirror. The silvery grey hair, grown to a smooth well-cut bob, looked chic and was flattering. She'd lost nearly a stone in weight and invested in a whole new wardrobe. He'd have had to be blind not to have noticed! Perhaps it was simply that her new image had made him take a new look at her and that he was missing their old way of life. If so he was destined to be disappointed. Nothing would induce her to return to that old anxious degrading existence. As she pulled into the drive, she saw the bench she'd been sitting on when Nick had come home more than two years before and made his outrageous request. Even now, she could still feel an echo of the pain and shock and knew that her confrontation with Cass Wivenhoe had been the turning point.

As she made herself a cup of tea, however, she wondered whether the first cracks had shown when Hattie bought the mill. She remembered how she'd envied Hattie's freedom and her determination to start a new life. Perhaps the affair with Cass had merely served as the catalyst; shown up the weaknesses and made her face the truths that she'd lived with but refused to recognise all those years. Well, she'd recognised them now and with a vengeance! The question was: where was it all leading?

Sarah wandered into the little morning room and bent to poke the fire and added some more coal. She felt that she was in a kind of limbo; that she'd kicked free of her old life but was not fully sure what the new one held for her. Resigning from her committees had been an almost impulsive action. She saw it as another step along the way and hoped, now, that it had been the right thing to do. They had taken up so much of her time but what would she put in their place? She knew that her affair with John Marriott was no more than that nor would she have wanted it to go further. Sarah shook her head. There was no point in worrying about it. In due course something would happen to show her the way forward. Meanwhile she was enjoying herself. For the moment she must be content with that.

Nick bumped into John as he was about to leave the office. He noticed that John was looking pretty good considering he was practically at retirement age and Nick experienced one of his twinges of ambition. He allowed himself to obey an impulse.

'How are you, John? Cold old night but the evenings are drawing out at last. Come on back and have a drink and a spot of supper.'

'Well, now.' John hesitated. 'That's a very handsome offer.' He smiled a little. 'Don't you think it might be a bit of a shock for Sarah?'

'Rubbish!' cried Nick. 'She'll love to see you. Anyway, Sarah's unshockable! I won't take no for an answer. We haven't seen you for ages. Not socially, anyway.'

'Then I accept with pleasure. I know the way so I'll see you later.'

John seemed rather amused by such impetuous insistence and Nick hoped that Sarah wouldn't be put out and show him up. Once he could have relied on her absolutely – especially with John being the senior partner and knowing Nick's long-held ambition in that particular direction – but these days . . . Nick slipped back into his office and dialled out.

'Sarah? It's Nick.'

'Oh, hello. What's the problem? Got a late client?'

He heard a touch of sarcasm in her voice and suddenly realised how often in their married life he'd rung with that excuse ready on his lips.

'No, it's just to warn you that John Marriott will be coming to supper.'

'John *Marriott*?' She sounded so astounded that he felt obliged to hurry into explanations.

'He was looking a bit down, poor old fellow, and I just made the offer. More out of politeness than anything else. He jumped at it! Couldn't back out, could I?'

'That's OK, Nick.' Sarah sounded faintly amused and he felt deeply relieved. 'It'll be . . . fun.'

'Good. That's excellent. What about supper?'

'That's not a problem. See you later.'

Nick hung up and went out to the car park. John's car had already gone and he wondered if he'd decided to go home to change. He drove away quickly, hoping to arrive home before him and to make absolutely certain that everything was in order.

John had gone home but not only to change. He, too, rang Sarah. 'Nick's invited me to supper,' he said. 'I thought you should be prewarned.'

'Thoughtful of you.' He heard her laugh. 'Nick's just phoned.'

'Aha. So he didn't think you'd be too pleased after all.'

'Probably. Should be quite entertaining.'

'If you say so. I feel extraordinarily nervous.'

They both laughed.

'Don't worry,' said Sarah. 'I told him we ran into each other last week and had lunch together. That'll let us out if either of us slips up.'

'I'm not certain I'm cut out for this sort of subterfuge,' said John plaintively.

'Too late to worry about that now,' she replied heartlessly. '*Courage, mon brave!*'

John hung up and went to change his suit for something less formal. He wasn't really nervous, in fact he felt quite ebullient.

'Life in the old dog yet,' he told Margaret's patiently smiling face and went to choose a bottle of wine from his cellar before hurrying out to the car.

Nick enjoyed the first part of his evening enormously. He'd almost forgotten what it was like to play the host and devoted husband at the same time and his enjoyment merely served to make him all the more determined to make a new start with Sarah.

'Don't you think she's looking well, John?' he asked, a proprietorial hand on Sarah's shoulder, on his way to open another bottle of wine. 'Those sailing weekends you gave us last summer have done her good.'

John gave Sarah what Nick could only describe as a very odd look, although he couldn't quite analyse it.

'I think she looks ravishing,' he said so seriously that Nick turned away to hide a little smile at his extravagance and missed the intimate look that passed between the other two.

'She's giving up some of this committee work,' Nick told him. 'I'm all for it. She's devoted all her life to it. Time she concentrated on me for a change.'

John shot an involuntary look at Sarah, who continued to look at her plate.

'You'll be sorely missed,' he told her and she gave him a brief smile. 'Margaret always said that you were indefatigable.'

'It exhausts her,' said Nick disapprovingly. 'This last year she's been all over the place, working early and late, never stopping.'

'You're exactly the same, Nick,' said Sarah sweetly. 'All those meetings in the evenings and at the weekends. Sometimes I hardly see you for weeks at a time. My work is merely in self-defence.'

Nick flushed a dark red but John stepped in and saved his embarrassment.

'So what shall you be doing instead of your committees, Sarah?'

'Enjoying myself,' she answered briefly and winked saucily at him as Nick wrestled with the corkscrew.

Nick filled the glasses feeling that he'd had a narrow escape. Thank God John hadn't picked him up on it and asked who these clients were. It was almost as if Sarah had dropped him in it on purpose but it was too preposterous an idea to consider. She knew very well that when John retired it would be in his power to nominate his successor. He was the senior partner and it was his grandfather, along with Charles Murchison, who'd been the founder members. There were no Murchisons left now and John was the last Marriott. Nick had long harboured a desire to step into his shoes and the last thing he needed was for Sarah to sow the seeds of doubt in John's mind. He considered mentioning a case or two which could possibly have led to work outside office hours but rejected it. If a brick was dropped it was best not to kick it about. He redoubled his efforts as the attentive host and husband.

'What about that plan of yours to take over the second-hand

bookshop in Tavistock?' John asked idly but immediately looked horrified and glanced quickly at Nick.

'Bookshop?' Nick took in John's distress and looked at Sarah. He felt a strange pricking unease. 'What's all this about?'

'Nothing in particular.' Sarah remained cool although she didn't meet his eyes. 'I've been told that Alex Gillespie's looking for a buyer. I'd just heard about it when I bumped into John last week. I told you we had lunch together, Nick. I was discussing it with him.' She shrugged. 'It was just a passing whim. I forgot about it almost immediately.'

It all sounded perfectly reasonable but for some reason the uneasiness continued. There was a faintly strained atmosphere which Nick couldn't quite dispel and presently he went out to make the coffee. Halfway to the kitchen, he remembered that John disliked drinking coffee late in the evening and turned back to ask if he would prefer tea. Just beyond the door he paused. They were laughing together; little gasping giggles that burst forth almost hysterically. Disbelievingly, Nick peered cautiously through the half-open door. Sarah had stretched her arm across the table and John had taken her hand between both of his and was holding it against his lips. There was something both intimate and relaxed in the gesture and Nick stood quite still, hardly able to believe his eyes. Sarah and John had never been on particularly friendly terms, certainly not as friendly as their present attitude suggested.

He retreated a step or two, his eyes still fixed on them, and deliberately made a noise as though he were returning from the kitchen. Sarah snatched her hand away and John automatically ran his fingers over his face and hair as though to wipe away any expression that might betray him. Nick composed his own features with difficulty and asked his question about John's tea. Back in the kitchen he stood for some considerable time before he pulled himself together and switched the kettle on. So that was the answer to the whole mystery of Sarah's new looks and different attitudes! John Marriott of all people! In the moment of suspicion last summer he'd wondered whether she might be using his cottage for an assignation but it had never occurred to him for a single second that it might be with John himself!

He clenched his hands in his pockets and wondered what he should do. A lesser man might rush in and confront them but Nick instinctively decided to bide his time. He must be absolutely sure of his facts. He remembered the blunder about the bookshop and guessed exactly what had happened. He made the coffee and tea slowly and carefully. After all, he was in a sensitive position. He could well imagine Sarah's derisive remarks if he were to call her loyalty into question and there was still the matter of John's retirement and his choice of successor.

Unable to resist the urge, Nick slipped back quietly into the hall and positioned himself so as to be able to spy on the pair at the table. Sarah sat with her chin in her hands, her eyes on the table whilst John leaned forward, talking to her in a quiet undertone, his hands gesticulating, shaping words. Nick watched for a moment but, just as he was about to turn away, his eyes dropped a little and he caught his breath with a gasp. John's long legs were stretched out under the table, crossed at the ankle. On top of them rested Sarah's. One of her shoes had been discarded and her bare foot moved up and down John's leg in a frankly sensuous caress. Even as Nick stared, John leaned down and seized her ankle and she bent forward laughing at him. Something made them turn suddenly to the door, John swiftly releasing her leg and Sarah seeking for her shoe with her bare toe.

Nick went back to the kitchen feeling angry, jealous and hurt. He could barely take it in. That Sarah should be unfaithful was quite amazing enough. But to be unfaithful with John Marriott – John Marriott of all people! – made it seem, somehow, a double treachery. And that they should show such little caution and restraint whilst John was a guest in Nick's own house was quite unforgivable. Controlling his emotions with difficulty, Nick put the tea and coffee things on to a tray and carried them into the dining room. They both smiled at him but now he was not deceived and, as he poured the coffee and John's tea and talked lightly of this and that, his mind was reeling as it tried to come to terms with this shocking and completely unexpected turn of events.

'Sorry about the bookshop business,' said John next morning on the telephone to Sarah. 'I don't think he suspected anything, did he?'

'I don't much care if he did,' replied Sarah. 'Good job I'd covered us though. Honestly. Nil out of ten for deception and lying.'

'Sorry.' John pretended penitence. 'I haven't had much practice at deception and lying.'

'I thought you'd been a lawyer for the last forty years!' retorted Sarah and grinned as she hung up.

Presently she telephoned Nick. 'Marian's just phoned,' she said. 'Asked me over for the weekend after next. I know she bores you rigid so I'll pop over on my own. She's not too well, so I'd like to go. Not a problem, is it?'

'No, not a problem. Weekend after next?'

'That's it. Just a short one. Saturday morning till Sunday night.'

'Could you put it in my diary? Fine. See you tonight.'

A little later Nick met John on his way back from lunch. John patted him on the shoulder and smiled at him warmly.

'Lovely evening, Nick. Thanks very much. Give my regards to Sarah and my thanks, will you?'

'Of course I will. We both loved having you. We must do it more often. Oh!' Nick turned back, smiting his brow. 'Nearly forgot. How about some golf? Weekend after next. Saturday or Sunday, either's fine with me. We haven't had a round for months.'

'Ah.' John looked profoundly uncomfortable. 'Can't, dear boy. Not a chance. Got people staying. The Anstruthers are down.'

'Really?' Nick raised his brows. 'Down a lot lately, aren't they? Never mind. Perhaps another day.'

They parted and Nick went into his room and very nearly slammed the door. He sat down at his desk and began to think very carefully indeed.

Chapter Thirty

Hands in pockets and with her old brown felt hat pulled well down, Hattie strolled along the embankment at Dartmouth. The strong March winds gusted in from the sea and screaming gulls mobbed a fishing boat as it came chugging up the river. Threatening clouds scudded before the wind and the intermittent sunshine gleamed down on the choppy grey water where boats rolled restlessly on their moorings. Hattie stared out to sea, beyond the castle at the mouth of the Dart, until her eyes watered in the cold wind. She found it hard to believe that she'd been at the mill for nearly five years yet she couldn't, now, imagine any other way of life. It was true that the letting of the cottages was proving more of a problem than she'd hoped and she wished that she could find tenants who not only fitted in with the existing community but wanted to stay for reasonable amounts of time. She'd done well with James but she was beginning to wonder whether she would ever achieve her ideal. As Sarah had said long ago, when you lived just across the yard from your tenants it was important that you liked them.

As she watched the Lower Ferry chugging back from Kingswear, Hattie wondered if, after all, she should have stuck to holiday lets. It was probably possible to cope with even difficult people for a fortnight at a time and at least they wouldn't break your heart when they left. With a grimace at her foolishness Hattie stopped peering for a boat that might be *Westering*, sailing in from Castle Point, and turned back. As she approached the car, parked further along the embankment, another problem assailed her. Soon she must think seriously about changing the car. Her old faithful Renault 4 seemed to sag visibly beneath the combined weight of the Admiral and the month's shopping and she remembered the local mechanic's warning about rust in the chassis.

As she drove slowly back, she faced the fact that she could no longer allow herself the luxury of letting the cottages to only those people to whom she felt attracted. She must harden her heart. It was extremely unlikely that James would ever return to the creek.

He'd written a letter to them all quite soon after his arrival in Oxford and he'd sent cards at Christmas but she suspected that his communications would arrive further and further apart until they ceased and that would be an end to it. As for Joss . . . Hattie took a deep breath and pulled out to overtake a man who was plodding along the road with a rucksack on his back. She glanced at him briefly as she passed and saw that he was very young, just a boy, nevertheless she decided that it was pointless to offer him a lift since she was about to turn off the main road at the Sportsman's Arms. Her thoughts drifted back to Joss. They'd all received cards from him at different times and from different points across the Mediterranean; brief reports of survival and always with the news that he was moving on. Toby suggested that they should send letters to the next likely harbour authority on his route but Hattie had resisted the temptation so far. If Joss wished to hear from them then no doubt he'd supply an address.

She turned down the lane that led to the mill, reminding herself for the thousandth time of his promise. He would come back. She crushed down the insidious little voice that whispered 'as long as nothing happens to him', parked the car and released the Admiral who leaped out and ran round checking that nothing exciting had happened in his absence. The yard was deserted. After James had gone she'd let the cottage to a young couple from the naval college who were waiting for their quarter to be refurbished and who had moved out a few days previously. Meanwhile, Hester was still havering as to what she should do and where they should go. Hattie knew that she wasn't really happy here and that Ned's aversion to water had become a very real fear but Hester seemed unable to come to a final decision.

Hattie began to carry the shopping into the mill. Very soon, she suspected, she'd have two empty cottages on her hands and the cycle would start again. As she packed away her supplies she knew she could no longer pick and choose. She also knew that she was desperately hoping to keep a bolt hole for Joss if he should return but wondered how she could hope to do that indefinitely. At least, should he ever return, he could live on his boat whilst he waited for a tenancy to end. The Admiral came into the kitchen and pushed his nose into the shopping bag on the table. Hattie noticed with a shock that his muzzle was beginning to show signs of grey and, with a jab of terror, she put her arms round his neck and buried her face in his thick warm coat. He stood quite still, tail gently wagging, whilst she hugged him, quite used to being treated as a recipient of outpoured emotion up and down the creek. Daisy had spent hours weeping quietly into his coat since James had left, Hester sat silently hugging him for long minutes at a time, whilst Ned often sought him out and sat beside him whilst he read his schoolbooks.

Hattie sighed heavily as she stood upright, giving the Admiral a final pat. She must stop dithering and get another advertisement into the local paper. She simply couldn't afford to have a cottage standing empty.

Hester drove back from Dittisham, having dropped Ned off to spend the day with Richard. Richard's mother had persuaded her to stop for a cup of coffee and Hester had enjoyed the friendly chat. Yet when it came to really becoming part of the local community – joining the PTA, going along to the Women's Institute, supporting the coffee mornings – Hester felt a strange sense of unreality. Part of her knew that she didn't belong here any more; that it had been an interlude that was now finished. Despite Ned's terrible ordeal and the scene with Joss, Hester knew that she was glad that she'd come. In some way, all the inhabitants of Abbot's Mill Creek had contributed to a healing process and at last she knew she could face both herself and life again with confidence.

Part of her felt deeply guilty about Joss. No matter what everyone said about Joss's determination to go off on his voyage, Hester still wondered whether he would ever have left. No doubt he would have taken *Westering* for short trips but he'd been away now for nine months and there was no word as to when he might return. There was never any message for her in the cards that the others received and she suspected that he would never come back whilst she was still at the cottage. Yet how would he know that she'd gone?

Hester shook her head as she approached the turning down to the mill. She noticed a young man with a knapsack coming towards her from the Dartmouth direction and, as she swung down the narrow lane, she felt a brief, eerie sensation of *déjà vu*. Pulling into the yard she saw that Hattie was back from her shopping expedition and considered popping in on her. Almost immediately she decided against it. She knew that Hattie was waiting for her to make up her mind as to whether she should go or stay and she felt unequal to making an attempt to sort out her feelings. It was as if she were waiting for something which, having arrived, would then point her in the right direction.

As she went indoors, she smiled at the fancifulness of this idea and wondered whether to telephone her father and suggest that she and Ned should join him for Easter even earlier than they'd planned. She knew that he'd be delighted to have them but still something held her back. She wandered upstairs to make the beds and down again to hoover the sitting room and clear up the kitchen. As she worked, her mind revolved round the continual problems that the lack of money presents. She'd always been surprised that Phil continued to support Ned – guessing that he'd had many battles with his mother over it – and she'd had a letter from him recently telling her that Ned was welcome to go out for a visit.

Fear had clutched at her heart. Was this some ploy to take Ned, as well as Jeremy, from her? She'd written back a carefully thought out reply which thanked Phil as usual for his financial support but regretted that Ned was too young as yet to undertake such a gruelling journey. Perhaps when he was older . . . As she ironed the white shirts she wore at the café, Hester brooded over the events that had spoiled her life. If only she could have coped better with Phil's infidelities, with the loneliness and terrible sense of inadequacy that ate away at her confidence and had finally driven her to use Jeremy as a scapegoat for his father's betrayals and her own weaknesses. At least she was able, now, to keep it all in proportion and look at it clearly but oh! how much she would give to turn back the clock and start again.

When she'd said as much to Hattie, that cynic had merely pointed out that she'd almost certainly do the same things over again. After all, nothing would have changed. The pressure, the desperation, the exhaustion; all these would still be present. It was only the wisdom born of experience and hindsight, she'd said, that leads us to believe that if we had our time over again we'd do it all better.

Then, Hester had said rather childishly, I'd like to do it again with wisdom and hindsight!

Hattie's response had been true to character. Pooey! she'd said. Why waste time going back? Why not use your experience and wisdom to go forward?

Irritatingly, there had been no answer to this but Hester, hanging her shirts carefully in the airing cupboard, smiled with affection and gratitude for Hattie's philosophies. The ring at the bell brought her out of her reverie and she went downstairs, hoping it might be Miggy coming in for a chat. She opened the door and stood looking at the hiker she'd seen earlier. He stared at her with such an avid expression of hope on his face that for a moment she couldn't speak. Again she felt a sharp sense of *déjà vu*; of sudden recognition.

'My God!' she whispered. 'Jeremy!' and her hands went out instinctively to her elder son.

'Oh, Mum,' said Jeremy, his face trembling into tears. 'I thought I'd never get here. Oh, Mum!' And he wriggled out of his rucksack and ran into her arms.

'It seems,' Miggy told Toby much later when he came back from the boatyard, 'that Hester's dad sent him out the money for his fare with a letter to Phil. Phil had been trying to persuade his mother that Jeremy should come for a visit but she'd refused to cough up.'

'Try to remember that I'm old and tired,' Toby said, 'and speak in words of one syllable only. Does Jeremy actually remember Hester?'

Miggy pushed a glass of wine into his hand. 'It seems that he's always wanted to see her again. He's never forgotten her. But old Mrs Strange wouldn't let him go. She holds the purse strings. Phil promised him that when he was old enough and they could spare the money he would be given the opportunity but until then he must abide by his grandmother's rules. Hester's father sending Jeremy the money and telling him how much he'd like to see him was the thing that pushed it over the edge.'

'And why did no one warn Hester?' Toby sipped appreciatively. 'That's better. I'm beginning to feel more human. Go on, then. It must have been one hell of a shock for her!'

'She was in tears when she phoned.' Miggy's own lips trembled a little as she remembered Hester's deliriously happy and incoherent voice. 'Apparently he was terrified that she might refuse to see him so he insisted it was kept a secret. He went straight to his grandfather in London and then came on down here with instructions as to how to find the mill. Hester actually saw him on the road. So did Hattie. He hitched out from the train at Totnes and someone brought him along to Dartmouth. They dropped him off at the wrong place and he had to walk back.'

'It's amazing, isn't it?' Toby was much struck by this recital. 'After all these years! What? Eight years? Ten? He must have forgotten that she was unkind to him.'

'I don't know.' Miggy looked thoughtful. 'Even if he remembers, it probably doesn't matter. Underneath it all they love each other. They're bound by ties of blood. Maybe some instinctive sense tells him that it wasn't him so much as the situation she couldn't cope with. After all, people put up with amazing things from the people they love. Look what I have to deal with!'

'I shall treat that remark with the contempt it deserves. I suppose Marigold is in bed?'

'Ages ago. And Daisy is watching television. She had her supper on a tray. You're very late.' Miggy topped up his glass and began to lay the table. 'Problems?'

'Oh, I don't know.' Toby rubbed his eyes and shook his head. 'Jerry is determined that he wants out and is trying to persuade me to buy him out.'

'But could you manage all on your own?' Miggy looked concerned as she set out the dishes. 'Jerry does a lot of the boat building work himself, doesn't he?'

'Yes he does.' Toby drummed his fingers on the table. 'I'd certainly have to replace him. I can cope with the administrative side but I'd need someone to take over from him.'

'Can you afford to buy him out?' Miggy sat down opposite and began to pile food on to his plate.

'Not really.' Toby set to, hungrily. 'But I don't want just anyone who thinks they can run a boatyard buying themselves in.'

'It's such a pity. Why is he set on going?'

'That blasted girlfriend of his has been left a house upcountry. She's determined to go and live in it and that's that. So Jerry's going to have to go too or lose her. Anyway, I think he's had enough down here. Says he'd like a bit of the bright lights and something more of a challenge. Must be crazy!'

'Oh dear.' Miggy watched him sympathetically. 'What a bore.'

'Well, it is a bit. I've asked him to give me a few weeks to think it over. Maybe something will turn up.'

It was nearly two o'clock in the morning when Hester, quite unable to sleep, let herself out quietly and wandered on to the quay. The night was clear but moonless and the mist drifted and spread itself over the water so that the black shapes of the trees appeared to be floating on it. Hester hugged herself within her shawl, her heart too full for thought. Her joy sang through her veins and in her head until she was dizzy with it. Jeremy had come back: without prompting or persuading he had come in search of her. Nothing that she had done had been so terrible that he wasn't prepared to forgive or forget. Of course there had been no time yet for any really serious talk. He'd had to meet Ned and certain explanations had taken place but, to begin with, there was just this releasing, glorious happiness.

Certain remarks had shown her the way his mind was working. As he grew up he'd begun to believe that *he* was to blame for things and that he'd been sent away because she didn't want him. Hester had been obliged to keep herself well under control at this point. She needed to discover just how much was Jeremy's own childish imaginings and how much might be attributed to his grandmother's propaganda. She was determined not to rush in with pleas for forgiveness, which might frighten him, nor accusations against those people whom he loved. He had come back to her of his own free will and now was her opportunity to practise the wisdom and experience she'd spoken of to Hattie.

She exulted in the thought of him, tall and strong and very like Phil. For her, this physical resemblance might be a drawback, she could see that, but one with which she must learn to live. As he talked to them at supper, she'd also seen glimpses of her father in him and this recognition delighted her. Now they could all go to London for Easter; a family together again under one roof.

The tide was rising and the water lapped gently against the quay. Hester realised that she was shivering and that the air was clammy and cold. Her shawl was spangled with moisture and she felt quite suddenly exhausted. She slipped silently back to the cottage, shook out her shawl and, on quiet feet, climbed the stairs and went back to bed.

Chapter Thirty-One

Gradually Nick's broodings crystallised into two separate ambitions; the first was to keep Sarah as his wife and the second was to become the senior partner of Murchison, Marriott. All through the spring he juggled these two desires with his longing to confront John and Sarah and show them that he knew exactly what was going on. He hated living with the knowledge that they believed they'd duped him and longed to expose them; but how to do it without risking losing all that he most valued? Several times he attempted to trap them but each time they eluded him and when he imagined the scene that must necessarily follow such an exposure he could only be glad that they'd succeeded. After these abortive attempts Nick decided to rethink the whole thing and was now reluctantly coming to the conclusion that, although it would have been more satisfying to wrong-foot them, thus making them the guilty parties, if he wanted to succeed in his ambitions then a completely different approach was needed.

Sarah's reborn love for sailing meant that, with the summer coming on, she would be more and more at John's cottage which now, apparently, he was showing no inclination to sell. She was a very proficient sailor, having grown up on the Hamble in a sailing community, but John's forty-foot motor-sailer was beyond her abilities which meant that her sailing was restricted to those occasions when they could sail together. As often as he could now, Nick made himself one of the party. He was an experienced sailor and he was quick to see that Sarah had forgotten this and was impressed with his knowledge and handling of the boat. An idea began to form at the back of his mind which took better shape after spending most of one Sunday at the mill.

'You haven't got any other nice young lawyers like James, have you, Nick?' Hattie asked as they sat lazily with their after-lunch coffee.

Sarah raised her eyebrows. 'I should have said he was a bit too young for you,' she said, and then laughed as she remembered how the two of them and James had got drunk together. How long ago it seemed!

'I'm talking about a tenant for my cottage,' said Hattie severely. 'I'm finding all this landlord business a bit tiresome.'

'Told you so!' said Sarah promptly. 'I said right at the beginning that it would be too much for you!'

'Oh, don't be such a know-all!' cried Hattie, pouring Nick a brandy. 'I've managed for five years, dammit! It's just so difficult to get decent long-term tenants.'

'Your problem is that you have to view them as neighbours as well as tenants,' agreed Nick thoughtfully. 'Ever thought of selling?'

'No!' Hattie stared at him in alarm. 'It would be exactly the same problem except that I'd lose control. Even if I got a good buyer I couldn't stop them selling on to some ghastly person who mends motorbikes and plays pop music all night!'

'True.' Nick seemed lost in speculation.

'It's such a pity,' said Sarah. 'James was perfect, wasn't he? And Hester's not a problem, surely?'

Hattie smiled to herself as she saw how Sarah had mellowed over the last eighteen months. How critical she'd been of these young women who left their faithless husbands! Now her sympathies had been aroused and she'd been deeply moved by Hester's situation and the story of her reconciliation with Jeremy.

'No, Hester's not a problem. Well, only in that she's decided finally to go back to London. It's been agreed that Jeremy shall come and live with her and they're going to move in with her father. It's the right thing for all of them, there's no doubt about that, but it means I've got two cottages vacant again. Or I shall have when she goes. I simply can't afford to have them empty.'

'Poor Hattie.' Sarah frowned. 'I'll have to think. Maybe some of my friends have got children setting up home who would like to move in. It's a lovely place and the cottages are sweet. It's a pity you daren't sell. They'd make charming holiday homes. On the water with their own moorings. You'd make a packet!'

'Don't tempt me!' wailed Hattie. 'I simply can't risk it. But if you could rack your brains I'd be very grateful.'

'I'll certainly do that.' Nick seemed to come back from a great distance. He smiled at her. 'Leave it with me and I'll see what I can do.'

'Thanks. And now I suggest we leave Nick to concentrate on

his brandy and the Sunday papers and you and I take Jellicoe for a stroll.'

'Fair enough,' said Sarah.

She patted Nick on the shoulder as she passed his chair and he reached up to touch her hand. This by-play was not lost on Hattie.

'Things better between you?' she asked as they strolled out into the cool misty afternoon. 'You seem less . . . well, less antagonistic.'

'I have been giving him a bit of a rough time,' admitted Sarah. 'And I have to say, if I'm honest, that he's taken it on the chin.'

'With his track record, I can't see that he had much choice,' said Hattie drily.

'Probably not.' Sarah shrugged. 'I just feel he's grown up a bit. He doesn't do the heavy bit. You know? Sulky and deeply wounded. And he doesn't act the martyr either.' She laughed suddenly. 'I feel quite fond of him,' she said. 'It's rather taken me by surprise.'

'Oh, honestly!'

'I know. But to tell you the truth I think I'm going to finish with John fairly soon.'

'Oh?' Hattie looked surprised. 'Bit sudden, isn't it?'

'Probably. I don't know. I think I needed to get something out of my system and now it's all over. Rather like an illness. I'm very fond of him and I'd like to stay friends but the magic's gone.'

'And what about John? Does he feel the same?'

'I'm afraid not. He's lonely, of course, and he likes the companionship. So do I but I think Nick's more than ready to supply that now if I want him to.'

'And do you want him to?'

Sarah was silent for so long that Hattie turned to look at her.

'I'm nervous, I suppose,' she said at last. 'I'm afraid that the old ways may start up all over again. And whilst I don't feel the same way about him as I did, nevertheless it would be extremely boring.'

Hattie nodded. 'Fair enough,' she said. 'So now what?'

'So we give it a bit longer,' replied Sarah. 'Just till I'm absolutely sure!'

Hester and Ned left the creek at the end of Ned's summer term. Ned was very happy to be going to his grandfather's roomy house which was full of books and within easy reach of the fascinating museums and libraries that appealed to him so much. Hester was surprised that Phil had been so ready to help, making no obstacles in allowing Jeremy to return to his mother. She wondered if he had accepted how much misery his own behaviour had caused her and consequently that he had been responsible for her treatment of Jeremy. She knew that he'd always been embarrassed by his mother's high-handed seizing of her grandson and suspected that he was ashamed that he'd let Hester carry the burden of guilt for so long. Whatever might be the reason, he was doing everything he could to make her path easy and she could only assume that, now Mrs Strange was getting older, Phil was beginning to take from her a certain amount of control. Hester had written and told him that he was welcome to come over for visits whenever he should feel so inclined.

Hester had now had a long talk with Jeremy. He explained that he'd felt that he'd been the cause of the rows and arguments and had assumed that Hester didn't want him or his father. He'd always been very jealous of Ned, who'd been allowed to stay in England, and for a long while had hated the brother he'd never seen. It was only when Jeremy got older, and Phil had finally realised how he was feeling and thinking, that he had told Jeremy the whole story. He hadn't spared himself apparently and Jeremy realised at last that he could rid himself of his guilt and travel to England to find his mother.

Everyone was delighted for them. Since Ned's accident, it was clear to Hattie and the Dakerses that neither Hester nor Ned was happy at the creek but now, at last, the future had opened up clear and bright with promise and, though they were sad to lose them, they gathered to wave them off on the journey to London and a new life.

Hattie now had two empty cottages. She'd had one or two old friends staying on holiday after the young couple had left and at least it had kept the cottage occupied and brought in a little rent. Now, she knew she must make a sensible effort and get them both let out. Still postponing the evil hour, she decided to redecorate them. After all, she justified it to herself, after five years they needed it! Whilst she was in the middle of it – she couldn't afford Bert Crabtree this time – Nick arrived out of the blue.

'This is an unexpected pleasure,' she said as she washed her paintbrushes and dried her hands on the roller towel behind the kitchen door. 'At least, I hope it's a pleasure?'

'I hope so too.' He looked rather serious but he smiled a little at Hattie with paint in her hair and on her Guernsey and dust on the knees of her old cords. 'I've got a proposition to put to you.'

Hattie raised her eyebrows and opened her mouth but thought better of it and closed it again. He smiled then, a genuinely affectionate smile, and Hattie acknowledged privately that he really was a very attractive man.

'Speak,' she said. 'You have my undivided attention.'

'You know all about Sarah's affair with John Marriott, of course.' It was a statement and Hattie remained silent. 'I'm not expecting you to incriminate anyone. I merely want to get our terms of reference right. I've been trying to find a way for Sarah and me to go forward together.' He put his elbows on the table and laced his fingers. 'If she'd wanted to leave me she could have done it long ago, so I'm assuming that she's decided to stay.' He put his chin on his hands and raised his eyebrows. 'Do you have any information that suggests my assumption is incorrect?'

'Don't play the lawyer with me, Nick!' said Hattie crossly. 'Tell me what you want.'

He sighed. 'Very well. The bones of it are that I'd like to buy one of your cottages as a holiday home for me and Sarah and I'd like to have a boat built for her, or buy her one, that she can moor here and sail whenever she feels like it.'

He opened his eyes at Hattie's dumbfounded silence and looked faintly amused. 'Well?' he said at last. 'Is that clear enough for you?'

Hattie drew breath, shook her head and let the breath out in a great gasp. 'Good heavens, Nick! I don't quite know what to say'.

'I know you don't want to sell,' he said rapidly, 'and I know why. We can put in a clause which prevents either of us selling without your permission and giving you a right to veto any buyer if we should all three agree to sell. Would that satisfy you?'

'I suppose so.' Hattie still looked dazed. 'Wait a minute. Does Sarah know about this?'

'No.' Nick sat back in his chair and stretched his legs out under the table. 'I needed to check that you'd go along with it. Sarah needs a new interest. She's given up a great deal of her charity work and she's always had a great love for sailing and the water. At the moment she's reliant on John for getting away and I'd like to make her independent.'

'I hope you don't think that I'd be prepared to act as a watchdog?'

Nick gave an exclamation of disgust. 'Of course not! I simply feel that she's ready to finish with John but she's not quite ready to trust me yet.' He looked at her and she stared back. 'Oh, she could.' He answered the unspoken question. 'But I can't expect her to believe it. She needs a halfway house and I think this is it. It's too expensive to consider renting a cottage as such a long-term proposition but I'll gladly buy at the market price. She can come over and be close to you but independent. And she can sail in the creek until she builds up her confidence again. I can come too when I feel it's what she wants.'

'It's a very . . . generous idea, Nick,' said Hattie slowly. 'I'm very tempted, provided you put that clause in. What happens if you should both die unexpectedly?'

Nick burst out laughing. 'What a business woman you are, Hattie. Let us say that we can draw up a codicil giving you first refusal to buy it back out of the estate but I shouldn't worry about it. Both Sarah and I are extremely fond of you, you know.'

As his meaning became clear to her she grew very red under his steady gaze and got hastily to her feet.

'I need a drink,' she said, squeezing into the larder past the slumbering Admiral and seizing a bottle from the shelf. 'This has come as a bit of a shock.'

'I'm sorry about that.' Nick stood up and took the corkscrew from her. 'Let me do that. Well? What do you say to my proposition?'

'It would answer so many problems,' said Hattie slowly. She looked at him sharply. 'You said that *you* wanted to buy the cottage, Nick. Don't think me rude but can you possibly afford it? Outright?'

'I think so.' Nick extracted the cork and poured the wine. 'My mother died last year and although she didn't leave much it would be enough for the cottage and the boat. Just about.'

Hattie thought about her conversation with Sarah when they'd walked in the woods after Sunday lunch. She knew quite certainly that Nick was proposing to do exactly the right thing and she felt a great surge of affection for him. It would be fun to have Sarah coming over for jollies and holidays and a great burden would be lifted financially. Meanwhile, she still had the other cottage to do with as she pleased.

'I think it's a wonderful idea,' she said, 'and I think it's exactly what Sarah needs.'

At the tone in her voice he looked at her sharply and she nodded at him. Relief washed over him and he smiled at her gratefully.

'You'll do it then?'

'I'll do it. I'll get a valuation done so we have an idea of the price and I'll let you know. But, Nick . . .' She hesitated, unwilling to throw cold water on his obvious happiness. 'You'll tell Sarah first?'

'I shall ask her,' he corrected her. 'There would be no point in doing it if she doesn't like the idea. I must just pray that my instincts are in correct working order.'

Hattie raised her glass to him. 'If it's any comfort, and from what I've heard, I think they're working overtime.'

He touched his glass to hers. 'I hope you're right,' he said quietly. 'It's about time, isn't it?'

Hattie drank deeply, feeling awkward. She felt poised between the two of them and hoped to keep her loyalty to Sarah intact whilst showing her approval and affection to Nick.

'Let me know what she says?' she asked as he put his glass down and prepared to leave. 'You're welcome to stay to lunch, you know.'

'No, I must be off.' He kissed her cheek. 'Bless you, Hattie. Get that valuation done!'

He drove away and Hattie went back to her painting, her spirits rising. She would have given anything to be a fly on the wall during Sarah and Nick's next conversation. It was only later, as she ate her solitary supper, that she realised that, if Nick bought the cottage, her decorating had been an unnecessary and tiring expense and she felt a moment's irritation before her sense of humour returned.

Chapter Thirty-Two

Miggy sat in the summerhouse enjoying the warm September sunshine and thinking about Daisy. Although James had been gone for almost a year she knew that Daisy still thought about him, holding on to his promise that he would come down to see them all. Miggy, feeling quite sure that James was too busy settling into his new life and his new career to give them a thought, wondered how she could encourage Daisy to forget him. It was strange that so young a girl should have set her heart so firmly on a man ten years her senior. She knew that James had only ever seen Daisy as a child and that she, herself, had been the object of his romantic passion, although they'd never spoken of it and she'd never acknowledged it. Fortunately Daisy had never noticed and Miggy blessed her daughter's lack of observation and her tendency to live in her own world. His gift of the Mirror dinghy had been a touching and generous gesture even if it had served to convince Daisy that he would come back.

Marigold completed the circle of the lawn on her small tricycle and paused to wave to her mother. Miggy waved back and, after a moment's consideration, Marigold set off on another lap. There was a fence now at the edge of the lawn, to prevent any accidents, and Miggy shut her eyes, turned her face up to the sun and relaxed. There was no doubt that Daisy had been deeply disappointed when James had made no effort to make the trip to the West Country during the summer. Toby pointed out that he would only have a short holiday and that Oxford was a long way off but Daisy was not comforted. She was old enough to know that, if James really wanted to come, he'd make the effort. Since Miggy and Toby knew this too there was little they could say.

Miggy sighed, her heart going out to her child. It had been a relief when Georgia had arrived, wild with joy at obtaining her degree, and very ready to take Daisy out of herself. They went off on little jaunts together and, having discovered that Arcadia had moved from Stoke Fleming into Dartmouth, spent hours poring over the wonderful clothes and chatting to Betty, the delightfully flamboyant owner. At nearly fifteen, Daisy was ready to be initiated into the joys of make-up, clothes and other feminine excitements and Miggy was relieved that Georgia was prepared to spend time with her young stepsister. Georgia, having lived under the shadow of Ruth's beauty and confidence, enjoyed being looked up to and giving advice and they all missed her when she went back to London. If it weren't for Ruth, Miggy would have suggested that Daisy went to stay with her for a weekend but she didn't trust Ruth and there was an end to it.

Marigold arrived on her tricycle and watched her mother dozing in the sun. Abandoning her transport, she came into the summerhouse and sat in the other big basket-weave chair. Some biscuits still remained from the mid-morning snack they'd shared and, reaching out a cautious hand, she took two and subsided back in the chair. Miggy, well aware of these proceedings, continued to brood over Daisy. Academically she was only average and neither Toby nor Miggy could quite see her fitting into the working world.

'She's the old-fashioned sort who should marry a jolly, outdoor sort of chap and live in a rambling old house with lots of kids and dogs,' said Toby when they'd been discussing a career for her. 'The thought of her working in an office or a shop is quite terrifying! She'll either be lost in a daydream or seized with a wonderful but totally impractical idea for revolutionising the place.'

Georgia had suggested a year at one of the colleges that offered cookery and home-keeping courses. Daisy could live in which would give her the opportunity to meet new people and learn a few new skills. Miggy was interested and Daisy enchanted. It was only later that Miggy realised that there was one of these select colleges in Oxford and it was this very one which Daisy asked her to approach. Miggy shifted in her chair a little and finally made up her mind. After all, it was two years away and by then Daisy might have got over her infatuation for James and, if not, it would certainly decide it one way or the other. James would have to deal with it himself if Daisy turned up on his doorstep.

Miggy opened her eyes and looked at Marigold who was now curled up fast asleep in the other chair. She was very like Daisy to look at but, mercifully, without Daisy's over-active imagination. Even by three years old Daisy had invented the other world in which she virtually lived with imaginary friends and animals. Miggy decided that she would write to the college in Oxford and obtain the prospectus. It would give Daisy something to think about and plan for apart from keeping the dinghy in immaculate condition against James's return. It would concentrate her mind and encourage her to work hard at school and, those things aside, it was all Miggy could think of to offer her.

Sarah paused in her walk back home along the lane to lean on the five-bar gate and stare out across the pale golden stubble. The village was hidden in the misty blue trees beyond the further hedge and only the squat grey tower of the church could be seen and a spiral of smoke ascending idly into the still, quiet air. A pheasant, almost gaudy amongst the muted autumnal shades, ran along beneath the hedge, its glossy green head bobbing as it went, and a flock of starlings swooped above the field and scattered down the valley out of sight. Sarah was soothed by this gentle landscape, feeling pressure and expectations fall away, and knowing a desire to be merely herself; not John's mistress or Nick's wife but simply Sarah.

When she'd woken that morning she'd felt a sudden irritation with her life. The years had passed in a flurry of meetings, lunches, weekend parties and, more lately, in having an affair; she knew an impatience with it all. She was bored with regular trips to the hairdresser to preserve the shape of her new hairstyle, irritated by the necessity to make her face up to match it and tired of worrying about what she was going to wear. It had been fun for a brief period, exciting and different, but the novelty was wearing off. This morning, she'd ignored the softly flattering, pretty new clothes and dragged out an old well-worn tweed and a shapelessly comfortable jersey and worked happily in the garden before eating an un-calorie-conscious lunch. Later, she'd strolled away down the lane, following the bridle path across the fields, her countrywoman's eyes taking in the turn of the season, the colours and the sounds, and feeling contentedly at peace with herself.

Now, leaning on the gate, her calmed, relaxed mind drifted back to her earlier thoughts. The affair with John had come to an end. She knew now that she would never leave Nick. It was too dramatic a gesture, too extravagant and self-indulgent, but she still wished for some path that would lead them back together gradually and naturally. He'd been odd of late, secretive and preoccupied. She might have suspected that he had embarked on another affair except that the pattern was quite different and he was at home too much. If he knew about her affair with John he'd said nothing but neither was he pursuing the courtship routine that he'd tried previously. He was simply friendly, amusing, attentive and kind.

As Sarah turned away from the pastoral scene and walked on, she caught herself remembering that happy time they'd known together before Cass Wivenhoe had appeared on the scene. They couldn't go back, that was never possible, but perhaps they could go forward. If only she could think of some means of carrying them over this hiatus. As she turned in at the gate she was surprised to see Nick's car in the drive. Surely it was rather early for him? With a sense of apprehension she hurried into the house and found him coming out of the drawing room with a drink in his hand. She opened her eyes at him, drawing down the corners of her mouth, and he smiled, slightly shame-faced, as if she'd caught him out at something shocking.

'That sort of day?' she suggested. 'You're early.'

'I wondered where you were,' he said, and she knew that he'd feared she was with John.

For a moment she felt a true regret for her betrayal and a shaft of tenderness pierced her. 'I went for a walk,' she said. 'It's such a perfect autumn day.'

He took in the old, familiar, shabby clothes and recognised the expression of contentment on her unmade-up face.

'You look lovely,' he said quietly, and she knew exactly what he was trying to say and his sincerity forbade any false disclaimers or pretended misunderstanding on her part.

'Thank you.' She accepted his tribute. 'I think I'll join you.'

They went together into the drawing room.

'I wanted to have a talk with you,' he said as he poured her a gin and tonic.

'Why not?' Mentally she reviewed all the things he might be going to say and sat down on the large deep sofa.

'I've been thinking very carefully about us.' He remained standing. 'And I've had an idea. This is based on the assumption that you wish to remain married to me so if I'm taking too much for granted, now's the time to say so.'

Sarah glanced up at him, certain now that he knew about her affair with John. She realised that he didn't want to raise the subject and felt a sense of gratitude and relief. She realised, too, that he was very nervous and felt another stab of remorse mixed with affection.

'You're not taking too much for granted,' she said. 'I have no desire to leave you.'

'Thank you,' he said after a moment. 'In that case I'll explain my idea. Firstly, I've been thinking that we might consider having another holiday cottage but much closer to home. Secondly, I'm well aware that over the last two years you've rekindled your love for sailing so it occurs to me that we could attempt to kill two birds with one stone. Are you with me so far?'

'Yes,' she said slowly. 'Yes, I think so. What have you got in mind?'

'One of Hattie's cottages,' he answered. 'You could go when I'm tied up in the week and we could go together at weekends and you could keep a boat on the creek. I thought we could look into buying you a small one that you could handle on your own. You could be independent but close to friends and I could join you easily and quickly. If you wanted me to,' he added hastily and humbly.

Resisting an almost forgotten desire to go and put her arms round him, Sarah forced herself to stick to the point. 'Hattie would never sell,' she said. 'She told you that when we had lunch with her.'

'She's changed her mind,' he told her with a certain amount of satisfaction. 'She's agreed to sell, providing we include a clause promising not to sell it on without her permission. I imagine you'd be prepared to agree to that?'

'Well, of course.' Sarah stared at him in amazement. 'You've taken me completely by surprise.'

'I have to say that that was part of the plan.' He smiled at her. 'I wanted to be sure Hattie would play ball. She's sick to death of finding tenants but, with that clause in place, very happy to have her oldest friend across the yard. And we'd have a mooring, too.'

'But, Nick . . .' Still Sarah hesitated, despite the great excitement that was building inside her. 'Can we afford this?'

'I don't know what *you* can afford,' he said indifferently. '*I'm* affording this. My mother's will has been proved at last and I want to take the opportunity of repaying some of the incredible generosity you've shown me . . . Please,' he added.

'Oh, Nick . . .'

'If it's what you want,' he said rapidly. 'If it would make you happy.' He swallowed the last of his Scotch and went to refill his glass.

Sarah got up and went to him. 'It sounds perfect!' She said it with such sincerity that he stood his glass down and turned back to her.

'Really?' He longed to take her in his arms but was scared that he might destroy the delicate mechanism that was beginning to repair the relationship.

Sarah nodded. 'It's a brilliant idea. I'd love it. And a little boat. Oh, Nick! What fun!'

'I thought Toby might help us out there. He'd know what was up for sale, I expect, and if not he'd be able to build one for you. Or at least the boatyard would.'

'For us, Nick. Our boat, not just mine.'

'I'd like us to think of it as yours.' He smiled at her. 'Your first boat's rather special. Like your first car. When I retire perhaps we'll think again. Get one like John's that we can go out to sea with and on trips across the Channel. Meanwhile, you need one to use in the river.'

'We'll share it,' said Sarah, and she reached up and kissed him. 'Thank you, Nick. I accept your incredible offer with delight.'

Wisely, he made no attempt to cash in on her gratitude but simply fetched her glass and poured her another drink.

'To Mill Cottage,' he said, and touched his glass to hers. 'I don't know which one yet. Hattie says you'll have to go and choose. They're both much of a muchness.'

'Oh, I can't wait.' She grinned up at him with such genuine happiness that he felt almost sick with relief. 'When can we go? The cottages are empty, aren't they? Could we go this weekend?'

'You could go before that if you want to.' He was determined not to muscle in. It was essential that she had space and time to herself and he knew how easy it was to give it away out of gratitude or guilt. 'She always likes to see you. Go and have lunch with her and have a look over the cottages and then we'll go again at the weekend just to be on the safe side. You need time to think about it carefully. Two visits would be quite sensible.'

Touched by his thoughtfulness and wisdom, she smiled at him. 'I might do that. So she's been in on the secret all along?'

'I had to persuade her to sell but I didn't want to raise any hopes. It's not easy to find a small cottage with a mooring on a safe stretch of water.'

'Go and phone her, Nick. Tell her she's got a buyer.'

He hesitated. 'Don't you want to do it?'

'You go first. Finish your business arrangements and then I'll have a chat.'

'Fair enough.' He went out taking his drink with him.

Sarah remained where she was, trying to take in all the aspects of Nick's offer. She'd been quite certain that Nick would keep his inheritance, hoping for the chance of buying John Marriotts share. Now Nick would be unable to afford it and, although he'd be able to borrow the money, it was as if he'd made the choice between the coveted position of senior partner and his marriage. She was deeply moved: he had shown her the path forward and she intended to take it with no more backward glances.

Chapter Thirty-Three

Hattie sat beside her bedroom fire, rocking gently in her chair. She'd given up all pretence of reading and, with the book lying unheeded on her lap, stared into the glowing heart of the fire and let her thoughts have free rein. She was both relieved and sad now that she'd relinquished one of her precious cottages to Sarah and Nick. It was a sensible thing to do; easing the financial pressure whilst removing the anxiety of finding two lots of tenants who could afford the rent and were pleasant neighbours. Because the cottages had no gardens, parents with young children were terrified lest their offspring might fall into the creek unless continually supervised and Hattie was reluctant to turn the place into a kind of Colditz which would ruin the appearance and atmosphere. Since this reduced the number of suitable tenants, it was easier to have only one cottage to worry about. At the same time she was sad to have lost control, to be unable to walk out of the door knowing that she owned all that surrounded her and could do as she pleased with it.

The wind was rising. It beat round the mill and rattled at the window, and Hattie pulled her shawl closer round her shoulders and bent to poke at the logs. Her thoughts carried her back to her first year at the mill and the storm in which Evan had died. She remembered how Sarah had telephoned her, warning her of the approaching gale, and how she, Hattie, had joked about *The Mill on the Floss*, secretly relieved that Joss was safe in the cottage. What an old fool she was! How much she still missed him! From the beginning there had been an empathy between them, starting with their shared service background and moving into close friendship. It had come as a shock to her that she could experience the agonies of maternal love without physically becoming a mother. Joss was the son she'd never had; the child she'd lost. Emotions she'd pushed down deep inside had slowly emerged but even she hadn't realised the depth of them until the night that he'd sailed.

She'd hoped that Hester would keep Joss in the creek and instead she'd driven him away. Sixteen months he'd been gone and no word of his return. His postcards told her nothing, except that he was still alive, and pride forbade her to attempt to communicate with him. He must return of his own free will or not at all. She guessed that Joss had come to look upon them all – Hester included – as a substitute for the family who'd rejected him. She felt quite sure that his mother's disapproval of his leaving the Army and living on a boat must have made it impossible for him to admit to his feelings of fear and inadequacy and he'd needed time and seclusion to come to terms with himself. The voyage had been necessary, both to get it out of his system and to maintain his pride, and now they must wait to see what had come out of it.

Those first early terrors for his safety had receded with time, bound up as they were with Ned's accident and all the trauma of that day, but rarely did Hattie look out from her bedroom window or glance down the creek as she crossed the quay without hoping to see *Westering* back on her mooring, the brown sails harbour-stowed and Joss rowing easily across to the hard. She'd hoped that he might come back before the winter arrived, which was another reason for keeping the second cottage unoccupied. Now it looked as though he wouldn't be requiring it.

Hattie pushed herself up out of the rocking chair and went to the window, holding aside the curtain. The tide was out and moonlight gleamed on the mud. Ragged clouds raced before the wind, obscuring the moon's face, and she thought of the *Abigail*, or what remained of her, a burned out hulk lying abandoned at her moorings. Hattie shivered, dropping the curtain, and went to build up the fire and place the guard around it. She climbed into her colourful nest, bolstering herself about with cushions and quilts, and switched out the lamp. The shadows danced and moved upon the walls and she remembered sharing this room with Daisy the night that Marigold had been born, three years before, and how they'd eaten the midnight feast. She felt an odd identity with Daisy who waited patiently for James's return as she, Hattie, waited for Joss.

What fools our emotions make of us, thought Hattie, as her mind drifted towards sleep. I'm nearly sixty, much too old to start being motherly. And Daisy's barely fifteen and too young to start being seriously in love.

She remembered how Miggy and Daisy had taken refuge at

the mill cottage when Ruth had decided she wanted Toby back; saw again the luminous expression on Hester's face when she'd brought Jeremy to be introduced. She recalled, too, Janice sitting beside Brian's hospital bed and with what terror and courage she'd received the news that he'd never walk again. As sleep overtook her she saw James crouching beside the Admiral and saying, 'Hi there, Jelly baby,' but her last waking thought was of Sarah, sitting at the refectory table, and her voice saying, 'I think it's going to be OK this time, Hattie. I really think it is.'

As the sale of the cottage proceeded Sarah decided to approach John herself regarding the matter of the senior partnership. She brooded long on the best way to deal with it without coming to any satisfactory conclusion. John had been deeply hurt by her decision to end the affair and he was finding it very hard indeed to accept her explanations. She realised how lonely he was and knew now that any suspicions she'd had that he might have played Margaret false were quite unfounded. After years of a dull, quiet marriage, he'd fallen in love with an almost forgotten passion. Their affair had temporarily restored his youth, the 'stolen fruit' aspect lending an excitement to their liaison, accompanied by a pleasant sensation of self-righteousness in paying Nick out for his disgraceful behaviour to Sarah over the years. He'd been unable to hide his bitterness when she'd told him that she and Nick were going to try again and she guessed that retirement had temporarily lost its fears for him when he'd thought that she was going to be his constant companion for the years to come. It occurred to her that he might even have suggested that, once he was retired, she should divorce Nick and marry him. Sarah felt guilty and very sorry for John but for her it was finished and there was no point in prolonging the agony.

She hadn't discussed the senior partnership with Nick. He'd been rather quiet of late and she guessed that he was weighing his chances and wondering when John was going to approach him, as surely he must. It occurred to her that John might be holding back, wondering if Nick could afford it. He knew, now, about the plans for the cottage and the boat and he might have assumed that Nick was in no position to consider it. Unable to bear the suspense any longer, Sarah telephoned him one Sunday morning when Nick was playing golf.

'Marriott.' His testy voice took her by surprise, so familiar had she become with the special tone he used to her.

'John. It's Sarah.'

'Sarah.' He sounded surprised, cautious, hopeful. 'This is an unexpected pleasure.'

'Oh, John,' she said regretfully, 'it's probably not going to be that much of a pleasure, I'm afraid. It's a tremendous cheek, actually. I want to ask a favour.'

'Oh my dearest girl.' His voice was warmer now, nearly intimate. 'You know there's nothing I wouldn't give you if it's in my power. It's wonderful to hear your voice.'

Sarah grimaced, instinctively shuddering at the horror that is aroused by an appeal to a love that is utterly dead.

'Not when you hear what it is I want to talk about,' she said flatly. 'It's about the senior partnership, John.' There was a complete silence and Sarah hurried on, her heart thumping. 'I just wanted you to know that if it's worry that he may not have the money that's preventing you from approaching Nick, it needn't bother you.'

There was another silence and when John spoke his voice was dry and very formal. 'This is all rather irregular . . .'

'I know that,' said Sarah quickly. 'I just hoped that we're on close enough terms for me to be able to bend the rules.'

'And are we?' The question was heavy with meaning.

'How . . . how d'you mean?' Sarah's confusion was painfully apparent.

'Are we on close enough terms, Sarah?' The intimacy was back. 'I thought you'd decided that it was all over between us.'

'Well . . . yes, that's true but . . .' Sarah floundered, embarrassed and confused. 'Surely we can still be friends?'

'Ah. Friends. Such an ambiguous word.' The intimacy was gone, resentment in its place. 'I shall be perfectly honest with you and say that, when I thought you and I had a future together, I considered offering Nick my share as a . . . well, let us call it a kind of compensation.'

'And now?'

'Now I have remembered my reasons for judging Nick as unsuitable for the position of senior partner.'

'Which are?'

He laughed a little, showing surprise that she expected to be admitted into his confidence. 'Since you insist, I'm sure I don't need to remind you of the incidents in Nick's past which make him undesirable as the senior partner for an old and very reputable law practice.'

'But you were prepared to take that risk when we were . . . lovers.' She brought the word out with difficulty.

'When I thought we had a future together,' he corrected her.

'And now you've changed your mind?'

He hesitated. 'Have you anything to say that might make me see the situation in its former light?' His voice held the suggestion of a promise.

'No.' She felt a surge of revulsion. 'Nothing.'

'Then that is how the matter stands.'

'I see.' A thought flashed into her mind. 'Does Nick know of your decision?'

'Not yet. I'm still considering the position carefully.'

'I see. And you feel it unlikely that you'll revise your opinion? About Nick's suitability?'

'Do you feel it unlikely that you'll revise your decision about our future together?'

'Blackmail, John?' She managed to inject a light-hearted note into her voice.

He laughed gently. 'Hardly, Sarah. I merely wish to have my terms of reference quite clear.'

'It's over, John. Quite over.'

'Then we all know where we stand.' He replaced the receiver.

Trembling, Sarah went back to the kitchen. She was shocked, unable to believe that he was capable of such hypocrisy, and horrified at the thought of Nick's disappointment. She wondered how he'd take it and how he would discover that he'd been by-passed, knowing that she could never tell him that she'd telephoned John. Perhaps Nick had already given up the hope, knowing that he had no money with which to buy the share. She was moved anew by Nick's generous action in giving her the cottage, feeling both touched and guilty. She wondered whether John would have offered the position to Nick if their affair had never taken place and it only now occurred to her that the sacredness of the position hadn't deterred John from a liaison with her. She suspected that this talk of Nick's past was purely specious, that John was merely taking revenge and that she would have to stand by and watch him exact his pound of flesh.

As it happened, Nick was still hopeful that he would be offered the position. He knew that he was the obvious choice and that the rest of the practice expected it. Neither he nor John had exchanged any word or look which acknowledged John's affair with Sarah and, now that it was over, Nick hoped that it could be forgotten. It certainly never occurred to him that he could be punished for being the innocent party.

On the Monday morning after Sarah's telephone call, John called Nick into his office. Heart beating erratically, hopes high, Nick obeyed the summons. This must be it!

'Sit down, won't you, Nick?' John surveyed him expressionlessly across the expanse of his desk, enjoying the power he was able to exercise.

'Thanks.' Nick sat, wondering exactly how John was feeling now that the affair was at an end. Even now he didn't know which one of them had called a halt or if it had been by mutual agreement. 'Haven't seen you for while.'

'I've been busy. As you know my retirement's close at hand and I've been making plans.' John looked upon Nick's confidence and felt a surge of pleasure fill his bitter breast. 'Plans which, I'm sorry to tell you, do not include you, Nick.'

He watched almost greedily as the smile on Nick's handsome face wavered a little to be replaced by a slightly puzzled expression.

'Sorry.' Nick frowned and shook his head a little. 'I'm not quite with you.'

'No?' John raised his eyebrows and smiled. How sweet revenge was proving! 'Well, I must make myself clear.'

'Please.' Nick watched him, a terrible doubt forming in his mind.

'I feel it is only proper that you should hear from me that David Corbett has been offered and has accepted the position of senior partner within Murchison, Marriott.' His smile widened almost rapaciously as he took in Nick's shock and disappointment.

'*David* . . . ?' He was silent.

John inclined his head – and waited.

Nick tried to laugh it off. 'David Corbett? Is there any point in asking why he's been selected over my head when I've been here twice as long, have three times the client base . . . ?' He shook his head, managing to look both mortified and disgusted.

'My dear Nick.' John smiled almost tenderly upon him, delighted to have the opportunity to twist the knife still deeper. 'Could you seriously have thought it possible that the position might be offered to you?' He, in his turn, shook his head, managing to look both incredulous and amused. 'With your reputation?' He sighed regretfully. 'The senior partner, like Caesar's wife, must be above suspicion. With your rather sordid history, it was quite out of the question.'

He watched Nick's anger with interest, saw him battle with the urge to confront him with his own affair whilst holding this exalted position, and smiled when Nick closed his lips resolutely upon discussing Sarah with him.

'I see. In that case thank you for giving me prior warning.' Nick had himself under control. 'I gather there's no more to be said.'

'On my part, nothing at all.'

They stared at each other.

'Then I'll get on.' Nick got to his feet, hesitated and went out closing the door gently behind him.

Sarah was sorting out curtains when he arrived home. They were hoping to exchange contracts by Christmas and she was busy selecting furniture and hangings. She took one look at his face and abandoned the curtains, knowing exactly what had happened.

'I've had a bit of a shock.' He was still managing to keep himself under control. 'They've appointed David Corbett as senior partner.'

He watched her, trying to assess her disappointment.

'Oh, Nick, I'm so sorry.' She stared at him, full of compassion and guilt. She bit her lip, guessing at the humiliation he must be feeling and how the tongues must be wagging in the office. 'Oh, Nick. It's my fault. If only . . .'

'No!' He spoke so strongly that she was silenced. 'It's got nothing to do with you. He made it quite clear that it was because of my "rather sordid history".' He emphasised the words and she knew he was quoting and felt a stab of rage at John's hypocrisy. 'I'm sorry, Sarah. I know you must be disappointed, too.'

There was no self-pity in the apology and she felt a wave of admiration for him.

'Nick,' she began but he shook his head.

'Try to see it like this,' he said, 'everything that has happened has been directly or indirectly caused by my past behaviour. Everything! D'you see?'

She stared at him. She knew that he was absolving her of any guilt that she might feel, showing her that he recognised that her affair with John was the result of his own betrayals. It was the truth and she realised that nothing less than the truth would do here.

She nodded. 'Yes, I see. I'm sorry, nevertheless. John is

making you pay for the fact that I've finished with him. He's a hypocrite.'

Nick felt a ray of comfort warm his heart. So she had thrown him over and John was taking his revenge. It was a high price to pay but he held to his own view: without his continued infidelities, that terrible scene he'd forced her to play with Cass, Sarah would never have ceased to love him. He smiled at her and she went to him and slipped her arm into his.

Chapter Thirty-Four

Toby strolled back from the boatyard feeling pleased with life. Winter was nearly here but the autumn had been a calm, peaceful affair, so far, with none of the usual gales or storms. He thought of all the plans that were maturing and smiled to himself. He could hardly believe that it was less than six years since he'd first met Miggy in the Royal Castle, so impossible was it to imagine life without her or the girls. He remembered Daisy as a skinny child, manhandling his heavy dinghy round the creek, and Georgia, a sullen and overweight schoolgirl, freezing them out until Miggy's warmth had melted the ice. Toby marvelled at the way women changed almost overnight. Georgia had a job in advertising and was doing very well and obviously loving every minute of it but he could still recall his surprise when she'd come down for the holidays after that first year at Canford, graceful, pretty, vivacious, having been translated from childhood to womanhood between one season and the next.

Now Daisy was performing the same miracle. She looked so like Miggy that it caught his heart; tall and slender, pale-skinned and delicate-boned. Her bright curls were the same coppery shade but her eyes were honey-brown – Patrick's legacy – and set differently from Miggy's green ones. She still loved to sail and row and swim but there was a dreaminess about her now, a secretive shyness, that touched him and evoked his natural protectiveness.

He looked down over the creek to the mill and thought of Hattie. He was delighted that she had sold her cottage to her old friend Sarah who, to everyone's relief, had long since abandoned her attitude of disapproval towards Miggy. It was a pity that people generally had to fall prey to their own weaknesses before they could understand or sympathise with others who had made mistakes but at least Sarah showed no tendencies to be hypocritical. Now, Hattie only had one cottage to worry about and, if all went according to plan, the other cottage would soon be occupied.

Toby gave a great sigh of pleasure as he watched the heron, still and watchful, almost invisible beneath the overhanging trees. The *Abigail*'s hulk was barely visible in the shadows of the smaller creek and his happiness was touched, briefly, by darker memories. He descended the hill and turned in to the cottage. Miggy was ironing in the kitchen whilst Marigold sat in the empty laundry basket, surrounded by toys and books. He swept her up in his arms, kissing her, and she shrieked indignantly, demanding to be returned to her games. He gave her a last kiss, put her back amongst her playthings and went to give Miggy a hug.

'All well?' She smiled at him, sharing in his excitement.

'All's very well.' He kissed her, too. 'Like a cup of tea?'

'I'd love one. You're very early.'

'I know.' He went to fill the kettle. 'I couldn't stand the waiting any longer.'

She laughed quietly. 'What an old softy you are!'

'Can't help it.' He grinned at her. 'You wouldn't want it any other way.'

'How true!' She continued to iron in silence for some moments whilst Marigold droned to her toys.

'Thank goodness the weather's held up.' Toby glanced at the window. 'It'll be dark soon.'

Miggy finished the last garment and unplugged the iron. 'Let's go into the sitting room,' she said. 'Bring my tea. We may as well wait in comfort.'

Hattie accompanied Sarah out into the mill yard. They hugged each other and Sarah drove away up the lane. Hattie listened until the sound of her engine had died away and the silence of the winter afternoon filled the creek once more. The brilliance of the sunset was fading, although the western sky was still suffused with a rosy glow. Seawards, the mist was rising, drifting down over the hills so that it became one with the water, the bare branches of the trees etched a ghostly grey against the soft pearly white. Hattie, with the Admiral at her heels, strolled into the orchard and along to the mill pond which was now a haven for water birds and other kinds of wildlife. She smiled to herself as she remembered the winter that Joss had cleared out the mill pond, digging out the years of silt, complaining vociferously and unceasingly throughout.

She called to the Admiral, who was making the roosting ducks uneasy, and wandered back through the orchard, thinking of Sarah. It must have been a blow to Nick's self-esteem to see the senior partnership given to another partner. At the same time, it might have been just what was needed to bring Nick and Sarah back together. She had been impressed by Nick's insight into Sarah's needs and she agreed that the cottage, along with the boat, was an excellent idea and just what Sarah required. Nevertheless, this crushing of Nick's hopes had drawn them closer and, if Nick could come to terms with it, it might be the best thing that could have happened. It had been illuminating to hear Sarah, furious on Nick's behalf, full of admiration for his stoical acceptance of it, and Hattie had seen them as a couple again rather than as two people living together.

It would be fun to have Sarah coming to and fro. She was such good company these days, easy and amusing, her earlier fussings and criticisms forgotten and Hattie had no doubts now that she would fit in with their little community. Miggy was no longer anxious in her company and Toby was delighted with the order from Nick for the little dayboat. Hattie glanced at the empty cottages as she wandered past, not destined to be empty for much longer. Contracts should be exchanged very soon now and then Sarah would be visiting regularly, moving things in, making it comfortable. As for the other one, Toby had a friend who wanted to rent it. Hattie had been a little cautious and Toby had been rather vague but she'd agreed to hold it until the friend could get down to see it. After all, a friend of Toby's was likely to be as suitable as anyone replying to an advertisement. She shook her head at herself, knowing her caution and unwillingness to commit herself was because she'd still hoped that Joss might return and she would have had a bolt hole ready for him.

Deep in thought, she followed along behind the Admiral who had pottered ahead on to the quay. The light was fading now and the creek was a ghostly, eerie place. She leaned on the wall for a moment and then frowned. The sound of an engine, muffled by the fog, echoed in the silence. She stared into the gathering dusk and saw the spectral shape of a boat emerging from the mist, coming up on the tide. Her brown sails were casually stowed, her masts bare and she seemed hardly to disturb the silvery gleam of water as she moved forward. The engine slowed as she came alongside the mooring buoy, a shadowy figure caught it with casual ease, and presently *Westering* was swinging at her old moorings.

Joss came up on to the foredeck and stared across the darkening creek. Hattie straightened up, her heart thudding, her mouth dry, and raised her hand.

'Hattie?' He couldn't quite disguise the joy of homecoming but his voice was as careless as he could make it.

'I hope nobody from BRNC saw you come past like that!' Her voice shook. 'They have their sails harbour-stowed before they get to Bayard's Cove. Not hanging all over the place like that.'

'That's because the Navy never sail their boats. They only know how to use an engine.' Joss was calmly getting the dinghy away. 'I only took 'em down at the end of the creek. Ran out of wind.'

'What sort of an ETA do you call this?'

'Never gave you one. Only the Navy issues ETAs they can't hope to keep.' Joss was rowing with easy strokes across the widening strip of water to the slip. 'The Army keeps its word. I said I'd be back.'

Hattie followed the Admiral out on to the slip. The great dog ran down into the water in his excitement, his tail wagging, and Hattie swiped the tears from her cheeks and swallowed desperately. Joss shipped his oars, ran his hand over the Admiral's head and pulled his ears.

'Get this great brute out of my way,' he called. 'He'll be in here with me in a minute. Dammit, he'll have me overboard!'

'Pooey!' cried Hattie shakily. 'Been halfway round the world and you can't cope with a mere dog . . .'

She called the Admiral to her and Joss climbed over the side and pulled the dinghy well up the slip, tying her painter to a ringbolt. He straightened up and they looked at one another.

'Welcome back, Joss,' said Hattie.

'Ah. It's good to be home,' he said and held out his arms to her.

It was much later that Hattie discovered that it was Daisy who had been Joss's contact whilst he'd been at sea. He'd written to her at school in an attempt to find out everything that happened in his absence and she'd told him about Jeremy arriving and Hester's final departure.

'Daisy was impartial, you see,' he explained to Hattie. 'I feared that you might imagine that I was breaking my heart and try to persuade Hester to stay and I felt that keeping absolute silence was the only way that our true feelings would emerge. I know now that Hester was looking for a loving happy family and I was looking for an excuse to stay here without losing face. The happy family bit was attractive too but I was all wrong for Hester and Ned and it didn't take long for her to realise that, once I was out of the way.'

'I think she knew it all along,' agreed Hattie unresentfully. 'And I take your point about us all writing to you and keeping the emotions too worked up. But why not Toby?'

'Toby's too much of a romantic,' said Joss at once. 'He'd have liked to keep everyone here, an even bigger happy family. Anyway, he'd have been unable to hide it from Miggy and she's Hester's friend. Daisy just reported things as they happened so that I knew you were all OK and I also knew when the coast was clear. Then she wrote and told me that Toby's partner was leaving and that's when I wrote to Toby. I was already on my way back then but I didn't want you to know in case I was held up by bad weather and delayed until the spring.'

'And you were Toby's friend who wanted the cottage.' Hattie was too relieved that he was safe and too happy to have him back to mind that she'd been deceived. 'So now you're a partner at the boatyard?'

'I am. I'm going to see my mother and tell her that I'm going to be almost respectable and hope that she'll give me her blessing. I think the only thing that Hester and I had in common was being rejected by our families. Thank God Jeremy came back!'

'She's so happy.' Hattie was glad to be able to tell him that. 'She's got her family now, all together under one roof with her father in London.'

'Jellicoe's looking older.' Joss looked round the kitchen. It was exactly as he had pictured it during those lonely nights at sea. 'He's fatter, too.'

'What d'you expect?' asked Hattie indignantly. 'We're all eighteen months older. I'm an old age pensioner, I'll have you know.'

'Don't angle for sympathy from me, woman.' He grinned at her. 'Get the booze out and let's have all the gossip. Daisy's too young to write a really juicy letter. What's all this about Sarah buying a cottage? And what about James? I did gather that Daisy still sees him as Young Lochinvar come out of the West in a Mirror dinghy.'

'Poor child,' said Hattie pointedly, beating the Admiral by a short head to the larder. 'She's learned very young that men are born liars.'

'Save her a lot of trouble later on.' He watched her fill his glass. 'It'll be nice to be back in the cottage, Hattie. I must say it's like a palace after eighteen months on *Westering*.'

'You won't get rid of her, though?' She sat opposite again and looked at his thin face. The Admiral wasn't the only one who looked older. 'She needs a bit of attention, by the look of her.'

'Plenty of time to do that,' he said comfortably. 'But I shan't live on board again for a while. You'll have to draw me up a proper lease this time. I can't afford to buy the cottage like Sarah and Nick.'

Hattie sipped her drink thoughtfully. 'It's none of my business,' she said at last, 'but have you got enough to buy the partnership?'

Their eyes locked and she feared that she'd gone too far. She must remember that he was an independent young man on whom she had no claims whatever. He saw the anxiety in her face and smiled.

'I'm borrowing it,' he told her. 'Toby's made it as easy as he can for me but I don't want any favours.'

'No,' she said quickly. 'No, I see that. It's just . . . if things get difficult . . . Well, I've got a bit of extra now I've sold the cottage. That's all.'

'I'll bear it in mind,' he told her. 'Thanks, Hattie.'

Later still, when he'd gone to see Toby and Miggy, Hattie checked the cottage over and made up the bed with aired sheets. She knew he wouldn't want too much fuss, so she made it look as welcoming as she could and left it at that. Outside the moon had risen and hung cold and bright above the milky swathes of mist that lay along the water. *Westering* looked like a ghost ship floating in the soft whiteness and the thickly wooded shoulders of the promontory were inky black against the midnight blue of the overarching sky. The tide was full now, lapping gently at the wall of the quay and reaching high up on to the slip where Joss's dinghy was just afloat.

Miggy had told her to join them as soon as she'd checked the cottage but Hattie realised that her heart was too full and her emotions too near the surface to expose them even to her dearest friends. The Admiral came close to her and sat heavily against her legs and she bent down to stroke him, glad of his company which was all she required at the moment. Her family were around her, close at hand, and she could go in now and be at peace, quietly revelling in her happiness. She gave the Admiral a last pat.

'Come on, Jellicoe,' she murmured. 'Bedtime for you and me.'

They crossed the quay together and, with a last glance across the moonlit creek, Hattie followed the Admiral into the mill and closed the door behind them.

Epilogue

1986

James started up the engine and followed the winding lane down to the head of the creek. Now that he was back he simply couldn't understand why he hadn't made the effort before. After all, he'd come down for Annie and Peter's housewarming party at Strete. Of course, he'd been at university with Peter . . . James knew that he was making excuses for himself and felt ashamed. He *should* have made an effort. Everything had been so new and so exciting and time had just raced by but at least he'd stayed in touch; Christmas cards and the occasional letter to Daisy. He remembered that she was supposed to be coming to Oxford to do some sort of domestic science course so at least he would be able to show her around and make up for his laziness. He thought of Miggy again and, despite several girlfriends and a quite serious affair, his heart quickened at the remembrance. Strange how that youthful passion had lingered; a young man's romantic ideal of womanhood.

He drove past the mill pond and slowed at the gateway to the mill. Should he just pull in? A sturdy Peugeot Estate was parked where Hattie's Renault 4 had stood and James cautiously drove in and pulled up beside it. To his delight the Admiral was stretched out in the sunshine and, as James got out of the car, he hauled himself to his feet and came over, tail wagging. James bent to stroke him, noticing the increased girth and greying muzzle.

'Hello, Jelly baby,' he said softly. 'Remember me?'

It seemed that the Admiral did. After a reunion which was very satisfactory to both parties James straightened up and glanced around. He looked with affection at the cottages, remembering how happy he'd been there, and wondered where everyone might be on a Monday morning. The mill door was open as usual but, instead of putting his head inside and calling, James followed the Admiral who had set off for the hard. As he reached the edge of the quay, James caught his breath. Miggy was coming along the hard, walking easily in an old denim skirt, her shirt sleeves rolled up and faded sandshoes on her feet. The bright curls shone in the sunshine and her face was turned towards the creek. He remembered her tall grace and the tilt of the chin and he felt the old heart-stopping jolt. The Admiral had reached her now and she paused to talk to him, bending to hug him, her cheek against his huge head. As she straightened she saw James watching her and, as her face lit up with joy and her hands went out instinctively towards him, he realised his mistake.

'Oh, James! You're late.' Daisy's voice shook. 'I thought you were never coming.'

'Couldn't help it!' He ran to meet her, seizing her outstretched hands and looking into her honey-brown eyes. 'Messrs Whinge, Whinge, Bellyache and Moan have really kept me at it.'

'Shoulder to the wheel?'

'Oh, Daisy,' he said. 'Nose to the grindstone. But never mind. I'm here now.'